THE
WOLF
&THE
WILD
FLOWER

ELLA FIELDS

ISBN: 9798364372475

Editor: Jenny Sims, Editing4Indies
Formatting: Stacey Blake, Champagne Book Design
Cover design: Sarah Hansen, Okay Creations

For the hearts who had to bleed out to learn how to beat again

PART ONE
THE BEGINNING

ONE

Aster

T
HE SLEEPING SUN BROUGHT A FLOOD OF NEWCOMERS TO THE tavern.

Chatter grew in volume, providing more precious moments of escape. My eyes remained clasped upon the golden liquid in the glass before me as I fell into the woes and highs of the mundane lives surrounding me.

Until the subject changed.

Not for the first time today, talk of bloodshed reached my ears.

Whispered and gleeful exchanges of battle and vengeance began to circulate at nearby tables with far too much ease. Such casual care-lessness made it clear that those within this tavern—within this city of Vordane—had never known what it was to watch all they loved burn.

As night bloomed in full and drink loosened more lips, what I'd assumed and heard proved true. This kingdom I'd chosen to visit had been doing the burning.

My blood cooled more by the minute, though there was no need for it. This was not my city. This was not my home.

The thought of returning to my own had me topping up my wine, the decanter hitting the table with a clank when the atmosphere shifted. The sparse candlelight flickered and flared. A hum, gentle yet deepening, infiltrated the dim tavern moments before its source.

Patrons glanced up when a male was shoved inside the door, laughing even as he turned to growl at the two males who entered behind him.

Wolves.

Their scent and the crimson markings of a royal army upon their black tunics and cloaks gave them away. It had been said that most wolves in this territory were warriors in the king's infamous legions.

Fear and awe mixed into a heady wave of ice-layered warmth from the city dwellers. For the beasts masquerading as typical fae males were anything but. One could learn a lot from merely observing and listening, and since arriving in the city only this morning, I'd gleaned a surprising amount of information about the kingdom of Vordane.

These wolves were both saviors and nightmares—stars-bent on shredding souls and livelihoods in their neighboring kingdom of Sinshell.

What Vordane's king hoped to attain from such brutality wasn't for me to discern. Though a part of me did long to give the seemingly unconcerned faeries of this kingdom a glimpse at just how devastatingly destructive bloodshed forged from hatred could be.

Interest in the wolves soon waned, the attention of most creatures given back to their liquor and companions. Two females seated along the wall in a booth by the door leaned closer to one another, their smiles and flushing cheeks earning them a glance from one of the warriors.

Hit with a hint of nostalgia for the excitement, the sweet-fragranced wonder the females fed to the musty air, I tried on a smile of my own.

It wobbled, my lips good for nothing more than fusing to the wineglass I gave to them.

I drained it, then scooped a handful of peppered nuts from the small bowl before me. The silver-haired bartender had kindly delivered it with the decanter of wine to my lone table in the corner when he'd noticed that I was in no hurry to leave. Uncanny yet not so wildly improbable, the flavored nuts tasted the same as our own. I'd hoped they wouldn't, but hoping was futile.

I could run. I could cross an ocean to hide amongst unknowing strangers and allow desperation to make me believe my brief escape would help. That it would make it hurt less or even offer some perspective.

But it hadn't worked. Not yet. Perhaps it wouldn't at all. So I ate, and I drank.

Feeling eyes upon me, I looked up to find there was only one.

A male with dark shoulder-length hair tied at his nape had seated himself beside a golden-haired female in the booth. He was missing an eye. A scar, severe and hooked, slashed through his sealed eyelid.

The females didn't seem to mind, offering broad smiles when he looked at them.

I was willing to wager the disfigurement deterred no one, his every feature sculpted with alluringly fierce edges. Dark hair peppered thick over his jawline. His cheeks sat high, intense enough to suggest many a knuckle had shattered upon trying to inflict him harm, and his lone eye resembled moss after the rain.

He was both utterly terrifying and beautiful.

Two things I'd gorged on for years, only to now find myself in hiding from the heartbreak of it all.

Yes, they'd enjoy him, I thought, offering a small smile when the male returned his attention to me. And so they should. They should enjoy everything he was before looking for something more trustworthy—something a little more tame.

Forcing my eyes to the deep blue of the decanter, I refilled my glass and dropped my chin to my hand to watch two males flirt with one another at the opposite end of the musty room.

It was everywhere.

The inescapable poison of lust and love. I could indeed run as far as I desired. I could hide in foreign lands amongst beings so much like myself that they might never know who I was. And I could feed myself all the lies in the world.

But just like the creatures surrounding me, I would always run straight back.

The air curled and pressed in warning, chilling my skin a split second before the empty chair at my table protested, yanked forcefully and then taken by a giant. "Drowning your sorrows?"

Him.

His voice was low, as deep as the darkest depths of the sea, and edged with rough precision. Not a voice many would dare ignore.

I tilted my head to study that scar of his. The thick, unmerciful slash. "Quite the war medallion you've got there."

"Not from battle." Seemingly taken aback by my immediate addressing of his trauma, he'd tensed. "Now answer my question."

I raised a brow, secretly thrilled by his audacity. Then again, he had no idea who I was. Which thrilled me even more. "I don't believe I asked you a question."

Dark brows hovered low, his tongue darting out to quickly wet his lips. Lovely lips. Thick but not so full that they stole from his fearsome persona. A persona that probably earned him whatever he wished, judging by the way he stared at me, as if suddenly unsure how he should proceed.

I ended his torment with a smile, easing back in my chair. "I'm merely enjoying a drink."

"You reek of misery."

I paused, the wine halfway to my lips. "A hunter, are we?"

His slow smirk was deadly affirmation. "If that's what you need."

It was impossible to stop the jolt of energy that scorched through me, heating things I'd thought might long stay cold.

His nostrils twitched a moment before his lips stretched into a devastating grin. He could scent it. A true predator.

A wolf.

I should've been ashamed at how easily I'd reacted—and that I'd reacted at all. But I had a feeling this male could say anything, so long as it was wrapped in the right intention, and most would find surrender the only option.

"What makes you think I need anything?"

He pursed his lips, then gave me a pointed look. No, he need not say it.

I still waited, smiling into my glass.

"You know I can smell you."

I nodded, swirling the liquid. "And what exactly is it that you smell?" I was playing a dangerous game, but I found myself too relieved by the distraction to care. Too thankful for the knowledge that misery needn't be my only companion after days spent with the torture of believing it was all I now had.

The glint in his eye should've been warning enough as he declared with utter seriousness, "My next meal."

Wine sprayed from my nose. I coughed, laughing so hard I couldn't breathe.

The stranger seized the opportunity to move closer, his fingers pulling back the curtain of my hair. The tickling, barely-there touch was a caress over every sensitive part of me. I coughed again, startled by its power.

"You okay?" His mouth twitched. "You really need to get out more if you think a bastard like me is funny."

"Perfect," I wheezed, dabbing beneath my eyes and coughing one last time.

He nodded, lips still wriggling, but he didn't move away. "Indeed." He watched me, that eye stealing mine and narrowing. "Who are you?"

"Most males usually ask for a name."

"Have a lot of experience in finding new bedmates, do you?"

As if he already knew the answer, his features didn't change when I shook my head. "I'll admit to being the committed type." I picked up my wine, feeling his arm at the back of my chair like a fire-warmed blanket. Taking a sip, I carefully set it down while saying, "I have a feeling you're not."

He whistled. "Beautiful and judgmental." My lips parted, an

apology ready to spill forth when he gently flicked his fingers under my chin and grinned. "And absolutely right." I laughed a little more, but it died when he said, "Give me your name."

There was no hesitation, the half-lie spoken smoothly. "Aster."

He cocked his head, a smirk joining his purred words. "A wildflower."

"Dearest commander," one of his friends hollered. "I am sorry to inform you that we simply must be taking our leave."

The other laughed. "Not sorry at all."

Scowling, the male beside me looked at the door.

His two friends exited the tavern with the females he'd been sitting with before joining me. One male with shoulder-length hair grinned and made a vulgar gesture, but rather than bristle over the loss of his nightly prey, the wolf beside me just made one in return and watched them go.

I cleared my throat, knowing I should have taken the opportunity to leave—to move away at the very least—yet I didn't. It was as if his heat had fused to my own, and to part would guarantee the return of winter to my bones. "Looks like they stole your next meal."

"Come now." The wolf looked back at me with a wicked glow in his eye. "We both know as soon as I noticed you that I would not be leaving with anyone else."

Smiling, I ducked my head, unsure what to do with this persistent faerie warrior but certain I shouldn't allow myself to feel any guilt when he stood and dumped some coins onto the table. "Take a walk with me."

I looked up at him. "To your bed, I presume?"

His eye flashed, but he only held out his hand.

It hung between us, giant and calloused and stiff, as though he wasn't accustomed to doing such a thing for anyone. "I didn't take you for a well-mannered male." Yet I placed my hand within his.

It was swallowed, his grip gentle but firm as he gave a tug, and I rose from my seat. My head spun, reminding me of the wine I'd consumed over the past few hours.

Another slight tug and I was forced to lay my hand upon his hard chest and tilt my head back to see him when he murmured, "I'm the furthest thing from well-mannered, wildflower." His head lowered, nose skimming my hair. I shivered when he groaned. "You smell like honey."

"I thought you scented something else," I quipped, but the words were but a whisper.

"Oh, there's still plenty of that too."

Laughing, I found myself clenching the hand still holding mine, my fingers curling into the coarse fabric of his midnight black tunic as though I would fall back into dark nothing without this unlikely savior. "Better get me some fresh air, then."

True to his word, we took to the damp city streets of Vordane.

They were less clustered than when I'd arrived. Some stragglers drank and laughed in groups, while others dined late outside restaurants. The moisture from the afternoon rainfall created a glow upon the cobblestone, weeds and shrubs and flowers lining the cracks and shopfronts still gleaming.

In whites and yellows and blues, they shivered and swayed.

My hand stayed tucked in the embrace of the wolf's. My heart remained torn but determined to stay afloat. And as he appeased the curiosity I couldn't shake, I felt myself slowly forgetting anything that wasn't him.

Recalling what his friend had said upon leaving the tavern, I broke the warm silence. "A commander," I said as though I knew anything at all. "Impressive." Though I'd gleaned that the ruler of this kingdom I'd decided to visit was stars-bent on seeking vengeance against their neighboring realm, I knew little else.

We had too many monsters of our own to concern ourselves with the problems of others.

The commander didn't preen like a peacock, though I highly doubted he was capable. But he did give my hand a slight squeeze. "To the rest of you, maybe." His tone held an undercurrent of apathy and something else. Perhaps discomfort.

"Have you lost many of your brethren to this war with Sinshell?"

"More than we'd anticipated," he said, rough. "And I've a feeling it'll only get worse." As though worried he'd said too much, he attempted to change the subject. "Why haven't I seen you before?"

But I wasn't yet ready to decide what lies to feed him, and I wasn't ready to let him escape what he wished to avoid. "Do you enjoy attacking your own ilk?"

The wolf tensed. I expected him to drop my hand and maybe even glower at me in outrage. Instead, he stared straight ahead to the sparkling river at the street's end.

I quickly added, "I mean, I assume it would be extremely difficult…"

"We do what we're born to do," he evaded, tone clipped and stoic. "Protect and serve. We will bleed them dry for what they stole from our king and for the future they took from our people."

I nodded, having heard the tale from my father quite some time ago.

The way he had spoken of this realm was partly why I'd decided to hide here. Over the fire, he'd told me the story of a young crimson king who had lost his parents to a battle that never should have happened. A battle with the golden fae who resided across the ravine that divided this continent of Nodoya.

A grave and culture-altering loss.

Regardless, I didn't believe it warranted the extremes the king now hungered to deliver. Then again, I had seen firsthand that war of any kind never solved much of anything.

The softest heart, Rorn would say, *wrapped in a thick layer of impenetrable gold.*

Yet you quickly found your way in, I'd forever reminded him, the surest way to earn a blinding smile from him.

Another tug on my hand brought me back from thoughts I couldn't have. Not yet. Not when it was all still so fresh and too much to digest. Not when I needed anything other than the ache of him. "Where'd you go just now?"

The wolf commander had stopped us outside of a small bookstore. "What do you mean?" I studied the faded etching of a stack of books upon the wooden sign hanging over the flaking brown door. A door in a city that wasn't my own. A male who wasn't my own touching me.

My chest flooded with cold as what I was doing began to rattle through me like a slow-to-take poison.

But before I could move away and concoct an excuse for my behavior—and an excuse to leave—the warrior's low timbre froze my spiral. "Your heart pounds." Taking a step closer, he drew my gaze and cocked his head, studying me. "Afraid of a little vengeance, wildflower?"

Wildflower.

It was then I understood what the name meant, and I felt both foolish and dizzyingly giddy. I liked it. I had no right to like it.

I loosened my hand in his to let go.

Instead, I found myself turning it over. Tracing the tiny scars and rough skin, I wondered over each one, of how injured he'd been in his lifetime to have earned such marks. And I wondered if months from now, the battered and bleeding organ within my chest might appear the same.

I wasn't sure which future scared me more—one filled with healing and forgiveness or a continued wilting existence.

"Actually," I said, my heart racing with a lighter patter. "I'm beginning to think vengeance has an unexpected…" I paused over a raised scar in the shape of a cross. "Allure."

The wolf rasped, "That so?"

I threaded my fingers through his thick ones and gazed up at him with my lip between my teeth. "Yes." His eye swirled, the emerald darkened with every shallow rise of his chest, and when he gripped my cheek, I didn't move away.

Closing my eyes, I awaited the fall of his lips on mine.

I expected rough, hot, urgent—a claiming of some kind. What I received was a gentle, shaken press of silk, sliding soft as he breathed me in. "I want to know you." His whispered words heated in every way I needed. "Why do I want to know you?"

I couldn't answer that, nor why I burned hotter at the thought of it. At the idea of this war-hungry wolf wanting something in a way he perhaps hadn't before and feeling confused by it.

I couldn't answer, but I could do what I grew more and more desperate to.

I could kiss him back.

With my hands roaming up his chest, brushing over his broad shoulders to his neck, I looped them there and pushed my body against his, my lips against his.

Unlike him, I wasn't gentle. I didn't want to melt.

If I was doing this, then I wanted to burn.

Bruising enough to draw blood, I meshed my mouth to his and opened it to explore the warmth and the velvet of his tongue. Our teeth caught, our breaths meeting and our hands grabbing. Mine clasped the back of his neck and head, nails scoring through his shockingly soft hair to his scalp.

I was tall for a female, but he was more than a head taller than me. It didn't matter when the hands squeezing my hip and delving into my hair fell away to grip my thighs and lift me from the ground. Instinctively, I curled my legs around his waist.

"May I have you?" he whispered to my cheek, the gentle words a violent contrast to his unyielding grip. He held me as if unwilling to let me go, his hardness meeting my core through my skirts.

I didn't think. I didn't let doubts creep in. Not when he pulled back to look at me. Not when that one desperate look, the hunger in his eye, made it impossible to want, let alone think of anything else. "Please do."

"Thank the fucking stars," he rushed out, the words squashed against my lips when his stole mine.

He walked uphill without falter, seeming to know exactly where he was going.

The wheels of a wagon squeaked by, and other city dwellers likely passed us, too, but when I tried to pull away, I was denied. He captured the back of my head, trapping me. I laughed, surprised to find I liked being told no.

We floated up a set of spiraling metal stairs, and when he finally removed his lips from mine, it was to kick open the door to a dark apartment. A woodsy scent and that of old books enveloped me. As I tucked my nose into his neck while he locked the door, I discovered it was him.

A faint trace of mint—no, pine. Pine and something smoky, something unnameable.

It was a drug. A potion that went straight to my head, made worse when he dropped me onto a ginormous bed riddled with the scent. Before I could so much as glimpse the entirety of the bookshelves encircling the room, the wolf was above me, staring down at me intently as he dragged a hand up my leg.

My skirts were taken with it. As was my breath, hitching when he reached the apex of my thighs. Something sharp grazed my skin.

My eyes widened when I realized what it was. A claw. When I realized that I was truly going to bed with a stranger.

I was going to bed with a wolf.

It was then, with him so close, with nothing else within my thoughts and sight but him, that I wholly absorbed this creature. All that he was and how I felt small for quite possibly the first time in my life. His sheer size, muscle packed on muscle, was to blame.

The power behind such strength radiated from him like a slow to grow fire, emanating an unearthly energy that was impossible to ignore.

A touch cruel and knowing, he smirked and placed his other hand by my head, expelling a breath through his nostrils. "I've no patience for undergarments."

Indeed, they then tore right over my center.

The claw retracted, replaced with the roughened pad of his finger at the top of my mound. Eye steadfast on mine, he took his time tracing the tear he'd made. I shivered. He swallowed thickly when he parted me. "Stars, you're soaked."

I raised a brow. "Is that a bad thing?" We both knew it wasn't.

He grinned, then groaned when he reached my opening, and his finger slipped inside. "Fuck." He sat back on his knees, pushed my skirts over my stomach, and barked, "Open these pretty thighs wide." I did, and his chest rose as he hissed in a breath through his teeth. "Wider. Fuck yes." With another groan, his eye flicked to my face as he began to lazily fuck me with his finger.

Sparks ignited when he pulled it free and lifted it to his mouth. His gaze refused to stray from mine as he sucked every morsel of me from the thick digit. Assaulted by another shiver, this one violent, I whispered, "I think I just…" I swallowed, my limbs tingling. "Maybe a little."

He leaned over me. "Climaxed?" That earned me a furrow of his brow and a dark chuckle. The sound raised gooseflesh on my bare thighs. "We can't have you unsure now, wildflower."

That name again, coupled with his touch returning, his palm rubbing over me, and his finger inside me, gifted me with mindless want. "Need you," I rasped. "Inside me."

"Not until I've seen these legs shake."

The slight desperation in his voice made me almost envious of his control. Biting my lip, I tugged down the neckline of my gown, exposing my breasts.

The wolf cursed, but his movements didn't cease. He tortured me harder, palm pressing and his finger curling when my hands gripped my breasts.

Exhilaration, a burning I'd never felt trailing through my torso to my core, emboldened. *This must be why*, I mused silently. The freedom to be whoever you wanted, to let go entirely, had to be part of the reason people enjoyed bedding strangers.

It had to be why Rorn had destroyed me by doing so.

The commander's thickened voice caused my hands to slacken.

"If you undo me this thoroughly while still half clothed, I'm a little concerned about what might happen when I tear this dress from you."

"You mustn't wreck it," I panted, panic attempting to distract at the mere thought. "I don't have another."

His eye narrowed, his curiosity brimming. But I gasped, arching into his slow thrusts and chasing the high he was taking his time to deliver.

"Fine," he clipped at the same time he flicked me.

I mewled, hands shaking as my fingers clawed for purchase in the bedding and my hips bucked. My low moans soon turned into a muted scream when his hot mouth latched onto me, tongue dipping at my entrance to lap at what he'd done.

My thighs clamped over his head. My body contorted, the sensations too much.

He pushed them wide open and shattered me so completely, I was a boneless, writhing, dizzied mess.

"Taste just like honey, too," he said, forcing himself away some minutes that felt like hours later. Maybe it was. I wouldn't know.

All I knew was that by the time his mouth ceased learning me, I was ready again, greedy again, so when his head came within reaching distance, I lifted my weak arms to grasp his cheeks. "Show me," I said, his eye boring into mine. "How I taste. How we both taste."

He cursed before sliding his lips over mine.

The undergarments disappeared entirely.

My dress ripped, his hands rough and mine urgent as we tugged and pulled at our clothing until we were rolling over the bed to free ourselves from their confines, unable to separate for longer than a second.

Pushed to my back, he hooked my thigh over his. The wolf inside the male looming over me shined down at me through his eye, pheromones seeping through his smooth skin. His forehead pressed to mine. My fingers got lost, searching and sliding over his toned hips, his tapered sides, and roaming over the twitching mass of muscle in his arms.

"Going to fuck you now."

My voice was foreign, husky. "Please do."

"Won't be sweet or gentle"—he exhaled roughly—"nor will the next time I have you."

I traced the harsh cut of his square jaw and watched his sooty lashes flutter. "Do you like to fuck multiple times in one night?"

"Yes," he croaked, and he dragged his cock through the wet at my center. "But I can't take a break with you. Doubt I can leave you alone for a stars-damned second." Noting my shock, he kissed my nose, the unexpected action warming my chest. "Okay with that?"

"More than okay." I'd barely finished talking when the ability to was robbed from me.

In one fluid, controlled thrust, his body joined with mine.

A drawn-out, graveled curse washed over my cheek as he seated himself inside me.

I was familiar with his size—his length and his girth.

What I wasn't familiar with were the strange feelings evoked by the connection.

Right, it sang. *Perfect,* it crooned. A melody thrummed inside my chest, euphoric in a way that made me forget the reason for it was someone I didn't even know. Pleasure erupted through my bloodstream and pressed tickling fingers against my skin. Gooseflesh rose, and my exhale shook.

The warrior eased out of me, then slammed back in and circled his hips. I moaned, and I molded to him. I bloomed like never before beneath him. Even as a growl ripped from his throat and he did as promised...

He destroyed me in every unexpected way.

His teeth sank into my lip, blood pooling before being stolen by his tongue. His swallow and approving rumble sang through each fire-filled limb. His large palm covered my breast and squeezed, then reached out to clench the headboard, and the bed met the wall.

Books rattled upon shelves and something clattered from the nightstand to the floor.

I was teetering within moments, scratching at his back as I began to shudder. He pulled his mouth from mine to stuff his face between my shoulder and neck. Teeth gripped my skin, threatening but going no further. Nipping and retreating, they followed the powerful, animalistic movements of his body.

A silent scream scraped my throat raw. My legs tightened around his hips when it became too much—when he growled his pleasure at my body's intense response to his.

That growl grew deeper. Deadlier. It erupted from his chest as he stilled and trembled above me, his hand leaving the headboard to clasp my cheek and jaw.

Breathing ragged, he lifted his head to fuse our lips.

My mind whirled. My heartbeat thundered. My nails slowly left his skin.

Dissolved so completely, all I could do was lay there while he kissed me. Hard, and evidently still hungry, he parted my lips and covered each with his before he licked at my tongue.

Cold washed in, blistering enough that I found myself reaching for him when he pulled away. "Want you on your knees now."

I didn't argue. I didn't falter. I didn't even offer him a sultry glance before doing exactly as he wished. The fact that I hadn't challenged him at all, that I *wanted* to please him, and that I needed him inside me again so soon should have more than concerned me. It should have sickened me.

None of it did any such thing.

The sound echoed before the sting arrived, and then his mouth was there, dragging and licking at the cheek he'd slapped. He hummed, leaning away to rub it. Then both hands squeezed my rear and hauled me back toward him.

"Sit," he said, gruff with desire and spearing at my core from behind.

I did, and he released his length when the tip encountered my opening to help me slowly swallow him with his hands at my hips.

"Good. So fucking good." He curled my hair over my shoulder to whisper in my ear, "Are you always this obedient, wildflower?"

Unsure how to answer that, all I managed was a shake of my head.

A pleased hum accompanied a press of his lips to my skin. "Never have I enjoyed anything the way I'm enjoying you."

I gripped the arm encircling my waist, burning and never more glad for it. Veins and muscle protruded beneath my touch, his mouth and tongue sliding over my shoulder. "Tell me if it's too much."

"It's too much," I heard myself say without thinking, followed quickly by, "but don't you dare make me leave."

He seemed to understand what I'd meant and stilled. His other hand crawled over my chest to my chin and turned it. I gazed at his lips, wanting them on mine. "Let me see those gray eyes."

I rose and then slid back down on his shaft, lifting my lashes.

His hand descended my body, my own still clutching his forearm, and he touched me. A touch so gentle and precise, my breath hitched, breaking across his lips. The question was hoarse, his gaze narrowed and searching mine. "Where in the stars did you come from?"

I just smiled and cupped his stubble-lined jaw, then silenced his curiosity with my mouth on his.

TWO

Aster

ANGER WAS MORE POWERFUL THAN GUILT.

Yet the latter lingered. It poked beneath my skin like a dull blade unable to wholly penetrate.

And so I clung to the anger. I let it blend with the heady arrival of flutters that left my chest to wreak havoc through every extremity when I turned away from the window beside the bed and rolled into the warrior holding me.

His arm tightened, and I waited for it. Though I'd never experienced anything like this before, I'd heard that the morning after spending the night with a stranger could bring some awkwardness.

But the wolf did not tense. He did not need a moment to remember who he was holding and what we'd done.

My nose was smooshed into his chest as he grabbed me by the rear, his other hand sliding beneath me to tangle in my hair. I stilled when he murmured, "Three, two, one…"

It was then I heard the footsteps thundering up the stairs outside.

"Scythe, what the fuck?" The hollered words were accompanied by an unnecessary bang on the door. "Serrin's yapping Dade's ear off about your attitude again. Get the fuck up and to the barracks—" A barked chuckle sounded after a sudden pause. "*Who* have you got in there? Must be extra tasty if you haven't kicked them to the street already."

I pushed against the wolf's smooth skin, his chest hair tickling my nose, but he pushed me back against him. "Your legion awaits you," I whispered, lips rubbing over his pectoral.

"Too late to give a fuck," he rumbled. "Not that I had any to give in the first place."

Indeed, enough light filtered into the room, even with the drapes closed, to let us know it was nearing midday.

Another thud, followed by, "Fuck you, asshole," and then pounding down the stairs. "Not cleaning up your mess this time."

"Scythe," I said to his chest, not in question but tasting the name. "Not your birth-given name."

"No," he said, curt enough that I knew not to ask him to tell me what it was.

That was fine. He could keep his secret, for I had no choice but to keep all of my own.

He squeezed my ass. I giggled into his chest and allowed my hand to drift down the broad expanse of his back.

He made a sound close to a purr that stirred the hair atop my head, and clutched me closer. "I really like holding you." Such simple words. Too simple to warrant the wildfire they caused inside my heart, the violent rush within my veins, when he murmured, "And how you feel against me."

I closed my eyes, wishing I could sink beneath his skin and start anew. A different life. A different male. A different collection of memories.

A different, wide-open future.

Unable to respond, I feathered my fingers over his back. They dipped into ridges between muscle, the indent of his spine, and over a thick scar.

I shifted my thigh, allowing him to better scent what I wanted— what I needed.

I needed what he was so unknowingly skilled at gifting me. The ability to forget.

The tempo of his heart increased under my cheek. He lifted my leg high enough that when he reached between us, he could touch me. He could feel me. He could feel exactly what he did to me. "Fuck, Aster." Languidly, he dragged his finger through me. "Are you not sore?"

I shivered at the way sleep lingered and thickened his tone. The way it made each word roll into another, and huskier. "Not sore enough."

A chesty growl, and then that finger plunged inside me. "Soaked. Have I kept you wanting?" Moving slow, deliriously slow, he curled and twisted, stroked me with teasing precision before retreating to do so all over again.

"Waiting," I managed after a shaken breath.

A smile wrapped around his words. "My sincerest apologies."

"I'll bet you never apologize for anything, wolf."

He chuckled, low and deep. "Not wrong about that. Roll over."

But I liked being pressed so firmly against him, where everything was dark and warm and delicious and safe. An illusion. A veil shielding what awaited me beyond.

My eyes flashed open when his touch left my core. He clasped my face, some of my hair woven through his fingers, and tilted it until his nose could skim my cheek. "Comfortable, wildflower?"

Sparks replaced the beat of my heart. Tearing myself away just long enough to roll over earned me another chuckle.

My gaze drifted to the tattered plaid armchair by the window, then to the books neatly piled on the nightstand next to me. Pieces of this male were few, but there were enough to make me want to fit them together.

Vacant thoughts I shouldn't have had were erased when he lifted my leg and his chest molded to my back. A rumbled, "Stars, I've been missing this," washed over my shoulder as he eased his length inside my body.

He stayed there for a swelling moment while roughened fingers ghosted over my arm and down my ribs, allowing me to adjust after a night spent filled with him. "It's been maybe five hours."

"Five hours too long." Those fingers tickled across my stomach toward my breast, then squeezed. "Perfect size." My breasts weren't overly large, but they were what I considered to be a subtle handful. To which he confirmed. "Fit in my hands like they were made to."

Bonds mean nothing when you were made for me.

The memory of one of Rorn's many heated declarations charged through my mind, my heart, my very soul, and with such ferocity that I whimpered.

The wolf inside me thankfully mistook it for pleasure and began to move.

He took his time, and I was tempted to push back into him— to push him to the bed and force him into distracting me more thoroughly. Yet again, he surprised me, somehow knowing what I needed without knowing much of me at all.

His lips marked my shoulder with gentle fire. His hips rotated with delirious finesse.

Before too long, my breathing grew labored, my bones began to burn and tremble, and I was falling. I was falling into this stranger with more gratitude than guilt, more thankful than he would ever possibly know.

He caught me before following, our bodies still joined as his hand roamed over my chest and stomach, and I soon succumbed to sleep.

Starlight sprinkled through the gap in the tattered drapes when I woke alone and wrapped in the gray and white bedding.

I rolled to my back, then sat up when I failed to sense another beating heart inside the apartment.

The bed I'd been left in shared space with a rectangular dining table. It resembled a workbench, the wooden top worn and the metal legs rusted. Two wooden chairs with chipped red paint perched at either end. Through an arched doorway behind it was a small kitchen.

Pastel blue and cream paint peeled in patches from the cupboards, the tiled countertops holding little more than a stovetop and a small collection of mismatched glass jars.

My limbs protested as I crawled to the edge of the oversized bed.

Stretching them, I stared down at the rumpled sheets, the few feathers floating upon them from the pillows. I chewed my lip as I re-called biting into one just hours ago, my stomach upon the bed while I was entered ruthlessly from behind.

An experienced and demanding lover, most certainly. The wolf had made that abundantly clear more times than I dared to count. Yet there was a softer, unexpectedly devoted side to him that made my chest squirm when I thought of him sharing all he was with some-one else.

I scolded myself and plucked my gown from the woven and faded crimson carpet. I'd need to mend it. I'd also need to bathe before I left—to soak myself clean of the scent of the male with a name that matched his scarred eye.

Scythe.

But the idea of returning home after what I'd done, after what Rorn had done, hollowed my chest. Acid slowly seeped inside to fill the void he'd so brutally given me.

I stood, unwilling to let it. Not yet. But the memories of what I'd fled from, of all I'd never once expected to break, quaked my knees.

"You've ruined it. Ruined me. Ruined it all."

"You're being shortsighted. Nothing is ever irreparable, Bloom."

"We are, Rorn, and you've no one but yourself to blame. I don't want this. Not like this."

Fury had replaced the fear in his eyes. "You think to leave this life? To leave me?" Rorn had scoffed. "We both know that's impossible. I'll give you what time you need, but your promises are as inescapable as I am."

Before I could utter a retort about his broken promises, he was gone.

Words, I thought, lost to the brittle imagery of Rorn stalking away from me as though he held ownership over who I was and all I could do, were useless.

For the male I'd run from was right. I could tell him that we were no longer and that what he'd done was unforgivable until it robbed me of sanity, but it would mean nothing.

I still, and I always would, belong to him.

With the bedsheet tucked around me, I spread my gown over my lap and did my best to repair the shoulder and the bust. Not exceptionally experienced at mending but determined to at least tap into that part of my mother's lineage during the lonely winters while growing up, I'd learned to make do.

A tepid warmth gathered in my fingertips, the frayed edges of the torn material crawling and tightening as they rejoined beneath the gentle coaxing of my touch.

My plans to bathe and dress and force myself to leave before Scythe's return were foiled when the air in the room grew charged. Shadows collected by the dining table, thickening and separating to reveal a tall, incredibly muscular male in a tight black tunic and leather vest.

The wolf could warp.

My heartbeat kicked as I pondered his lineage, and I deduced he likely carried traces of noble blood.

Inwardly, I rolled my eyes. Of course, he did. It wasn't enough that he could murder with a flick of his claws. The stars had felt the need to give him the ability to be even more deadly.

His vest creaked. The crimson stitching of his tunic threatened to burst at his biceps when he lifted a gleaming silver tray of food and gestured to the table. His gaze swam over me, as if checking all of me was still here.

He blinked, almost shy as he roughly said, "Thought you might need something to eat."

Steam rose from the chicken and roast vegetables when he removed the lid shielding the plate. "Where did you get that?"

"The Keep," he said, and before I could ask more, he came for me to steal my chin. "Hello, wildflower."

My head tipped right back, and my lips parted when his thumb brushed beneath my mouth. That fluttering returned with a vengeance. "Hello, wolf."

He smirked, then dropped his hand to grab mine. I was tugged to my feet, the sheet held to my chest, though I didn't know why. He'd seen everything—parts of me I'd only ever shared with one creature.

A kiss, a barely-there placement of softness over my cheek, had never felt so menacing. "Sit," he commanded. "Eat."

With my heart hammering, I swallowed and thanked him, sliding into the chair he'd untucked.

He left me with my turmoil and the delicious food I was suddenly not so hungry to eat, his boots heavy over the wood floor as they carried him to the small bathing room next to the kitchen. Tears sprang unexpectedly when I heard water filling a tub, then his returning steps.

I ducked my head and snatched the fork from the tray, forcing myself to eat to better hide my inconsistent emotions.

The cheese sauce was unlike any I'd tasted at home, rich and creamy without overpowering the herb-laced chicken. Hunger returned with a force that made my stomach growl.

Chuckling, the wolf poured me a glass of water. "When was the last time you ate?"

Except for some fruit and bread from the city market stalls the morning prior and some peppered nuts at the tavern, I hadn't. Though I knew to say so would displease him. "Yesterday," I simply said, then gestured to the empty space at the table before him when he took a seat, the wood of the chair groaning. "You're not eating?"

"I ate at the Keep," he said, pushing the water toward me.

So the royal home of Vordane was called a keep. I smiled my gratitude and took a sip, finding I couldn't meet his watchful gaze. "Did you fix your mess?"

He huffed. "Dramatic is Fang's surname."

I set the water down. "And what is yours?"

When he didn't respond, I looked up and found his hands curled together over the table. His eye was a brighter green this evening, like the stained glass of the windows back at home. "Don't have one."

"I don't believe you." But I didn't press and continued eating, wondering how this would work. Did I merely say thank you and then leave? Was I supposed to wait until he next disappeared so it wasn't awkward for either of us?

Before I could build the courage to suggest it was time I returned home, Scythe rose and traipsed to the bathing room. "I've drawn you a bath."

The fork shook, clattering against my teeth as I delivered my next mouthful. I shoveled it in, chewing slowly as I listened to him open a cupboard and unscrew something.

Shit.

Swallowing, I reached for more water and emptied what remained of the glass. "You really don't need to do that or any of this," I said, proud of the polite strength in my tone. "I appreciate your kindness, but it's unnecessary." Lifting the napkin to my lips, I stood and dabbed at my mouth. "There's no need to worry or fuss. I know it's certainly past time I took my leave."

Scythe turned to lean against the chipped doorframe of the bathing room, holding a small towel in his large hands. He twisted it, eyeing me with a curl to his lips. "You've never done this before."

The way he'd stated that truth rather than asked grated a little. I pulled my shoulders up and opened my mouth.

His smirk bloomed into a word-stealing smile. "If I wanted you to leave, you would know, and you would've done so last night." A slight lift of his shoulder. "Or in the early hours of this morning."

I blinked, then scowled. "And do you treat most females in such a way?"

"Most don't care," he said absently. "I'm a fun time, a wild ride, the untamable." He half-rolled his eye. "I don't encourage anything more, so"—he shrugged again—"it works fine. Despite what Fang said, they just…" He scratched at his stubble-coated cheek. "Well, they see themselves out, really."

Anger shocked me where I stood trapped between the seat and the table.

I didn't know why. I didn't even know him. But what I did know, I wanted more of, and that shamed me. Though not enough to do what I knew I should have already done and walk away.

"But you," he said while I grappled with thin scraps of resolve. "You're different." He erased the space between us. The towel dropped to the table, and his head lowered to mine. "I already suspect that I'll be the one doing the taming here."

"Scythe," I whispered, my eyelids fluttering when his hands molded perfectly to the flare of my hips. "I really should go."

"Why?" He dragged his lips over my cheekbone and inhaled deep. "You're afraid." He paused, those keen senses mercifully unable to read my thoughts. "Of what?"

"You," I said, and it wasn't a lie.

He was grinning when I allowed myself to peer up at him, to touch his waist. I told myself it was to steady my feet over the ground that had begun to shake beneath them. I already knew I'd tell myself some dangerous things just to touch this peculiar yet intoxicating warrior.

I would tell myself that I was allowed to, as I would never have been here in the first place if it weren't for Rorn's betrayal. That I could take what I wanted if it meant making my altered—*ruined*—future more bearable to face.

I would tell myself that I deserved to feel good, to feel alive after days spent with nothing but breath-robbing misery.

Scythe twitched beneath the gentle brush of my fingers over his lower back. I tilted my chin with the help of his fingers.

Another kiss, softer than any I'd had before, instantly warmed the coldest parts of me. The wolf aligned our lips, breathed me in, pressed, then rubbed his silken mouth side to side over mine. Our noses bumped, the finger under my chin stroking so tenderly, a flood of heat spread right through me and straight to my core.

Scenting what he'd done, he smiled against my mouth. "Stay. Just one more night."

I kissed him and dragged my teeth over his bottom lip, the smooth, slight thickness of his mouth too addictive. "Just one?"

"Forever would be ideal, but we'll work our way up to that."

"I…" My heart skidded to a halt, then roared, and I broke away before he could sense what he'd done. I cleared my throat, dropped the bedsheet to the floor, and grabbed the towel. "Let me ponder it while I bathe."

His deep voice held a hint of laughter as his gaze burned my skin from behind. "Whatever you need, wildflower."

The bathing room was tiny and reminiscent of the one we'd had growing up in the cottage. The tub was big enough for a male but, unlike his bed, most certainly not a beast. A privy sat in the corner with a small basin on a cracked porcelain stand between it and the tub.

Rather than recoil at the mildewed and chipped tiles on the wall, the shallow space I hadn't thought I'd ever find myself inside of again, a vintage part of me awoke with a smile, and I climbed into the tub.

My fingers skipped over the rusted rim toward the cracked, cream tiles, leaving damp trails behind. Opulence was divine, there was no doubt about it, but there was something to be said for the quainter things in this eternally dramatic life.

When I returned, Scythe was seated on the end of the bed, my gown draped across his lap.

Seemingly lost in thought, he rubbed at the mauve velvet bodice, large fingers disturbing the ivory ribbon ties. "I've not seen a gown like this here. Simple, versatile," he said, as if to himself, "yet still elegantly beautiful."

"I'm glad you approve, but I'll be needing it back," I said with a smile. Though really, I'd have been perfectly happy to remain in the coarse towel that was soaked in his scent.

His lips curved, then parted when his head lifted. "I don't know," he said, gaze wandering from my scrunching toes and over my legs, taking its time to reach my own as he drank all of me in, "I think we should make sure it stays in one piece."

I bit my lips to keep from laughing.

"I see you've mended it." Curiosity lingered in those rough words as he stood and crossed the crimson carpet to the dining table. There, he carefully draped the dress over the back of a chair. "Though not very well." It was more of an honest observation than an insult.

"It will do." My heart pattered at the gentle way he adjusted the garment to keep it from further creasing. "Scythe." I wasn't sure why it was so hard to say when typically, I had no trouble saying exactly what I felt. Perhaps it was because it wasn't what I wanted. I didn't want to leave. "I should…"

He moved within a blink of my eyes, and I felt him behind me, his hands over my hips and his warm breath at my shoulder. A lingering kiss was pressed to my skin, and then he was gone, leaving a hiss and low laugh in his wake as I stood naked in the middle of his apartment.

He'd stolen the towel, giving me little choice but to don my gown.

Water splashed, and the thought of him lathering himself with soap, cleansing me from his body, stilled me before the table.

"Touch that dress, and I'll treat my claws to it until it falls from you in shredded ribbons."

I gaped at the bathing room, unable to see him, yet I knew he was wearing a smug smile. "I've nothing else to wear, you beast. My undergarments were ruined, and they've conveniently disappeared."

He sounded delighted. "Best be climbing into bed, then."

"Do you get a thrill out of being so bossy?" That he was a commander for one of his king's legions should have already warned me of that being true.

My question earned me a rich but sadly too-short laugh. My chest filled at the sound. "Just reminding you of what you want to do, seeing as you still need a little help to commit."

He was right. It was both maddening and ridiculous. Yet as I placed my hand over the gown, knowing I could snatch it and warp back to a secluded part of the woods near the towers to put it on, I hesitated.

I hesitated long enough to freeze entirely, my eyes closing as what awaited me infiltrated.

Bloom, we must talk.

I'd known.

I'd known for days that something had been wrong. Rorn had returned from overseeing a large soldier rotation more haunted than when he'd left. I'd been informed it had been a successful journey with little to no skirmishes, save for an encounter with a pack of wild hounds.

But the weeklong venture in swapping out troops to guard against another wave of mortal soldiers farther breaching the border had nonetheless eventuated into something heartbreaking.

Certain I wouldn't survive knowing exactly what had happened, I'd walked away. I'd avoided him every day since he'd tensed at the sight of me waiting to greet him from across the river when he'd returned. Those frostbitten blue eyes hadn't smiled, hadn't looked upon me with any of the typical relief I'd come to expect with his arrival home.

They'd been empty of everything I'd needed and adored, and replaced with nothing I wanted to know.

Avoidance was futile. I was eventually cornered, the guilt too much for him to carry, it seemed. He'd needed to purge it.

He'd needed to destroy me to unburden himself.

And so I'd stood there, taking each word for the blows to the chest they'd been. He hadn't realized how quickly I was bleeding out, nor the way I struggled to find my next breath. No—too busy vomiting apologies and promises and unforgivable truths, Rorn had barely noticed me at all.

It wasn't until he'd placed his guilt upon me, until he'd used the one thing I'd thought we'd both wanted against me in his quest to cleanse his soul, that I'd finally moved.

"The constant talk of babes and the eternal disappointment we insist on enduring... I need an heir, Bloom. Wistensia needs one. We must move forward by any means possible."

Those words became knives I'd been unable to pull free from my heart.

But I hadn't walked away. Before Rorn's slow to widen eyes, I'd merely vanished.

I'd returned at nightfall to find him seated on the end of our bed in our chambers, his eyes pillowed with shadows.

"Bloom," he'd said, rising instantly.

And that had been when I'd told him we were no longer.

That had been when he'd stripped the worry from his features to replace it with cold ire—to remind me of all I'd once so desperately wished for. To ensure I was aware of what I could now never escape.

I'd then vanished entirely with his chilling exit.

Neither of us had ever crossed the Night Sea to visit Nodoya.

I'd found my destination weeks prior to his betrayal out of sheer curiosity while thumbing through an old tome of known fae cities of the world in the library. Recalling the story my father had shared of Nodoya's first war, I'd taken the book with me to my parlor.

The images of a river-edged diamond city I'd painted from the description and the map of a land that rose toward the sky as though it were a chest of jewels unearthed by the sea had been tucked within a pile of other paintings.

So unless Rorn discovered them and took a wild guess, he would never know where I was.

He wouldn't find me.

I closed my eyes and drew in a deep, shaken breath. When I opened them, I was turned into a damp chest.

Scythe gently lifted my chin, his intense scrutiny of my features nearly comical. "Aster, if you truly wish to leave, then I'll take you wherever you damned well need to go. I'll take you straight home." His teeth scraped his bottom lip. "I didn't mean—"

"It's not you," I said in a rush. "It's not this. I swear."

His brows lowered, the harsh rise and fall of his chest slowly calming. He cupped my cheek, brushing a rogue tear with his thumb. "Then what the fuck just happened?"

I slid my hand over his, leaning into his hard body. "Memories." He scowled, seeming to know what I would say next. "It's fine." Taking his hand, I kissed his palm.

His gaze softened marginally. Our nakedness became apparent then, his nostrils flaring, and I squeaked as I was swept off my feet and taken to the bed. In the center, he curled my body into his and pressed his lips to my forehead. "What in the stars are you running from, wildflower?"

"Everything," I admitted, my head settling upon his rock-hard bicep.

"Sounds promising," he grumbled, evidently annoyed at my failure to share with him.

Laughing, I tilted my head back to see him, and his glower fell away beneath the pads of my searching fingers. I traced his brow, the bridge of his strong nose and its tiny bump, then his plush lips. He was both wild yet refined, a contradiction that shouldn't work. But oh, how it did. "You're beautiful."

"Not something I've been called before, but thank you." He huffed. "I think."

"I mean it," I insisted, already imagining revisiting all that he was on parchment. Impossible, I knew, to capture the entirety of him. When I reached his scarred eyelid, he stilled. "Even this."

"Liar," he hissed, taking my hand and nipping at the tip of my finger.

I stole my hand back to return my fingers to his face, and he laughed silently.

I avoided touching the scar, but I couldn't keep from touching the corner of the sealed eye nor from marveling at what must have been agony. Traumatizing.

The longer and closer I looked, the more evident it became that someone had pried his eye from his face. "Who did this to you?" For they hadn't merely gouged it from his head—this warrior had been marked by such brutality that it could have killed him.

"Do I detect a little wrath there, wildflower?"

"You won't say. I already know you won't."

"The details are murky, and even if I wanted to, there's no point in sharing them." He sighed, threading his fingers through mine and holding our hands between us. "I like the look of murder in your eyes." He dragged his teeth over his lip. "A rare, stormy sunrise blue, but don't waste it on me."

I melted into him, and his lone eye heated. "You're far sweeter than you look, wolf."

He barked out a laugh. "Furthest thing from sweet," he said, his grin positively wolfish. He kissed my knuckles, then released my hand to move some strands of hair from my face. "It was a long time ago. I was young, so I managed."

"You simply managed?" I asked, a touch incredulous and unable to hide it.

"Don't fret, wildflower." Stroking the curve of my cheek, he admitted, "I've never missed it, not in the way I should. There are other things I would've chosen in a heartbeat over having it healed. All were impossible, so I learned to live without everything I once had with an aggression that enables me to better guard what I do have."

I pressed against him, wanting more but knowing better than to force him. "You lost loved ones."

He nodded but said nothing more on that. His finger and eye traced my lower lip, his voice a quiet rumble. "My other senses became stronger—so much clearer than that of those I grew and trained alongside. My instincts have never led me wrong, and I can't help but feel as though I wouldn't have risen to the highest rank possible if I hadn't been forced to fight twice as hard as my brethren."

A warrior indeed.

"Now," he said, his hand sweeping over my curves to caress and grip my rear. "Tell me what brought you to that tavern."

I couldn't. But I could lie while wondering if maybe it was not a lie at all.

I kissed him with a whispered, "I was looking for you."

THREE

Aster

WIDE AWAKE AND ALONE FOR HOURS THE FOLLOWING morning, I paced Scythe's apartment as though I'd been imprisoned in a cell of my own making.

Acknowledging that I wanted to know more about this wolf and that I couldn't stand my own company and the ache it brought forth— nor the idea of returning to a home that was no longer—left me feeling more tangled in knots than that of my waist-length hair.

I swept my fingers through it to try to rid the tangles from the previous night but soon gave in when they snagged and shook. I dressed and undressed and dressed again, and though nettles pierced my chest and vinegar singed my eyes, I began to warp home.

I stopped before the shadows of time could envelop me, and on the edge of the unmade bed, I fell limp.

I sat and stared at nothing while trying to forget everything.

Birdsong crept in through the crack in the blurred glass of the kitchen window, turning my attention to the contents of this stranger's home. To the books and the meagre belongings scattered throughout the shelves.

I wondered if it were fair to think of him as a stranger. If that were even possible after all the many ways our bodies had learned one another.

Looking at the copious spines, the filigree and the faded text, and the split covers, I wondered why it felt as if this male had never truly felt like a stranger at all.

The wolf returned before midday, his hair sweat-slicked. A glorious smile set his eye aglow and seized my heartbeat when he observed me eating crackers with a book in hand at his dining table.

I'd expected his giant collection to include texts pertaining mostly to battle or even politics. I'd been half wrong. As luck would have it, the novel I'd chosen was fictional and utterly engrossing. "I cannot remember why I stopped reading during the day," I uttered aloud by way of greeting. "It's so much more enjoyable, knowing there are more hours available to do so."

I surmised the inclination had been snuffed when replaced with painting. A more acceptable daily pastime for someone like me.

Scythe hummed. After a moment of silence, of studying me so intently I felt my skin heat in patches from his gaze, he clipped out, "I like this."

I refused to acknowledge that, nor the part of me that liked it too. Instead, I said, "You have no food. Just some nuts and dried meats and"—I lifted the jar with its few remaining crackers—"these."

"I eat most of my meals at the Keep." He grabbed the book, inspecting the title with raised brows. "One of my favorites."

"I might have picked the one that told me so."

"You've a good nose for someone who can't shift." Placing the book back in my hand, he crouched down before me and ordered gruffly, "Kiss me."

I did, breathless instantly. Even though he kept it gentle—sweet—it was no less intoxicating. Leaving me dazed, the legion commander tore off his leathered training gear and said on his way to the bathing room, "Let me get cleaned up. I want to take you somewhere."

Assuming this place had something to do with food, I waited

impatiently upon the bed, but I would soon find my hopes crushed and replaced with something unexpected.

Something a little bit like love.

For along the river heading north toward the royal Keep sat a patch of dense forest. Within the forest, not a mile from the riverside path trailing to the city we'd left behind, a small cottage greeted us.

A butter-stone chimney winked beneath the sun through the trees.

My chest filled with elated warmth, a nostalgic tug for what had been a different lifetime ago. I didn't wait. I walked closer to take in its ivy-coated entirety. Leaves encircled the chimney and drainpipes, and vines climbed over and around the arched windows.

The red-painted door was faded. The gardens were overgrown and in need of weeding. The cobblestone path that began between two shabby topiary trees was cracked and slippery with moss.

And all of it was the best form of medicine I never would have thought I'd need.

An assortment of birds sipped from the algae-covered birdbath that stood forgotten within the gardens.

Although quiet enough that I hadn't heard his approach, I still knew Scythe stood behind me. "This is…"

"Go on in," he urged gently when I failed to find words, my fingers clenching my skirts.

Inside, bookshelves made from branches and uneven slabs of wood lined half of the large circular room between the three arched windows. Roses, crimson with emerald leaves, stained their glass. The kitchen nook awaited next to the door, the backsplash and counter tiles a patterned mixture of creamy lavender and blue.

Fresh fruit gleamed in the wooden bowl upon the tilted top of a round dining table. He'd been here earlier. Which was confirmed by the half-set table and the pan upon the stove. Whatever this magical place was, it was his. His scent smothered as if cemented between the cracks in every stone.

I looked back to the shelves, blurting, "More books."

"Haven't read them all yet."

"How would you have the time, being gone for days on end for your king…" Staring at the novels, I felt my heart pinch, remembering some of the names scrawled upon the title pages inside others I'd flicked through back in his apartment. "They aren't yours."

My observation and accusation invited silence.

When Scythe finally spoke, his tone remained even and matter-of-fact. "Some of my brethren seek jewels and other valuables on raids. I take the books and the booze." He moved to the sink with a casual agility that drew my eyes, seemingly without a care for what he'd done.

Their heartbreak. Their homes. Their priceless possessions and lives…

My ears rang with the screams and anguish of those I'd left behind.

The sickness of guilt was a weight that would never leave, no matter how much I reminded myself that I couldn't change anything. How he could slaughter lives and livelihoods in the name of vengeance, I couldn't and refused to understand.

I swallowed, my voice quiet as I tried and failed to mask my distaste. "While I cannot say I like how you came to possess them, I do like that combination." The reminder of what he was, of what he did to assumingly helpless souls, had chilled me to the bone.

Scythe looked over at me as though sensing as much, but he wisely said nothing. He remained still and awaited my next move with unreadable and lupine features.

I forced myself to avert my gaze as the male who focused so keenly on me refused to hide what he truly was.

A predator keeping watch on his prey.

In an effort to rid the unwelcome cold and the increased tempo of my heart, I roamed the cottage. Some moments later, my mind still riddled with the terror of the helpless and the dying, he mercifully lit the stove, the scent of sizzling meat soon following.

When the fighting had moved from assassination attempts to

outright displays of violent force in our kingdom, my father had said no two sides were ever faultless in war.

As the king's favored general, he'd then been forced to start taking me to royal events while he worked, rather than leave me to our quiet life within the woods. During those frightening, formative years, the years in which I'd matured, I'd found myself a prince.

And it was during the months before my father's death that I'd agreed to marry him.

I had to wonder what my father would think of it all now, and if he'd somehow known what would come to pass. He'd not seemed happy with our engagement. He'd expressed that he was relieved I would be taken care of—that I would be safe—and little else. Then again, with the exception of a fresh slab of venison he'd hunted himself, the fearsome general had never been overly thrilled by much.

A smile untucked my lips from my teeth.

Perhaps that was why I felt so drawn to this wolf who went by the odd name of Scythe. For they were similar, and not merely because he was a shifter just as my father had been, but due to their frank belief that there was no right or wrong.

There was only duty. A primal loyalty to see to what must be done.

No lies and no games.

Next to the kitchen, two leather armchairs sat between the windows. A tree stump with books upon it served as a tea table. On the large oval carpet beneath the rickety dining table was a pair of ginormous combat boots, freshly scrubbed. There were only two chairs to lounge and eat in, so I assumed the warrior wasn't one to have visitors often.

The very idea made me snort as I pictured the rugged male serving anyone tea and cakes.

He knocked me from my musings. "Have you found something amusing?"

"I've certainly found something," I muttered with a smile he couldn't see. "And it would seem he's a bit of a contradiction."

He huffed. "The booze stays untouched."

"You don't drink liquor?" Casting back through my muddled mind, I couldn't remember seeing him with a drink in the tavern.

"No. Take a seat."

How he knew I was unsure of what to do with myself, I didn't know. But I assumed it had something to do with those keen senses. So I did as I was told, grateful to have something to do at all when he turned with a plate in hand. A hand so large, it made the average-sized porcelain appear too small.

I fastened my gaze to the table, to the cutlery and glass of water already waiting. "Then wouldn't it be better to get rid of it?" Unable to stop myself, I scolded gently, "Or perhaps not to take it at all."

His lips curled as he set a giant cut of beef before me. "I find keeping temptation within arm's reach at all times serves me better."

I swallowed, though I hadn't yet eaten a thing, and blinked at his broad back.

Forcing my eyes from his fluid movements, I sliced into the still-bloody meat. I half feared I could waste most of this eternal life just watching him. "So is this some type of wintry retreat for you?"

"It's my home." He dumped another piece of meat into the pan and a plate into the sink, already filled with soapy water. "The apartment is mine too, but it's mostly used for…" He trailed off with an endearingly uncomfortable clearing of his throat.

"For taking someone, or…" I smirked and amended, "Perhaps multiple someones home?"

"For when I need to stay in the city."

"The city is not too far from here," I needlessly prodded.

"It is when you're wounded or exhausted, and yes," he relented, crossing his arms over his chest and leaning against the sink, "when you just want to fuck."

Those thick arms, the muscle threatening to rip the crimson stitching of his tunic, almost distracted me from what he'd said. I wished they had. My nose crinkled at the thought of sharing that space, that bed, with even so much as a memory.

Hypocrite, I silently berated myself. I was being criminally absurd.

"Hence why I thought it was time I brought you here." The softer way he'd spoken alluded to a vulnerability that confirmed this was a space he didn't share with anyone before he said so himself. "Not many know I live here, and that's how I prefer it."

Yet he wanted to share it with me.

My heart tumbled and trembled.

I ate to keep from asking anything else that might propel me into more trouble. I'd already landed in too much. As it was, I still wasn't sure if I should be grateful or extremely worried about this situation.

A situation I'd encouraged. That I'd greedily brought upon myself.

Eating with uncontrollable speed, I settled on both and tried to refrain from licking the plate.

Before I could, it was snatched from under my nose. I frowned but made myself say, "Thank you." The plate returned a moment later with another slab of meat. I stared at it, then up at the wolf, my neck protesting due to his height. "I've had plenty."

He just grunted, "Eat, Aster," then turned for the door. He had to duck to fit through it, and I didn't know why, but I found it so humorous I had to bite back a laugh.

Deciding to show a little delayed appreciation, I scrubbed my plate, the glass, and even the pan he'd left to soak in the water. I set them all on the countertop to dry just as a loud crack came from outside. Pushing the dusty lace curtain aside with my damp fingers, I saw nothing but vines and the weed-infested path leading into the woods.

So I followed the sound as it continued through the front garden and to the side of the cottage. In a small clearing surrounded by a cluster of redwood trees, a shirtless Scythe raised an axe and brought it down upon the waiting chunk of wood atop a tree stump.

Breath dried over my tongue, gluing it to my mouth as I attempted to warn him of my presence. There was no need. He knew I was there, and he wiped at his mouth as he turned.

His gaze roamed up my body to settle on my face. "Had enough to eat?"

I nodded, freeing a breath slowly while moving to a grouping of rocks encircling what looked to have once been a firepit. He watched me take a seat, my hands spreading over the smooth stone beneath me, then he began collecting the wood he'd chopped.

The sun had warmed enough that he should've been sweating. Yet he carried the wood with ease to the side of the cottage where more had already been stacked, his skin dry. I tried to trap it, the need to know, but it escaped in a tentative rush. "Have you eaten enough?"

"Ate at the Keep while you were still snoring."

Aghast, I almost shouted to the treetops, "I do not snore."

He snorted. "Okay."

"I don't." Rorn had never said I snored. I'd only asked a million times when I'd woken to find him smirking down at me as though I'd sung a terrible ballad in my sleep. Then again, if he excelled at one thing, it was duplicity.

Rather than think it sweet that he'd tried to save me from embarrassment, a fresh wave of anger scraped at my innards.

Scythe pulled the axe from the stump like one would a knife through warmed butter, and I had to wonder if much escaped the commander when he started to say with barely veiled humor, "It's not that bad, wild—"

"Don't," I warned before I could stop myself, my fingers joining and clenching in my lap.

He turned to face me with his head tilted, the axe falling limp at his side. "Don't what?"

"Lie."

He watched me for three failed breaths. Then he nodded, spinning the axe in his hands with a crooked smile. "You snore like a drunk bumblebee."

I rolled my lips between my teeth to keep from smiling in return and failed. "I suppose that isn't too terrible."

"Compared to a camp of wolves?" He grinned wide and swung the axe in a loop. "Pure bliss to the ears, wildflower," he said gruffly and plucked up another hunk of wood to hack.

Content to watch him, although I knew it was wrong to indulge even more than I already had, I did just that. Though it soon became apparent it wasn't merely the flex of his muscles that captured my unwavering attention or the tendrils of dark hair that escaped the leather tie at his nape to lick at his peppered jawline.

It was him.

Something about this blunt and violent warrior of few words put me at ease and drowned me in a strange heat that had nothing to do with wanting to bed him. Though I couldn't deny that I wanted to bed him until the stars ceased to return and that I held little to no regret for having done so many times already.

Stars save me. The shame I felt was due to not feeling ashamed at all.

"So," the wolf said, startling me a little, "ready to tell me why you're visiting Vordane?"

Stunned, I blurted foolishly, "What makes you think I'm not from here?"

He didn't answer, and fear tapped softly at my chest.

He knew, and with enough certainty that I felt more foolish for believing he would think me one of his fellow crimson fae. "Is that why you're letting me stay?" I pressed hesitantly. "Because you wish to know what I'm doing here?"

He was quiet for so long that I didn't know if he'd answer.

"You know damned well that's not why I want you to stay." I frowned, a squirming ensuing in my stomach. A crack echoed as the wood split and fell to the grass. "But tell me something."

"What is it you wish to know?" I asked a touch too playfully for the serious response he gave.

He left the axe in the stump, the blade embedded in the wood, then walked over to join me. "Everything, but I'll settle for knowing if you'll be safe should you decide to run back home."

The word run caught my attention, but it couldn't hold it as my eyes danced over the maze of abdominals to his wide chest, wanting to stick themselves to him. To count every dark hair and scar. I met his amused gaze and grinned, unapologetic though I should've felt every shade of ashamed.

His amusement fell as I took my time to answer, watching his lips slacken while marveling over the fact that he truly seemed to care. "I'll be safe, wolf."

Rorn would never hurt me—not physically. Nor would he allow anyone else to. I once thought that made him nothing short of magical.

Then I learned there were numerous ways to bleed.

Scythe watched me for a minute that made me wonder if he didn't believe me. Soon fearing that perhaps he saw right through me, I looked down at the rock and traced a light crack beside my thigh. "I don't want to, but I do need to leave."

He was quiet for a moment, but his gaze still burned upon me.

Twigs and grass crunched as he walked back to the cottage. "You evidently came here for a good reason, so don't go letting me foil your plans if you need to stay a while longer. I've got plenty of shit to tend to with Dade and the legion anyway."

Dade. The way he spoke of his king alarmed me. Such familiarity alluded to friendship, and I belatedly realized they indeed would be very familiar. They were brethren—wolves.

I followed Scythe inside, watching as he washed his hands before fetching a glass of water. "More murder and maiming?"

It didn't seem real. Not now that I'd spent a few nights with him. That he was capable of such atrocities. I was a fool indeed. Conveniently forgetful, too, it would seem. For I'd witnessed seemingly good people do terrible things for years, especially recently.

Maybe the good were merely serpents with too many glittering skins, and the bad were more trustworthy.

Scythe shut off the faucet but didn't look at me as he said, "Probably best you don't ask."

"There's no need to ask, though, is there?" I closed the door and walked deeper into the cottage. "Not when I know."

He stiffened. "You're upset."

"I just don't understand."

"There's nothing to understand, wildflower. It's war."

"A quest for revenge," I murmured, trailing my fingers over the spines of all his stolen books. His silence confirmed. "But when does it end?"

"When he says it does."

He being his tyrannical king. Dade.

"Then what will you do?"

His lack of instant response gave me pause, and I spun to find him watching me with his arms crossed over that impressive chest. His features gave nothing away, not unless he wished them to. A trained beast indeed. "If I'm still breathing, I'll continue to serve as legion commander to my king."

"Still breathing?" I asked in sudden and sickening horror. "Why do such a thing?" Unsure why, I felt compelled to know. "Surely, you do not enjoy it."

"Serving Dade and protecting my people?"

"No," I said, taking my time to cross the room. "Hunting and hurting your own ilk."

His expression remained emotionless. "They're golden fae." The word *golden* was said as though it were cursed.

"Fae all the same."

"Are you uncomfortable staying in a hunter's home, wildflower?" I blinked, halting when he advanced, a glint darkening his eye. "Because I'm not forcing you to."

Shocked, I stilled painfully. "Do you now wish for me to leave?"

"No." His veneer cracked, his jaw rotating. "You know I don't want that."

"To simply cease asking you questions you do not like, then?"

His forehead creased as he declared earnestly, "You can ask me whatever you want."

"Then define uncomfortable for me," I said, my lips wriggling into a smile when he stopped right before me.

"Your heart races," the wolf said, so low it was nearly a graveled rasp. "Whenever I get too close."

"Does it?" I whispered, though we both knew I was well aware.

He hummed, his fingers collecting my own and pulling me to his chest. "It's flying..." Warm breath singed my temple and stirred my hair as he murmured, "or stopping entirely."

"What's it doing right now?" I asked, even after I'd felt it stop beating.

His fingers released mine to skim down my side. I shivered. "It's waiting to see what I'll do to you." His lips moved down to my cheek, where he whispered heatedly with a smile in his voice, "Breathe, wildflower."

I did, and a tiny noise escaped with the rush of air, my knees quaking.

A low chuckle lingered with his rapid exit, tendrils of shadow mixing with my panted breaths.

The wolf didn't return until well after midnight.

He climbed into bed carefully until he realized that I wasn't sleeping.

He asked no questions. He simply pulled me close, his fingers smoothing down my back and over my hair. The last thing I remembered was my breath evening against his chest as my tears dried upon my cheeks.

Scythe was gone when I woke late in the morning, and I tried to spend the day reading and sorting through my thoughts. I failed. Anxiety twisted my insides and shortened every inhale. So I cleaned. The cupboards, the windows, the countertops. None of it was in dire need of attention, but I couldn't face it all yet.

I couldn't make myself leave, and I couldn't relax, knowing I shouldn't stay.

I was halfway through dusting the bookshelves when the wolf returned. Cloth in hand, I spun to face the door at the sound of a female's voice, but it didn't open.

"...not arguing. I'm just failing to understand why the secrecy is necessary."

"It just is."

"Do you wish to keep people thinking the wrong thing? Because that's cruel, Scythe, even for you."

"No, that's not..." He growled, then cursed. "Look, I just need you to make some fucking gowns. That's it. Nothing else. I'm not asking you to smuggle her into the Keep."

"And what will Dade say when he discovers your secret? Because he will eventually."

My fingers curled, nails digging into the cloth and my palm.

"It's none of his business. It's no one's business but mine," Scythe said, the words clipped, then he paused. "She's waiting."

The door opened a second later, and I smiled as if I hadn't heard a word they'd said, all the while knowing it gave me away entirely. "Uh, hello."

A lithe female with long brown curls stepped into the cottage, a small bag in tow. Tilting her head, she returned my smile with a beautiful broad one of her own. "Hello, indeed." Looking back at Scythe, who scowled in a way that suggested she shut her mouth, she snorted and walked over to the dining table.

The wolf cleared his throat. "This is Olivianna, the king's personal seamstress. I've asked her to make a dress or two for you."

"He's requested five, actually."

Scythe glowered, his jaw rigid as he scraped a hand through his hair, forgetting it was tied and setting thick strands loose.

The king's seamstress?

Oh no. *Oh stars no.*

My head shook, panic and something akin to sadness seizing my chest in a breath-robbing vise. "I don't need any," I stammered out. "That's very kind of you both, but truly, I'm fine." He couldn't do this for me. It wouldn't be fair, and it was incredibly unnecessary.

Scythe's eye narrowed, assessing me. "She's already here, and someone is minding her babe, so it's best not to waste her time."

"He's right." Oliviana studied the dress I'd been wearing for days with golden-brown eyes. "This was terribly last minute, so I've had to leave him at the bakery down the street from my shop. If I don't hurry, he will be up all night with a stomachache. Pilma loves to spoil him with treats his tiny stomach isn't ready for." Tapping her chin, she asked, "Just where did you purchase that gown?"

Unsure what to say, I said nothing.

"Velvet and cotton." She blinked. "Genius, but undoubtedly doomed if you keep wearing it." With a *thwunk,* she plonked her tiny but heavy bag onto the dining table. It tilted even more in protest. "What's your favorite color, Aster? I refuse to believe it's custard and mauve."

Scythe must have informed her of my name in a conversation I'd unfortunately missed.

I peered down at the colors of my gown, wondering what was wrong with them, all the while still trying to process what was happening.

"Well?" Oliviana prompted.

Scythe chewed his thumbnail, the action shocking and unlike him enough to keep my tongue tied. But when I forced it to work, I couldn't find an answer. "I don't know."

The brilliant array of browns and copper in the dressmaker's skirts moved with her like a waterfall under her command as she turned, measuring string in hand and her dark brows poised high. "You don't know?"

Scythe was eyeing me warily again when I dared a glance at him. For help, maybe. I wasn't sure. But staring at him, I blurted, "Green. Emerald green."

Oliviana's eyes flicked between us, and my cheeks flushed when she muttered under her breath, knowing full well that we could hear, "Of course it is."

The wolf's attention began to burn, but I refused to look at him. Instead, I combed my fingers through my hair, wondering if this seamstress had a brush in her little leather bag.

Not a moment after I surrendered and dropped the dusting cloth so that Olivianna could take my measurements, the door closed.

Olivianna cleared her throat, her words barely audible. "He's been good to you?"

"Yes," I said instantly. "Very."

She hummed, moving the string across my hips and smiling. "Just checking."

"Why would you need to?" I asked, keeping my tone light to show I was merely curious.

"Many wolves have known tempers or reputations for being self-ish assholes," she said, her voice hopefully still too low for Scythe to hear. "Then there are those like our fierce commander outside who are known to have both."

"Both?" I blinked as her nose came within a few breaths from mine, her eyes wide as she measured my bust without even looking.

"Demons," she hissed. "Multiple shadows at his back."

My gaze tore from hers to swing to the door. "His eye?"

"No one knows for certain, but whatever happened left more than what we can see on his face."

Moving back to the table, she dipped her quill in a portable vial of ink and jotted my measurements down onto a small pad of parchment. "Those hips and that bust..." she said with a smile over her shoulder. "Even without the rest, I can see why he's doing his utmost to keep you."

I frowned, heat drenching my neck and cheeks. "Oh, it's nothing like—"

Turning to me, she pressed her finger to her lips, her eyes darting to the window. A brief glimpse of raven hair made me smile as I wondered what in the stars this wolf was doing.

Wonder was soon swallowed by dread with Olivianna's next question. "Where are you from? You're not local, or I'd have seen such a dress before." Pursing her lips, she tapped the end of the quill to her cheek, studying me. "A farming region? But you're incredibly well spoken." Her eyes narrowed at my shoulders. "That posture. Regal, almost."

My blood cooled too quickly, the heat rushing from my head to my toes and leaving me rocking while not moving at all. "I. . ." Words failed me. My lungs tightened with my throat.

I shouldn't be here.

What was I doing? Standing in this cottage, in this forest, in this kingdom, allowing this warrior inside my body and to buy me gowns I did not deserve nor need—

The door opened. "Done yet?"

Dizzy with fear and relief, I reached for the back of the armchair to steady myself as soon as Olivianna twirled to her belongings. "I believe I have enough." Packing her things, she asked the commander pointedly, "Do you?"

Scythe just glared at her, and she released a weak laugh.

With an expression I couldn't understand, followed by a wink over her shoulder, she called, "Lovely to meet you, Aster dear. I'll have something for you to try by next week."

Next week?

The shock of her words, the slow to thaw ice within my veins, rendered me incapable of uttering gratitude or a farewell.

The closing door knocked me from one spiral to another. He was paying her, and quite handsomely given who she worked for and what she'd said to him in jest. He was purchasing expensive clothing I would likely never wear.

What in the stars was I fucking doing?

Just because I couldn't bear all Rorn had done did not mean I should remain here and take advantage of this mystery of a male who insisted on doing things—

Fingers clasped my chin. A hand gripped my waist. "Breathe."

I couldn't.

Not enough. Not until he picked me up to put me in the armchair. But my hands refused to unclench from his tunic, so he sat with me in his lap.

I didn't care. It didn't matter.

I'd already taken whatever this was entirely too far. Farther than I'd have ever thought imaginable. It was growing painfully clear that no matter what I did, I wasn't escaping anything. All of it was too thoroughly entwined around me, squeezing no matter what move I made. As if I'd been wrapped in razor wire and my fate was simply to bleed.

But I wasn't alone.

Perhaps, I didn't have to be. Maybe, this was how Rorn had felt— torn to too many shreds to remember what was right and wrong.

Attempting to allow empathy for him, attempting to understand why he'd hurt me so irreparably at all, caused my eyes to well with tears. I gripped Scythe tighter, and his hold on me tightened, too. He rubbed my back while I tried to focus on drawing even breaths.

He said nothing. He just held me.

Me. A strange female who'd crept into his city and into his life. Yet swallowed in his embrace, somehow, none of the insanity felt insane at all.

FOUR

Aster

I T WAS WRONG TO SNOOP THROUGH SCYTHE'S BELONGINGS, SO I
decided to call it exploring.

Down the short hall at the back of the cottage was a bathing
room that wasn't much bigger than the one in his apartment and a
single bedchamber.

At first glimpse, I'd thought the room was incredibly small. That
was until I absorbed the sheer magnitude of the bed, which was larger
than the giant one in his apartment. Large enough for four males, it
swallowed nearly all the space in the room.

Large enough for a faerie wolf.

Nightstands sat on either side of it, a tall arched window behind
the bed, and a chest of drawers squashed into the corner opposite
the door.

The cottage door opened. "Wildflower."

I quickly placed the emerald stone back where I'd found it. Or
rather, where I'd felt it inside the top drawer of his dresser while I'd
been wiping it free of dust. "Yes?"

"Was beginning to think you might have come to your senses
and ran," Scythe said, and though it was in jest, we were well aware

that none of this made sense. We knew rations of one another, yet it felt as if we could survive on those for an eternity.

We both knew we couldn't.

"I lost all sense a few nights ago," I reminded him with a coy smile.

He grinned, eye moving to the drawers behind me. Looking back at me, he offered his hand. "Come. Time to feed you."

I placed my hand in his and laughed when he pulled me against his chest. "You do like doing that."

"Nothing has made me happier"—he tipped up my chin—"than filling your cunt with me and your stomach with food."

I shivered. No matter how lewd and antiquated his declaration, I loved it all the same.

The roughened pad of his finger stroked beneath my chin while his gaze danced with mine. A moment before our lips touched, he moved his to my cheek and breathed me in instead. "I was gone too long," he whispered quickly as though afraid of voicing it.

"You were gone for a few hours," I pointed out, smiling slightly.

After I'd calmed down, he'd read a chapter aloud to me from the book I'd been reading while I'd remained in his lap. Then he'd drawn me a bath while explaining that he had been expected at the Keep some time ago.

Yet he'd lingered in the doorway.

I'd thought he'd merely wished to see me undress until I'd noted the rigidness to his lips and jaw. The curling of his fingers and the heavy height of his broad shoulders.

I'd then promised him I was fine. Judging by the way his eye had observed all of me, he hadn't seemed to believe me. As if watching me and inwardly battling with all the questions I could feel gathering like a storm inside him had only made him feel worse, he'd torn away from the doorframe with a twisting of his features and vanished.

A grunt left him now, his fingers trailing down my throat and his lips to my ear.

Understanding dawned, and I clasped his waist to steady myself, but I couldn't keep my exhale from breaking. "Have you ever missed someone before, wolf?" I knew before asking what the answer would be, but I selfishly still longed to hear it.

"No." Greedily, I soaked up his admission with my next breath, my eyes closing. "Your slippers are by the door." He left me to wash up in the bathing room, and I smiled even as apprehension settled like a layer of ice beneath my skin.

Not ten minutes later, we left the trees and headed down the slow-sloping hill toward the heart of the diamond-shaped city.

I was well aware that Scythe wished to distract and lighten my heart after my earlier episode, for we'd yet to venture out together. I'd not asked for different or taken offense, as I sensed he wasn't hiding me for his own benefit but for mine.

I kept my hands clasped loosely before me, and he kept his at his sides unless gesturing to some of the stalls and shops while telling me what they supplied.

Many a vendor and passerby nodded in respect upon seeing him, but just as many ducked their heads out of what I assumed to be fear. Regardless, Scythe acknowledged no one.

Such arrogance bothered me. Upon glancing at him to say so, I found him looking only at me.

He quickly averted his attention to the street and steered me around a mound of horse dung.

People clustered in small groups outside of bakeries and restaurants. Wagons overflowing with fresh produce ambled carefully through the foot traffic. Dough, fresh fruit, and notes of cinnamon and flora traveled upon the gathering breeze. And when we turned down an alleyway near the end of the street to enter another, I was met with a wave of fresh seafood, cheese, and wine.

"Fish?" the wolf asked, noting my curiosity as I looked at the markets across the street before the river. "Jayron makes an incomparable fish pie. Some say it's because his grandfather was half fish himself."

"A merman?" I hadn't seen any, but my father had often humored me when I was young with stories of the few who'd dwelled in our rivers decades before I was born.

Scythe lifted a shoulder. "He never comments when asked, but I think he likes to let people talk to keep business flowing."

"Clever." I pursed my lips, tempted by the scent. "But I find myself in the mood for something sweet."

"Maybe after you eat something proper," he said, so utterly serious that I swallowed a laugh. He noticed and frowned. "What amuses you?"

Forgetting myself, I leaned into him as we came to a stop in the small line at the stall. "You're very assertive, and although I shouldn't, I do find it endearing."

"Endearing?" he asked as if I'd called him a wet sock.

I did laugh then, clasping his thick arm and earning a look from two females standing before us. I straightened, making to pull away, but Scythe slid his hand around mine.

My stomach rioted for reasons that had nothing to do with hunger as his roughened skin tickled, fingers sliding over my own with slow intent before he linked them. I couldn't keep from gazing up at him. But he tipped his chin in greeting to the vendor and squeezed my hand.

Indeed, he wasn't concerned about being seen with me at all. He was just trying to follow my lead—to keep me comfortable.

To keep me with him.

Tension drifted from my shoulders, from nearly all of me as Scythe purchased our food, and we ate while walking along the riverfront. "I didn't think wolves enjoyed fish."

He licked his finger, and the sight of it returned a different tension to my limbs. "Some are stuck with archaic taste, while others use their brains."

"Like you," I said, smirking.

He stared at my mouth, his lips parting. "Like me," he finally said. "If something tastes good, you eat it." He grinned when my own lips parted.

I peeled my eyes from him and looked at the water, needing to. My mind felt layered in cotton the longer I indulged my senses, that wild heat unfurling from my stomach and spreading. Even my fingertips warmed and grew numb, almost itched.

The water gave a brief respite. Nothing had made me long for home until then, and even so, it was but a tiny nudge for that familiar, magical comfort. For the glass river that stretched for miles beneath the base of the mountains, winding through the woods to meet with the sea.

The river before us was a royal blue. Sunlight bounced off its gently lapping surface in sparks.

Younglings sat upon one of the small wharfs, attempting to fish. I smiled, slowing where the cobblestone gave way to grass and ferns. "Are they using apricots?"

Scythe, already finished eating, licked more remnants from his fingers as he squinted toward the younglings. He huffed while I struggled to breathe momentarily. "Last time I saw them, it was sugar cubes."

"Someone is having too much fun," I said with a husked laugh. "Feeding them false information."

"You want a babe?"

The question was so abrupt that I stopped moving altogether.

Scythe stopped too, his eye narrowed and assessing, as though worried he'd spoken out of turn.

The clawing need that had grown near painful slipped away and left me chilled to the bone. Though maybe, I'd just done too thorough a job of trying to ignore the different longing I could never quite shake. "I do," I confessed, all humor gone. "Though I don't know if that's what the stars have in store for me."

We both knew my words hinted at trying—at failing—to conceive but he thankfully let it be with a low clearing of his throat. "It's not solely the stars who decide what you will have, Aster."

Wet filmed my vision, but he took my hand as if it had always been his to take, and we continued on toward a smattering of trees at the end of the river-lined street. More woods and more dense than the forest housing the cottage above the city. The trees stretched as far as I could see, clogging the outside of this city like ancient sentinels.

We didn't enter them. Scythe took a left, then waited patiently while I sniffed and studied the flowers at a cart on the street corner. The vendor smiled as I yammered on about their rare coloring, but she stiffened when Scythe's form darkened the stall behind me.

"Those fawny brown ones," he said and dumped some coins onto the window's counter.

The female gathered the flowers and tied them with twine before handing them over with a shake to her hand. I grinned, bringing them to my nose and inhaling. "I've never seen violas this color before."

"Similar to your hair," Scythe muttered so quickly that I nearly missed it.

With my fingers stroking the petals, I tried to make my heart settle as we skirted a carriage and entered another alleyway, heading toward the city's center.

"Still want something sweet?"

"I'm fine," I said, though I was anything but—my innards twisted into a never before felt chaos. It rendered me incapable of focusing on any singular emotion, left me floating as if I'd escaped my life via a dream I'd soon wake from. "I just have a sweet tooth."

"Kept away from sweets growing up?"

I grinned down at the flowers. "My father was somewhat of a simple male."

"Eat what you want," he said with a smirk when I looked over. "You're far from a youngling now."

"Indeed. In fact, I do wonder if I'm older than you."

I assumed age was not an issue for those of faerie blood on this continent either, as most of us could live for thousands of years. But I was picking, wanting to see if he'd fray at all. I needed him to give me a reason to run from this place I shouldn't be clinging so tightly to.

But it would seem my needles were too blunt.

"Thirty years as of last week," he said. "Is that experienced enough for you?" He clasped my elbow, tugging me around a puddle of thickened mud and spoiled milk. Pulling me close, he whispered, "We both know it is."

I flushed, unable to remember the last time I'd grown heated in the cheeks so often. Too often, considering I was five years older than he. It coaxed a wild smile from me, then laughter when Scythe dragged me into an alcove in the alleyway, steam rising from the fogged window behind us.

I was pressed against the wall, the flowers falling limp in my hand, when he said, "Open your mouth."

A hardened sweet was placed over my tongue, his gaze heating when it curled around it. His hands framed my face. His lips fell over mine. Unbearably still, he breathed me in with a low rumble coating his throat. A harsh exhale later, he opened my mouth with his tongue to scoop the sweet into his.

Before I could melt into the stone, he pulled me down the alleyway toward the street.

I was still reeling, my mind as fogged as the windows we'd left behind.

As if knowing, he took advantage of that by asking, "Tell me where you're from." He threw it out there so suddenly that it was clear not knowing had plagued him.

"Wistensia," I said, and the reveal felt like a betrayal somehow, even as some relief arrived from having finally said it.

Abruptly, he stopped at the end of the alley and turned to me with questions flooding his eye. "Across the Night Sea."

I nodded.

A tilt of his head. "Why come here?"

"For a break, I guess you could say." It wasn't a lie, and thankfully, he seemed to sense that as those broad shoulders dropped a fraction.

Still, his gaze held a gleam of wariness. "I know there's far more to it than that."

I lowered my eyes and ran a hand through my hair. The beast watched me, his curiosity falling into suspicion with my continued silence.

"Aster, did you sail here?" I shook my head and looked up to find his brows flattened. "You warped." At my failure to respond, he confirmed, "You're of high-born blood."

That could mean anything. A fact he was all too aware of.

Those with a smidge of noble descent in their lineage were sometimes born with abilities many of our kind didn't have. "Then I suppose you are too," I fired back, being that he too could manipulate the energy rifts to move from one place to another. He could warp.

My statement broke the fierce set of his jaw, and I splayed my palms over the rough stone wall behind me as he advanced and cocked his head.

The motion was pure predator.

And I'd never felt more tiny, more like prey, as his hands pressed into the stone and his arms caged me. "Fine." Using his nose, he tilted up my chin, then skimmed it over my jawline. "Keep your secrets," he whispered, rough. "For now." His lips climbed over my chin, hovering over mine. "Open your beautiful mouth."

Instinctively and instantly, I did. Another hardened sweet, this one buttermilk, was passed to me via his tongue.

I hadn't seen him reach for any, too distracted by everything I shouldn't feel and the consequences I couldn't yet bear to grasp. Too addicted to the way his lips fit perfectly against mine, the soft yet undeniable claiming within every sliding caress.

"One more night," he rasped, the demand more of a plea.

Breathless already, I fell deeper into my demise. "One more."

"Chicken or beef?"

"Both," I said, without knowing why he'd asked, and stared down at my bare legs. My fingers brushed over the tunic I'd changed into. It had been left to dry over the back of the dining chair, the material heavy yet not uncomfortable.

We'd returned to the cottage mere minutes ago, Scythe's glances hungry and his hold on my hand unwavering as we'd trekked back uphill to the trees. I'd almost expected not to make it through the door.

To have been pushed up against it with my skirts around my waist at the very least.

But with a rotten, toe-curling smirk, he'd released me to pluck a bottle of wine from the cupboard. He'd set it on the dining table with a grumbled, "This one's not stolen."

I'd smiled, thankful he couldn't see as he poured me a glass and then started the fire. It wasn't much, just a comment, but it had shown he'd listened.

At his continued silence, I ceased fussing with the violas I'd placed in a milk jug upon the table. I picked up the wine he'd left for me, asking, "And you?"

"Both," he grunted.

"Hungry again?" I asked, smirking.

"Eternally, apparently," he murmured, so low I nearly didn't catch it. "Gold or silver?"

I hesitated and wondered if a few measly questions could really do any damage after everything we'd already done together. "Silver." I decided to ask a question of my own. "Blue or green?"

All I heard was myself swallow. With the glass of wine perched at my lips, I turned to the short hall leading to the bathing room, thinking he wouldn't answer me.

Then he finally did. "Neither. Naked or clothed?"

I laughed, full-bodied and now understanding this game of his. "Clever."

"Not an answer."

"What's the stone for?" I asked, mainly to keep my eyes from sticking to his perfect rear, those muscular thighs, as he left the bedchamber and crossed the hall to the bathing room. "The one in your chest of drawers."

"Been snooping, have we?" But he didn't sound displeased. Merely amused. Water sloshed, followed by silence, then, "Come here."

I dragged my finger around the chipped rim of the wineglass. "That's not an answer."

This beast I'd grown far too fond of had a rather alarming amount of liquor within his otherwise near-empty cupboards indeed. I hadn't pressed him to tell me more about the collection, and I also hadn't protested when he'd presented the wine.

I'd reminded myself that his demons and addictions and his life were none of my concern.

Yet the desire to know more, to know as much as possible, still tormented. As if I were being tugged down a road I knew I couldn't allow myself to travel, I was trying and failing to remain at the crossroads. A battle against the urge to spoil myself stupid before retreating to that of which I could never escape.

A battle I was losing.

"Come here, and I'll answer."

I scowled, water trickling from inside the shadowed bathing room. Commander indeed.

Cedar-and-oat-scented bubbles frothed against the edges of the tub and floated toward the cracked ceiling. Candlelight flickered from two corners.

Wine in hand, I leaned a shoulder against the doorframe and watched his lips curl, though his eye was shut. "This looks cozy."

"The rock is the only thing I have of my mother."

"Sentimental then," I said, taking a sip of wine. Since I hadn't seen any other treasures or portraits, I knew I had to be right.

He groaned, those giant legs half exposed as he squeezed his upper torso deeper into the tub. "If that's what you wish to call it. Do you make a habit of warping wherever you like?" he asked. "Or was this the first time?"

Something told me he already knew it was far from the first time I'd made myself disappear. "Sometimes, I just…" I tapped my nail against the glass. "I need to visit another place."

"To take a break," he said, his eye opening. "On another continent. How?"

To warp meant you had to be familiar with an area. You couldn't just hope to wind up somewhere you'd never seen safely.

"I haven't actually been to many others, but I read a lot, and I paint what is described if there are no pictures. Detailed images are usually enough."

"That's a nasty little trick if I ever heard one, not to mention dangerous." But he was grinning, wolfish and evidently intrigued. His grin waned as he then said with lowered brows, "What makes you feel the need to disappear, wildflower?"

Unsure what to say but wanting to give him something, I admitted, "Survival."

His gaze immediately darkened, and I smiled before he could unleash the worry and fury rolling from his form in heated waves. "Nothing like that." He waited as I tried to find the right words. "When I'm feeling overwhelmed, sometimes it helps to go someplace else."

He was quiet for a long stretch before saying, "Makes sense."

And the way he'd said it, gentle and affirming, made me wonder if the horrifying missions he conducted for his king stemmed from more than just loyalty.

"Come here," he said again.

I smirked, veiling it behind the wine as I drank some more. "But I'm enjoying the view."

Though it was drawled playfully, he said with utter seriousness, "Why watch when you can touch?"

I snorted, coughing a little. "I'm also enjoying the wine."

The way the green of his eye glowed brighter in the candlelight made my skin twitch. "You look good in a tunic." He eyed my body languidly, pausing upon my bare legs. "Especially mine."

I refrained from ensuring the too-large material wasn't gaping over my chest, uncaring if it was.

The air warmed further, each breath burning hotter as the wolf swiped a hand over his face and into his dark hair. The thick strands were slicked back over his head to display every devastating inch of his fierce features. Water beaded over his forehead and slid down his rock-hewn cheeks to settle at his parted lips.

Why, with every prolonged glance at him, my chest swelled more and more, I couldn't dare to decipher. He'd already had me, and far too many times. Yet when he stared at me, the rushing weight of anticipation, heady as though it were the very first time, threatened to both burn and drown me.

"I'm..." I swallowed and turned. "I'm going to go finish my wine now."

Water crashed. Sleek movement at my back. Then teeth pinched at my neck. "Not so fast."

I squealed, water splashing and engulfing my lower body as Scythe climbed back into the tub and took me with him. I slipped over his waist and chest. "Stars, are you *insane*?"

A grumble vibrated against my cheek as he pulled me close. "Apparently."

"I do think so." Sensing his meaning, I leaned back, the half-drenched tunic heavy and pulling. "I'll bet you've never kept anything this long."

His silence as he eyed my chest, then the fingers I dunked into the remnants of my wine, made me feel foolish for saying such a thing. Lifting my fingers from the glass, I dragged one down his bicep, tracing the dips and bulges as I memorized each patch of smooth skin.

Aimlessly, I continued to collect and spread the wine over every exposed part of him. The dark hairs upon his chest tickled beneath the pads of my fingers, the slow rhythmic pound of his heart calming my frayed thoughts.

His voice had thickened. "Do you not approve of the wine?"

"I approve so vehemently that I long to share it with something else I approve of." Fluttering my lashes, I added softly, "And rather highly at that."

His grin dazzled and doomed.

I forced myself to look away, though touching him was just as dangerous. Remaining still and relaxing more with every moment, despite the hunger that never seemed to want to leave us, he watched me quietly while I painted him with the vanilla frosted wine.

I liked it, existing without constant chatter of plans and worries and reassurances.

I tried and failed to remember the last time I was able to feel so at ease, and I struggled to figure out how that was even possible when just breathing the same air as this warrior wolf bubbled all the blood within me. When he was nothing I was allowed to keep.

He was both comfort and chaos. A threat to everything I thought I was.

And nothing I could conquer.

He demanded my surrender—and whether that be good or bad, he had no unearthly idea.

My mind quieted more with every gentle breath he expelled and every inch of skin I covered. My eyes traced the gooseflesh left in the wake of my eager fingers.

Scythe knocked me from the unexpected peace with a rough, "Who wounded your soul, wildflower?" His hands molded to my hips. "Tell me their name, and I'll make sure it's wiped from history."

I smiled, but I didn't dare meet his gaze as I thought about how to answer that. "It was my own foolish expectations, I suppose."

He said nothing for long moments. As though knowing I did not wish to talk about it, he gently squeezed my hips, his shockingly soft statement causing my eyes to sting. "Expect me to never hurt any part of you."

"Scythe." I stilled, growing both warm and chilled.

But he shushed me and said, "You're an artist."

"Funny," I retorted dryly, then looked up to find his expression held not a trace of humor. He'd meant it. I rolled my lips between my teeth and refrained from moving over the twitching hardness snug against my core. "What gave me away?"

He blinked. "The easing of your features." He didn't stop there. Water splashed when he reached for my hand, his large one swallowing it as he brought my fingers to his lips. Gently, I traced their softness while he murmured, "The way your fingers and wrist move. The way the tempo of your heart slows."

Said fingers and heart paused. "And how would you know of such subtle tells?"

"Mariana," he said, the name jarring me. "She likes to draw and paint."

I raised a brow, jealousy blooming like an unwanted visitor within my chest.

Before it could spread throughout my veins to stiffen my limbs, he smirked. "She's somewhat of a mother to me, wildflower."

Delighted by this information, I smiled. "More," I whispered, afraid and desperate.

As though sensing that, he kissed each fingertip, then returned them to the glass of wine. He spoke while I continued to decorate his skin. "Mariana is Fang's mother."

"The wolf who came knocking the other morning?"

He hummed in confirmation. "The pest is like a brother in every sense of the word. Mariana and her husband, Berk, raised me." He paused. I wondered if he was considering if he should say more, and then I pondered his hesitation. "They took me in when I was quite young."

Looking at his missing eye, I tilted my head and watched his jaw firm. So this wasn't something he shared with most, I surmised, not if his scars had anything to do with it.

And his silence made it clear that they certainly did.

Snatching my fingers, he brought them to his mouth again and rubbed. "Let me take you to bed and read to you."

I smiled once more, even as something sorrowful still lingered from his words, and set the wine outside of the tub on the tiles. "Not yet. First"—I pulled my fingers free and shivered when his teeth gently nipped them—"I must clean you up."

He cursed when I lowered my head to his torso and began to lick away every drop of wine.

My tongue roamed the delicious dips and deep crevices of his chest. His breath became a rumble that I felt in my core when I reached his abdominals. Before I could wrap my hand around his cock, Scythe cursed and ordered, "Lift your arms."

Reluctantly, I straightened and did as I was told.

THE WOLF & THE WILDFLOWER | 63

The wet tunic was pulled from my body. With a slap, it hit the floor beside the tub. For seconds that split each burning exhale, the wolf's lone eye crawled over my breasts, his lip caught between his teeth.

I remained still as a large hand rose from my hip to my breast. His calloused finger tickled, stroking with a barely-there touch that caused my nipples to bead as though they reached for his attention. "I don't know why I've been blessed like this," he murmured, his finger trailing up my chest to my chin. I lifted my gaze to find his own waiting. "But I'm certainly not going to let them know they've fucked up."

Tempted to smile, I found I couldn't when his touch reached my cheek. My eyes fluttered closed, his fingers whispering over the curve of my cheekbone. When they opened, his lips parted, and his brows lowered. "Beautiful," he rasped.

I'd felt what it was to be adored. More so, I'd known what it was to have declarations given so often that I hadn't realized it wasn't the quality of one's words that mattered.

Until now.

Until this wolf collected my body to his as if needing it for more than just a satiating of his arousal—as if he needed to tell me all he was feeling without words.

As if words were not enough to describe it.

My arms looped around his neck, and his mouth fused to mine as he carried me from the bathing room. He didn't take us into the bedchamber. He lowered before the fire he'd built upon our return to the cottage.

"Your lovely ass will get cold," I warned, inhaling his scent at his collarbone and shivering when his hands feathered down my sides and up my back. My legs tightened around his waist, his cock nestled against my stomach.

He kissed my shoulder. "It'll quickly warm up."

I laughed. "Will it now?"

He hummed and pressed me tighter against him, and for some minutes, he simply held me. The gentle adoration of his fingers and hands over my body both liquified and thickened my blood. I melted against him though I was growing restless, murmuring, "Are you going to fuck me?"

"Soon," he grunted.

Frowning, I lifted my head from the crook of his neck to stare at him. He smirked when my eyes narrowed. "Hungry, wildflower?"

I brushed a thick strand of hair from his face and traced the violent edge of his cheek as I tucked it behind his ear. "I'm not quite sure what I am anymore."

Growing wholly still, he watched me intently while my eyes and fingers explored his cruel beauty. After a minute, he relaxed beneath me. "Is that a bad thing?" he belatedly asked.

I paused at his mouth, and his lips parted when I smiled and ran my finger over his lush bottom lip. "It doesn't feel like it." Laying my forehead against his, I skimmed my lips over his cheek. "I'm wondering if that's all that matters."

His rough exhale hitched. The hands at my back trembled when I stroked his nose with mine and then pulled myself up with my hands on his shoulders.

He reached between us to feed his cock to my body. I lowered onto it, my teeth catching my lip as I was slowly stretched and filled. Taking my chin, Scythe untucked my lip and groaned. "Nothing has ever felt so fucking good."

I agreed with a slight nod, my arms twining around his neck again.

He gripped my hips and stole my mouth with his. I opened for his tongue and met it with my own. With tentative touches that matched the slow rocking of my hips, they dueled and danced as I tried to work all of him inside my body.

Scythe cursed, tearing away to grip the back of my head and kiss along my jaw. His arm banded tight at my lower back and pushed me down on him.

I moaned at the burn, at the burst of fire that filled every vein, and clasped his neck and hair as my back arched. A low growl, and then I was tilted backward, forced to take every inch of him. The hungry heat of his lips and tongue was everywhere—upon my breasts, my clavicle, and then my throat.

Holding me suspended over him, the wolf used the arm at my lower back to rock me over his cock. The burn subsided into a growing inferno as he ground me against him and remained planted deep.

When I tugged at his thick hair, wanting the closeness back, his mouth left my throat, but he didn't leave my body. He kept us joined as he laid me down, my head cradled in his large palm. He held himself above me with his forearm resting beside my head on the fire-warmed stone.

His nostrils flared when my legs climbed over his ass, my feet digging with every circle of his powerful hips. I wanted his mouth on mine, but more than that, I wanted to watch him as he ruined me by finally withdrawing to begin a rhythm of slow thrusts.

Firelight highlighted the shadows of his muscles and the rigid state of his jaw as his glowing gaze remained fixed on my face. My hands trailed over the bulging masses in his arms, and he shivered. I reached his upper back, then froze, cursing.

Scythe chuckled, low and throaty, slamming harder as he entered my body.

I moaned, my thighs trembling.

He skimmed his nose over my cheek. "Good?"

I swallowed, exhaling, "Yes," when his thrusts gentled again. "Scythe, I need…"

"Not yet," he said, and then he rose until I was once again seated within his lap. Breath tumbled from me, fast and searing. He clasped the side of my face, thick fingers tangling in my hair, and kissed my nose. "Breathe, wildflower."

I inhaled deep and released it. Every part of me awakened and throbbing and desperate. "That's it," he crooned roughly, his thumb rubbing my cheekbone. "Now kiss me."

I squashed his lips with mine, and my breasts to his chest. He caressed my back and held the base of my neck while his other arm tightened around my waist. A nip at my upper lip, then he ordered, "Now fuck me."

I moved, relief sweeping through me in a dizzying rush when I crested the wave of pleasure he'd had me ignore. A relief so torrential that it hurt in the best possible way.

I cried out against his mouth.

His chuckle was wicked, his satisfaction a pleased rumble while his fingers petted my hair and back.

Before I could fully recover, I was taken to the floor again.

In silence that was only broken by the grunting beast of a male atop me and the sounds of pleasure he wrung from me, I was thoroughly studied and fucked until he gave me a reprieve and found his own release.

A reprieve I wasn't sure I wanted as I gazed up at him in breathless wonder.

Later, the moon so high in the sky it was beyond view of the window behind the bed, I tried to understand what this overwhelming attachment was.

Scythe's head laid in my lap for my fingers to better roam through his thick hair—and for him to pause each chapter to kiss and inhale my stomach.

He read with a quiet but sturdy confidence. The cadence of his deep voice hypnotized me. So much so, I lost track of the story due to losing myself to the sound of it, and to the way his lips shaped around each word.

He was nothing I would have ever imagined wanting, yet I found myself comfortably fascinated with every piece of him.

This wasn't merely lust, and I could no longer call it a distraction. As I traced a small scar along his hairline, I knew it was no longer revenge, either.

It was obsession.

FIVE

Aster

S CYTHE HAD TO TEND TO HIS LEGION FOR MUCH OF THE NEXT day, leaving me to my thoughts in the warmth of his cottage once more.

This time, there was no fighting off attacks of panic, but there was still a desire to ignore the onslaught of fear I found in his absence. I tried to read and failed, deciding I'd rather wait for him to read that particular book with me. Then I decided to clean the bathing room.

I almost jumped out of my skin when I returned the cleaning supplies to the cupboard beneath the kitchen sink.

"You're a terrible fucking singer."

Flushing from my cheeks to my toes, I slowly rose with a laugh. "I know."

Scythe peeled away from the door he'd been leaning against to watch me for stars only knew how long and advanced.

He stroked his fingers over the heat in my cheeks and smirked. "Kiss me." I rose onto my toes and pressed my lips to his. He breathed me in, his mouth parting but otherwise still beneath mine. Pulling back, he brushed his lips across my cheek as he whispered, "I want to hear it anyway."

"My singing?" I asked, confused as he kicked off his boots at the door.

"Every sound you make, every single thing you do..." He stalked to the bathing room. "Need it all."

He left me there with my ears echoing the stalled, thunderous beat of my heart, a sponge still in my hand. I stared down at it, then back at the hall, unsure how so few words—such simple statements—could burrow deeper than years of heartfelt proclamations.

Irritated, but knowing it had nothing to do with the wolf, I squeezed every drop of water from the sponge as if it were a different male's heart. Only when my fingers cramped did I take a deep breath and force myself to take a few more.

I set the sponge on the windowsill and washed my hands, then snatched the book from the armchair and took it with me to Scythe's bedchamber while he bathed.

He entered, damp and naked, some minutes later. "What's got you bothered?"

How he even knew... I shook my head. "Nothing," I said and withheld a sigh as I turned the page, though I hadn't read a word. I'd been waiting. Waiting and stewing and uncomfortable in my own skin.

Scythe huffed and dumped a dagger upon the nightstand. Gently, he plucked the book from my hands and climbed onto the bed with grace a creature of his size should not have. He patted his lap, and I shook my head again.

He raised a brow but didn't argue as I lay beside him instead.

Opening to where we'd last read to, he stared at the page a long moment before asking, "Was it what I said?" At my scrunched expression, he scratched the thickening stubble at his jaw. "The singing comment."

"No," I said instantly.

Seeming so adorably uncertain, Scythe looked down at me with a furrowed brow. "I know I should be more careful, but I didn't mean to..."

"Careful?"

He waved a hand, groaning with his sigh. "I shouldn't use honesty as an excuse to be an asshole."

Unable to help it, I laughed and sat up. I took the book and set it on the bed, then pulled the blankets down and his legs open to fit between them. "You're not an asshole."

The wolf smirked. "No lies, wildflower."

"You're not," I said, crawling over him to push my nose to his. "Not to me, anyway. I was not offended. I can't sing, but I like doing it, so all that matters is that you like hearing it."

He chewed his lip, his eye searching mine. "You're certain?"

I kissed him. "I promise."

"Then what's bothering you?"

I knew I would need to admit something in order for him to truly believe he hadn't upset me. "You're not incredibly romantic," I said and laughed when he scowled. "But I'm beginning to fear that's not what I need, and that maybe"—I kissed him softly—"what I need is something else entirely."

He stared for a broiling smattering of seconds, and then he kissed me back.

I tore away and retreated down his body to settle between his legs. He hissed through his teeth when I wrapped my hand around his cock. "Tell me what scares you, wolf."

"Nothing."

I arched a brow and flattened my tongue over the base of his erection. He cursed and tensed. With my eyes on his hardened expression, I dragged my tongue up his shaft and stopped when I reached the engorged head. "Nothing at all?"

His fists uncurled beside him, and he reached out to shift a strand of hair from my face. "Guess that changed when I first saw you."

"I scare you?" I asked, bewildered.

"You fucking terrify me, wildflower."

I blinked, absorbing that as I stroked and licked him.

Even without such an admission from him, crouched between

this mighty creature's knees, his giant form allowing me to toy and tease him however I wished, I'd never felt more powerful.

And as I swallowed as much of him as I could manage, choking but unwilling to quit while he groaned and shuddered beneath me, I realized the absurdity of it when I compared the feeling to all and who I was in the kingdom I'd run from.

Scythe's fingers scrunched into my hair, tugging. His hands pushed and pulled my mouth on and off him until I'd captured every last drop of pleasure I'd forced from his body. I swallowed and sat up, and he did too.

Thick fingers swept my tangled hair over my shoulders, then captured my chin. His thumb wiped at the seed that'd dribbled from my mouth. Focus fastened on my lips, he painted them with it, his voice husked as he ordered, "Lick."

I licked each lip slowly and felt him grow hard against my stomach.

I didn't wait to be told what to do next. I turned on all fours beside him and arched my back. The wolf chuckled and reached out to touch me from behind. "Need something, wildflower?"

"I can do it myself if you're too tired, wolf."

He was up in a heartbeat, and I grinned into the bedding. Then I gasped when my ass was smacked and a finger was plunged deep inside me. "That simply won't do when you're this aroused."

"No," I agreed.

"My mouth or my cock?"

"Cock."

He groaned. "Say that again."

"Put your cock inside…" My command fell into a whimpered exhale when he ended my misery and mercifully filled me.

"Better?" he asked, and I was gifted another chuckle when I gave him a garbled response.

In quick and deep thrusts, he delivered me to a rapid ruin that was halted from arriving when he paused. About to protest, I was then hauled up as he leaned back onto his haunches and scooped my hair aside. "Want to hold you when you break," he muttered to my shoulder, and indeed, his arm enveloped my stomach.

I gripped it as he rocked up into me and kissed the curve of my shoulder. His teeth sank into my skin, the sting soothed by his lips and tongue. "Sing for me, wildflower."

I laughed at his choice of words, but it was stolen by a moan when he reached down to slide his forefinger over my clit, and I fractured. He held me to him, kissing my neck and shoulder while I trembled and saw stars behind my closed eyelids.

"This isn't normal, is it?" I rasped, swallowing.

Scythe hummed, his hand sliding over my stomach to cup my breast. "You desire something normal?"

Unable to help it, I smiled as I admitted, "Actually, I do."

He stilled, but only momentarily. Taking my chin, he turned my mouth to his and tucked my hair behind my ear, tracing the arch. His question was hesitant, quiet. "Would you settle for natural?"

I frowned as I studied his lupine eye, his rugged features. "Why?"

His smile revealed and broke something I hadn't known I'd possessed. "We both know nothing has ever felt this right." He kissed me, deep and branding, and I was grateful.

I wouldn't have known what to say to that—wouldn't have known how to refute it when it was irrefutable.

He moved me over him with an unhurried finesse that reawakened my body far too soon. I slumped back against him, his stubble tickling as he continued to hold and taste me, and waited for my heart to slow.

It never did.

It was as if time failed to exist in this new world I'd fled to. That, or perhaps we were both aware that even though we would live for hundreds and hundreds of years, it was still far too fleeting.

Hours after feeding and hydrating me, when we should have been sleeping, the wolf set the book he'd been reading to me upon the nightstand and looked down at me. "What does normal mean to you?"

Exhaustion had cloaked but hadn't yet taken me, and so I said the first thing that entered my murky mind. "Chickens."

"Chickens?"

I leaned back in the embrace of his arm to better see him. "Do you not like chickens, wolf?"

He made a face. "To eat, yeah."

I laughed. "Well, I want them as pets." Imagining it out loud, I said, "I want them roaming around, leaving eggs for me to collect..." I reached up to brush my fingers over his furrowed brow. "You'd cook them, of course."

He huffed, his features easing. "Of course." Taking my hand, he kissed it. "What else?"

"Perhaps a vegetable garden."

He rubbed my knuckles over his lips. "Already have one of those."

"I believe it's in no giving state."

"I'll fix it."

My chest squeezed. I rolled to my stomach, half sprawled over him. "Would you?"

Scythe traced the bridge of my nose with his finger. "Yes." A singular word that meant more than a hundred.

Attempting to quell the rise of threatening emotions, I closed my eyes momentarily, then opened them and asked, "What of you? Does your ideal normal include hunting and murdering for your king for the rest of your days?"

Perhaps it was unfair of me to flatten all he'd brought to the surface within me by reminding myself of what he was—of what he did and would continue to do—but I needed to try.

Scythe licked his teeth and stroked my cheek, undeterred. "I know you do not approve, but even if I had another option, I would still lead and protect. I'm a wolf. It's in my blood."

I took his hand and kissed his battle-roughened skin. "It is not the leading and protecting that I do not approve of." I turned his hand to kiss his palm. "But fine, you would still serve your king in your ideal world."

"It's not ideal, Aster."

I frowned up at him. "But—"

I was pulled over top of him. "Not until I know you'll always be the first thing I see when I wake each day."

Tears pooled in my eyes.

If he noticed, he said nothing. He kissed me, and I let him. I greedily took everything he gave, for I would need it all to replace the pieces of me he'd robbed without mercy.

The commander was summoned to his king before dawn.

He didn't return until deep into the following evening, damp and in a clean tunic and britches. As though he'd thought to shield me from any evidence of battle or other forms of violence.

Sweet, I thought with a smirk, though it still clung to him like a copper smoke. "Think I'd run screaming from you, wolf?"

"I'd hunt you down." His tone might have been light, but it held an unshakable warning within.

I fought back a shiver, thinking it wise to move away from the subject. At least a little. "Your boots are still covered in mud and someone's innards."

He cursed, kicking them off. "We had to—"

"Terrorize some more golden faeries?" His lack of response and the flattening of his features were confirmation enough. I scooted over the bed, my tone sugar with a bite of venom. "Tell me again, my beastly warrior, what exactly have these poor creatures done to you? Not to your king," I said when he opened his mouth, "but to you?"

Unable to answer, perhaps unwilling to acknowledge even to himself that whatever reason he had wasn't something he entirely agreed with, his jaw clenched. "I'd rather we don't talk of such things." Attempting to veer from the subject, and nearly succeeding, his eye gleamed as he rumbled, "Still wearing me."

I was indeed still too fond of his tunic. I smiled. "Peering into those shadowed corners does nothing good for the guilt, does it?"

"Not sure what you mean." He dumped his dagger upon the nightstand, as well as some coins. "Guilt and I steer well clear of one another. Besides, few people died today. We even brought some back."

"To interrogate?"

Scythe huffed. "They surrendered. They'll now be set up with housing here in Vordane."

I failed to mask my surprise. "What is the point of this vengeance upon Sinshell if you're not slaughtering them all?"

"To take it all, wildflower, everything they hold dear," he said, cold and plain. "The way they did us."

Those words. I had to wonder if, in the end, it was always the same—a ruler's desire for bloodshed.

Sitting up, I studied Scythe with a tilt of my head.

He lifted a brow, endlessly patient while he waited to see what I was up to.

I hooked my finger, beckoning him closer.

He narrowed his eye, but the intensity of his features gradually melted as he stripped out of his tunic and pants. Stoic and hard, his entire physique mouthwateringly impressive, he stood naked before the bed. "What do you need?"

He wasn't expecting it, so it thrilled me to say, "I need you to change for me."

He frowned. "To shift?" At my nod, surprise lit his eye. "You've never seen fae in beast form before?"

"I have," I said, and numerous times at that. "But I've never seen you."

He blinked. "You're sure?"

I nodded. "I want to see you." I crawled to the edge of the bed when he expelled a rough breath. "You cannot scare me, wolf."

He smirked.

A heartbeat later, he reformed before my very eyes. In tendrils of shadow and warping, cracked movements, the male who'd found me in the dark tavern a handful of nights ago disappeared.

Standing in his place, his muzzle reaching my head and his body blocking the doorway of the bedchamber, was a giant black wolf.

The scar, his missing eye, and the violent green of the other were all that remained unchanged, as well as the fast beating tempo of his heart.

Breath bloomed and burst over my lips when he lowered his hind legs and sat down.

A long, tufted tail swished. A pink tongue darted out, revealing a quick flash of huge, dagger-sharp white teeth.

"Stars," I exhaled. "You're unlike anything I've seen before." And that was the truth. Having grown up with one, I'd seen plenty of faerie wolves during my years, but not one of them came close to the one watching me with an intense glowing fixation.

Far larger than any fae beast I'd known, he had to be almost twice the size of the average wolf. The energy radiating from him like a crackling, threatening fire would make most run.

It only lured me closer.

I leaned close enough to brush my fingers over the velvet of his ears, slowly exploring the dense softness of the fur behind them and over his head. "A mane," I whispered. "A crown of fur." His nose nudged at my fingers when they retreated, and I laughed, tracing his giant muzzle in wonder.

Warm air rushed from his nostrils, followed by a pleased, rumbling growl.

A longing to kiss that snout took hold, although his head was twice the size of mine and his snout nearly as long as my forearm. My heart stopped as soon as my lips touched the fur above his nose.

And he melted beneath my hands.

Before I realized his intent, I was flat on my back upon the bed. Scythe loomed above me, pulling the tunic from my body. Buttons popped and the fabric tore with a quick scream.

There was nothing beneath, and though he'd likely already known that, it didn't stop him from groaning and dragging his hands up my legs and over my thighs. He pushed them wide. His thumbs dragged down their insides, and my breath caught when they reached my center and opened me.

With a hunger in his eye, he leaned forward and blew a heated breath over my slick flesh.

I choked on a gasp, and he pushed his hands over my stomach to my breasts. He squeezed, then lowered to an elbow and circled my nipple with his thumb, his gaze fixed on mine. "You should know better than to kiss a wolf."

"I've been doing a lot of things I normally don't do," I said without thinking.

Scythe narrowed his eye. "That so?" He watched my lashes flutter while his fingers slid over my stomach, circled and tickled their way back down to where I needed him. Mouth curving when my hips rose to meet his forefinger at my entrance, he said, "Like me?" He toyed and teased, watching as I struggled to form an answer.

I moaned, and he gave in, sliding his finger inside me with a growled, "Fuck, I'm obsessed with this perfect cunt. Kiss me."

Snatching the back of his head, I brought his mouth to mine and did just that, rocking into his rubbing, twisting movements and wanting so much more while never wanting him to stop.

As if reading my mind, he pulled the digit free and aligned his hips with mine. Our lips refused to unstitch, his hand seeking mine and clasping them both tight above my head as he slowly, torturously, entered my body.

"More?" he rasped, but all I could do was quiver, my lips shaking against his. He smirked, gaze lupine. "You're so fucking swollen, wildflower. Soaking my cock in pure, blood-rushing gold." He shivered, his teeth catching my lip.

His hand clenched tighter around mine when I attempted to touch him, needing to—needing him to move.

Then he did. His forehead rolled against my own, an utterly inhuman noise falling from between his lips into mine as he mercifully filled me completely. More torturous seconds passed, the glint in his eye wicked and knowing. Knowing that I was so desperate, my thighs climbing his body, that as soon as he moved…

He covered my cry with his mouth, whispering me into pieces, "That's a good little flower. Come." He shivered again atop me as I shook and whimpered. "Stars, you murder me."

Then he truly moved, sudden and coaxing. He kissed me, and he moved inside me with the knowledge of exactly what I needed. With a roll of his hips, a careful stretching and filling that ensured every pleasure point awakened, hungered, and spasmed.

I'd always been so naïvely certain of most things in this life— what I felt, who I needed, and what I'd never do.

Yet when Scythe's mouth left mine to kiss and suck and nip at my neck, and he whispered, "I don't want just one more night, I want them all, Aster," everything I was, everything I'd always thought I'd be, ceased to exist.

A new soul, scarred and bruised and hungry for someone and things I never saw coming, bloomed in place of who I once was.

But as midnight neared and I lay half draped over this male who was never meant to be anything more than a talented stranger, our fingers entwined over his stomach and the book he'd been reading to me forgotten in the bedding, I swallowed back the urge to cry.

The female I used to be might have been gone, shattered beneath the brutality of another male's actions, but that didn't mean I could leave the skin I'd begun to shed.

I couldn't hide from him forever.

Too much longer, and I knew Rorn wouldn't just tear through the countryside and into dangerous, war-ruined territory, but he'd calculate the days. He would soon realize I'd never disappeared for this long before.

Too much longer, and he would begin to hunt.

I'd hunt you down, the male holding me so close it was hard to believe we'd ever been strangers had said.

The threat of tears advanced with force.

I needed to make sure that didn't happen.

Vordane and its smiteful king and the wolf beneath me were too much for our kingdom to survive. If Rorn came here, if he brought our warriors and his wrath...

Stars only knew what might eventuate from it all.

We were barely surviving the hatred of humans we'd once welcomed and trusted. We wouldn't survive the cunning and vengeful nature of the fae.

I closed my eyes, kept my breathing even, and reluctantly called forth the beginning of the end. "Scythe?"

He gave a hummed rumble.

"I have to go, wolf..." I swallowed thickly. "And soon."

He tensed. "Why?" A grunted, sleep-thickened bark.

I would have to lie, and so I did. "I have a pet raccoon who's probably fretting."

His finger stilled at my lower back. Rather than wiggle to make him continue stroking, I waited as he made a sound of amusement and said, "A raccoon?"

"Her name is Nibbles." I leaned back into his arm to read his expression, to see if he believed me, a part of me desperately hoping he wouldn't.

He snorted and pressed his lips together. "Okay, but she's a raccoon." He said the words slowly. "She's probably fine."

Looking up at the male holding me a little tighter than moments before, however that was possible, I withheld a sigh at seeing the stubborn glint in his eye.

It was time to deliver the truth if I wanted him to make this easier for me. For us both, really.

And I so desperately wanted this to be easier.

For if he knew, he'd certainly balk. He might even get so angry he'd demand I leave right away. Then I could return home with nothing but memories to keep me warm during the cold nights ahead. No need for anything else. For ties I couldn't keep.

"Scythe," I said gently. Perhaps too gently.

He tensed again. Seeming to sense I was about to say something he couldn't excuse away and ignore, each word was clipped. "What is it?"

"I don't have a raccoon." I couldn't look at him. I knew that made me a coward, but I wouldn't be able to carry the memory of his reaction with me, too. "I have a husband."

He ceased breathing, every particle of air in the room stilling with him.

Then he coughed, croaking out, "Did you just say *husband?*"

Fear made it easier to leave his warmth and sit up. He didn't stop me, rolling away himself to the side of the bed.

He raked his hands through his hair. "Fuck." The pale moonlight dripped through the window to display the clenched muscles of his back. "I knew you were tangled up in something, but..." He groaned and pinched the bridge of his nose. "Fuck, Aster."

"I'm sorry." Words poured from me like water I couldn't capture. "He betrayed me, and I didn't know what to do, how to even so much as breathe near him, so I ran away, and then I—"

"Then you found me in a tavern and decided to get that vengeance you were talking about."

"No." I shook my head, but I couldn't lie now. "I mean yes, it might have started out that way..." More words I shouldn't have freed trembled loose. "We both know it's no longer that simple."

Scythe released a dry, scathing laugh, then rose and tore open one of the drawers. "You're fucking right it's not simple." He slammed the drawer hard enough to crack the wood, his next words growled. "You're fucking *married*, Aster." Forcing his legs into a pair of pants, he then grabbed the tunic from the floor.

I wasn't sure what he was doing, but although I couldn't have hoped for a better escape, it now sickened me to think it would end like this. The precious collection of days, the life-changing nights...

All of it ruined.

Yet when I opened my mouth, I could find nothing to say. This was what I'd needed. What had to happen. It was working. There was no making it better.

I couldn't. Not only was that likely impossible, but it had to be this way.

"I truly am sorry," I rasped. "For withholding the truth." I couldn't bring myself to apologize for the rest—for the time with him I'd wrongly stolen. Even if I could, I wouldn't.

As though he'd sensed as much, Scythe turned in the doorway.

The fury that'd hardened his violent features eased as he stared at me. I started to say his name, my clenched fingers unfurling over the bed, but he blinked slowly and shook his head.

Vengeance might have been my excuse, but it was something else entirely that had brought us together.

Something cruel and unjust in its timing and delivery.

Shadow began to separate from the corners of the room, forming around him like ribbons of sheer gauze. "Just..." With one last pained glance at me, he released a rough breath. "I don't know, Aster. I need a fucking minute."

Despite knowing I should've left as soon as he did, I didn't. Like the selfish and reckless fool I'd become, I waited.

I stayed for what remained of the night and the early hours of the incoming day.

Only when the sun had climbed to its full height did I finally force myself back into my gown that had yet again been so carefully draped over a dining chair.

Only then did I wholly surrender to a fate I could never escape.

I warped home.

SIX

Scythe

MARRIED.
Fucking married.
I'd known something awful had happened to her. Many a miserable soul hid in taverns over the city and the countryside, but it had been a long time since I'd encountered heartache as smothering as Aster's.

At first, I'd wanted to grab one of those females in the tavern and leave to escape it, but then I'd looked across the low-lit room. Upon seeing the source of such suffocating doom, I'd forgotten there were even females seated beside me at all.

She might have been miserable, but fuck if she wasn't the best damned thing I'd ever laid an eye on.

I'd wanted her. I'd taken her. I'd claimed her. I'd thought that despite whatever secrets and problems ailed her, she was mine.

That it was irrefutable.

Perhaps it still was. Maybe I just needed to ask the hard questions—figure out how we could somehow move forward.

He'd betrayed her, she'd said, this husband I would need to get rid of. I couldn't assume his betrayal meant she would simply leave the asshole for me, but I didn't know if I didn't ask. Problem was, I'd been too furious to ask. Too shocked to think of a way out of this worst-case scenario.

And so I'd sat in that same tavern, staring at that same corner table between the two windows, and I'd imagined her there. I'd imagined what I might have said if things had been different—if I'd have known from the start that she was spoken for.

But I didn't need to imagine the change in her since that night, nor the irrevocable pull that had only tightened between us during our time together.

Resolved, I'd downed a carafe of water and a plate of chicken before heading to the Keep to get my legion sorted so I could head home to Aster. We would talk. She would tell me everything, and somehow, we would figure this shit out.

Never had I been in such a hurry to leave the Keep or my brethren as I had been this past week. Home was nothing but a place to sleep. A place to rest before returning to the same routines that'd both saved and doomed me.

But with Aster waiting, I made myself scarce as soon as I could get away with doing so.

It was a mistake to think that day would be anything like the previous ones. For when I reached the cottage, she wasn't there.

The bed was made. The books we'd read had been returned to their homes on the shelves. The few dishes we'd last used were drying on the counter. Her honeyed scent lingered over everything.

I stalked outside, but her scent there was old. She hadn't left the cottage via the door.

Which meant she'd warped.

Turning back inside, I discovered exactly where she'd left me. My fingers reached for thin air by the dining table where her gown had hung over the chair, my heart sitting in my throat.

The curse I'd known better than to believe was a blessing meant for me was just...

She was just gone.

"I wasn't fond of the dumplings either," Berk said, dropping with a groan into the armchair next to mine. "Too salty."

I smirked. "They were fine."

He hummed. I could feel his eyes upon me, but I kept staring at the fire, annoyed that I still couldn't shake the cold that'd seeped inside my bones. "You're acting stranger than usual. Care to share why?"

It clawed deep—just how much had changed since our family dinner last week.

I hadn't seen her coming. Unexpectedly, I'd found something priceless, and before I could make sense of what it all was and what more I could do to keep it, I'd fucking lost it.

Gone.

Telling anyone was pointless. Not to mention more than I thought myself capable of enduring.

I said instead, "So you failed to convince Mariana to let you join Fang's next assignment?"

Fang hadn't shown up at dinner tonight, busy preparing for the journey northeast with his legion at first light.

Mariana was right to put her foot down.

Having spent the better part of the past three decades learning how to walk again, her war veteran husband and mate had no business going anywhere with our legions. After receiving a spinal injury and broken neck during the first war, there was only so much our blood and magic and time could do. Berk still had days when he could barely move at all.

Berk scoffed. "What do you think? And don't change the subject. Just because I'm bored shitless doesn't mean I'm patient. Spit it out. I've no interest in dancing."

"Yet you wish to join your son and a legion of warriors in battle." Feeling his ire, I looked over at him and sipped the water I'd been clutching, wishing it were something with enough bite to distract.

Nothing would be enough.

As predicted, Berk was glaring, but his jaw loosened when his eyes dipped over my face. "If I'd have known you'd end up being such a wiseass, I'd have left you to bleed on that beach."

I grinned, as I always did whenever he spoke of things we both knew were bullshit.

His eye twitched, his glare softening. "Oh, fuck off."

"Stars," Mariana hollered. "Must you poison our ears so profusely, Berk?"

With a wave of his hand, the door to the sitting room slammed closed. "Sixty-two years. You'd think she'd let me be by now."

"She enjoys it too much," I said, and a tightness twisted the organ in my chest. I drank some more and stared back at the crackling flames.

For some minutes, the only sound came from the fire, both of us lost to its lure.

"Who is she then?"

I didn't startle. Didn't so much as blink. I knew better than to give anything away under the watchful eye of an ex-commander. "Who?"

"Don't play stupid. I already know you're a fool."

I chuckled. The stale sound died rapidly.

I tossed back the last of the water, wishing again for whiskey. The burn wouldn't be enough to kill the thoughts he'd pulled to the surface. The memories I'd spent the previous night and today dodging and running from by spending every minute at the Keep.

It didn't matter where I was. Gray eyes had chased me from sleep and during each waking hour.

I couldn't forget them—couldn't forget any part of her—and I knew I never would. The caramel hair, feather-soft over her bare shoulders and tits, tangled and damp between my fingers. The secretive smile that filled my chest with an elation I'd never felt before. The laughter constantly tripping the beat of my heart. The comforting weight of her in my arms while she dreamed.

The fucking scent of honey that had yet to leave the apartment or cottage, nor the taste of her—that sugar-laced venom.

It took every ounce of the brutal training I'd had to keep the roaring sorrow inside me from showing.

"No one," I eventually murmured when I felt as if I could trust my voice. "We both know I'll never venture down any road like that." Hollow words, yet I'd said them with conviction. Until little over a week ago, I'd been sure of it, too. Now, the stars had made it more certain than the next sunrise.

Berk sat with that a moment, drumming his fingers over the armrest. "Sometimes we don't willingly venture." He lowered his voice and leaned over the arm of the chair to whisper, "It's forced upon us, and we're fucking dragged the entire way."

I couldn't help but snort.

He sat back with a wince, the door to the sitting room thrown open.

Mariana held a tray of tea, her brown eyes fixed on her mate. "I do hope you like that chair," she said, setting the tray on the table between us. "You're sleeping on it."

"The truth hurts, sweets," Berk sang after her, though his tone was weak.

"Uh-huh." She pulled the door closed. "So will that back of yours in the morning."

Berk cursed and closed his eyes.

For the first time since Aster left, I laughed in earnest, though I soon sobered.

It was time to give in to the curiosity. Just a little. Just enough to move on and hope the growing ache she'd left me with would soon reach its peak before letting up. "Have you heard much about what goes on over there?"

Berk grunted and opened his eyes. "Where?"

I refrained from gritting my teeth. "You know where." He'd mentioned more than once that he was still in casual contact with a distant relative from the isle. And with little to fill his days, the veteran made it his business to know everyone's business.

"Oh, right." He straightened in the chair. "Not much has changed.

The humans still cause a stir. The bloodshed continues." Dark eyes scrutinized me. "Why?"

I ignored his question. "Still?"

"That human king won't stop until vengeance for the death of his family has been met," he said, as if I were daft, then threw his hand out. "Everyone so much as connected to his bloodline was wiped out."

"Yet somehow he survived."

"Well, the emerald fae thought him dead, of course, but I heard he was raised within the butchered lands of the isle until he grew strong enough to build an army and take back one of his family's strongholds. What was his name? Merlin?"

My spine began to lock.

"No," Berk said, tapping at his crooked nose. "Marvis? Stars, I don't fucking know. Something stupid like that."

"So he won't stop." I licked my teeth, pondering that. "How much vengeance does he desire exactly?"

"Fuck knows, but given the duration of it all, and that the emerald king still lives, he still hasn't accomplished it."

I went to sip my water, forgetting that it was empty.

"Hard to believe they once existed peacefully, those humans and the emerald fae," Berk said after a tense minute had passed. "That for a great length of time, humans were welcomed and even *celebrated*," he hacked, "for the trade and entertainment they offered those ignorant faeries."

"Just as the golden royals have encouraged with those in Errin," I said, referring to the two kingdoms across the ravine that split through our continent of Nodoya. Errin, the human territory, shared a portion of the continent with the fae kingdom of Sinshell.

Berk nodded. "That will tear a chunk out of their asses, just you wait."

Indeed, I concurred silently.

"Do you know much of the tale?" Berk asked.

Knowing he was itching to speak it, I shook my head. Berk had few things left he enjoyed, and one of them was sharing stories.

He dug straight in. "Apparently, it was this Marvis' grandfather who was one of the first to perish from the plague that swept across the Isle of Emerald. Loving neighbors and companions then became enemies. We do not fall prey to illness, so of course, the fae were to blame. The human royals and many within their kingdom believed they had been cursed by faeries, and they began to retaliate. The emerald king went to the new human king to ask for help in putting an end to the madness, but he and his warriors were slain, and his son, Helvectus, was then crowned king."

I refrained from shifting in the chair.

"But this plague continued to take human lives. Helvectus was unable to squash their grief and anger with niceties such as peace talks and the offer of remedies, nor did the young king harbor the patience of his late father. Fearing the illness would spread, more humans arrived by the boatload from neighboring mortal lands to assist in ridding the Isle of Emerald of such evil creatures." Berk laughed, dry and rasped. "A grave mistake, for Helvectus had had enough."

"So it was he, the late emerald king, who had Marvis's family destroyed," I needlessly affirmed.

Berk nodded, gazing at the fire. "Fed up, Helvectus killed every single one of them himself, including that of any relatives, then he and his brethren destroyed their palace. Things settled for some years, but it was only a matter of time before Marvis and his military grew, and such brashness caught up with King Helvectus..." Sighing, he waved his hand. "His younger brother was then crowned king. And on and on it shall go until no royal blood remains."

Another minute passed in silence before he added quietly, "Talk may state that this King Marvis wants to avenge the death of his family, but some things are more valuable than vengeance. Many mortals cannot tolerate having faeries for neighbors, for they do not wish to live in fear."

We both sat with that truth for searing moments, the slow thud of my heart warning me to cool down. To move away from the fire. From this entire conversation I'd stupidly encouraged.

From this sickness I couldn't remember ever feeling before.

"I truly do not think it will cease," Berk murmured. "The fighting. Not until one side has thoroughly conquered the other. Like pests that won't die. You leave a few breathing"—he scratched at the bristle lining his jaw—"well, you earn yourself hundreds more."

Gnawing worry tried to drown the anger as I sat there, doing my best not to let any of it show.

Aster knew exactly where to find me. She had the ability to come to me whenever she wished.

Yet I knew she would not return.

She'd chosen *him*. Her husband. Whoever the fuck the idiot piece of undeserving shit was.

It was probably best I didn't know, and that she'd told me next to nothing about the life she'd run from. How like the blasted stars, to deliver an untouchable fate. They themselves knew all too well that I would never dare set foot upon the soil of that place again.

That I couldn't. Not even for her.

"You haven't asked about Wistensia in years," Berk said, barely above a whisper.

Think I'd run screaming from you, wolf?

I'd hunt you down.

I stared at the fire, the tea untouched and growing cold. "I know."

SEVEN

Aster

T HERE HAD BEEN NO SIGN OF RORN WHEN I'D ARRIVED IN OUR rooms at the towers.

Being late afternoon, it would have been the last place anyone would typically find him. But he hadn't been in the towers at all, I'd discovered after finally working up the courage to trek downstairs.

Theenon, steward to the Jade family, had twisted from the window in the dining hall, his orange-brown eyes wide with surprise. "Majesty." I'd smiled and taken a seat at the long, empty oak table. Seemingly stupefied by my sudden return and lack of explanation for my absence, he'd sputtered, "Where in the skies have you been this time?"

"I just needed…" I scrunched my nose. "Some fresh air."

"Fresh air? It's been *six days*," he'd stressed, clenching the gnarled wood in the back of the opposite chair. "We may be accustomed to these disappearing acts of yours, my queen, but this one was too much. Rorn was in a wild state before he was called to the graveyard."

Despite everything, I'd been unable to keep from stiffening with alarm. "The city?" He hadn't needed to help the warriors who protected the decimated land between the two kingdoms of the isle in some months. That he'd needed to return did not bode well, and likely with many warriors to assist.

"You didn't hear? Two battalions breached the graveyard via the sea caves three days ago." He'd made a sound of disgust and smoothed a hand over his bald head. "Bloodthirsty pests."

I'd swallowed and nodded. "No, I hadn't heard." When it became apparent that I wasn't willing to say more, Theenon had taken it upon himself to head to the kitchens to inform Dudley, our head cook, of my return.

And I'd left for our chambers to soak myself clean. As if a bath would make any sort of difference.

Sighing, I slid deeper into the water.

Home.

Rorn had ruined that for me, but surprisingly, it still lingered—the feelings of comfort, contentment. So much so, that a rapid drowsiness overcame me, and I startled awake when I was plucked from the cooled water by strong hands.

Trapped within the filmy haze of sleep, it was so easy to forget. To ignore what he'd done and what I'd done since. It was too easy to tuck my nose into his crisp winter-scented neck and to drape my arm over his shoulders.

Rorn, still holding me, lowered to the bed.

I forced my heavy eyelids open wider. "You're back."

His rush of breath gave away the vibrating tension, the anxiety roiling like a storm within him. "I should be saying that about you." His throat bobbed. "Bloom, where have you—"

"The Graveyard," I said, not wanting to talk of betrayals—of the wolf's scent that still stained like a curse I'd never rid upon my skin. "Theenon told me you returned to the city. Why? You know that is what they want, to catch you without enough strength behind you. You must cease journeying so far."

"It was only a small wave." Armed murderers who hoped to reduce the Jade line to ashes would never be considered something small, and he knew it, yet he still insisted on downplaying. "The threat has eased."

The threat would never ease.

So long as we lived, the kingdom of Wistensia, and much of the Isle of Emerald, would continue to be butchered by those who loathed and feared our kind.

Silence trickled into the chamber. Not even the warm notes of late spring upon the evening breeze washing in through the cracked, arched windows were enough to eradicate the chill blanketing us both. My blood thickened to sludge, my eyes gritty as I pulled away and rose to dig my palms into them.

I couldn't do this.

I couldn't do this, yet there was nothing else to be done. No other way.

I was a queen. A monarch with responsibilities. A torn soul with a shattered heart. A dreamer who'd been given everything I'd ever dared to want.

I was a typical treacherous faerie fool who'd sought revenge without knowing what it would cost.

And now, it was time to pay the suffocating price.

"Astrantia." Rorn's smooth timbre, the question within his warning as I stood and walked to the window, should've concerned me. "You're tired. Come back to bed."

"You should bathe," I said, numb and blinking down at the glass river. My eyes traced its curves around the base of the hills—a jeweled serpent in the grass through the patches of forest on either side. "You reek of death."

You reek of misery.

I closed my eyes, tight and wincing. Forced the memory of dim lighting and the first glimpse of that arrogant, wolfish grin to melt from my mind.

But it took too long, leaving behind a venomous taste that burned each shallow breath. So long, that I hadn't sensed my king arrive behind me.

"I love you," Rorn said, fingertips ghosting down my arms. My damp hair was shifted over my shoulder for his mouth to graze the bare skin of the other. "Stars, I love you so much." The regret and conviction roughening his voice almost had me falling back into him.

Almost.

I turned, blinking up at this male of whom I'd sworn my life to, and I marveled at what stood before me as I'd done thousands of times before.

Frosted blue eyes held a sheen, following the sweep of my own over his features. His long, thin nose was bruised from battle but already healing, and those soft, supple lips parted with a short burst of breath.

I traced the sharp rise of his cheeks with my thumbs, my wonder dulling as it melded with dismay. My fingers hovered over the thick arches of his brows, the same shade of soot as the hair rustled by the breeze to dance over his shoulders. His long lashes feathered the palm of my hand.

He'd always been majestic. Devastatingly divine.

And from the moment our lips had first touched when I was all of seventeen years, he'd been mine.

Had this female he'd lain with known that?

Had she been aware of just how young I'd been when I'd handed all I was to him? Had she touched him like this? With an appreciation for all that he was while wondering how the stars could possibly think her enough for him?

Had she known she wasn't merely bedding a king but a soul darkened by deeds that tainted his sleep and constantly robbed the color from his eyes? Had she known he wasn't just a priceless piece of art—a young god to lust over—but that he was also a useless queen's entire universe?

Her every reason for who she was?

Whoever this female was, had she known how irrevocably lost she would render me by enjoying the male I'd made my world? By stealing what wasn't hers to take?

"Bloom, say something," Rorn rasped and gently took my touch from his face by taking my wrists. "Where have you been?"

The flaring of his nostrils as he studied me with growing fury, the impatience that sparked in his beautiful eyes as he dared to open his mouth to demand *anything* of me...

It made me smile.

His mouth closed at the sight, and I rose to my toes while sliding my hands up his chest.

"Did it feel good, my king?" I purred to his ear. "Did it feel like one of the biggest rushes you've ever experienced in your life?" My fingers slid down his chest.

Rorn's frame tensed when they stopped atop the waistband of his pants.

I dragged a finger from one toned hip to the other. "Did you feel like you might just combust into stardust, never to return because it was just so..." I exhaled into his neck. "Fucking," I moaned, "thrilling?" I laughed, low and without humor, when he didn't answer, and then I stepped back.

His eyes, so bright blue they'd turned to ice, sank into mine. "You didn't." That deep, richly dignified voice cracked. "Tell me you didn't." He frowned, as if struggling to believe what he already knew. "Do not toy with me, Astrantia."

Adrenaline faded rapidly. As did the satisfaction it had so briefly given.

My lack of response was all the confirmation he needed.

But before his ire caught fire, I asked him, "Do you remember what you said to me the night you tossed your guilt at my feet like a weapon?" Unlike him, I wouldn't make excuses. But I would blame him just as he'd blamed me. "I'm certain you can recall reminding me of my failure to give you what you need. After years spent trying to be all you needed, desperate to give you the heir you desire while trying to fix this broken realm, after so many years by your side..."

He swallowed, the sound of it harsh.

"All these years, Rorn." My voice dried to a rasp. "All my love and unwavering devotion, and you said I cared for *nothing* but my fuck-ing womb, so you would see to it that our anguish ceased." I sniffed, whispering and loathing the taste of repeating it all. "You also said you would do it again if necessary. As if that would somehow make me grateful. As if I would not see that you need an heir more than you'll ever need me."

"Bloom, that's not true. You're the reason for every-fucking-thing I do."

Once, I might have believed that. For so long, I'd blindly believed every word that left his traitorous mouth.

The pieces of me he'd torn apart wished I still could, if only to alleviate the pain.

"Liar. I was the furthest thing from your mind when you fucked her. You didn't think of me or this kingdom," I seethed, my voice ris-ing. "You thought of no one but yourself."

"Astrantia," he gritted, scarcely a whispered growl, for he'd loathe for anyone to overhear. "You're angry and hurting, so you are refus-ing to understand." He raised his hands when I opened my mouth to snarl at him. "The need for a babe has caused us to veer off path. Stars, can you not see how true that is now?"

"I never saw anything but you—"

He spoke over me. "It's going to destroy you, Bloom. It's going to destroy *us*." He sighed and lowered his voice. "I will admit it was wrong of me to explain myself in such an indelicate way, but I was right to have said that this is what is best. We need to take a different approach to get what we want. It's honestly that simple—"

"Simple?" I almost shouted. "How fucking dare you—"

"Bloom, if you would please just *try* to understand—"

"Enough. I will hear no more of the same poisonous excuses." I stabbed my finger into his chest. "You blamed me for warming anoth-er's bed, my foolish king, and now?" My smile shook with my heart. "Now I get to do the same to you."

I left before he could stop me. Before the tears flooding my eyes could fall.

Footsteps clacked upon the stone stairs.

Most of the carpets had been removed after the towers were set upon by a small unit of mortal soldiers two summers ago, leaving the drafty rock-hewn walls even colder during the icy months. The humans had all been slain in the halls and on the stairs before Rorn had even opened the doors to our rooms, his sword in hand and half naked.

If you looked closely, you could still see the crimson specks within the mortar.

Those humans had been the first and the last to breach our walls. The last of them to die had said they'd scaled the northern mountains beyond the towers. Many of his comrades had fallen during their journey, lost to the perilous and steep terrain. Which had left just twelve to fire iron arrows into the chests of our guards in the rear courtyard before they'd encountered more guards inside our home.

There were now shifter sentinels living in packs within the mountains.

Theenon knocked once on the open door to my painting parlor. "Majesty, might I tempt you with a walk in the gardens?"

"Not today, Theenon."

He lingered, the sun glinting with the shine of his head. "It's a beautiful day."

I curled my legs over the window seat, smiling because he knew I was well aware of that. "I know."

His wiry brows scrunched. "Some lunch, then?"

I shook my head, and he bowed, taking his leave.

I stared at the door, my eyes fastened on the bronze handle. Perhaps fear was to blame, but I failed to understand how I hadn't seen it before. Why I hadn't realized just how lonely love had left me until I'd tried desperately to cling to the rubble of what it had once been.

Since my return to Wistensia some days ago, I'd walked the meadows surrounding the towers as dawn had rolled in. I'd received the usual smiles from the groundskeepers and other staff as I'd plucked at the clover and wildflowers with aimless intent.

I'd reentered the towers filled with color, with a fresh vow to try. Each morning I woke after failing to dream, to sleep much at all, I felt that vow grow stronger. As if it might eventually prove successful if I could just hold on long enough for time to pass.

But upon reaching the rooms Rorn had prepared for me as a wedding gift, easels precisely placed to capture every changing shade of light, I'd find myself draining into darkness once again.

Still I stayed, unwilling to venture downstairs to the quiet halls of the mostly empty fortress. There was no comfort to be found in the chilled, echoing rooms and in the familiar yet ever-fleeting faces of the staff.

I'd barely been a princess. A queen was all I'd ever been.

For too many years.

Looking back, I struggled to remember who I'd been before Rorn. I'd been young. Perhaps too young, as my father had warned. I'd been careless, most certainly, yet so confident.

But from the moment I'd first laid eyes on Rorn, I'd been in love. From the second he'd touched my fingers with his, I'd been impatient. From the heart-seizing minute before his lips had first introduced themselves to mine, I'd been in his arms.

Forever in his arms.

Even as he'd worked, I'd worked right alongside him. As he'd trained, I'd trained with him or watched while trying to replicate the wonder before me on parchment. When he'd traveled, I'd always accompanied him, no matter the distance nor the risk.

Over the past few years, that had all changed.

The slow erosion had never alarmed me. I'd been too determined to further daydream my life away—content to lose myself to the promise of a future I couldn't see while anxiously awaiting a full womb.

Ever since I'd accompanied my father to the jewel ball at the dreamy age of sixteen, Rorn Jade had been all I'd known, all I'd ever wanted, and I'd never once cared a thing for the consequences. Not once had I acknowledged the danger of tying myself to one soul in such extremes. For I'd had no reason to.

Until he'd given me too many.

Now, he was out there while I remained in here. Alone with all we'd once been.

Days spent dreaming, months of nothing but us and believing the world lay waiting at our feet, turned dark when Rorn's older brother, Helvectus, was slain in battle at Bone Cove. Helvectus and his few troops were ambushed while greeting whom they'd thought were visiting officials in the harbor.

We'd had no warning. No time to send more warriors. No time to stop them.

A unit of over fifty mortals killed almost every creature in sight. They'd then decimated our seaside city before setting up camp in preparation to march farther inland.

Beyond the window I laid my head against, beyond the ever-stretching miles of greenery containing villages and farmland, laid a wasteland of valleys and homes and a fallen city that had been so aptly named. Upon seeing it for the first time after the human soldiers who'd destroyed it had been defeated, I remembered thinking that perhaps someone had known.

Perhaps our ancestors, upon giving portions of the isle life in the form of names, had been warned of what all those once spacious streets and crowded shops would eventually become.

And so they'd named it Graveyard City.

For it was now scorched earth and sand-swept debris, the bones of many souls forever trapped beneath the ruins.

Warned indeed, I had thought as I'd stood upon a sandy knoll at the young age of eighteen. Freshly wed and so perilously in love, I'd soaked in all the destruction mere weeks after Helvectus' passing, shaken to my core.

A prophecy wrapped within a name.

I wasn't sure whether to laugh or cry or surrender to both. For it had been at that same jewel ball where I'd first laid eyes on my prince turned king that I'd been given a warning myself.

Not once had I looked at his older brother, King Helvectus, when the sorceress with eyes and hair of pure crimson had warned me that my true love would be a faerie king.

My heart had known. It could only have been Rorn. So I embraced her warning as magical fate, and I'd welcomed it with all I had to give.

In return, I'd been handed everything, only to eventually rot with nothing.

I'd foolishly believed we would live as we'd wanted. Two souls free to adventure and hide and love. I'd thought if Rorn would one day become king, then that day would only arrive when we were both ready.

Raised a dreamer by a warrior who so often had to leave me with nothing but my stories and paintings and wild imagination for guardianship—I'd never felt more naïve for letting my heart run so far away from me.

Rorn and his most trusted returned at nightfall, catching me unawares in the throne room.

Their footsteps ceased as three sets of eyes fell upon me.

"Majesty," Rollins said with a swift bow. "Good to see you." I forced a small smile, and the captain gestured over his shoulder. "I was just heading for the barracks."

Halthorne, our mapmaker and a longtime friend of Rorn's, was slow to follow. Finally sensing the rising tension between his king and queen, he wisely excused himself.

The doors closed.

"Hello, husband."

Rorn just stared at me, his face marred with sweat and sun and a trace of fury.

"Nothing to say?" I tapped at the rose fashioned from gold at the end of my throne's armrest. So rarely, with the exception of formal gatherings and visitors, did we now sit in this empty, soulless room.

Rorn turned to leave.

Still too enraged, then, I surmised.

"It will wear off soon." I couldn't help myself—found the temptation too irresistible. "The anger. You'll soon enter this lovely fog of numbness. You might even find yourself capable of forgetting, if only for fleeting moments of time."

"Stars, Astrantia." Rorn whirled, booted steps echoing as he stormed across the stone floor. "You think to torment me further with venomous words?"

Placing my hand beneath my chin, I brushed a finger over my lips. "Do you believe you've been tormented enough for your transgressions, my king?"

His ire faded, brows pulling low. "That's not what I meant—"

"I wish to know something." I rose and descended the steps to stand before him.

His eyes flared when I reached between us to palm his growing erection.

"When you pushed this lovely cock inside this female you chose, did you think I would forgive you?" I stroked my nail over the rock-hard bulge. "Did you think my love for you was so vast that your pitiful reasoning would make perfect sense?"

Rorn stiffened, coiling to take a step back.

I squeezed him through his pants and he hissed. "Did you think you could be just like your father? Have yourself a doting wife and also do whatever you please while outside of these towers?"

"You know I thought none of that," he seethed between his teeth. "Nothing like that at all."

"You're right," I said with a flat laugh. Releasing him, I strode to the doors. "To think anything of the sort, you'd have needed to think of me at all."

The doors to the throne room slammed with a harsh wind. Besides warping, maneuvering air was Rorn's only magical ability—and that he'd been given what he considered scraps from his powerful royal lineage bothered him endlessly.

His heated presence loomed at my back. "I did it for us. For you.

So you will admit to lying in order to hurt me with your claims of giving yourself to another, and you will stop this."

"Stop what?" I asked, apathetic.

He saw right through it, his hands grasping my hips and turning me. "Punishing me. Pushing me away."

"Then you shouldn't have given me reason to." Forced against the doors by his body, I shoved at his chest. "Release me."

His eyes flashed, bright with intent. "Never."

"Don't you dare even think—"

His mouth stole mine before I could finish speaking, the violent prying of his lips rendering me useless for searing moments.

I'd never known that bliss and torture could be one and the same. Not until I caught fire and disintegrated beneath the heart-splitting familiarity of his touch, his claiming hands at my cheek and hip. His taste, the crisp sweetness, both poisoned and revived.

He was the antidote to the wasting soul inside me, but he was also the cause of its slow demise.

Fire scorched a trail up my throat in the form of untamable, snide words. I tore free, gasping, "The touch of your lips won't erase what another's has done."

Rorn froze, and it was all I needed to drift into mist, to leave him alone and grappling with the double meaning of what I'd said.

EIGHT

Aster

THERE WAS NOTHING SUBTLE ABOUT HEARTBREAK.

It crawled through the walls, chased me outdoors—neither sun or rain able to change the way it discolored everything.

In the weeks since I'd returned from Vordane, I'd learned the decaying of a heart could touch the entire world. Its power was such that even those around me would often tense in discomfort.

Theenon began to check on me less frequently. When he did, I'd do my best to tame my emotions, to keep him from stiffening to stone while he awaited the same refusals from me.

As the days dwindled forward to carry us into a future too uncertain to find ourselves grateful for, the heartbreak began to morph into something new yet equally as deadly. Longing had tangled with sorrow, and the sorrow welcomed a need I couldn't quench.

I'd thought it would lessen. I'd expected each passing day and night away from Scythe to help deliver me toward something resembling relief. Instead, the restless and listless cycle of want and sadness repeated every minute of every hour of every day that slipped away into the void.

While lost to the flat brush strokes of his wolf's mane upon the easel before me, I half-wondered if the growing burn within my chest would worsen when met by the slow-traveling ache within my bones.

A risk, I knew, to wound Rorn further should he discover what I'd given into—the recreation of my vengeance. I didn't dare paint his face, the long dark hair, the moss green eye and those full, soft lips. Nor did I dare spill his blinding, wolfish grin and the way it lit his eye onto the parchment.

The mere thought of doing such a thing—of seeing him when I could never again truly see him—weakened my knees and squeezed my lungs in a vise of my own making.

No, denying myself wasn't merely to protect Rorn, who didn't deserve as much.

It was self-preservation.

So I painted Scythe's wolf form instead, not expecting the warming of my blood to push at my skin with every piece of appearing fur. As always, my hands shook when I came close to completion. But this time, I stopped myself from ripping the parchment from the easel and tearing it to tatters.

Hungry, wildflower?

Breathing through my nose, I dropped the brush into the pot of clouded water and crossed to the window to watch the moonlight dance with the shadows between the trees over the river.

The towers were silent, allowing Rorn's soft snores on the floor below to flood the stairwell.

In the sitting room beneath my parlor, he laid sprawled across the chaise, maps and empty wineglasses upon the table. Watching him at rest, the strands of dark hair that veiled his cheek, the rhythmic rise and fall of his chest, it was easy to remember.

To remember this young king had been handed a kingdom and the task of protecting it before he knew what that would rob from him.

His father had also been a young king. He'd barely reached one hundred and fifty years when he'd tried to end the unforeseen brutality between human and faerie. Being that he'd sought peace—for the human royals to cease all violence and placing blame upon the fae for the plague that had befallen their people—he'd taken only his guard with him.

He was slain upon being welcomed into the previous human king's stronghold.

His portrait hung upon the wall above the fireplace next to his first-born son, Helvectus. Their twin gazes stared down at me, both touched by the stars with one eye a deep blue and the other an emerald green. The rare orbs were a sign of the alpha king.

Helvectus, with his long golden hair and his mismatched eyes, stared at me now as he had when he'd last passed me upon the stairs of this very tower—with a darkness of duty in one eye and the gleam of mischief in the other.

Helvectus had never married. Never mated nor procreated.

Rorn used to say it was due to his brother's inclination to have himself as many bed partners as he wished. But I'd once overheard Helvectus admit to Theenon that he'd never subject any mate, wife, or offspring to the curse that he and his father had unknowingly placed upon this family and the isle.

I'd once thought Rorn's brother selfish for it. Though I'd never implied as much, I'd thought him utterly obnoxious and insufferable for the way he had lived his life. Now, I was beginning to understand that perhaps we were the selfish ones.

Those who desired more no matter the cost.

All those years ago, Rorn had sworn he was ready to rule. But looking at him now, unable to escape where we'd ended up, perhaps he hadn't been. Perhaps he still wasn't.

He needed an heir. We needed a successor. If something happened to us—if the towers and the protection of this kingdom fell into the wrong hands…

There was no longer enough of our ilk left to take it back.

Too many had died or fled for safer lands with their families. An island once swarming with thousands of fae folk had now been whittled down to hundreds.

One broken heart was nothing when faced with the loss of everything.

Regardless, just the sight of him raked claws down my chest. Disgust and something sickening, something between anger and resentment, hollowed my lungs. I peeled off the stone doorframe and traipsed back upstairs to my paints. Not to paint, but to sleep.

I hadn't returned to our bed since arriving home, and seemingly doing his utmost to avoid me, Rorn hadn't tried to make me.

Home.

Its comforts no longer comforted. No longer glistened with faulty, fleeting promises that, somehow, everything would be okay. Time had proven there was no way of making that so. There was no more hope to gorge ourselves on. We were in too many differing pieces to fix.

And in the end, none of that mattered. I was still a wife. More importantly, I was still a queen.

I was still stuck.

"You know, I wasn't entirely sure I believed you when you told me." Rorn's tone held an edge that suggested he'd been watching me for some unnoticed moments. "Didn't believe you could actually do such a thing to me at all, let alone out of spite."

I didn't startle, but I placed the brush into the pot of water and met my husband's frosted eyes. "Well, now you know."

"You betrayed me out of spite," he said again, features twisting with incredulity. "But I betrayed you for *you*."

Blinking slowly at him, I had to refrain from laughing. From asking if he'd always been this arrogantly delusional, or if perhaps I'd been too in love to see it until now.

Instead, I wiped my hands over my paint dotted skirts and said, "You know I would never have agreed to…" I could barely conjure the words without that pit of forming rage getting the better of me. I gave in, setting some of it loose. "I would never be okay with something that contains the power to destroy me more than my inability to give you an heir."

Rorn's jaw ticked. Behind his closed lips, his tongue dragged over his teeth.

He eyed my soiled skirts, of which I typically went to great lengths to keep clean. "Who was it?" he finally said with a calm I did not trust.

"No one you know."

"Astrantia," he warned.

The gritted use of my name had me expelling a rush of breath and shifting upon the stool to fully face him.

Leaning against the doorframe to my parlor, his hair and tunic dusted with raindrops and his gaze unwavering, he unclenched his jaw. "I will ask you one last time."

I should've been alarmed, afraid even.

I felt nothing but that awakening pinch within my chest. "Why?"

"Why?" he repeated with a harsh laugh. "You know damned well that you promised his death the moment you let him touch you."

I nodded, smiling slightly at the thought. Rorn was a fierce warrior, to be sure, but the ability to shift had not been granted to him like it had for many others in his family, and so I didn't like his chances. Nor did I like the idea of either male injuring themselves. "You're still there, then."

"There?" he asked, irritated. "Where?"

"Anger," I said, turning back to my easel. Looking beyond it to the bay window, I gently rolled my neck. "It will pass soon."

I could almost hear his teeth grind. "If you truly believe there will come a day when I won't wish to know who he is, then you're indeed lying about having been with another at all, or you've forgotten who the fuck I am."

"I haven't forgotten," I said, gentle but firm. "I merely cannot remember ever agreeing to marry a male who'd so easily disregard my own heart for the sake of his cock and pride."

A prolonged minute of silence screamed and strangled.

"His fucking name, Astrantia," Rorn ordered, each word enunciated with a rare, worrying sharpness. "Now."

"I do not know it," I said, the half-truth falling from my lips with ease. "Even if I did, it wouldn't matter. It wouldn't change anything." Smirking down at the paint-stained fingers in my lap, I laughed, the sound choked and wet. "You'll never find him, Rorn."

The emerald king snarled and crossed the room in an instant.

A stunned inhale was trapped in my throat when he gripped my neck. Rage whitened his eyes, his every feature, and rolled from him in waves. "I will find him, and when I do..."

Just when I'd thought he might let that rage and his strength get the better of him and tighten his hold on my neck, he kissed me.

Bruising hands plucked me from the stool to set me on the window seat. Grabbing at my skirts for access to my thighs, they were too fast, too knowing to stop. "When I do," he continued, "mark my words, wife, he will bleed out while watching me take you."

"Rorn." Horror swept through me, emptied my lungs of enough air. "Rorn, we can't," I rasped when he laid a knee upon the seat and dragged me closer, pulling me against him.

"We can because you're mine." He shoved my leg around his waist, his lips fighting with mine. His energy clouded and clashed with mine. Our desire and need to take and erase and destroy left us breathless and biting.

His cock rubbed me through his pants, rocked and pressed and gathered sparks to send them flying. Blood filled my mouth, the sour taste of wrong and the sweetest touch of perfect.

I began to unravel. Unrelenting, his mouth trapped all sound and breath with a wicked rumble from his chest that ceased when he groaned and I clenched. Right before the wave of pleasure could crest within me, Rorn reared back to free himself from his pants.

Breathe, wildflower.

Cold drenched me from head to toe. I broke through the haze of unwanted pleasure and growled, shoving Rorn away before he could enter my body.

He didn't leave.

He stared at me with a cruelty to his eyes I'd never glimpsed before.

Then he stole my mouth and fisted his cock, pumping as I tried not to lose myself to my never-ending ruin. "You would deny yourself?" he broke away to whisper, his lips roaming my cheek to my neck. "You need to come, Bloom. I can smell it. Feel it in the tremble of your skin."

The fog cleared entirely, and this time, I didn't push or fight. I merely stood from the cushioned window seat, abrupt and uncaring.

Cock still in hand, Rorn stumbled back to his knees, knocking brushes from the easel behind him and spirting his release over the floor with a curse.

The silence roared as we both panted and stared.

"This has to fucking stop. It's been weeks, Astrantia. We're so much more than this mess, and it's time we both remember that." The words were more of a plea than a command. "Forgive me," he ordered, shuffling to me on his knees.

My eyes widened at the sight. "Rorn…"

"Forgive me and I know I can find a way to forgive you."

My head shook. He made it sound so easy, so temptingly doable. "I don't know how," I said, barely a sound as tears stole my voice.

"We'll help each other." He rose and clutched my cheeks, brushed at the wet staining them and vowed, "We will make it through this." I nodded, found that I wanted to believe him even though I didn't. I didn't believe him at all. "We will."

I placed my hand over his at my cheek. "Rorn."

"We need to try, Bloom. We have to. If not for ourselves then for the sake of this stars-damned kingdom."

He was right.

He was wrong for using the weight of responsibility against me. For reminding me that I was trapped. But that didn't mean it wasn't true.

I couldn't go on like this.

Deep down, I knew it would only continue to destroy me. I had to start accepting all that had happened and move forward. I had to tell myself that forgiveness took time, and that I didn't truly want the one-eyed wolf. That my reasons for thinking I did were unjust.

I wanted Scythe because he was forbidden.

I wanted him because he hadn't yet betrayed me. I wanted him because he made me feel things that my promised love had rarely ever scraped the surface of. I wanted him because I was in lust and in search for something more. I wanted him because he represented a life I thought I might prefer.

The wolf was nothing more than a distraction from the pain of what was real.

This was real. It might have been irreparably broken, but it was still mine. All these broken pieces still belonged to me. This king was still mine, as he was always meant to be. He was all I'd ever wanted. He was all I'd ever have.

Anything else was fleeting and impossible.

NINE

Aster

HOPE SHIMMERED WITHIN THE SUNLIGHT, WARMING MY cheeks and chest.

The path downhill was well-worn, wildflowers waving at my skirts. My guard walked behind me, in talk amongst themselves. I didn't mind, and I resisted the temptation to pluck more flowers to place within my basket, for I was off to see an old friend of my own.

Shayleen lived in the village across the river, but her stall had a permanent home in the market by the bridge. It had been too long since I'd last seen her, and after spending weeks with only my anguish for company, I decided that maybe it wasn't too late to revisit parts of myself I'd left behind upon marrying Rorn.

Rorn had promised he wouldn't so much as stand too close to another female, let alone continue to try to create the heir I could not provide with another. I believed him. I believed him yet I still couldn't seem to forgive him, no matter how ready he seemed to forgive me.

Maybe I would never forgive him.

I'd tried to return to our rooms, but I'd lasted mere hours before the attempt to close the icy distance between us had ended in another interrogation of what I'd done and who I'd done it with. I'd since retreated to my painting parlor.

Dinner was often spent in stilted silence, breakfast a forgotten memory due to the late hour I woke after each night of fitful sleep.

I feared we were lost. Somewhere beneath our actions, we'd lost who and what we'd been.

When I'd said as much to Rorn last night over dinner, he'd countered with, "So we rebuild." Taking my hand across the table, he'd stated with soft sincerity, "We simply start again."

I'd stared at our interlaced fingers, my eyes dry yet the threat of tears closing my throat.

There was no other option. There was nothing else. There was only the two of us desperately trying to cling to something for the sake of what was, and for the sake of others.

And so I'd agreed to a game of chess after dessert.

It had been silent, tense, for the most part, but as the fire had warmed the sitting room and the wine our bodies, we'd begun to smile. We'd begun to laugh. And when Rorn had bid me good night with a gentle brush of his lips over my cheek, his fingers trailing through my hair over my upper arm, I'd felt it.

I still felt it now—that slight flare of hope in my chest as we trekked the rockier slopes of the downward path, the market now within sight upon the river's edge.

The bridge was dotted with horses and carts and glowing greenery around the posts and railings. Traders and civilians walked the rock-laden roads beyond that would take them south of the isle via the northern woods. Leaves danced across the curving wood, crunched beneath hooves and boots, and gathered in soggy piles along the river bank.

A smile bloomed, along with a furthering lightness within my chest. Fresh fruit and vegetables, and chicken pie, floated upon the breeze from the small collection of stalls.

We wound between them, Illon plucking an apple from a cart and tossing two coppers to the vendor. The other two guards caught up with me when I stopped to purchase a pie, and eyed our surroundings with keen focus. There was likely little need for them to fret, nor to follow me at all, given the few times danger had managed to come to the towers, or even this close.

But it had still happened, so they were still wary. I was thankful, but also thankful for the privacy they offered by waiting outside once we'd reached the rusted hut with sunflowers dancing either side of the door.

Inside, the overwhelming perfume of Shayleen's remaining stock engulfed me. I inhaled it deep and skimmed my fingers over a cluster of marigolds. I withdrew my hand when I saw them.

Violas.

The sight of them singed, both my eyes and heart.

Through the door in the back of the small shop entered a female with white-blond hair shorn close to her scalp. "Shayleen," I said, smiling instantly, even as my chest continued to twinge.

The feeling worsened when she adjusted the babe on her hip, his pudgy fist at his mouth. Blinking over at me, she dropped the pail she'd been holding. "Aster, oh my stars." Her eyes widened as she made to curtsy. "My apologies, Majesty."

I waved her off. "Unnecessary." We stared at one another, and I could've kicked myself for coming unprepared. For not knowing what to say. "It's been so long, I know, but I just thought I'd say hello…" I lifted the basket. "And I couldn't resist the chicken pie."

Her shock waning, she nodded and offered a weak smile. "No one can surpass Jon when it comes to pie."

"No one," I agreed, and my gaze lowered to the babe in her arms. "Congratulations. What's his name?"

"Quain," she said. "And thank you. I've two more at home. Beatrice is almost four summers now, and Santon is two."

"Are they with your husband?"

"No, he's dead," she said, and with such speed it was as if she didn't want the word to touch her lips. "His mother lives with me now. She minds them." Smiling sadly at Quain, she brushed some of his unruly blond tufts from his forehead. "This one won't be weaned for a while yet, so he's created a somewhat permanent home on my hip."

"I'm so sorry, Shayleen."

"Me too," she whispered, and moved to the counter at the window by the door. Setting her son upon a blanket there, she got to work on removing petals from damaged flowers, and opening tiny sacks.

I had no idea what to say next, if there was anything else to say, nor if my presence was what this soul needed. I didn't know why, but I asked, "Was it in battle?"

"He was returning from a short run, and it was too late to turn back when they saw them upon the shoreline. He and most of his crew were slaughtered hours before the king's patrol reached the docks."

Her husband had been a fisherman, that much I knew, but I'd never met him. I never would.

We'd both been so young the last time I'd visited Shayleen with news of my fairy tale prince. Too young, perhaps, to ever guess at just how unpredictable life would become in this place we'd always called home.

"Are you faring okay?" I asked, knowing she knew what I was offering. "I can have a delivery sent, and make sure you—"

"The king cannot afford to give all of us coin, Astrantia. I know that better than most. Besides"—she tossed a stem onto a tray filled with others and began counting seeds from a bowl—"we manage fine. Unlike most."

Her tone implied that my time would've been better spent seeing to other widows, and to the younglings now bereft of parents. I didn't tell her I had. That the running of the orphanage and its funds were overseen personally by Theenon, the king, and myself.

But it wasn't enough. I could see now that nothing would ever be enough unless the violence ceased. An heir wouldn't help. They would merely inherit this heartbreak.

I stared at Shayleen's son when he smiled at me, toothless and new and rosy-cheeked.

"Aster?"

"Hmm?" I tore my eyes from the babe and blinked at the open

window, the sunlight blinding and blurring in contrast to the shaded hut.

"Are you okay? You're looking a little pale."

I cleared my throat and gave my head a shake. "Fine, sorry."

"Don't be."

I smiled, but her attention was given back to her task, and my stomach was weighted, my chest tight.

A moment passed, followed by too many more, before Shayleen finally said gently, "Well, I really must get these seeds organized before this little goblin of mine grows grumpy again."

"I could help," I said, and found I meant it, eager to see if perhaps it would rid the insidious churning within me.

"I cannot allow that, my queen, but I do thank you for the offer."

With that, she smiled and curtsied, then plucked her son from the counter to retrieve the pail she'd dropped upon my arrival.

It would seem I'd out-stayed my welcome, if I'd been welcome at all, so I turned for the door with a heavy heart. "Take care, Shayleen."

"Aster," she called.

I turned back, shielding my eyes from the harsh glow of the sun with my hand. "You take care, okay?"

I frowned, but she was gone before I could read her expression.

The journey back to the towers was quiet, and I was once again thankful for the males who left me to my own musings. Though I could've definitely done with the distraction, I wasn't sure what would have vacated my mouth if I were to open it.

Wailing or screaming.

Years spent playing hide-and-seek, catching butterflies, and braiding hair with flowers while we regaled one another with fictional tales of love and danger and magic still lingered in my fondest memories.

Growing up, my father had made sure we'd had no neighbors in the forest within the foothills of the towers, but I'd still attended classes a few days a week in the village. Shayleen had been the only one brave enough to befriend the general's daughter, and I'd foolishly swept those years of friendship aside as soon as I'd laid eyes on my future husband.

Perhaps life would've drawn us in two differing directions regardless, yet I couldn't help but feel as if this sudden sense of loneliness was no one's fault but my own. I'd been ignoring the way it wrapped around my heart in a cold squeeze for weeks on end, but there was no ignoring it after today.

I was alone and that likely wouldn't change, so there was no use in feeling sorry for myself.

It was time to make peace with it.

The males chattered and laughed, crossing the fields to the western road leading to the towers. Shining like onyx spears jutting toward the cloud-dusted sky, the rock-hewn sentinels I had stared at longingly while growing up watched over the northern half of the isle.

Now, they were my home.

The smallest of the three square towers was wrapped in too much leafy greenery to glimpse the emerald Rosetta windows, while the two beside it mirrored one another in size.

When we reached the little bridge that gave passage over the creek to the empty courtyard, I stopped to stare up at the giant tower on the left. The tower containing my parlor and our rooms.

He was there. I could sense it.

Crossing the gurgling water, I gathered my skirts away from the pebbles over the drive and willed that tiny spark of hope to return. Urged it to drown out the sadness that somehow felt even more encompassing.

I still had him. My king. It would never be the same, I knew, but perhaps it shouldn't be.

Perhaps, I thought, nodding to my guard as they bowed and left for the barracks, we could somehow make it even better than before. Perhaps, we could take our hurt and create something so formidable, we would be untouchable to all. Even our enemies.

We could rebuild, as Rorn had said.

The spark returned, and I smiled.

Upstairs, I discovered Rorn was indeed in our rooms. Head bent low, he sat upon the chest at the end of our bed with his hands clasped between his knees.

"I hope you're hungry." I frowned when he refused to look at me. "Rorn?"

"Not at all." His rasped, humorless laugh sank my heart. He lifted a shaking hand to his forehead, then cursed and dropped it. "Bloom, I'm not quite sure how to say this..."

The room swirled, sunlight mixing with shadow.

The basket of wildflowers and chicken pie fell to the floor before the confession could leave his mouth.

"It worked." Red-rimmed, his gaze rose from the mess I'd made to meet with mine. "She carries my heir."

PART TWO
ROTTEN GOLD

TEN

Aster

SHE LOOKED NOTHING LIKE ME.

It was all I could manage to think upon first glimpsing the slender, raven-haired, and wide-eyed creature.

Nothing.

I didn't know if that should have concerned or pleased me. Though I supposed I was expected to be pleased. For Rorn's treachery had indeed not been in vain.

No longer would I need to suffer through the vicious arrival of each cycle. No longer would I need to plead with the healers to find what was broken within me and fix it, only for them to continually tell me it was just the way things were—and for far too many of our kind.

I couldn't decide what I was as the female without an empty womb was given a room in the staff quarters beneath the first floor of the towers.

All I knew was that I was anything but happy.

My husband's seed had filled this stranger's body. A male that didn't belong to her had given this thief something that would never be mine.

For weeks now, I'd only seen her from afar.

For just as long, I'd avoided Rorn's touch and company by staying with my paintings. Alone with my wilted heart and empty thoughts—I'd succumbed to the odd feeling of feeling nothing at all.

No amount of apologizing would change anything. Not even the few times my king had gazed at me from his knees with tears flooding his eyes, a sight I'd never thought to see, could rouse the courage within me to care.

For days, Theenon did not climb the stairs to check on me, but rather, he'd send one of the guards or kitchen-hands to deliver my meals.

Many of them went untouched. It'd taken days to find the desire to eat. Survival, whatever it was I was even surviving for, eventually had me forcing down small bites of fruit and bread.

The scythe moon sat in the corner of the bay window.

There was one thing to be grateful for. The ache and sense of missing something I hadn't known was so vital had finally departed with the arrival of Rorn's pregnant lover. There was no room for longing for the wolf.

But I wasn't grateful.

I was simply… nothing.

My barely touched dinner sat waiting by the door. I'd deliver it to the kitchens later when the occupants of the towers were slumbering and I could pretend to roam the halls as if nothing might harm me.

My gaze slowly crossed the parlor to the door at the sound of footsteps.

Theenon. His mouth was etched in a thin line, hands tucked before him as he stood at the door that had been left ajar. "Majesty," he said, his eyes assessing.

I looked back to the window, to the land beyond.

Perhaps I could be of use somewhere out there. It had never been more clear that the title of queen meant little here in these royal towers. Maybe I'd cut off my locks and dress differently. Maybe I could try to be something else for a while.

Remembering with heated color what had happened the last time

I'd tried to escape my life, I squashed the thought. It was but another useless wondering my solitude and weary soul liked to tempt me with.

"It's good to see you," I said, aware that it was flat.

"I wish I could say the same to you."

I snorted, surprised by the sound. "I know. I need to bathe." It had likely been a few days. I couldn't recall. The times I'd found the energy to wash, I would wait until I knew the king was long gone before sneaking up the stairs to our rooms.

"No," Theenon said. "You need to leave this parlor. I've drawn you a bath in the guest rooms below to give you privacy and a change of scenery."

"Theenon," I started.

"It's already done. Do you wish to waste the water?"

"Give it to somebody else."

He said nothing for a stretched moment, then sighed. "Very well."

Guilt pricked at my eyes, but I closed them and laid down over the window seat with my head against the cool glass.

I woke some hours later with a need for water and the privy. After using the latter, I collected my dinner tray and decided it was probably safe to take it back to the kitchens.

Shadows grew deeper with each step down the winding stairs, the green tapestry rustled by the howling wind outside as it stole through the cracks between the stone and windows. Rain loomed upon the stale summer air. Flame bounced in the sconces upon the walls of the hall.

My heart pattered like the wings of a trapped bird.

Bypassing the great ballroom that entwined all three towers, I hurried down the hall of the smaller tower. Soft murmurings could be heard from the staff quarters below, and I pondered over the idea of them all befriending the pregnant female who now lived amongst them.

I hadn't been introduced. I hadn't learned her name. I hadn't listened for it. I hadn't thought I'd want to know.

Rorn wouldn't dare, yet that he hadn't even thought to ask me what I might prefer also cut deep. As if his two lovers were to be kept separate at all times.

Pets within their rightful cages.

Embarrassed beyond measure at the thought of our people—of anyone—knowing what had become of us, and learning what I'd now been reduced to...

My fingers clenched the tray. I welcomed it. I nearly smiled as anger rushed through me to warm the metal, thankful for the rage that burned through my limbs.

At the end of the hall, I veered left and took the stairs down to the kitchens. They were half underground, the rooms for the staff even lower, and mercifully empty.

I scraped the leftover food into the compost and placed the dishes by the sink before quickly stealing a carafe of water and hurrying back to the stairs.

I should've taken the wine instead, but the last time I'd done so, someone had tattled. Rorn had then decided to pay my parlor a visit out of concern. I didn't want his concern. It was far too late for him to finally show any regard for my well-being. Furthermore, I didn't want to see him.

Avoidance was futile. A game that could only be played for so long.

My blood ran cold when I reached the bottom step. His voice traveled down the hall above, hushed and angry.

I slunk back into the kitchens against the stone wall, the carafe hugged tight to my chest as if it could somehow protect me from what I was overhearing.

"You did this to me, and you think to simply dump me down here to hide me as if I'm the one who did it to myself?" The female voice hissed just above a whisper, "As if I asked for any of this?"

Shockingly snide, Rorn responded with, "You speak as if you had no say at all in the matter, Carelda."

Carelda.

The name rang through me like a war bell, hollowing what remained of my heart.

"The matter?" Carelda half-laughed. "That's what this babe means to you? What I mean to you? We are not a problem you can simply hide from, Rorn. This is horrifically cruel, and I do not remember bedding a cruel male."

"I am your king, and you would do well to address me as nothing else."

Silence froze the musty air. I quit breathing, fearing my struggle to do so would potentially give me away.

"And I never said you were a problem," he spoke again, softer now. "But I've given you more than you had, more than I think is fair, considering what I am is a married male. A fact of which you seem to be forgetting."

"Oh, you remember that now? For you did an impressive job forgetting yourself over the course of those three nights, my *king*." Carelda spoke over Rorn when he attempted to respond. "Does the queen even know?"

I slid down the wall, the rock tearing at my nightgown and scraping the skin of my arms.

Three nights.

Carelda.

His iced responses now seemed warm as he growled with low venom, "Aster is none of your concern, and you'd be wise to never speak of her again." His steps clipped down the hall.

Three nights.

Carelda called after him. "I don't want this." Her statement dripped with heartache and desperation, enough that my own heart clenched more in response.

Rorn's steps faltered. "You want everything. You said so yourself."

"But I didn't think that would mean..." She paused, finishing quietly, "I didn't think at all."

Rorn was silent, then his steps sounded again. Moments later, softer footfalls headed down the stairs, followed by a door closing.

Rushing to the sink, I heaved, but the little food I'd eaten refused to budge, leaving me nauseated and choking on nothing. One thought circulated my mind repeatedly.

Who was he?

I no longer knew. For he wasn't anything I remembered.

The male I'd come to know these past months was nothing but a lying, merciless asshole.

If Rorn intended to take the babe from this Carelda and leave it at that, then it was clear he'd most certainly not informed her. And after what I'd witnessed from him of late, I had a harrowing feeling that he never intended to tell her much at all.

That he had no idea what to do with any of us.

ELEVEN

Aster

"NO ONE HAS SEEN HER, AND THOSE WHO CLAIM THEY have say she appears like a ghost," Urina said inside the doors to the terrace. "Darting about and hiding before anyone can get a proper glimpse or talk to her."

"You know her father was odd too," Fregson said without care for his volume. "Always so quiet and stoic."

Urina snorted. "He wasn't odd, but indeed, there was something different about him. In any case, the way he left our queen to fend for herself in those woods day in and day out likely hasn't helped matters." She tutted. "She was far too young. Now look at her."

"You think she's losing touch with herself?"

Water sloshed. A clang sounded.

Then Urina said gently, "That's what many are whispering, and though it's mostly in jest, I do fear they might be right."

Their voices faded as they moved on to clean elsewhere.

I remained where I was upon the grass between the pond and the bed of roses just beyond the terrace. The moon was heavy but not so full that anyone paid me any notice when walking past the doors to the gardens.

Some of the sentinels had paused, one had even asked if I'd

needed anything, but they otherwise kept to their duties of patrolling the grounds and the rolling hillsides.

And here I'd thought that choosing to sit outside in the moonlight was a healthier option.

Glossing my fingers over the stem of the rose curling closer to me, I watched it shiver in response. Perhaps I was indeed losing my mind. Perhaps it had begun long ago. A relief, I thought, to have an answer—perhaps an antidote—for all of this.

Howls struck the silence.

The echo of warriors communicating with one another was typically a knife grazing every organ. A reminder of my father and of another male I'd never had yet had lost all the same. Now, those howls were something of a balm over a burn, as I allowed the memory of those precious days in Vordane to tumble forth.

As I allowed them to take me away.

If I wasn't careful, my emotions would carry me into the void—straight into that book-lined cottage with its tousled bedding and crooked dining table and tiny bathing room. I couldn't dare entertain the thought of giving in.

A respite must remain all it truly was.

Standing, I waded back through the circular rows of white roses to the central tower. Most would be retired for the evening, and I found spending time outdoors before attempting sleep each night helped.

Flame bobbed in the two sconces by the doors, the rest of the entry hall quiet and giving way to shadows. I followed them into the deeper dark toward the king's tower. Our tower. My place of refuge and turmoil.

My spine locked when I rounded the end of the hall to meet the stairs.

There, in a threadbare nightgown, her shoulder-length hair sleek in the dim light, stood Carelda.

Vivid copper eyes widened upon me, large and framed with sooty lashes. Her lips, thin yet perfectly shaped, parted. Those pretty eyes welled.

Against my will, I felt my own eyes do the same. The sting of tears worsened when they dropped to her stomach.

The thief placed a protective hand over the bump there, and my world tilted even more.

I cleared my throat and blinked, lifting my chin as I forced myself to say, "Hello."

Carelda cursed softly, then muttered useless apologies as she curtsied.

I smiled. It was brief, and the foreign action hurt more than I'd guessed it would. My voice was rasped, but my words were thankfully clear. "We needn't bother with formalities."

She frowned slightly.

I shifted some tangled hair behind my ear. "You carry my husband's..." I could not say it. The word slammed into my teeth, refusing to leave.

"Your Majesty, I'm..." she started, her doe-eyes flooding.

"Don't," I demanded. "We both know you're not sorry, nor should you be." I swallowed thickly. "You've been blessed." Then I forced a smile that made a tear fall down her cheek. "But if you'll excuse me..."

I said nothing else, could say no more if I'd truly tried, and hurried upstairs.

He didn't knock this time.

Rorn entered without pause, but he halted in the center of the parlor at the sight of me on the chaise.

I didn't look at him. I stared down at the remnants of my cold tea. "King."

"Stars, Bloom. You..." He swallowed.

"Look ravishing, I know," I said dryly, then sipped the tea. "No need for flattery."

At his silence, I looked up to find him smirking.

"Don't do that."

"Do what?" he asked.

I sighed. "Do you need something?"

"Yes," he said instantly. "You."

I scowled, taking in the worry at his mouth and eyes. Then I laughed.

Cool and fractured, it poured out of me as I stood and rounded the table filled with lunch and scrunched piles of dead flowers and parchment. "It's never been so abundantly clear that you do not."

"I know this has been exceptionally difficult for you, but you know it changes nothing."

"This?" I spat. "*They* change everything," I surprised myself by shouting. Chest heaving, I tried to calm down as he stood there and watched me, assessed me, searching for a way in beneath the rubble he'd made of me. "Everything, Rorn."

"She will have the babe and then she—"

"She?" I repeated. "*She* carries your precious heir. *She* has broken your marriage. *She* has changed our entire lives." Breath panted from me. "You will say her fucking name."

His eyes narrowed, words now gritted. "Carelda hasn't changed anything. She will have the babe and then she will leave."

"No," I said.

Shocked, he blinked. Almost laughed. "No?"

"I could not have said the word any clearer, my king."

Rorn shook his head. "I fear I do not understand."

Staring at him, it was growing painfully obvious that perhaps he never would understand. "Just go, please."

"Not until I know what I can do to finally make you better—"

"Nothing," I snapped, and turned for the easel I'd prepped this morning. "There is nothing you can do, so kindly take your false concerns and irksome troubles elsewhere."

"Astrantia, what am I to do? Tell me," he said, shockingly hoarse. "If you wish Carelda gone, then tell me and I will make it so immediately."

I turned back. "What are you to do?"

He frowned, nodding.

I snatched the teacup and sent it soaring across the room.

He ducked. It met the wall. Porcelain and tea sprayed the stone as he gaped at me, wide-eyed.

"What are *you* to do?" I laughed. "What am I supposed to do?" I advanced on him, growling, "Tell me, Rorn. *You* tell *me* how in the fucking stars I'm supposed to go on like this because I mean it…" I clutched his tunic, the emerald stitching snapping. "I mean it when I say I want to know."

"Bloom," he rasped, his eyes wet.

I shook him, barely moving him an inch. "I *need* to know because there is nothing. I have been reduced to *nothing*." I sniffed and whispered, "You took it all, every fucking thing I had, all I was, and the worst part?" He watched a tear roll down my cheek. "I just let you. I just…" The sobering fact drained me, my fingers loosening their hold. "Believing it was fated by the stars, I just let it all happen to me."

Rorn caught my wrist as I made to leave, but I pulled free and ran down the stairs.

"Bloom," he roared, following and too fast for me to outrun.

So I used the only remaining power I had—I disappeared.

The docks were empty.

A lone boat was tethered and bobbing over the calming waves.

This entire portion of the isle was empty, the city and the harbor still in shambles. Wood, rock, and miscellaneous belongings that hadn't been scavenged dotted the shoreline and the alleyways beyond.

Eerie silence crept through The Graveyard with the sea-salted breeze. Silent, but not still. Beneath each crumbling shop and overturned broken wagon, the bones and souls of those slain here lingered.

I wondered if they too were trapped. If perhaps one day when this city was rebuilt, they may find some semblance of peace.

Maybe, they would simply prefer to stay.

Moving deeper down what had once been the city's main street, I kept my eyes off the ground. The last time I'd visited, the sight of toys and portraits had snuck so thoroughly beneath my skin, I'd never forgotten what each looked like.

They didn't want us to forget, Rorn had said. They wanted us to ensure such devastation never happened again.

And we had, but barely. The siege on the city and the surrounding towns and villages was something none of us had been prepared for.

The only reason the humans we'd once deemed friends hadn't managed worse was because they lacked the abilities and force that had been gifted to our kind—and because of those I could hear now in the forests and along the coastline. The units of wolves on patrol.

The faint scent of smoke rose in the distance from a campfire. I walked toward it. Not to visit with them, but merely for something to do.

Sand and glass and rock crunched under my bare feet. Though I hoped I would, I felt none of it as I continued to the street's end and down the coastal road. The connected piles of broken and crumbling shops soon turned into vacated and destroyed homes.

Staring northeast at the sea, I could feel it. A tug at the bones. A song of the soul in the form of the wind whispering over the ocean. The temptation to return. The aching desire to run to what I'd run from and never once look back at this life again.

To better ignore it, I warped to the mountainous terrain of the towers.

Months had passed. There was little point in returning to a land that wasn't my own for a male who had likely moved on. There was little point in giving in to daydreams and memories of something I could not have.

For the only way a monarch such as myself could escape their duties was death.

Leaves still danced at my feet from my arrival in the forest when I heard it.

Shouting.

Slinking back against a tree, I waited for the caravan of warriors to pass by. Blood stained the air. Some of them were injured.

There'd been no activity in the city—of which had always been considered the first point of entry to the Isle of Emerald. Though hunters typically loitered farther inland. Survivors from previous skirmishes would wait for more of their murderous human friends to cross their path so that they might attack us and stand more chance at survival or safely journey home to their kingdom of Pelvorn.

The warriors—wolves—often found them before that happened. But that didn't mean all of them escaped such things unscathed.

Quietly, I crept closer to the road.

Two, maybe three, faeries were being hauled uphill via horseback. "Run ahead, Malex," one of them hollered. "Warn them we're coming, be sure they're ready." His voice then turned hushed as he crooned something that sounded like, "Hang on, Vee, you hear me? Just wait."

Unless gifted so by their heritage, few emerald wolves could warp.

My father had never known who that particular ancestor had been in our own lineage, but he'd always said those blessed in such a way by the stars should use it to help those who were not.

I'd done a rather poor job of that—of upholding his honor at all of late.

Merely thinking of what he'd say, the hard expression that would befall his features if he could see me now…

I exposed myself, the warriors cursing and halting when I appeared before them on the road. "Majesty? What are you—"

"Give her to me."

Knowing what I intended to do, their shock faded quickly to relief.

The male, likely her mate judging by the cloying scent of his fear, gently brought the injured female to me. Courtesy of spending so much time idle, I hadn't the strength to move her, but I was able to hold her tightly to me. I nodded to the males as the void swept in. "Go."

Her heartbeat was weak. Blood smattered her braid and armor. Most of it had already dried, but when I appeared in the infirmary and the surprised healers snapped into action and took her to the closest bed, I looked down to find fresh blood all over my gown.

Swallowing, I swiped my hands over my bodice and followed them. "There are two more coming, but Vee is the worst."

Nesalla, the elder healer, balked when I joined him at one of the twenty beds lining the wall. Half of them were filled with resting patients. "My queen, I am grateful, but is there something else you need?"

"I wish to help."

"Oh." Unraveling bandages at the cupboard beside the bed while another healer arrived and began stripping the armor from the too-still female, he paused and blinked at me. "We are quite capable, Majesty. Thank you."

"I know you are." I caught his hand and squeezed. "But you will let me help."

Nesalla's shrewd gaze gentled as he studied me closely. After a moment, he turned my hand to place a pot of patchwork cream within, then squeezed it in return. "Okay, my queen."

Admittedly, I was not adept at healing much of anything, but I was quick on my feet and willing to be of use in any way I was able.

Even if it involved cleaning bedpans and washing pus and blood from bedding and bandages. The tasks, as mundane as most of them were when the infirmary wasn't too full, kept the sanity that lingered with stubborn claws from fleeing entirely.

I was well aware I couldn't keep finding new places to hide, tasks to make me feel as though I had some type of purpose. But I wasn't sure what else there was for me to do when I wasn't sure what else there was for me at all.

Rorn had given up on trying to call me away from the healers and their fascinating remedies and potions. It became a game of counting the days as he added more between each visit. Sometimes, a week would pass before I would see him. Sometimes, I would merely see him. He would watch me, and then he would leave.

And then it finally happened.

Carelda was brought to the infirmary by Theenon, crying and clutching at her stomach. "He's coming," the steward said.

He.

How she'd known what she was having, I didn't know. A mother's intuition, perhaps. The reminder that I'd likely never know for certain—never experience it myself—belatedly forced my feet from the rooms.

Hours dragged by, and with the dawn of evening came the arrival of screams I'd wager could be heard for miles.

On the stairs of our tower, I sat and waited as the moon rose and the stars twinkled through the floral green glass in the window behind me.

Rorn found me there, looking weary and rumpled with a glass of wine in hand. He eyed the open door to my parlor behind me, then tilted his head. "Why are you sitting out here?"

"I'm not quite sure." I frowned as he drank. "Why aren't you with Carelda?"

The look he gave me was one of reproach and confusion. "My place is not at her side."

I couldn't have said it politely if I'd tried, and I didn't want to. "But that is your son."

That he did not refute that he was indeed being gifted a son said he'd already known. "I will meet him when they've rested." He walked by me and the parlor, then continued to our rooms above.

But I couldn't ignore the anguish I'd seen hardening his jaw and darkening his shadowed eyes.

"Rorn." He didn't turn back, but he did stop. "Stars, Rorn. Go and be with her. You want to, I can tell, so cease being a stubborn coward."

He set loose a rough chuckle and turned to glare at me. "You're wrong and entirely out of line to suggest…" He stopped and blew out a harsh breath. A groan followed. "Fuck, Astrantia." Our eyes locked, torment bleeding from his own.

Finally, he moved. He handed me what remained of his wine and continued down the stairs.

Watching him go, I couldn't decide if I was glad he'd listened or what it meant that he had. The wine warmed in my hand as I slumped against the stone.

Carelda's screaming continued long into the night.

To give birth, to merely carry a babe to term, came with higher risk for those of faerie blood. My own mother had perished after delivering me. Maybe that was what kept me rooted to the stone steps, my limbs long numb.

I'd never known her, yet I couldn't keep from imagining what she might make of this life of mine. The one she'd sacrificed herself to give.

When I woke, the wine was seeping into the cracks of the steps, the glass having fallen from my hand. The first hints of sunrise leaked into the towers, followed shortly by something else.

The magical, heart-scoring wail of new life.

TWELVE

Aster

RORN, LOOKING LESS PALE BUT NO LESS EXHAUSTED, VISITED my parlor two days after his son was born. "Would you like to meet him?"

The grape I'd just chewed stuck to my throat when I swallowed. I placed the bowl down beside me on the chaise and tried to make sense of what I now had to do. Nothing made sense anymore, but that was not the fault of an innocent new soul.

So I sipped some water and nodded.

It was what was expected of me, after all.

Rorn's eyes gleamed, his lips parting as if he would say something else.

I stood but did not move, and he closed his mouth.

Wise, I thought, as I trailed him downstairs and through the lower levels of the towers. If he'd said anything else, I would likely have stayed in the parlor.

His hair was in dire need of a wash, but his shoulders were loose and high, and he walked with that same arrogant grace.

A proud king. A proud father.

The burn in my eyes cleared when he reached the stairs to the kitchens and staff quarters. He was still keeping them tucked away, then. I'd feared as much from what I'd heard—the cries of a newborn still so distant at night.

I blinked into the dim stairwell, unable to move as I failed to think of what would have been better. A place in our rooms? The babe's basket set just so on the chest at the end of the bed where I'd always imagined I'd one day place my own?

Laughter, accompanied by cooing and fussing and a short cry, echoed up the stairs.

Rorn cursed. "Bloom, wait."

"Another day," I lied, in hopes he did not follow as I returned to the parlor.

A piercing scream woke me from my unintended nap and curdled my blood.

It was not the scream of an infant.

Lurching from the chaise, I hurried out of the parlor and down the stairs as I heard another, followed closely by shouted pleas.

The commotion was coming from the entrance to the towers.

A group of guards, not wanting to let me pass but doing so reluctantly, stepped aside to reveal Rorn standing in the middle of the drive.

Breath fled me so fast, my ears began to ring with my screeching heartbeat.

Carelda, her meagre belongings strewn across the pebbles, was being restrained by two guards. "You cannot keep him and not me," she seethed, noting my arrival as I slowly came to a stop mere feet away from the king. "He is *mine*." Her face was wet, heated, and her teeth bared as the two males struggled to escort her to the awaiting carriage.

"He will be well cared for, this I vow," Rorn promised, yet he would not even look at the distraught female. He spoke to the trees lining the drive, his hands clenched behind his back.

I stared at them, the squeezing, bruising grip purpling his fingers.

Stars, he wouldn't…

But he was.

"He needs me," Carelda cried. "My milk and my touch—you cannot do this, Rorn. Stop." She tripped backward, but the hold of the guards was too tight for her to fall. "*Please,*" she screamed, and in the few battles I'd witnessed, I'd never heard such pain. Not from the wounded. Not from the dying. Not even from the grieving.

It sliced through me to bind with my own—a growing drumbeat that caused my blood to churn and roar. "Let her go," I said before I was aware that I'd planned to say anything at all.

But my voice was brittle. I was ignored.

Rorn nodded to the guards, and they once again attempted to maneuver the squirming new mother into the carriage.

Carelda swung her legs and planted her bare feet on either side of the open door, howling and struggling like an animal being led to slaughter.

"Unhand her," I stepped forward and ordered Malex, who continued his attempts to pull her leg away from the carriage.

He was forced to stop when Pandel, the other warrior, ceased his own efforts. He looked from me to the king, unsure, and shifted in his boots.

I marched across the pebbles and almost shouted, "I said unhand her."

Before they could receive further instruction from Rorn, I snarled and tightened the ties on my robe, forgetting in my haste that I wasn't dressed. "You should be ashamed of yourselves." But I knew they were merely obeying orders given to them by their king.

A king who'd become more tyrant than true love.

Pandel's hold loosened, and I pushed Malex back. "Hands off. Now."

Carelda stumbled forward and latched onto my arm and hand. Her nails dug and sliced as if she'd now plead with me. I shushed her and shook my head.

Rorn kept his tone calm, gentle, as though he were speaking to a youngling. "Astrantia, I think it would be best if you returned to your parlor now. Freshen up and I'll ensure some lunch is delivered."

I whirled to my heart's broken promise, but his features remained still—cold. "You wish for me to freshen up while you get rid of your lover?"

His jaw flexed. "Leave, Astrantia."

I laughed. The sound stunned me. It also stunned the guards and Carelda, as well as those who'd left their tasks nearby to see what was happening. "I think I finally shall. In fact, I think I'll go with Carelda and never return."

Rorn's eyes flared a fiery blue. A warning.

He could warn me all he liked. I warned him right back by snatching Carelda's wrist. Together, we warped inside the towers.

To undermine the king, and to do so before many an observing eye, guaranteed severe consequences. But he knew as well as I did that there was nothing more he could do to hurt me.

"Insufferable, unbearable, disgusting..." Words kept tumbling from me in a free fall I could not stop as I paced the landing outside my parlor. Carelda watched, trembling. Then I froze and muttered, "This way."

Left with little choice, Carelda trailed me downstairs to the room I had in mind for her. A mistake, probably, to have her close. I couldn't muster the energy to care when it seemed the king wanted his son near and the female he once just had to have his fill of now out of sight.

"Where is he?" I asked, shoving open the door to the guest chambers.

As though he'd followed, Dudley, the cook, appeared on the stairs beneath us with a tiny, fussing babe in his giant arms. "Forgive me, my queen." He bowed. "But he was left in the lady's room, and he started crying. He won't stop. I didn't know what else to do..." He offered the infant, who let out a squawk.

Carelda retrieved her son with a sob. A thank you was rasped as she tucked his head beneath her chin and closed her eyes.

Never had I seen a look of such relief as she breathed him in. A contentment, a peace so rare yet so tangible I could almost touch it, dripped from her softening limbs, her body rocking slowly from side to side.

Feeling my attention on them, Carelda opened her eyes, her thick lashes soaked.

I cleared my throat and dismissed Dudley with a nod, who seemed grateful to escape all of this chaos and retreat to his kitchens.

The guest chambers were a little dusty but otherwise clean, and I got to work on removing the coverings from the bed and the chairs in the sitting area.

"Has he always been this way?"

The unexpected and tentative question jarred me—sent me back to memories of dream-like times. Unable to help it as I remembered the way Rorn had first looked at me from across the ballroom, then every room from that day forward, I informed her, "No." I sighed. "Not always."

Absorbing that for a minute, I suspected she was now wondering what had happened to change our king so much. For I also suspected Rorn had been anything but cruel to her during their first encounters.

The babe released a cough, then a wail, his tiny head bopping over his mother's chest.

"Why?" Carelda said, calming him at her bosom.

My heart warmed at the sight of his downy raven hair, the way his precious little hand splayed and bunched over Carelda's chest. I found I couldn't answer her, asking instead, "What did you name him?"

Confusion momentarily puckered her brows. "Oh, well…" She brushed her fingers over his head. "I haven't been able to decide on one." At my silence, she then added, "I know that's terrible. He's been with us for days now."

"A name is important. Take your time."

Theenon arrived with the babe's basket and bowed before setting it by the window.

"Why help me?" she asked again.

I gathered two blankets from the cupboard and unfolded one to place within the basket though it already contained some. "Would you rather the alternative?" Crossing the room, I laid the other blanket upon the small table before the armchair Carelda sat in.

"Of course, not, but—"

"Then please do not ask questions I cannot and do not wish to answer." I straightened and peered around, then looked at Carelda. Her cheeks were still stained red from her turmoil, her eyes murky and marred from exhaustion. "You won't be forced to leave. Theenon will have your belongings retrieved and assist you with anything else you might need."

Standing by the door, the steward nodded when I gave him a weak smile. His eyes shined in a way that made my chest tighten painfully. "Indeed, my queen. Anything they desire."

I was heading back upstairs when Carelda stopped me, calling softly, "Thank you." I made to keep walking when she said, "My queen."

I didn't and knew I couldn't look at her.

Feeling her gaze upon my back, I closed my eyes as my heart slowed, then I opened them and continued climbing.

Rorn awaited me on the chaise in the parlor, his fingers at his brow. "Do you have any idea what you've just done?"

"Your ego will have to soothe itself elsewhere." I perched at the window and unwrapped the banana I'd left there yesterday. "I'm not in the mood."

The fruit was taken from my hand before I could blink, Rorn's nose an inch from mine. "You might blame me for the demise of our love, and I shoulder that blame despite your own misdeeds, but this?"

I waited, half-wishing I might grow fearful—*stars, maybe even heated*—by the anger in his eyes.

But I felt nothing as he said, "This will only push us farther apart, Astrantia." When I failed to respond, his head tilted. "Though perhaps I am a fool for thinking otherwise, and that is what you truly want."

"My king," I said, not unkindly. "The distance between us grew too vast many months ago, and we both know it."

His eyes swirled over my face. "You punish me with words you do not mean."

"No." My fingers crawled over his hair-dusted jawline, a sad smile curling my lips. "I merely speak the truth."

His lashes fluttered. He straightened when I took my touch away. "You know I will do whatever it takes to see you happy again."

"Treating Carelda this way…" I shook my head and met his eyes as I said softly, "This isn't it."

His gaze swept to the floor. His words were a whisper. "I've lost you."

"Rorn." Rising, I stood close as I searched his narrowed eyes. "You've lost yourself." Taking his hand, I squeezed it. "Find him." I stepped back. "And before it's too late."

With a low snarl, he was gone.

THIRTEEN

Scythe

"**C**OMMANDER," TRES CALLED. "WE'RE LEAVING?"

"I am. You may do as you wish."

The village had already been vacated before our arrival, and judging by the state of some of the homes, many of them had been empty for a long time. "Waste of our fucking time."

But not completely.

I'd found some new books amongst the few belongings left behind by this particular community of elusive golden fae.

"File out," Tres called to the rest of the legion.

Flame ruptured from my palm. Though not as violent as our king's, it was enough. It wouldn't serve me to show off. I tossed it toward the barns along the eastern perimeter of the village, ensuring it would wipe out any crops that anyone nearby might be returning to tend to.

And so it went.

Another mission east across the gaping ravine to steal and destroy, followed by a long trek home. I didn't do my brethren the disrespect of warping back to the Keep when many of them could not. Not when there was no urgency. No need.

Nothing awaited me—save for the same old shit.

Only now, our king had found himself a mate.

A golden one, to make matters worse. Holed up in her special frilly rooms right next door to Dade's, the princess of Sinshell had yet to make peace with her fate. That she was beholden to Vordane's king despite how much she wished otherwise.

I couldn't say I blamed her. We had ruined and ravaged numerous parts of her precious kingdom. And we would continue to. Though not without reason.

But something told me that because of our king's obsession with the princess, that very reason—his entire life's purpose—would soon run dry.

So to say I didn't like the swan was putting it mildly. Though I wasn't yet sure if that were because she would be the end to the only thing that had kept me rising from bed each dawn, or if maybe, it was because she and Dade made me sick for reasons I'd spent well over a year trying to recover from.

I'd tasted joy. I'd bathed in its fleeting magic, believing I could somehow tame it. Keep it. Make it mine. In its swift absence, I'd learned that joy was merely like everything else in this world—just another form of poison that would leave you to rot after having its way with you.

I wanted to keep going. I *needed* to keep going.

Dade's vengeance on those who'd robbed him of his parents, and Vordane of their previous beloved rulers, meant more than vengeance to some of us.

It was an escape. An outlet for so much more than grief and fury. Without it, I wasn't sure what the fuck I'd do. Command a legion to patrol our lands and deal with minor squabbles? Skip rocks across the Night Sea in hopes they might smack into the windows of a certain female's home and she'd scent whom had sent them?

Insanity.

I'd lost more than sleep to the best female I'd ever had, the only creature I wanted to share space in this eternal life with. I'd damned near lost my fucking mind.

And I'd been searching for it ever since.

We arrived at the Keep two days later, tired, grumpy as shit, and with King fucking Dade nowhere to be found.

"He's taken the princess on an outing to the city," Fang supplied when I entered the war room and cursed at the piles of nonsense all over the meeting table.

"I hope they have themselves a delightful fucking time," I said, sarcasm heavy, and I dropped into the chair to begin writing up my report on a half-crumpled piece of parchment.

"Touchy," Fang remarked, running the end of his blade down the list of names for the following week's patrol along the northern end of the ravine. "That Princess Opal seems..."

"Naïve and untrustworthy," I stated helpfully.

"Well, okay." Fang sat back in his chair and cocked his head, studying me. "Don't hold back on my account."

I looked at the parchment. "Wipe that fucking smirk off your face."

"Make me, scar-face," Fang teased, and I growled. He chuckled. "You're not wrong, but the bird is his mate. So any harm she might cause will be of no great consequence."

I snorted and far too loudly. "You're a stars-damned idiot."

"While that may be so, I am still right."

Long minutes passed in silence while I finished writing. Then I rose to pin the nearly illegible report on the corkboard behind me. "Ever mated with someone?"

We both knew he hadn't, and so he stayed silent.

I'd reached the door when Fang said, "And you have?" The question was far too delayed, too careful, to have been made in jest.

He'd attempted to scour the depths of my thoughts for months after Aster had left, but to no avail. He'd long since given up, resigned to my moods after he'd experienced the very worst of them while we'd matured under the same roof.

"No, but the swan could still reject the bond." I walked on before he could ask anything else and warped back to the city.

The wind carried the warning.

A fierce caress that many of my brethren had wanted to ignore. Given the circumstances, I couldn't blame them.

But some of us hadn't, and there was no time to gauge just how much worse it could've been if we hadn't acted.

They arrived in swarming droves under the cover of darkness.

That their ships hadn't been seen by our warriors and spies posted at the cove and along the coastline could only mean two things. They were all long dead, and these human soldiers had timed their arrival to perfection.

For our king and half of our legions were not here in Vordane.

They were in Sinshell to protect Dade from any foul play because he was determined to marry his bird of a mate—their princess. A princess who, as far as any of us were aware, still hadn't even accepted their bond.

He was a stars-damned besotted fool.

And as we'd feared, a fool who'd seemingly played right into their hands. The kingdom of Sinshell wanted to hurt Dade as he had hurt them, so we'd all known they'd allowed him to wed their princess in order to get the peace and revenge they'd been desperately seeking.

But never could we have guessed that the golden ones possessed the power for something like this.

That they would trap Dade in Sinshell while foreign soldiers crawled through his kingdom as though they'd been given the key.

Not just any soldiers. Mortal soldiers who hungered to kill anything unlike them.

Years of controlled cruelty upon the kingdom who had ruined Dade's family, every inch of it inflicted by our own hands, had now turned into a giant fucking mess.

My sword met an axe. The claws on my other hand unsheathed to drag down another screaming soldier's face. Blood sprayed across my own and rushed down my arm beneath my sleeve.

Limbs and bodies, both human and fae, dotted the clearings of villages and the roads that stretched toward the city. Growing fires joined with new ones. The flames seemed to rise higher with the cacophony of screams and wails.

As mortal soldiers continued to swarm our land, it became clear that this wasn't just a lucky coincidence on their part. It was carefully constructed mayhem.

Females and younglings ran for the woods, and those who hadn't managed to were herded into livestock pens like cattle.

I kicked and sliced my way through the next throng of soldiers determined to cut me down, and then I warped to the pen in the distance. My blades struck as soon as I appeared between two men. Their crossbows fell with them, but the men behind them let their nocked arrows fly.

I roared as they made clumsy contact with some of the trapped females and charged at the soldiers. The sound mercifully attracted help from my brethren, and the red-rimmed night unfolded into a dark haze of bloodlust.

Blood-bathed terror crawled across our home, the percussion of it all unlike any I'd heard in battle before.

"You," said a human piece of scum from the ground beneath the blade I pushed to his jugular. "A chest of gold for your mangled head."

The distraction worked as he'd intended. A mace skimmed my side when I sensed it too late and failed to move fast enough.

Snarling, I welcomed my wolf form to better stem the bleeding and launched at the asshole's chest. Then I ripped out his throat. His friends ran like cowards looking for easier prey, and I shifted back before advancing to the next group of human fucks.

"You're the one who ought to be running, wolf," taunted the same human who still hadn't died.

I twisted back, the smoke-heavy wind burning my eye.

The man I hadn't finished stabbing in the throat gurgled, blood dribbling from his mouth, "Dead giveaway..." He coughed. "That scar."

Cold raced through my limbs and faltered the beating of my heart. I stepped closer and growled low, "Who sent you."

He grinned, revealing blood-covered teeth, then coughed again. "You seem to already k-know."

My teeth gnashed, but an incoming whistle of metal upon the air had me crouching to the side, and the idiot who'd aimed to kill me ended his comrade's suffering instead.

Realizing what he'd done, he made the fatal mistake of stilling over the man who'd thought to taunt me, his hand falling from his weapon in shock. From behind, I dug my blade into his gut before he could rise, and then I foolishly froze, too.

Howls sounded from the east.

Dade.

Not trapped after all. The king and the rest of our legions had returned.

Relief delivered me a renewed burst of energy. But looking at the carnage as I swung my sword to meet with an incoming dagger, I could only hope our king knew this was the real trap.

And nothing more.

FOURTEEN

Aster

THE MONTHS WASHED BY WITH THE UNEVEN PACE OF THE babe learning to walk within the halls of the towers.

I'd spent them confined to my quarters, painting, or working in the infirmary. So I seldom laid eyes on Rorn, but I did see a lot of his lover. Carelda was either chasing her son or carrying him, and as time went by, our awkward glances and encounters soon faded into tenuous greetings and smiles.

The babe had been named Helvectus, after Rorn's brother, the late king.

Whether it was Rorn who had decided on the name or Carelda, I hadn't heard. I had my suspicions, knowing all too well how it felt to have the king take matters into his own hands in a way that fooled one into thinking it was because he knew best. For both the kingdom and our hearts.

Time had made it somewhat easier to accept that Carelda was not to blame for the actions of a faithless male. Even if she had known he was married, and she surely had, I hadn't any room left for hatred. Not even for the king himself.

My whittled energy, and the remaining fragments of who I'd once been, were used solely to keep moving forward. Though there were days when I still wondered why I felt compelled to stay afloat at all.

There was no one dependent on me. No one who would lament losing me. The one soul who might have cared was now nothing but a blistering memory to keep me company at night.

And that was how I spent my days—endlessly avoiding the aching loss of something I never truly had and avoiding the loss of something I once believed would only ever be mine.

The night was for dreams.

Sometimes they'd bring tears as I'd lain awake in agony, knowing he would have moved on many times over. Sometimes they'd bring laughter and moans, muffled by pillows and blankets. Regardless of what I did, no matter how much I painted or drank or tried to be of use, the wolf would find a way to creep in.

Always and over and over, the inescapable imaginings would come.

Alone, I'd wake and struggle to find the strength to so much as climb to my feet. Alone, I'd force myself to eat. To move. To do anything other than surrender to that stalking darkness that had nearly swallowed me whole.

The attacks on our people and the failed missions to breach our royal lands had lessened.

Rorn and his warriors knew better than to believe the mortals were at last done with tormenting us. The unease we'd lived with that had stifled the towers for too long soon lowered to a steady, hesitant impatience.

For even after almost two months without a single skirmish reported, all of us knew it was only a matter of time.

Nesalla's voice rose in volume out in the hall. "What do you mean? Of course he's doing something about it. He has to be."

I crept back from the basket of clean bandages I'd been rolling at hearing Carelda's hushed response. "He's said nothing to me, but he's been locked in the council chambers for weeks with talk of it."

"I say better them than us," Milla, another healer commented. "Stars forgive me, but we desperately need this reprieve."

"Easy for you to say when you do not have relatives across the sea," Nesalla snapped, leaning against the door to the infirmary while biting into an apple. "All of it needs to stop, period. He must act now while they're preoccupied and end this."

"What do you speak of?"

None of them expected the queen who'd remained mostly silent for months to interrupt their conversation. They'd grown accustomed to having me organize things that didn't really require it, and loitering like an unwanted chaperone, forever in search of something to give my attention to.

"Majesty." Nesalla blinked, then blinked again. "We were just talking about how quiet it's been on the isle. How..." He grimaced. "Unusual it is, I suppose."

Carelda frowned at the healer and hoisted Helvectus higher upon her hip. "Rorn has been attending all these meetings with his council, discussing the whereabouts and the possible new motives of the mortal terrorists."

"The whereabouts," I repeated and walked closer. "New motives?"

With a look at Milla and Nesalla, Carelda then jerked her head to the hall, indicating that I walk with her. Eyes fell upon us, waiting and anticipating. Likely expecting me to snub the mother of my husband's son.

It gave me a small dose of satisfaction to join her, to prove them wrong in their judgment. Not that I could blame them for their assumptions. The feeling, although small, was so startling, so foreign, I'd nearly forgotten what it felt like to feel anything satisfying at all.

Helvectus squealed, his rosy cheeks rising as he threw his head to the side to give me a wet grin. It hurt to see him, to know who he belonged to. But what hurt the most was knowing I could never feel anything unkind toward him.

What hurt most of all was recognizing that I loved him, even if from a safe distance.

I returned his smile, and I then forced my eyes forward, nodding at one of the guards heading past who greeted us with a bow.

Carelda waited until he was out of earshot. "Hel snuck inside the chambers yesterday. I know it's wrong, but I lingered in the hall after overhearing that the mortals have indeed moved on."

"Moved on?" I could scarcely let myself believe it.

Carelda readjusted her squirming son. "It seems too good to be true, of course, so I stayed, hoping to know more because he won't tell me."

"Rorn will seldom discuss kingdom issues with his…" *His wife*, I nearly said, but she wasn't his wife.

I was.

And that wasn't entirely true. There was a time, though it had been some years ago, when he would tell me every thought he'd had, no matter how flippant and sensitive.

Understanding, Carelda slowed her pace. "So I've discovered. But if the humans have found entertainment elsewhere, then I am glad for it. We've endured enough."

Footsteps echoed down the stairwell up ahead. As quietly as I could, I asked, "But where did they go?"

"Across the Night Sea. I don't know for certain." She eyed the stairwell, then stopped. "Just that it has something to do with a swan who weaves golden clothing."

So baffled I nearly laughed, I made a face and bit my lips.

Carelda shrugged. "I know, but that's exactly what I heard."

"But how did Marvis even hear of such nonsense?" For surely, it was sadly nothing but nonsense. Our ilk were well versed in spinning fables and myths to lure and tempt the desperate and to weed out the wise.

"I'm assuming the mortal king has spies in this other realm, or he's been in contact with people there. Rorn sent his own spies to the south to see what they could find when it became clear the attacks had indeed stopped."

He'd sent our spies to Pelvorn, to Marvis's territory. A gigantic risk, and one he'd not taken in many years.

We both stiffened as the encroaching footfalls neared.

Rorn rounded the base of the stairwell, Rollins and Jyll, the war general who'd replaced my father, at his side. Then he halted with his back to us.

Slowly, Rorn turned. His lips parted, and his eyes narrowed. He looked back and forth between us, the greeting more of a question. "Ladies?"

I offered Carelda a thankful smile as I brushed my fingers over Helvectus's soft hair, his babbles following me back to the infirmary.

I'd expected Rorn to see to his son and his lover, being that he and Carelda seemed to have formed some type of stilted arrangement for the betterment of Helvectus.

And I needed time to process, to steal away to the library in search of this nonsensical swan business. For if Rorn believed in it enough to trust we were indeed experiencing a reprieve, perhaps even an end to the bloodshed, then maybe there was something to it after all.

One thing was certain—whoever this swan was, they evidently were not mortal. Which meant Marvis and his soldiers had potentially taken their bloodlust to another fae-inhabited continent.

"Bloom."

Shocked that he'd dared to follow me when he'd given up on me months ago, it felt as if I were pushing against an invisible tide to turn and face my husband. If I happened upon him in the towers, then I would head in the opposite direction. That was if he didn't redirect himself first.

It wasn't out of fear. It wasn't because I couldn't stomach seeing him.

It was because I no longer had it within me—the energy to battle—to so much as exist near him. But time away from him hadn't made it any more bearable. My heart dragged, and my body coiled as I fought the instinct to flee.

Rorn swallowed, his throat bobbing, and spoke before I gave in to the urge. "How are you?"

"Fine."

His eyes dipped over me. "You are looking somewhat better."

My brows jumped high.

Rorn cursed. "Apologies, I just..." I waited, having nothing to say and no desire to make this easier for him. His teeth flashed with his slight huff of laughter. "It would seem you still leave me without proper words." He stared, perhaps waiting, but it was in vain.

He excelled at sweet nothings, but I'd learned that was all they were.

"I miss you," he finally said on a ragged exhale, his shoulders lowering. "Stars, I miss you dreadfully."

"I miss you too," I said, and it wasn't a lie. It also didn't mean that anything would change.

I missed the lie I'd once lived so blissfully, believing it was fated magic. Some days, I'd find myself staring at the dining hall, the gardens, and even the doors to our rooms, aching with nostalgia. Aching with a vengeance that made me quiver with the need to scream until my lungs bled.

For although it had all indeed been a lie, it was preferable to the emptiness of the here and now.

"Have dinner with me." A gruff, rushed request.

My eyes widened. "I don't think that's—"

"Please."

An opportunity, as awful as it was of me to take it. A chance to find out more about Marvis. To seek answers about the swan.

I shouldn't have cared a thing for where the human armies had sailed to, but I had little to care for anymore. So I would appease my curiosity. "Okay."

FIFTEEN

Aster

THE LIBRARY WASN'T OF MUCH USE, AND I QUICKLY RAN OUT
of time.

Deciding to return afterward, I left the books I'd been perusing upon the table in my parlor and readied to meet with the king.

While I didn't wish to overdo it, I still made some effort. I chose a flowing apricot gown. The tunic-resembling sleeves billowed to my wrists, where they were cuffed with cotton in a dark orange that matched the faint beadwork in the loose bodice.

Rorn was already in the dining hall, his hands folded behind his back as he stared out the window.

He wore the same brown britches I'd seen him in earlier, but he'd changed into a fitted buttoned shirt of rich emerald. It would seem he had wished to make some sort of effort too, though I doubted his reasons were anything like my own.

Upon sensing my arrival, he murmured to the open stained glass of the window, "I had feared we'd never do this again."

"Dine together?" I asked, still rooted in the doorway as an oily sludge made a home within my limbs at the thought of moving toward the table.

At the thought of spending so much time so close to him.

Rorn huffed, lips curved as he turned and walked to the set table to untuck the chair beside his own. "That too, but I was referring to the wide open window, which is now one of many. Another sheer simplicity we had lost to keep danger at bay."

I nodded, forcing my bare feet to move. "And how long do we believe such simplicities will last?" I took the opportunity to press while he tucked me close to my waiting meal of quail, lemon-baked asparagus, and potato.

"I suppose we wait and see," he said, taking his seat.

I watched him pour us each a glass of wine, near hypnotized as the blood-red liquid splashed against the sides of the glass.

"Eat," he encouraged with a wave of his hand at my plate. "It smells and looks divine."

"Indeed," I concurred, unable to look at him.

As though he knew as much, he carved into his meal, steam rising from the bird, and then paused. "As do you."

That earned him what he sought, my eyes lifting from my food to meet his.

He was expecting me to say something. I couldn't. I offered a faint smile, failing to conjure words while he studied my features with a rapt focus that lightened the blue of his eyes.

I lowered my gaze to my meal, and though I wasn't so sure I could stomach it, I began to eat.

The silence screamed louder than the call of a night hawk streaming past the window toward the mountain peaks beyond. The king chose to end it with a slight clearing of his throat. "I was surprised to see you and Carelda together."

"I know."

"Dare I ask what it was you were discussing?"

I set my cutlery down and picked up the wine, swallowing a greedy sip before answering honestly. "You, of course." My eyes swung to him as I swirled the wine, and I smiled again at the sight of his lowered brows and stiff jaw. "Fear not, we shall not compare notes on bedding you."

He cursed, his knife falling to his plate with a clang. "Astrantia."

"She is quite lovely, though," I admitted, unable to help myself. "I can see the allure."

"I haven't fucked her since..."

I took another sip and lifted a brow, prompting, "Since?"

His silence and the clustering of his features as he gave his eyes to his food sickened me.

I laughed, the sound sour and a distraction from the churning in my stomach. "You've fucked her since her arrival at the towers, haven't you?"

"Not for some months," he said, and harsh enough to suggest he hated even having to say as much. A storm now clouding his eyes, he handed them back to me. "I meant it when I said I miss you. You know I need you and that I'll never stop wanting you."

"But never only me," I said, as the truth of that crystalized and added another layer of mortar to my chest. He didn't respond for some moments, and I saw the lie building in the clenching of his long fingers as they gripped his cutlery. I didn't want it. "It's okay. I do not wish for pretty lies."

He frowned. "But you misunderstand me."

I shook my head. "I think it's you who doesn't quite understand what it is you want, and I think perhaps it's been that way for far longer than either of us realize."

"I just told you what I want."

"Telling and showing are two entirely different things, my king," I said, though not unkindly, and I found my stomach eased as I drank more wine. "You've never been one to handle your emotions too well."

"Bloom..." he warned and picked up his wine. Staring into the glass, he sighed. "Never mind."

We ate in silence for tense minutes until I finally built the courage to ask what I wanted to know. "So Marvis and his armies..." I sipped more wine, Rorn eyeing my mouth as I swallowed and set the empty glass down. "Are we to merely assume that they've vanished?"

"You need not worry about all of that."

"But I once did," I said, unexpectedly soft and calling his eyes to mine when I continued, "You used to tell me everything."

His face fell as though he were just acknowledging that. As though he hadn't realized before now that he'd withdrawn from me long ago. I would have pitied him if it weren't for his ruthless selfishness.

"Years." I dug the blade in deeper. "You ceased bringing me into our daily affairs well before Carelda, Rorn."

He blinked, lashes lowering. "I know." He licked his teeth, and I waited to see if what I'd thrown onto the table between us might encourage him to talk, yet I felt little satisfaction when he did. "My," he started, then stopped and corrected himself. "Our spies have not long returned from Pelvorn with news of ships bearing Marvis's flag sailing to another continent."

Pelvorn being the human kingdom of the isle, whose inhabitants had made it a family tradition to torment us. "An entire fleet?"

"Multiple," he confirmed. "Further surveillance has revealed that they've set their sights on a more lucrative venture."

"And what is this venture?"

He lifted a brow, and his wine to his lips as he eyed me. "Nodoya."

It was written all over my face, I knew, though I tried to conceal it a failed heartbeat too late.

It couldn't have been helped as I tried to imagine what beneath the skies might encourage Marvis and his followers to sail that far east, and to a continent far larger than that they'd already brutalized.

Carefully but as carelessly as I could muster, I ripped my eyes from Rorn's and asked, "Do you know what they wish to find there?"

He took his time to answer, setting his glass down and twisting it side to side over the emerald table linen. "A few things," he murmured with a twitch to his lips. "Among them, a faerie princess who is rumored to weave gold into clothing."

"Gold?" I questioned, though I'd already heard as much from Carelda.

He hummed, eyes fixed to the stem of the glass he continuously twisted. "She can also change into a swan." He smiled, a breathy laugh leaving him on an exhale.

"But a myth, surely."

"Most myths are derived from truths, and it is said that the last golden fae of Nodoya to weave gold could indeed shift into a swan, but with such abilities comes severe consequences of course, and so she burned out."

"Burned out?"

As if in a trance, as if both in awe and seeing something I could not, he explained, "Eventually, those with such mythical powers might spend themselves recklessly. A glowing, ancient and time rectifying, can very well render them powerless. It will weaken them to the point of death should they desire to heal someone."

"Then what could the mortals want with a creature that will inevitably lose its value?"

"All the gold they can collect before it happens, I suppose," Rorn said evenly, his lashes steady and his finger now tracing the condensation upon the glass. "The two fae kingdoms of Nodoya are at war, but while they've been squabbling, it would seem the lone little human kingdom by the name of Errin in the south has been making plans of their own."

"Human kingdom," I repeated, blinking fast as I recalled the mention of it. It seemed so long ago that it was but a dream. Yet it took only a moment for me to garner just what those plans might be. The knowledge settled like rocks within my stomach. "The Errin royals have asked for Marvis's help?" I blurted, then shook my head. "To move against the two fae kingdoms?"

"One in particular," he said, tone absent, unseeing eyes upon the wine. "Though I suspect the kingdom of Vordane and its tyrant ruler are merely just an excuse to collect themselves a fuck ton of gold and a chance to do what they enjoy doing most…" His eyes rose, and he straightened to his full height in his chair as they dropped upon me with startling force. "Hunting faeries."

My lungs tightened beneath his cool gaze, the assessment of my every feature as he leaned forward and placed his elbow upon the table, a finger stroking over his clean-shaven jaw.

Even after all this time, I could still feel it. Not Rorn's, but Scythe's. The bristle that had grown thicker during my stay. The way it had felt beneath the pads of my fingers, scraping against my neck and shoulders, the delicate skin of my stomach and inner thighs...

I stood, rocking and knowing I could no longer mask the thundering echo in my chest. I couldn't just sit. Not here. Not anywhere. Not now. Not when I had to do what I'd silently sworn to never do again.

I had to leave. I had to go back.

Rorn's amused question trailed me to the doors. "Where are you going?"

I'd almost forgotten I'd been dining with him amidst his reveal of all this fear-fueling information. "I've something I need to do."

"Such as?"

His airy tone warned that it would be futile to lie. "Rorn, we need to inform them. I'll—"

The doors closed.

Rorn's chair slid over the stone behind me as he stood, and I stared at the wooden barriers before me. He knew a door couldn't stop me, but it was why he'd even want to entrap me that held me so perilously still.

Slow, measured steps clicked behind me. "Even if we could tell them anything, of which we cannot," Rorn said. "Why should we? No one has ever come to our aid."

"Rorn," I said—nearly begged. "I have to go."

"Don't be absurd. Besides, it's far too late. By the time we finally heard of this news, the ships were likely already within sight of Nodoya's shores."

My heart sank. I almost couldn't bear to ask, and I didn't need to. "When did you hear of this news?" He'd known for days. Possibly weeks.

My eyes squeezed closed. That would mean a war was already underway, or worse...

Long over.

Breath lodged tight in my chest, I waited for an answer I wasn't given.

Rorn stopped at my back with a hollow, sinister laugh. "He resides there, doesn't he? This male you've been slowly wasting away over."

"Wasting away?" I asked, incredulous as I whirled to face him.

"You heard me," he pushed between his teeth. He gazed at me down the bridge of his nose, a cloud of swirling ire within his eyes.

The words hissed, and I stabbed a finger at him. "You keep me in name only, even though you were the one to destroy everything we had. Even after all this time, you still expect forgiveness for crimes you'll commit again and again should it suit you. And although I've tried..." My chest rose and fell violently, my voice rasping. "I've tried, Rorn, and with all I fucking have left, *that* is why I've not had anything to do with you."

"But it's not the only reason, is it?"

Asshole.

I stepped back. "Fuck you, Rorn."

"But you won't, will you?" He smirked. "You won't fuck me at all. Not while you perish every night to dreams of another." If it was his mission to enrage me, it was working, and he knew it. He advanced until I was broiling fire pushed up against the closed doors, whispering heatedly, "You thought to deceive me, to hide your lover from me forevermore, but I saw it."

Unsure what he meant, and a breath away from slapping him as his head lowered closer to mine, I couldn't respond.

"Come on, Bloom." His bark of laughter was low and dark. "Did you think I wouldn't find out who he was? I promised you I would." His sharp smile blinded me with a hatred that swam bone deep when he dared to open his mouth again. "Your paintings of him and Vordane were discovered months ago, and your reaction to this news only further cements what I'd begun to suspect. He is there, and now"—he trailed a finger down my cheek, his lips falling into a sneer when it reached the corner of my mouth—"now you fear for his life enough to betray your own people."

"I would never betray them." How he could even say as much when I'd done as he'd said for them—wasted away for a short eternity. I'd given him and this doomed kingdom my heart, and more than that, it was the remnants of my soul that were bound to this place I could not escape that kept me here.

Rorn tutted. "To disrupt this peace we've gained is the work of a traitor."

"So behead me and be done with it," I snarled, for he'd need to find me first.

But as I attempted to call forth the ribbons of energy and time, to manipulate them into taking me back to a kingdom I'd never dared to believe I'd see again, nothing happened.

Rorn grinned. "I could never harm you, you know that." He sauntered back to the table to pluck my empty glass from it. "So unless you wish to sail, which I will certainly not allow, you'll be staying right here…" He dropped the wineglass to the table. It shattered, his venomous expression one I'd not seen before. "Where you belong, Astrantia. For unlike this thieving male who is but a fleeting pest in our long lifetime, I fucking love you, and I won't let you betray us."

My fingers tingled with empty warmth as I tried again and again to disappear. Panic heightened my fear and rose my voice. "What did you do?"

"I won't let you betray yourself."

"Rorn," I whispered, choked as I studied the thin air all around me, desperately needing it to thicken. To take me within its embrace and away from here.

"I won't let you betray *me*."

I ran at him, growling as I grabbed his shirt in my fists. "What did you do to me?"

Gently and smiling wide, he pried my fingers from his shirt and brought them to his mouth. He kissed them as tears blurred my vision, as I tried to comprehend all that he was doing.

All I'd never be able to do again.

"I've saved you," he said softly, so simply.

Without strength and eroding with dismay, I slid down his body to the floor. "Water wish," he informed. "From the only remaining creek known to produce it. You know it well, my daring, darling wife, being that you grew up in the forest mere miles from it."

A tasteless potion to render someone temporarily without abilities. The algae that provided the liquid was made illegal and destroyed many centuries ago after being abused for too long.

The wine. He'd drugged the wine.

Rorn stepped over me and strode to the doors. "Its effects will wear off in roughly a week's time, and by then…" He released an exhale, his tone hardening. "You will find there's no longer any point in endangering yourself."

The doors closed.

Hours turned into two days. Meals were delivered to my parlor by my husband only.

After countless failed attempts at pleading with him to let me go, and to find me the remedy to end this cruel punishment, I was left with no choice but to surrender.

I paced, and I cried. I ignored him.

I loathed him.

The unjustness of all he'd done, of all I'd endured out of responsibility and some foretold love…

It multiplied into a hatred so deep, my skin hummed with the burn that slowly reverberated from my chest. From a place deep within the soul.

It gathered and grew until I couldn't sit still without clawing at my skin.

I didn't sleep. I paced, and I painted.

Not even Theenon was permitted to visit me. I was alone, but not like before. Now, I was alone and aching and burning alive while wrapped within the cold embrace of my king's so-called devotion.

And so I let it break loose. All of it. Everything I'd suppressed and ignored and fought against for months and months on end to no avail.

Shaking all over, I found one of many paintings of a green eyed wolf.

One of the many I'd had to leave unfinished for I'd given him up, believing I'd had to, believing he wouldn't want me. That even if he still did, it would never work. That leaving him was for the best.

It no longer mattered if he didn't want me. It only mattered that he lived. So I set the painting upon the easel and wiped the wet from my face, and then I succumbed to the agony of completing it.

If I couldn't reach him, if this war that had moved to Vordane took him, then I would at least see him. I refused to forget him, no matter what it did to me. Attempting to had never worked anyway.

Every trembled brush stroke that brought him to life chipped away at something fundamental inside me. The mere sight of him—the sight of what I'd never have and of what I might never see again—cracked something irreparable inside me.

But I couldn't stop. Not until it was done. Not until that entity within had broken wide open.

Breathe, wildflower.

The carnage charged through each vein. It spasmed every muscle until the brush fell from my shaking fingers.

Until I was on my knees, my head thrown back with the force of its exit.

It erupted.

Tears flooded my eyes, my cheeks. Into fragments of screaming regret and fury, I exploded.

So did all of the glassware in the room.

Flying everywhere in dagger-sharp shards, it screamed with me. So loud the void to warp into didn't just form—it grew into a windstorm that blew out the flames in the sconces and the glass of the windows.

Shouting echoed through the void, but I was already slipping free and falling through the hole I'd somehow managed to create despite the potion I'd been tricked into drinking.

The door to the parlor crashed open, and I smiled as I disappeared before the eyes of our blurred guards.

Breathless, I fell to the floor before the gigantic bed in the small apartment of a wolf.

SIXTEEN

Aster

MY EARS RANG. MY VISION CLOUDED.

I blinked and rubbed my numb hands over my face, then winced when something sharp cut into my cheek.

Glass.

A piece was imbedded in the side of my palm. I pulled it free and barely felt the sting, nor the trickle of blood rolling through my fingers to the carpet as I placed my hands upon it and leaned forward.

I closed my eyes and willed my roaring heart to slow, the tears to cease falling.

Settled enough to see and think straight, I opened my eyes and allowed the echoing silence of the apartment to infiltrate. His scent was an instant balm and a toxin.

The door was closed.

The bed beside me was made with the same linens I'd spent countless nights dreaming of being entangled in. I pushed up to my knees and used the end of the bed to assist with rising on trembling legs. The kitchen nook looked untouched, just as it had been a year and a half ago.

I moved, striding to the empty bathing room and then back to the bed.

The only noticeable difference since telling its owner that I was married were the books. There were more. Some had been piled upon the dining table as though the wolf hadn't had the time or inclination to find room for them within the already crowded shelves.

He wasn't here.

A slow thud ricocheted through my head, and I swallowed thickly. Never had warping to another place ever hurt. Not even when I'd been young and I'd failed to make my intentions clear before entering the void. I'd ended up slamming into the base of the same tree I'd attempted to leave near our cottage in the woods.

That had left a bruise, on both my forehead and my ego, as my father had laughed for hours, but nothing else.

An acidic film coated my tongue. A haze fogged my every thought.

In the kitchen, a carafe of water sat beside the sink. I cared not how long it might have been there. I drained half of it while slumped against the countertop. With each swallow, the ringing in my ears decreased, and the volume of the city outside slowly rose.

I could wait, and it would have been wise to do so considering I'd just broken a potion's binds upon me. I had no idea how long the effects of doing such a thing might last—whether it would be hours or days, or if there would be other repercussions to come.

But I had to leave. I had to find him.

I dropped the carafe and took to the stairs leading down to the damp cobblestone streets.

A misty rain fell, casting the already unbalanced world I'd entered in a gray gloom. I clung to the railing at the bottom of the stairs, dizzy and blinking hard in an effort to clear it.

Wagons filled with stone passed by, carted downhill with large, armor-clad warriors following. Some carried shovels over their shoulders, others sacks of building materials.

From all of their sides and backs hung swords and blades.

One of them sniffed the air after releasing a barked bout of laughter with his comrade, his sharp hazel gaze darting to me. As he stared, the wind curled the red hair around his cheeks and revealed the dark shadows beneath his eyes.

Unmoving, I stared back, tempted to ask him for Scythe. Tempted to ask if it was over, and if I was too late.

But fear of the unknown kept me utterly, breathlessly still.

The wolf warrior peeled his attention from me as his group trundled on, and I released a wheezed breath. I coughed, smothering the sound of it with my hand. Something wet smeared my lips and cheek. I could chase them. Ask them of the commander's whereabouts and well-being. They would likely ask why I needed to know. Perhaps they'd even demand to know who I was.

I didn't care. That was why I was here. I had to know. Fear couldn't overpower the need I had to make sure he was okay. So I followed the wolves downhill, my gown billowing in the wind and my steps uneven.

Eyes fell over me like a suffocating blanket. Some shop owners and citizens paused in their conversations and movements as I stumbled past. Gritting my teeth, I tried to straighten my gait when my stomach clenched with cramping, and my vision once again turned against me.

Debris cut into my bare feet. But the wagons were still in sight. If I could just make myself—

"Aster?"

I stopped so suddenly, I nearly fell.

The female cursed, snatching my arm and helping me beneath an awning.

Helplessly, I watched with blurred eyes as the wagon, as Scythe's brethren, continued through the intersection at the end of the street and marched on toward the woods.

"Where are they…" I started, waving to the warriors. "I need them."

"What in the stars for?" The female took my wild hand, then slid her arm behind my back. "They're headed to the ruined village down the river. You're bleeding, Aster."

A youngling's voice broke through the fog. "Mama?"

Maybe he was there, then. At this ruined village. Maybe I could still reach them.

But as the fog faded and I gathered my breath, I realized that maybe I didn't need them. I blinked slowly, my eyelids made of sand, and looked at the female holding me. "Olivianna."

Her hair appeared to be shorter, but it was her.

Her honey colored eyes roamed my face, concern pinching at her pink lips. The seamstress nodded. "I'd ask where you've been, but right now we need to get you fixed up before someone comes asking questions of their own." A cursory glance behind me to the street confirmed that there were indeed curious eyes still upon me.

With Olivianna's assistance, we hobbled to the intersection and veered left around the corner to a white door with blue trim, her son trailing with questions she couldn't answer.

I steadied myself with a hand upon the doorframe while Olivianna fished a set of keys from a hidden pocket in her skirts.

A sign above us swayed with the gathering force of the wind, creaking. The tiny male, who looked to be no older than three or four years, tilted his head from behind his mother's skirts as she opened the door to the shop. His obsidian eyes roamed me with nose-scrunching suspicion.

Inside, Olivianna helped me to a velvet chaise in the corner of the material cluttered shop. A metal table sat before it, and two armchairs in a floral fabric either side. On the hexagonal table sat a glass vase of fresh lavender and lavender scented candles, the overwhelming scent permeating the small space.

"Close the door and lock it, Ryon," she instructed the youngling, who scratched at his golden-brown mop of curls and watched me from the doorway. "Then why don't you head upstairs to your crayons and draw our guest a picture."

"She's bleeding," said little Ryon, scowling at me as he closed and locked the door. "Why? More baddies? You promised they was gone."

"They are, and I don't yet know why she's bleeding, but I do know one of your beautiful pictures will go a long way in making her feel better."

When he didn't move, Olivianna placed her hands upon her hips. With her back to me, she gave her son a look I couldn't see.

He sighed, stomping past gowns that swished and up the wooden steps a moment later.

Olivianna turned, the layers of violet frills cascading from her waist like that of a spinning waterfall. Hypnotized and trying to better clear my vision, I blinked and stared and blinked some more. Her cream blouse, tucked into the elastic waistband, was speckled with blood.

"I ruined your blouse," I croaked.

Olivianna peered down at it, frowning. "You can make it up to me by telling me where you disappeared to. I've still got those gowns of yours, you know." Gathering her skirts, she headed upstairs as I recalled how I'd fretted when Scythe had asked her to make me some. "All five of them gathering dust and taking up much-needed space in my storeroom."

Guilt needled at my blistering skin.

A growing light lured my eyes to the window, and I winced as the sun breached the dark clouds. People passed and clustered out on the streets, going about their lives. It gave me a modicum of hope, but not enough that I could keep from asking when Olivianna returned with a bowl of water and a cloth, "Is he okay?"

"Lie down," she said, and I did so gladly. The tea-tree aroma of the water warned me of the sting before the cloth was dipped and wrung and pressed to my arm. "Scythe?"

"Yes," I said with a hiss, Olivianna dabbing at cuts I hadn't noticed until now.

"Define okay," she said with a snort, but when she found me waiting, she sighed. "He's just fine. Now tell me what happened."

Unable to hide my relief, I let it fall through my slumping body. "I broke a potion," I admitted a moment later. "I think."

Her golden eyes tipped up to mine. "You're lucky to be breathing."

I didn't argue that, though each breath was labored. She pressed me with more questions, but now that I knew he lived, the exhaustion attacked from all sides, tinting the edges of my vision with darkness.

Seemingly aware, Olivianna murmured, "They're mostly scratches, but your hand…" Turning it over in her own, she clucked her tongue. "That's deep enough to need assistance. May I?"

I nodded as best I could, my eyes falling closed. "So they came."

She cleaned the cut, asking, "Who?" as the cloth fell into the bowl with a slosh.

"Marvis' mortal army."

There was a long pause, warmth spreading over my hand from Olivianna's touch. My skin began to re-stitch, and though I tried to force open my eyes to witness it, I struggled to make out anything but her head of lustrous curls. "You're not from Nodoya at all, are you?"

"No," I whispered, feeling her attention shift to my face. But I couldn't keep my eyes open. "Forgive me, I haven't slept in a while."

Olivianna continued to stare at me, clearly wanting to ask why. To ask every burning question she had. But she relented with a loud exhale. "Sleep, we can talk when you wake."

Just knowing I was here and that he was alive was enough, and so I ceased fighting.

SEVENTEEN

Scythe

S TROKING THE PRICKLING LAYER OF HAIR AT MY JAW, I GLARED at Dade. "We need to show up on their doorstep and demand they tell us what the fuck they were thinking."

"And what else they might be planning," Fang added.

"And by demand I do mean kill their useless king and string the queen and those princesses up by their exuberant ball gowns until they spill all they know."

Fang paused in carving up an apple with his dagger to swing his eyes to me. "You've seen what they wear?"

I shrugged. "A time or two."

He snorted and continued with his torture of the fruit. "So we hang them from the ceiling, but how will they talk with all that pomp covering their faces?"

"You're right," I said, smirking despite not wanting to. "Won't be able to tell if one of them perishes from all the blood rushing to their heads if we cannot see past their skirts."

Fang chuckled. "A tragedy."

"Finished?" Dade drawled, a brow raised as he reclined in his chair beside Fang, who straightened and pulled a chunk of apple from his dagger with his teeth.

I just stared, awaiting the insipid order that was surely about to leave the king's mouth.

As though sensing I had little faith for whatever he might say, Dade leveled his whole attention on me. "We leave them be."

"We leave them..." I shook my head and sat forward. "What *the fuck?*" I'd been waiting for this damned meeting for nearly two weeks— ever since the last of the human soldiers had been ran off, captured, or killed—and this was his answer to all we'd endured?

"Easy," murmured Fang, ever the irritating voice of reason. "Let him speak before you combust."

But I continued to glower at our king. The same king I'd recently witnessed enter death before his mate had unleashed some ungodly glowing that'd pulled his softening ass back to the land of the living.

"They tried to kill you," I needlessly reminded him. "They would've killed as many of us as they could without hesitation, and the reason sits in that fucking castle in a kingdom they have proven they do not deserve to rule, and we're just going to let them be?" I asked, beyond incredulous.

"We don't yet know enough," said a soft voice from the door to the war room.

Stars, this shit just kept getting better and fucking better.

Both Fang and I watched, stupefied, as Opal entered the room with two steaming cups of tea and set one down before her mate.

Fang bit back his amusement with a choked-sounding cough, but I wasn't hiding a thing. I openly grinned at Dade as the swan procured a sugar cube from her hidden skirt pocket and placed it in our king's tea before taking a seat beside him.

The king stared right back at me, warning with fiery blue eyes not to say a word.

He should've known warning me would only make the temptation to pick at him more impossible to resist. "And here I'd thought you were sweet enough already, oh savage king."

Dade's teeth flashed in a cruel smile. Another warning.

Opal, tucking her chair in, stilled. "I couldn't find a tray," she said. "And I didn't know if either of you liked tea…"

"For future reference, I take two sugars," Fang supplied, evidently taking pity on our new golden-haired queen. He grinned as he made to snatch Dade's teacup for himself. "But one will do for now."

Dade snarled, claws unsheathing and falling into the wooden table like butter between Fang's fingers. "Back off."

Fang snickered and carefully plucked his fingers free, his attention given back to his apple.

I settled as best I could in the chair. It wasn't that Opal was female that had me on edge. It was the fact that up until now, it'd mostly just been the three of us and Dade's uncle. Serrin was now on his way to Sinshell to assist with repairing everything he'd instructed Dade and our legions to ruin.

In my humble opinion, he deserved far fucking worse for what he'd done to his nephew's mate. I'd have killed him with nothing but the feathers he'd plucked from Opal's shifted form, and I was certain Dade had wanted to.

But it would seem the king's heart had more than failed during the battle he'd barely survived. He'd let it take a different shape. Though I couldn't blame Dade entirely when his mate was responsible for his new, softer decision-making skills.

"Opal will be joining us during these meetings from this day forward." A statement—indisputable. I didn't care to fight it. Not even when Dade looked straight at me, expecting as much. He arched a brow when I did nothing but stare, then relaxed a fraction in his chair. "Good."

Opal's gaze lingered upon me, though I didn't look at her. I peered up at the damp ceiling and wondered what in the stars these idiots were going to do to make sure an attack of such magnitude never occurred here again.

I shouldn't have cared so much. It was over. But it was impossible not to when I struggled to see past the reasons the war might have happened in the first place.

Guilt and duty were a ruthless combination.

"The queen acted out of desperation for her daughter, and she sought vengeance for her mate," Dade said, referring to Opal's mother, who'd conspired with the human royals of Errin to rid Dade and many of us from this continent.

Dade was right. He had killed Queen Nikaya's husband, the late king of Sinshell.

I held no issue with letting Opal's mother be, but I took umbrage at merely leaving the human royals to show us what else they might be up to, and I voiced as much. "Regardless, we need to speak with Nikaya again," I said. "Ask her if there is anything more she might know and what she can maybe find out about Errin."

"I will," Opal said with steely promise thickening her words.

My nose twitched as I looked at her and found her studying me intently.

Dade stirred his tea. He made a show of it as he tapped the teaspoon against the rim of the teacup hard enough to nearly crack the porcelain.

He might've been softening at the edges, but I knew if I studied his female in return, he'd snap. Not wishing to place him on his ass in front of her, I smirked and averted my gaze. I held no interest in Opal. I held no interest in anyone aside from what I could glean of use from them.

And the kingdom of Sinshell's swan princess had proven to be far more useful and trustworthy than I ever could have imagined.

It was different now, the energy surrounding her—or lack thereof. As if the ancient glowing she'd performed on that battlefield from sheer heartache alone had stolen much of her magic from her.

I saw no harm in asking, and even if it caused some, I still wanted to know. "Your gold," I said, glancing back at Dade's mate briefly. "Can you still weave it?" She knew I referred to the ability she'd inherited from her Gracewood ancestors. The ability to produce gold thread within garments.

She knew, yet our new queen eyed her tea and took her precious time to answer while her mate glared at me. "I don't know."

"Have you attempted to?" Fang asked.

"Why should it matter?" Dade said through his teeth. "She's still healing."

"If you want her at these meetings," I said evenly. "Then you'd better get used to us talking to her."

Opal placed a hand upon Dade's fist. "He's right. Calm down."

Dade closed his eyes, his shoulders lowering marginally. When they opened, he set them on me. "Why do you care?"

Surely, I couldn't have been the sole reason an army of humans would cross the Night Sea. The resources, the danger, the uncertainty...

Let it be, my instincts warned, and I lifted a shoulder. "Merely curious." Rising, I said, "Well, if we're not making plans to torture some human royals for answers and their total submission, then I think I'll take my leave to torture something else..."

None of them stopped me as I left the war room and crossed the underbelly of the Keep to the dungeons, where weeping humans awaited the attention of my claws.

The few that still lived hadn't been incredibly forthcoming, but just in case, I'd made sure I was the only one permitted to pay them a visit.

Freshly bathed but unwilling to stay in the rooms I'd been given at the Keep, I warped back to the apartment to fall into bed.

Nothing was worse than wrapping a hand around my cock, only to have someone in the same guest wing ruin it with their snoring. That someone being Fang, who had no trouble falling asleep as soon as his obnoxious head hit the pillow.

Some of us needed to fucking unwind first.

All of that went straight to shit when I materialized inside the apartment.

My heart quieted to a racing patter in my chest. Every sense awoke with a ferocity and speed I hadn't experienced in a long fucking time.

The door was open, swaying with a creak in the wind.

Blood stained the air, and the carpet beneath my boots in the shape of half a hand print. The carafe I'd left by the sink yesterday now shone in broken pieces upon the kitchen floor.

My lungs tightened with each short inhale. Her honeyed scent was everywhere. Fresh.

Just hours old.

Unable to believe it, unsure what the fuck was happening—if it were real or a fever dream—I did the only thing my baser self would allow.

I hunted.

I trailed her scent outside to the stairs. Swiping the rain-damp railing where her blood had nearly dried, I sniffed it. I shivered from the taste when I licked it, my skin trembling in response.

Then I stalked down the sloping street into the fog.

After making progress in rebuilding the neighboring villages difficult for the past two days, the rain had ceased falling onto the city streets of Vordane, though the wet and the clouds still remained. They blanketed the stars and buildings, allowing the fire swaying in the street lamps to cast the city in an eerie glow.

City folk seldom lingered outside of their dwellings since the war that had come too perilously close to robbing them of their lives and homes, but a few males lumbered up the street with raucous laughter from the tavern at its end which remained open.

They attempted greetings. I ignored them, my focus stolen so thoroughly, they'd need to attempt to kill me to garner so much as a glance from me. Even then, I wouldn't stop. My mind had narrowed. The hunger within me had sharpened to a lethal point that wouldn't dull until I found the creature I was seeking.

The breeze carried her scent to the very end of the street. To the tavern.

I smirked, but soon frowned when it faded at the intersection. I backed up and retraced it to the city's most popular tailor—Olivianna's shop and apartment.

Blood marked the trim of the door.

I didn't knock. The door opened from my fury and need alone, slamming into the wall and sending rolls of fabric to the floor.

Olivianna gasped and stood, her hand on her chest. It dropped, her shoulders sagging when she saw me and said, "Scythe, you scared me."

I ignored her, struck still by the female curled upon the dressmaker's velvet chair.

Her hair was a mess and impossibly longer, a pillow and a blanket beneath her lithe yet curved frame. The pounding of my heart ceased as the organ swelled and pushed a searing breath through my slackened lips.

Some of those curves were noticeably less severe when she opened her gray eyes with a start and pushed herself up. I scowled, both hating and loving what I saw. She was here. She was not the same.

Then I crossed the room, ignoring Olivianna's protests to let the female be.

"She needs to rest," she said at my back.

I said nothing, just glared down at the creature who'd run from me without a backward glance. Who'd left me without a shred of thought for what the fuck I would do in her absence. Who'd changed my life in a matter of days only to leave me in the type of darkness I could never fucking escape on my own.

My heart restarted with a violent thud.

Those big eyes stared up at me from a thinner face, her cheekbones and lips more pronounced. The latter trembled as she dared to reach for me.

I took that soft hand and pulled her to her feet. The magic of her skin on mine threatened to undo me on the spot.

Aster fell into me and splayed a hand over my chest, fingers and eyes searching.

Before Olivianna could say another word, I ordered, "Tell no one of her," and then I lifted my thief of a female into my arms to take her home. "I mean it."

EIGHTEEN

Aster

IN SILENCE, THE WOLF CARRIED ME UPHILL TO THE APARTMENT.
Content to stare at him, to trace the hair that punctured the skin of his rigid jaw with my eyes, I didn't mind. I could scarcely believe it—that I was here and in his arms.

Noting the severe arch of his ear, I mumbled, "You cut your hair." I reached for the thick darkness he now wore cropped close to his scalp, but my heavy arm fell when we encountered the stairs.

The loss of the shoulder-length strands had hardened him, revealing his every fierce angle and breathtaking feature. I couldn't decide if I preferred it. I couldn't decide if anything but his mere existence mattered.

The apartment door slammed, and I stiffened.

"Are you hurt?" Was the first and only thing he said before throwing me down onto the bed.

I bounced, wincing as the ache that had dulled reminded me of its presence. "No, but I—"

"You dare return after all this time fucking reeking of another male?" A barked laugh punched from him, but it was void of any humor.

It was riddled with throaty disgust.

I pushed to my elbows. "Scythe—"

"Don't worry, I'll make careful work of remedying that. Though I must warn you"—he flicked his hand, and my eyes widened as black claws replaced his fingers—"there will be no saving this gown to better hide your transgressions, and I'm not fucking sorry."

Before I could speak, before I could understand what was about to happen, he climbed over me on the bed. I fell back to the pillows, and he hooked two claws into the neckline of my dress. Tickling, they gently scratched my skin as they tore through the material.

I tried and failed to form words.

My heart pounded too fast, too hard, and I knew it had nothing to do with the potion. It had everything to do with the wolf who ripped the gown free of my body.

Breath fled me when he rose and gripped the dress within his hands, his claws now sheathed. He split my gown in two screaming pieces.

In nothing but my lace undergarments, I tried again to sit up.

"Wouldn't do that if I were you," Scythe warned, and he then crawled over top of me to straddle my waist. With skilled swiftness, he took my wrist and used the material to tie it to the wooden head of the bed.

I found my voice then. "Wait—what are you doing?" Once secure, his thumb skimmed the inside of my wrist, but he didn't answer me. I shivered. "Do you mean to interrogate me, wolf?" I glared up at him, disbelief hitching my voice. "For what purpose?"

A cruel smirk lit his eye when I placed my free hand underneath me to keep it from him. He leaned down and whispered to my mouth, "Give me your hand, Aster."

Though the gleam in his eye and the wild energy radiating from him promised punishment, I knew he wouldn't hurt me. But I still tried to forestall whatever he had in mind. "We need to talk."

"Give me your fucking hand, Aster." When I refused, he flashed his teeth with a deadly grin.

Then he kissed me.

Just once. Hard and bruising, it rendered me limp and in need of more as the taste of him, the heat and scent of him infiltrated like a heady wine.

He groaned as he pulled away, my hand within his. He secured my wrist to the bed.

My teeth gnashed. "What in the stars do you intend to do with me?"

The beast ignored me. Sliding down my body, he dragged his nose between my breasts, over my stomach, and stopped between my thighs. He pushed them wide and dug his nose into my core.

His mouth followed. Warmth drenched me from within and without as he breathed me in with a shudder of his broad shoulders. "Fuck," he rasped.

I reached for him, forgetting my hands were tied, and almost whined.

Then he flattened his tongue and licked me slowly, stopping at my clit. He flicked it, and I moaned. A claw unsheathed again, teasing as it tore through the flimsy fabric of my slip. He plucked it from my body, rough enough to jerk me upon the bed.

Scythe brought it to his nose and inhaled with his eye closing, then tossed the material to the floor. "Go ahead and warp home, but mark my words. This time I will follow." He pressed his nose to mine, his lone eye aglow, and rumbled, "I'm in the mood to draw blood, and that husband of yours has been number one on my kill list for too damned long."

My heart ceased beating at hearing that, then pounded painfully when cold swept in as he rose.

He pulled his tunic from his body and unbuckled his pants. The sight of him, the enormity of all of him, was nothing like I remembered.

It was so much more—he was so much more—than my imagination was capable of containing.

His cock was hard, engorged and bobbing as he shifted down the bed.

"Miss me?" he taunted, a brow raised when my eyes quit feasting upon his lower abdomen and crawled up the muscular expanse of his torso to meet his feral gaze. He dragged his teeth over his lush lower lip, then looked at my thighs with his nostrils flaring. "Open nice and wide. Show me just how much."

Fear and anticipation swelled my tongue—my chest.

Though I knew he was without patience, he waited. He remained focused on my core while I shook. While I battled the need to talk to him and the desire to give him anything he wanted.

I couldn't deny him.

And I couldn't deny myself.

I didn't know what he was playing at, but I knew words meant little to this creature. If I wanted him, then I would need to play by his rules.

His lips parted when I opened for him, and he lowered to better look at me. "Good." A rough exhale quaked his giant shoulders. "So very good, and so fucking wet"—a finger brushed the sensitive flesh on either side of my core like one would the petals of a flower—"I'll bet you missed me a whole damned lot."

I quivered, and he leaned closer. He blew over me, and I moaned as he chuckled.

"So pink and swollen, wildflower. I'll bet all I need to do is…" His tongue dragged over me, through me, just once. When he reached my clit, I detonated with a shocked yelp. I moaned and twisted as he climbed over me and forced my head to still with his fingers clamped at my chin.

I squeezed my eyes shut, breathless and trying to close my thighs to finish riding out the unexpected orgasm.

Scythe forced them open with his knee, keeping me spread—depriving me. "Look at me." I did, and he held me there, eye bright with fury and hunger. His hold tight but not bruising as he watched me squirm and shudder beneath him. "Can he do this to you?"

"Scythe," I choked.

He grinned, menacing and beautiful, and lowered his head for his nose to skim over my jaw to my ear. "Can he make you feel as if you'll never be satisfied, like you'll forever need more even after you've just been fed the best meal of your life?"

His hips fell, the arm beside my head braced, the only warning I was given.

He entered me in one slow thrust. A moaned gasp vibrated within his throat and warmed my ear. "You're still clenching, wildflower." His inhale hissed when I spasmed. "That's it. Tell me I'm right while telling me fucking nothing at all."

He seated himself fully and chuckled when I exhaled a broken cry, unable to handle it. Unable to handle all of him—his size when I'd been empty for so long and all of the sensations ruining me again so soon.

"It would seem you're exceptionally good at that." He licked my jaw, turning his head to whisper to the side of my mouth, "So very good at pretending you don't know what this is, that you don't feel it, too." He withdrew, then slowly slid back in, his words groaned. "So good at believing you can survive without it when we both know you've tried and fucking failed."

"I tried," I started, stuttering a little. He couldn't say it. He shouldn't even be thinking about it. There was no point in making this worse. In all of my imaginings, I'd never once imagined this. That he would still want me like this. That he would dare behave like this. But he couldn't. "I did try, but Scythe…"

He moved his mouth to my neck, teeth grazing, tongue lapping. All the while, he stayed planted deep in my body. "I tried, too. Tried to let you." He circled his hips, ensuring he pressed and tortured everywhere I needed him to inside me, the fabric of his pants rubbing at my rear. "Turns out, I can't let you, Aster," he rasped. "I fucking can't. I won't." His teeth pierced my skin, sinking deep, and I knew.

Some intuitive part of me knew he was both affirming and destroying everything.

He stole from me, forced my hand entirely into a promise of reckoning—and with nothing but a slew of pleading whimpers, all I could do was let him.

I began to drown, and with a cry so loud I feared I might scream.

The wolf's hand covered my mouth, his fingers snug between my teeth. To my ear, he ordered, "Take me." His hips reared back and forth. A calculated attack on every pleasure point. "Fucking choke on me."

Grinding and thrusting and never slowing for a heartbeat, he left no room for me to pay attention to the multitude of feelings within me. He made it impossible to decide if I wanted him to stop when I needed him to continue to destroy me in ways I'd never known I'd so desperately want.

I whined, coming apart. My teeth sank into his fingers in warning.

He released a low, rumbling laugh. "That's a good little flower. Just like that." He groaned when I drew blood, his essence falling over my tongue and swimming down my throat. "More. Swallow every fucking drop, Aster."

Wild, I twisted and shook beneath him while he watched with glowing satisfaction—a hunter enjoying the demise of his prey. Garbled, I pleaded, though I didn't know what for as wave after wave of mind-bending pleasure consumed me.

My vision darkened. My heart ceased its dancing. My ears drowned in terrifying silence.

Then with a brightness so vivid it burned, all of it returned.

The shocking heat rocked me from head to toe. It reduced me to a shivering, barely breathing pile of limp flesh. All the while, the beast I'd angered continued to fuck me without mercy.

"Mine now." He sucked from my neck, then threw his head back and roared.

Muscle corded. Everywhere. Veins pulsed and sweat glistened upon every bulging inch of him.

There was no reprieve, no softening of his features, as the same violent darkness I'd endured shuddered through him. If anything, they'd turned more feral, more lupine, as he lowered his gaze and rocked his hips, ensuring every last drop of him spilled nowhere but inside me.

Withdrawing slowly, he hissed at the sight between my legs. Then he undid one of my restraints and smacked my thigh. "Roll over."

My voice was weak, useless. "Scythe, we need—"

"Quiet." He rolled and lifted me onto all fours by my hips.

On my knees, I turned to glare at him, but his hold was too tight to escape even if I'd wanted to. I didn't want to. Yet I still said, "You can't just keep fucking me."

His nostrils and eye flared. "Watch me."

Panic mixed with the overheating war inside my chest, robbing me of speech.

He flashed his canines, still red with my blood, with his wicked grin. "Bend over, wildflower."

"I should..." I swallowed, beginning to feel the consequences of our actions, his blood staining my tongue.

"You should bend the fuck over," he said softly. Far too softly. "Right now."

Again, I swallowed and awkwardly turned back. My hand was still tied to the wooden headboard.

"Everywhere he touched you, everywhere he so much as looked at you, will be covered in me. In the pleasure I've found with his beautiful, cruel wife."

"But you knew I couldn't stay—"

"I knew nothing but you, so don't bother trying that bullshit on." He barked, "Ass in the air," and smoothed his hand over each cheek when I complied.

Two fingers impaled me from behind, dunking in and out of me slow and deep. I moaned when they left, only to still when I felt them trail over my ass. Taking his time, Scythe painted it and my lower back in his seed.

"You've already marked me."

His laugh was caustic, and I shivered when he said, "You know that wasn't just a mark."

He continued to gather and spread himself over my body. My breasts were squeezed, and my nipples pinched, his heat scalding at my back. "Smelling so much better already."

Breaths left me in short, stilted puffs. My hips circled, every part of me awaiting something I shouldn't but feared I would forever want. The burn built into an inferno, the fury of it leaving me stained with sounds I tried and failed to stop.

My stomach clenched. My center ached. My mind emptied of everything but the hollowing desire to be filled. I wouldn't say it. I refused to.

I didn't need to.

"Have I kept you waiting?" Scythe purred and returned his touch between my legs. The merest skim of his finger over me evoked a moan. My stomach tightened, the wood of the bed protesting beneath my squeezing fingers. "Drenched." Lips pressed into my shoulder, then cold air washed in as I felt him sit back to study me. "Need me, don't you?"

When I didn't answer, he grunted, "Say it, Aster."

"I need you," I growled.

A chuckle unlike any I'd heard from him made my heart seize and my spine lock. His weight left the bed, and when I turned with my mouth agape, I found him buckling his pants and on the cusp of disappearing. "Remember that next time you think to try to forget me."

"I never forgot you. Not for a moment." I lowered to the bed, both cold and unbearably hot. "Where are you going?" He couldn't mean to leave me. Not like this—tied to his bed naked and aching with need. "Don't leave me."

The wolf tensed with his back to me. "I've got shit to tend to." The shadows stole him, and left me with his chilling threat, "Run from me again, mate. I fucking dare you."

The heat of his gaze pulled me from the waking tendrils of sleep.

The drapes were closed, the sun gliding through the sliver between to dance with the dust motes over the bedding.

In the armchair by the window, Scythe reclined with an ankle over his knee. His large booted foot bounced slowly. Fingers at his chin and lips, he stared. I stared back, my chest tightening at the sight of him.

This wasn't a dream. It was real. It had all been real. I was here.

With my mate.

The tension within me eased the longer I studied him. The longer I marveled at his heavy gaze, the bright emerald of his eye, and the stillness of his fierce features. Every part of me relaxed more with each breath as I let myself believe, however fleetingly, that I was right where I needed to be.

His forefinger brushed his upper lip, and he murmured with brutal softness, "Drunk bumblebee."

Sheepish, I smiled and curled into the bedding.

He bit his thumb, his focus moving to my mouth. "He knows you're here?"

I swallowed, not wanting to think about it, and clutched the pillow beneath my head. "I think so."

A moment passed, carrying with it the desire to ask him to join me, when he stated more than asked, "So he knows about me."

I licked my lips. "He knows enough."

Scythe stared again. Tension returned to my limbs when he concluded, "And he didn't just let you leave, did he?"

I didn't need to answer that, and so I didn't.

My wolf rubbed his upper lip. "How many times, Aster?"

Confused, I frowned. "What do you mean?"

"How many fucking times?"

Oh.

Oh.

To lie would be futile because he would see right through it. I didn't want to lie, but I didn't want to speak of it either. I wanted him to join me in bed, to feast upon me before we feasted on a meal, either here or in this beautiful, war-touched city.

It seemed some things might remain but a dream—a desperate memory—for Scythe's expression hardened. His jaw flexed. "Tell me how many times he fucked you, Aster."

"Once." I exhaled the word, then I winced as I recalled that one particular time. "Not long after I returned, though it didn't really get that far. We tried, but we didn't…" I cleared my throat. "He didn't get to…"

"He didn't stick his cock inside you," he stated with dangerous calm.

"No," I said, his foot stilling and the weight of his assessing gaze so heavy that I wanted to look away. I didn't, knowing that whatever it was he was doing, whatever he was seeking, it was necessary.

He needed to know, and I wanted to give him whatever he needed. But regardless of how he'd bound me to him by forcing me to accept the mating bond, I would only give him what I could. There was still only so much I could reveal without endangering us and causing a ripple effect that might spread too far.

"He still touched you," he surmised, voice graveled. "Put his hands and his mouth on you."

"He's my husband, Scythe. I didn't think I would return to Vordane, and we had to try to fix it…" I shook my head. "In the end, we never did try very hard. I gave up long ago." I released a tremulous breath. "I think we both gave up long ago."

"Because he fucked someone else."

I nodded, tracing a loose thread in the blanket. "Multiple times." I hesitated, tempted to say more, then decided it was best to leave it at that.

Scythe said nothing else for torturous minutes.

I knew he was waiting to see what else I would divulge, and like an addicted fool with the need to please my obsession, I whispered, "I couldn't…" A knot of anxiety formed at just the thought of returning, at remembering it was far from over. I would have to face him again. "I'm beginning to loathe him, wolf."

"Yet you stayed," he said, a quiet fury lacing the gentle words.

I closed my eyes. "I had no choice." *I will continue to have no choice,* I didn't say, though the temptation to berate him for what he'd done to us both laid hot and thick over my tongue.

If the past year and a half was harrowing, then what would the rest of our lives look like now that we'd bonded in a way that went beyond the bounds of marriage?

"Look at me, Aster."

I did, pulling the blankets to my chin and waiting as he studied me some more.

"You do not love him," he finally said, his thick brows furrowing hard enough to cause his scar to bunch slightly.

Perhaps for the first time, I said out loud, "Not in that way. Not…" My head shook, and I came close to laughing as the acceptance of the truth cemented deep within me—within my words. "Not anymore."

The fear of knowing I would need to see Rorn again stemmed from what once was. From what he'd done and what he might yet do.

Scythe blinked, tilting his head and folding his plush lips between his teeth. Then he leaned forward, the leather vest over his tunic creaking, and clasped his hands between his spread knees. "Why come back now?"

"I heard there was a battle. I needed to see you."

"Make sure I'm still breathing and then run home again?" His eye swept over my face. "To the husband of whom you do not love yet would still choose over your mate."

"It's not that simple."

A dark brow rose. "Why?"

I couldn't tell him. I couldn't explain everything the way he needed. It would only make things worse. I needed time to figure out how to reveal what I could to him—a way to make him understand without him understanding the things he could not.

He didn't push for a response.

The wolf who'd altered our entire lives so recklessly without even knowing the extent rose from the armchair. He stared down at me, and I twisted to better see him. My eyes roamed up his towering black-and-crimson-wrapped bulk to try to read what he might do next.

But I was given one last look that lingered at my mouth, his nostrils flaring as the air around him darkened before he vanished.

NINETEEN

Scythe

ASTER COULD LEAVE.

I would have little to no trouble finding her now that I'd made sure she was mine. My mate could return to her precious husband, but this time, it would not be without consequences.

Bloody and oh so beautiful consequences.

The mere thought of unleashing this rage—this hatred born from jealousy and something foreign I struggled to name—upon the asshole who hadn't appreciated what he'd had in a creature who wasn't even his to keep…

I shivered, a wave of pleasure rolling over me from head to fucking toe.

Yes, this mate of mine would need to tread very carefully indeed.

Dade appeared beneath the stairs in the Keep, but I continued down the hall as he said to the poor mutt who'd loitered too long near the bowl of fruit on the hall table, "Tres, find out who's responsible for my missing meals."

Aghast to have been given a lowly duty for a warrior, Tres sputtered, "Me? But I need to—"

"I do not recall making a request," Dade said, his tone now that of the alpha he was.

Tres cursed but muttered, "Of course, my king."

Dade caught up with me in the dank hall leading to the war room, his gaze a burn upon my back. "You've been busy."

"No." I pushed open the door to the musty room. "You merely spend too much time in your rooms with your bird to notice much of anything."

He ignored that, leaning against the doorframe while I plucked a fresh piece of parchment from the mountain of mess at the center of the table. "You smell strange."

I dipped the quill into an inkpot and smirked. All the while, I tried to keep my hackles from rising. "I might have skipped bathing," I lied far too smoothly. "You're welcome."

The crimson king's eyes dug into my profile like a serrated blade. "Not of filth."

"You're truly becoming so sweet, but I'm afraid you're spoken for."

He snarled, then paused, and I knew I'd stepped in shit before he realized it himself. He laughed, the sound one of disbelief. "A female, isn't it?"

I ignored him and continued with the list for my legion so that we could finish the repairs on the village outside of the city and move on to the next. "We need more supplies and fast."

"They're coming." Silence settled upon that thorn-covered wall between us—the one we'd never breach. Sighing, the king mercifully veered away from the subject.

At least, that was what he led me to believe.

"For two days now, my lunch seems to have gotten lost on its way to my rooms," he said. "You wouldn't happen to know anything about this mystery, would you?"

I cleared my throat to keep from laughing. "Not a damned thing."

He surveyed me in a silence more irritating than his grating interrogation tactics while I marked the list as priority and placed it over one Fang had recently left upon the board.

"Who is she?" Dade said when I marched for the door. "I won't ask again."

Fuck.

I stopped, knowing I couldn't avoid it—knowing that if I didn't give him something, he could very well look into what I was up to.

I met his eyes and unveiled a half-truth. "A foreigner. I found her roaming the city in a daze, so I took her home." Sure, there hadn't been as many women soldiers as there had been men in the human army, but there had been enough that he should have believed me.

"You just took her?" he repeated. "As captive?" His eyes danced when I nodded once. "Then why isn't she in the dungeon with the rest?"

To lie was easy when it could be mixed with a heady amount of honesty. "Because I'm enjoying her if you must know." I grinned. "A lot."

Dade's golden brows lowered, his gaze sharpening on mine. "And have you gleaned anything of use from her about the attack?"

"I've been a little busy, as you said."

"Busy fucking her."

Nerve instantly struck, I seethed in warning, "Busy rebuilding shit." I'd forgotten my place, and we were both aware of that as the air grew charged. Too often, it became a problem, especially over the past few years while I'd battled with more than just other creatures.

Though it physically hurt, I forced myself to back down.

But Dade only studied me with unveiled curiosity brightening his blue eyes. "Very well." Licking his teeth, he straightened from the door. "Do let me know as soon as you shake anything worth knowing free from this…" He smirked. "*Captive.*"

I inclined my head and took my leave. My claws, half unsheathed and piercing my curled palms, retracted when the blood king ordered at my back, "And stop pilfering my fucking lunches."

Another stolen meal sat waiting upon the table between the half-eaten bowl of grapes and the barely touched jug of freshly squeezed melon juice.

At least she'd finished the water and most of the meal from the day before. I could've had the Keep cooks make me an extra meal without much in the way of questioning, but there would be talk as soon as my back was turned.

I couldn't yet decide what I should do with this female of mine, let alone understand what her intentions for me might be, so I'd said nothing. I'd given no one a drop of anything. For I couldn't let anything or anyone ruin it.

I had to have her. I had to keep her. It lived within the marrow of my bones—the need to make sure she never left me again. I just didn't know how to make sure she wouldn't.

And so silence and as much secrecy as possible was best. For now.

Especially while I tried to drag myself out from this pit of rot I continuously fell into when I remembered she was married—that she had a life. One that did not include a one-eyed brute with nothing to offer except for himself.

My jaw clenched.

It was no wonder she had chosen him. A weeklong mating session had likely been enough for her to realize there was nothing else for me to give besides pleasure.

I was good for nothing else.

Regardless, I couldn't let her go. I refused to. A terror unlike any I'd felt in decades seized me at the mere thought of returning from my duties to find that she'd disappeared yet again.

So I'd continued to work. To keep from rousing questions I was never in the mood to answer and to keep from guarding her like a beast with a fresh kill.

I couldn't lose her, but I didn't know how I would keep her, and the resulting anxiety made it hard to fucking breathe.

My beautiful thief rose and quickly, as though she thought I was unaware that she was awake. "Don't go." That caramel hair was tangled around her shoulders in a tempting mess, just calling for my fingers to toy—to tug.

My lips twitched, but I said nothing.

Her dove-gray eyes narrowed, her heaving chest and racing heart slowing. I had to wonder if this whole mate thing had caused her to feel more anxious over my own whereabouts. For she'd certainly not cared so much before now.

"You're back." Eyeing where I sat at the dining table, the fresh food I'd placed upon it, she said, "With more food." Her sleep swollen cheeks flushed with irritation. "Is there something wrong with my appearance?"

"No," I snapped, taken aback.

"Then why all of this grand food?"

I looked down at my clasped hands. "You haven't been taking care of yourself. I can tell by your cheekbones and the hue of your skin." I probably shouldn't have, but I added quietly when I lifted my gaze, "Your stomach and thighs are not as fleshy and soft."

Her shoulders drooped, her eyes ashine with emotion I couldn't decipher. "So you're doing this." When I didn't give a response, she said gently, "I don't want all of this food, Scythe. I just want you to stay."

I eyed her breasts, which were sadly lost to one of my tunics, and inhaled deep. "You need to be fucked." Indeed, her need ripened the air the moment the words left my mouth.

"No, wolf," Aster said, and I scowled, confused. She needed my cock to fill her. I could practically taste her growing arousal. "What I need is for you to talk to me."

I tensed before I could control it and rose from the chair. "That would be unwise."

"Why?" she said, crawling from the bed and walking to me.

I stood firm, though I knew it would hurt so beautifully if she dared to touch me. "Because I have nothing good to say to you, wildflower."

"Say it anyway." At my silence, she urged, "Please."

"No," I barked, instantly regretting it when she stilled.

Sickened, at myself and by how much I needed to both take and escape her, I turned for the kitchen and didn't sense it—didn't expect it after grouching at her like I had—so I flinched when her fingers brushed my own. "What happened to you?"

I pulled away, moving far enough that I could begin to warp someplace else.

"Scythe…"

"You," I said quietly, too quietly, and froze before the dining table. "You happened. Years of fighting back shadows, and there you were. An unexpected light. Then you ripped it from me without warning, without even fucking waiting. You took it all without a care for anyone besides your fucking husband. Now you're here, and I…"

"What?" she carefully prodded, slowly advancing behind me.

"I don't trust it." I swallowed, the sound thick. "I don't trust you."

Then I disappeared.

TWENTY

Aster

MORE THAN JUST SCYTHE'S THICK HAIR HAD GONE.
Anything that had once remotely softened him was gone.
Now there was nothing but cold, studious venom within his gaze. An aggressive obsession to claim within his touch.

I'd have taken him any way he came if only he would let me.

He refused. I'd begun to fear that perhaps I repulsed him and that he'd regretted cementing the mating bond between us. I'd have never guessed that maybe, just maybe, I'd broken his heart.

It would seem I'd once again been painfully naïve, yet I also couldn't fault myself for thinking he hadn't cared. He was my mate. He was compelled to care even if he did not wish to. But I hadn't thought his feelings ran any deeper than that of his beastly instincts and his ego.

In all the months of misery I'd endured in Wistensia, I hadn't once thought that I wasn't alone. That he would be hurting with me. Maybe more than me.

He barely knew me. Yet he knew me in ways I'd not shown another soul in many years. I wouldn't delude myself into thinking he loved me, but I also couldn't forget that there were feelings, a smattering of stepping stones, that most encountered before falling into something as powerful as love.

196 | ELLA FIELDS

For I felt them, too. All of them. That perilous climb that would lead to a freefall—into a madness none of us wanted to fall into on our own.

Strange and more than a little off-putting, this confusion and anxiety and desperate longing. As I'd felt none of it in this way before.

I'd been in love before. I could never cheat myself or Rorn of what we'd once had by making it seem smaller now that I'd fallen out of that love.

But that love had been instant. A certainty upon the first meeting of our eyes.

And perhaps, too easy.

I pushed the new tray of food away. This one contained an array of nuts, banana pie, and a meat-loaded sandwich. I was certain it was delicious, but I'd eat some of it later.

As it was, I'd eaten twice as much as what had become my usual. The sight of the two other trays with their mostly eaten dishes awaiting collection angered more than it made me grateful for Scythe's odd way of caring for me. While I did love that he'd been fond of my curves, that didn't mean I had to appease him when it would only make me sick after eating so little for so long.

The anger climbed and spread the longer I stared while sipping a glass of water. His insistence on caring for me while not giving me what I truly needed had to end. If I had indeed wounded him as he'd suggested, then, somehow, I would just need to make things right.

As right as I possibly could.

I stood and set the water down, then I changed into the gown I'd tried to mend. It looked dreadful, courtesy of Scythe's claws and my poor mending skills, but it would have to do.

Then I warped to that cottage within the forest.

I knew within moments of steadying my feet upon the stone floor that he wasn't there, yet I still scoured everything I could see.

Nothing had changed.

Not one thing, I realized, alarm spiking through me as I crossed to the stump of a tea table and inspected the books. The same books that had been resting there the last time I'd stood in this very room of this very cottage.

The shelves lining the walls were untouched, dust gathering in a thick film. The kitchen was tidy but mainly due to it looking unused. I traipsed to the bedchamber. Pushing the door wide, I discovered the gigantic bed was made, the linen tucked tightly beneath the oversized mattress.

He was likely working with his legion then.

Unwilling to leave just yet, I wandered outside to the overgrown gardens and past the chopped wood lining the side of the moss-touched stone of the cottage. The axe stood against the stump, weeds sprouting around the blade.

The grass grew longer, thicker, beyond the cottage. It climbed in patches toward the trees and gathered around a pond.

I searched the trees and watched the sunlight dance with the shadows. Birds called to one another. Critters scurried through the brush. My shoulders loosened, each new breath taken easier than the last. I closed my eyes and just breathed—just felt it. A magic I'd never thought would grow so rare.

Peace. A calming, soul-soothing peace.

A shrieked cry shattered it. I startled, my eyes flying open.

"Help, you rotten toad," shouted a tiny figure in the pond before me.

"Quiet," another grouched from atop a little boat fashioned from lily pads. "Play dead."

"You'll be dead in a minute." The elf climbed back onto the lily pads, and shoved his companion.

His friend shoved him back. "Stop it," he hissed. "She'll see us."

"What are we going to do? Sit here like doomed idiots?"

I laughed, then stopped abruptly when both creatures froze.

Slowly, they turned my way. The wet one squeezing his top hat free of water blinked with large black eyes. "What do you want?"

"You're elves."

198 | ELLA FIELDS

"That depends who's asking," said the other creature, a reed in hand that he attempted to use to row their makeshift boat.

"She did not ask, idiot." The soggy one peered around. "Where's the beast?"

"The beast?" I questioned.

"The one-eyed demon with rocks for arms."

I withheld another laugh and informed, "He's not here."

The rowing elf paused and nearly shouted as he slumped with relief, "Oh, thank the stars."

His companion looked skyward, his sodden hat clutched to his chest. "They are indeed so magically merciful."

The rower narrowed his dark eyes on me. "But who are you?"

"I'm Aster, his…" My nose crinkled. That I would dare utter such a thing to these creatures when I could barely acknowledge it myself was absurd.

"His…?" the hat hugger prompted and scratched at his mop of wet, buttery hair.

"Don't prod." The rower glowered at him. "It's evidently sensitive."

I walked closer and crouched upon the muddy bank. "What are you two doing in there?"

"We were fishing until *someone* lost our rods," said the rower. "I'm Jats, and this is Kloon, the idiot who sent them sinking into the deep depths of the void."

I bit my lips to keep from smiling and spied one of the rods lingering just beneath the surface of the pond. Leaning closer, I plucked it out. "Here's one." I peered into the algae-covered gloom again, but I couldn't see the other.

I reached across the water to give the rod to Kloon, who blinked up at my hand as though it would squash him. I laughed. "Do you not want it?"

Eyeing the rod, then me, the elf nodded with his mouth agape. He snatched it, and I quickly retreated before I fell into the pond.

"Epitome of rude," Jats said, laying his reed over his brown trousers. "Say thank you."

"Thank you," murmured Kloon, who inspected the stick they'd trimmed and whittled into a fishing rod—some type of hair twined and caught around it.

I smiled and pushed to my feet, studying them for a moment. The last time I'd seen Little Folk, I'd barely been old enough to know what they were.

They typically dwelled within tree trunks and giant toadstools. Fiercely protective of their domains, most knew to take extreme caution when encountering them, lest they wished to lose some hair, clothing, and even footwear.

"Do you know where he might be?"

Jats scratched at his brown beard. "The wolf?" I nodded, and he laughed—a rough chime that ended when he stated, "Stars, no."

"Probably growling at some unfortunate soul," Kloon muttered low, as if fearing Scythe would hear.

"Or maiming them," Jats said. "Rumor has it his torturing tactics are positively grotesque, and that he's spent a lot of time in that nightmare of a keep's dungeon with the daring humans captured from the war."

My hopes drooped. That Keep was the one place I could not go.

Kloon shivered. "Beast indeed." Setting the rod over his lap, he mumbled, "Nothing but a grizzly, grumbling monster."

I couldn't help but laugh at that. "Why are you so afraid of Scythe?"

Kloon looked at me as though I'd asked something ludicrous.

Jats pursed his lips, then said, "I think the better question is, why in the bloody stars aren't you?"

"Don't pry," Kloon mocked. "*Sensitive.*"

Jats smacked his chest. Kloon released a miniature growl and threw himself at Jats. The two tumbled into the water, making a raucous and cursing.

I waited until they'd both reached their overturned boat, and then I smiled and left.

Daylight bled into evening, and though I longed to stay in the cottage to wait for this beast of mine, he might have thought I'd left if he returned to the apartment and I wasn't there.

So I went back. I ate some pie, and I tried to read some of his many books.

Then I took to the streets. There was one other creature who might know where I could find him or at least have a way of reaching him for me.

The downhill trek to Olivianna's was quiet and crisp, winter pressing its warning upon the air.

City dwellers were tucked inside their apartments and townhouses and businesses. Some roamed the streets in small groups, but there was a somberness to them, to the entire city, that hadn't been here when I last was.

War had touched them and, perhaps for many, for the first time.

Guilt needled, and again I reminded myself that I hadn't known what Marvis had been planning. That even if I had known ahead of time, I wouldn't have been able to stop it. Which, in turn, angered me. For if I'd discovered anything sooner, perhaps some lives could have been spared.

I kept my head down when a passing carriage ambled uphill, golden eyes searching the street from behind a velvet curtain. No matter how often I told myself that I was safe, and that Rorn wouldn't know where to find me, it didn't help.

Without the safety of Scythe's homes to hide within, I felt exposed. Raw and anxious all over again.

It was then I was forced to consider that perhaps it wasn't revealing myself to this city that was not my own that caused it, nor was it the fear of Rorn finding me—should he even be looking. It was just me.

I'd done this to myself.

For endless months, I'd hidden. I'd made sure very few souls saw me in order to somehow better protect myself. Now, it was hard to shake that need. The desire to escape as best I could behind walls and closed doors.

I swallowed over the tightening within my throat and lifted my chin.

But the street was now empty, void of even outdoor tables and displays before the restaurants and shopfronts I passed. I heard it, though—life beyond the doors and the cracked open windows.

Perhaps the people of Vordane just needed some time to hide and learn how to breathe amongst others again, too.

My bare feet slowed at the sight of that tavern, and I remembered that Olivianna's was nearby. I paused outside of the narrow, two-story building and inhaled the scent I'd carried within my memory of stale ale and spiced nuts. The murky windows of the tavern were damp and dimly lit, the occupants within boisterous.

Growing cold, I made to keep walking when a familiar scent trapped my next breath within my lungs, and I turned back.

Inside, I shouldered gently through a large throng of females. Nearly every table was occupied, laughter and cussing and even singing overwhelming my senses. But his scent had never been more unmistakable now that he'd bound us together.

I followed it, relied on that pull that was so much stronger than ever before, to the bar.

Scythe stood at its end in discussion with what smelled like another wolf. Sensing my approach, he stilled, then he turned just far enough to see me as I struggled to squeeze between a rowdy crowd of young males.

One of them hollered a greeting at me and offered his drink, of which I declined with a slight smile and a shake of my head. By the time I was free and nearing the end of the bar where Scythe stood, I could see the wolf had left him, but he wasn't alone.

A female with dark shoulder-length hair now hung from his arm. Another wolf, I noted when I inhaled her perfumed scent and saw the brighter hue of her pear-colored eyes.

She smirked at Scythe and shook her finger, saying something

I couldn't hear when one of the males behind me called to someone across the tavern.

My wolf wasn't looking at her. He was staring straight at me while he placed a hand upon the female's waist.

I scowled. My heart paused painfully.

Then he looked away to whisper something in her ear. The female's eyes closed, her lips parting.

My heart splintered. I hadn't known it was still whole enough to be harmed in such a way. I wasn't grateful to be made aware that it was. I didn't push back through the crowds of the tavern.

I warped my way outside and found myself standing before a familiar white door with blue trim.

My breaths came fast. Far too fast. I tried to slow them.

I shouldn't have warped here. There was no need to visit Oliviana now that I'd discovered where Scythe was...

Busy seducing another female. One with claws and fur.

I couldn't compete with that. I never wanted to compete with anything. I supposed this was my comeuppance for trying to take a little more of what I couldn't keep. As my father used to say, the stars would never fail to throw blades to the ground for the treacherous to eventually stumble upon.

I'd had one more night.

I'd made sure he was okay. There was no reason to linger outside of Oliviana's shop door, and there was certainly no reason to linger in this war-wounded city for another moment.

The door cracked open far enough to reveal Oliviana in a floor-length blue robe. "Aster?" she asked, a glass of wine in hand. "Oh, I suppose you're finally here for the gowns."

She threw open the door and traipsed into her shop, leaving me to follow. "I'd ask if you want some wine, but I think that would be redundant."

Remembering she had a young son, I was careful to close the door quietly behind me, for he might have been asleep upstairs given the hour.

Dresses and shirts and even some pants lined one wall, waiting upon hangers. Some were complete, and others seemed to await final touches. Rolls and mountains of fabric dotted the space I'd stumbled into bleeding and disorientated just a few days ago.

I crossed to the chaise I'd laid upon, unsure what else to do when Olivianna returned with another glass of wine. "Here," she said, and I took it as she eyed me up and down. "You're looking better, but I do hope you haven't been wearing that soiled dress since you arrived."

"No," I said, sipping the wine and taking a seat when she gestured for me to. "I've been wearing Scythe's tunics."

"We can't have that, either." She set her glass on the table and twirled back out of the shop.

A moment later, she returned, gowns in hand and blowing a ringlet from her cheek that had escaped her clipped updo. "I'd be offended that you hadn't thought to visit me again until now, but I suppose you and Scythe have had some ah…" Her nose scrunched. "Catching up to do."

"He's been busy," I stated simply.

Olivianna halted before the armchair, draping the gowns atop it. "The war has been keeping the lot of us busy." I drank while she surveyed me. "But he seemed angry. More so than usual, most certainly, when he came and stole you."

I stared at the fresh flowers upon the table, willing my eyes to stay dry. "He's…" A humorless laugh escaped as I settled on, "Displeased with me, yes."

"Because you left?" she asked carefully. I nodded, drinking more wine. A heavy half minute later, she sighed. "Are you okay?"

"I will be." And I wanted to believe that I would be, but I knew it was a lie. A blistering darkness threatened to overtake my soul once more, urging me to return to Wistensia to the misery I knew best. The misery I knew I could survive for I'd done so already.

"You know," Olivianna said absently. "I never thought I'd see the day that brute of a male tried to court anyone, yet here we are. Five stunning gowns later." She giggled and began to display each one. "If I do say so myself."

Indeed, they were stunning.

An array of cream, teal, and three in differing shades of emerald. All of them were simple, as though Scythe had requested they be similar to the gown I'd worn upon first visiting Vordane, but more beautiful than I ever could have imagined.

Loose and tame tufts of organza and silk spurted from the shoulders, and on two of the gowns, in full sleeves to flow gently to the wrist. The busts were velvet and satin, charming without looking too constricting, and the skirts a marvelous waterfall of swinging color.

And they would have cost Scythe an absolute fortune.

"Has he paid for them?"

"Yes, and he paid extra for me to keep them," Olivianna said, bringing the gowns closer so that I could inspect them.

My fingers trembled as I reached out, and I immediately pulled them back.

"Do you not approve?"

"No, I do," I said quickly. "They're simply gorgeous, but I suppose I just don't understand..."

She laughed. "He might be surly, but he is beyond smitten." There was a knowing pause as she placed the gowns over the armchair again. "Though I'm sure you're already more than aware."

"Courting," I murmured, recalling that she'd said that just minutes ago.

Olivianna hummed. "Almost adorable, isn't it? Unless it involves fucking one, Scythe has absolutely no idea what to do with a female." A light scoff. "Stars, he doesn't even know how to treat his brethren and friends. I'd blame the upbringing, you know, being conditioned to kill and destroy..."

"Conditioned?"

"You didn't know?" As if remembering that I was not from here, understanding dawned and she explained, "All crimson wolves are raised to serve the crown, and for the past handful of decades, that means being the beasts many think they were born to be. But that Scythe"—she waved her hand—"far worse than even that of the duty-doomed dimwit who sired Ryon."

"Ryon's father is a wolf?"

"Indeed." She reclaimed her wine from the table. "I half-hoped the war would take him, if only so I won't have to tell his son that his father wants nothing to do with him. Alas, he still breathes." A look at me and my stunned features had her laughing. "I think we'll be needing more wine for this conversation."

But the door burst open, and Olivianna jumped with a shriek. "You must stop doing that and learn to knock like a civilized male."

Shocked by Olivianna's fright, Scythe froze. Frowning, he asked, "Civilized?" He then looked at me.

With my heart pounding, I looked away, unsure what to do.

He clipped, "Come with me, Aster."

Olivianna's nervous energy cloaked the air, nearly overpowering that of the tension between the wolf and myself. "Perhaps give her a little space, commander."

"Perhaps mind your—"

"Don't you dare," I said quietly, but he heard and stilled when my head rose. "You will walk back out that door, knock and apologize, or simply keep walking."

"Will I, wildflower?" he taunted. "You know I'm not going anywhere unless you're coming with me."

"Oh, stars," Olivianna muttered, her fingers at her forehead. She downed the rest of her wine, and then reached for the decanter.

And studying him, the clenched fists at his sides, the unflinching stance of his towering form, and the resolute rise of his cruel jaw, I knew he spoke true.

I sighed. "I will meet you at the apartment. Olivianna and I were in the middle of a conversation."

Scythe stepped back against the wall and crossed his arms, and Olivianna snorted when he said, "Go ahead and finish it, then."

He couldn't be serious...

He smirked and raised a brow.

I glowered. "You're an asshole."

His eye widened, then narrowed with a gleam. "So I've been told."

"By your friend at the tavern?" I feigned counting the time. "I daresay she would be mad. Half an hour is far from your best."

Oliviana gasped.

Both of Scythe's brows rose, and his lips spread into a menacing grin. "Only one creature gets my best."

Anger roared through me, sending me to my feet and across the room. But I stopped before him, remembering where we were and the youngling upstairs. I swallowed and retreated a step, Scythe watching me with narrowed focus and his arms unfolding.

"I'm so sorry," I said to Oliviana, who didn't seem to mind the dramatics we'd brought into her home and shop at all.

Her lips pursed, her gaze darted between the two of us with bright delight.

Then I warped back to the apartment, unsteady on my feet as I locked myself within the bathing room.

Scythe's booted steps boomed over the wooden flooring as soon as I had the door closed.

I should've gone home. For although it didn't feel like home anymore, it was better than enduring this male's toxic, acidic hatred of me.

A hatred I knew I deserved to some extent—but he'd gone too far.

"Open the door."

I bent over the sink, fingers clutching the cracked porcelain.

"Aster."

I peered at the female staring back at me in the broken mirror, unsure who she was. Her cheekbones were sharp, her hair a tangled mass of cinnamon waves, and her eyes...

Damp and reddened and empty.

"Wildflower?"

My breath hitched, and my eyes further flooded as I wondered just how far he'd taken it with his friend in the tavern. As I surrendered to the perilous reality that he'd likely brought many a female back to this very apartment, and tonight he'd…

He'd rejected me.

No. Surely, that wasn't what he'd done. Not when he'd been the one to force the acceptance of the bond upon us.

Though that didn't mean it couldn't be severed.

"Fuck, Aster. Would you please open the door so that I can look at you."

A sad smile colored my lips. Unable to stop myself, I had to know, "Why do you always demand that?"

"Because," he started, and there was a giant pause before he finally said softly, "I need to know you're real. That I didn't just fucking dream you into an obsession I can't shake."

My lips quivered. My smile fell.

"Aster, please." His sigh was almost groaned. "Just open the damned door."

I closed my eyes over the tears, but a few snuck free. They tickled against my cheeks and chin, falling to splash against the porcelain.

"I needed you to wait."

I said nothing, though I knew what he meant.

He repeated himself. "I needed you to wait, and you left. You just…" A rough clearing of his throat sounded. "You were just gone."

More tears escaped. I swiped at my cheeks while pacing the length of the tub, too torn to know what to do.

"A door can't keep me from you, wildflower," he said with gentle lethality. "Nothing can."

I clasped the handle, then leaned back against the wood.

"Fine. Be angry. Hate me if need be," he said roughly. "But don't you dare leave." I slid down the door as he warned, "If you do, I can promise you won't like the repercussions." He remained some minutes longer but said nothing else.

He seemed to be listening—and I knew he was—as I did my best to quiet my quaked breaths upon my forearm. My teeth sank into the sleeve of my gown and the skin beneath.

I thought I'd already experienced what it was to be lost, and that once I survived, I would never feel so out of touch with myself again.

I'd never been more wrong, and this time, it felt worse.

It felt like a chasm had yawned open inside me, and it was filling higher by the breath with everything I'd contained for far too long.

"Aster," Scythe rasped, low and choked.

An aching moment later, he was gone.

TWENTY-ONE

Aster

SCYTHE DIDN'T RETURN BEFORE I SURRENDERED TO SLEEP, and he wasn't there in the morning.

A fresh meal awaited me on the dining table when I woke, but I couldn't so much as stomach the scent of it.

I knew better than to disregard his warning and return to Wistensia. I knew better than to think doing so wouldn't harm him again. Regardless, I should have left the moment I saw him touch another female.

Yet here I still was. A fool who hadn't learned anything.

After bathing, I went back to the cottage and to the pond where the elves had been. They were no longer there, but their boat was hidden amongst the tall grass at the water's edge. I wasn't sure what I was searching for. Perhaps a reason to stay, some clarity as to why I was still here, or the peace I'd felt upon visiting yesterday.

The breeze and the rustling of foliage and forest debris settled around me. An embrace that soothed but gave no answers.

A violent roar stilled the trees.

I leapt from the grass. A cold sweat swept over my skin when I heard footsteps crunching at the front of the cottage.

I hurried toward them, scenting him before I saw him.

Scythe stood upon the stepping stones leading to his home. His back to me, the heaving wolf dragged a hand over his head. Then he bent at the waist, retching but seemingly not evicting anything from his stomach.

He spat at the ground and wheezed, "Fuck."

"Scythe?" I questioned.

It was then I saw the bouquet of violas the same shade as my hair upon the grass by the door—the same bouquet he'd bought me during our small tour of the city.

Hesitantly, I made to collect them from the ground. I stopped when I noted the pouch of spilled sweets.

Trapped breath burned my throat when Scythe coughed and straightened. "I thought you were gone." Slowly, he turned as though worried I wasn't truly standing mere feet behind him. "I thought you'd…" He exhaled roughly and rubbed his large hand over his mouth and chin.

I'd never seen him look ill, so pale and worn that his eye looked like a jewel.

"I should be gone," I whispered, my lungs too tight as I drew in shallow breaths.

"Not again," he said, stepping closer. "You cannot leave like that again, Aster."

My eyes blurred. "You touched her, and with the intent to hurt me. I want to stay, but if I'm not going to be treated any different than what awaits me in Wistensia, then I will be forced to leave, wolf, and I won't look back."

"Don't," he gritted. "Don't say such things." He stopped before me and clasped my cheek with a quaking hand, his tone softening and scratched. "You would reject me again?"

I retreated, meeting the stone of the cottage. "You're not hearing me. You're not understanding." I couldn't control it, the need to lay it all bare before him. He'd gone too far—we both had taken this fated connection that should have remained ignored far too far.

There was no taking any of it back now, so I let go. "That…" I gestured behind me in the direction of the Night Sea. "That I have barely survived, but you?" I shook my head, tears flooding. "I won't. I know I won't. And I'm so fucking tired of merely trying to survive."

Seeming both stunned and horrified, his features hardened to stone. "What did he do to you?"

"I don't want to speak of him. I want to know if you heard me."

Scythe stepped forward. "You will tell me what he did—"

"Did you hear me or not?" I came close to shouting.

The intensity bled from his features, gentling them in a way I hadn't glimpsed since that one week we'd spent together, as he observed the tears I couldn't keep from spilling. "I don't know what to do here, Aster. I'm so lost, it's like I'm sinking. I feel sick with worry and anger and longing and all these fucking things I've never felt before, and I don't know what to do. I don't know what to do with any of it."

I reached behind me for the stone, for something to steady me.

Scythe noticed, and he stilled before me. He tracked the tears over my cheeks with a pained expression. "I'm a monster," he said, rough. "A beast without a single fucking clue, I know that, but I don't want to hurt you."

It was unfair of me to remind him, especially when I was the one who had left him. I said it anyway. "You once promised you never would."

"I never intended to. My ego took over." He licked his lips and cursed. "She was hanging about, and I took advantage of her interest only when I sensed your arrival."

I swiped my nose. "That's all?"

"That's all." He captured my cheeks, calloused thumbs sliding over the wet beneath my eyes. "You hurt me, Aster. You damned near fucking ruined me, and I've spent so long in pain that I wanted you to feel it, too. I failed to think about why you left. I failed to remember that you didn't even want to leave," he said, and I melted more with every low yet resolute word. "All I could see and feel and think was that you *did* leave."

"I thought you would have forgotten me," I whispered.

"I wanted to," he admitted. "I failed miserably, so I was never going to take it any further than what you saw. I just needed to gain back some control, to feel like I was in control, but I'm not." His mouth lifted a little. "I need to be, and I'm not, and I can't fucking stand it. Can't stand even admitting it, and I'm sorry."

That was it. Stark honesty. No matter how much it poisoned.

And poison it did.

"I'm not sure what's worse," I said thickly. "That I believe you or that I don't know if I want to." More tears escaped, and he wiped them away with his thumbs. "You're a risk. One I'm not so sure I'm strong enough to take."

His jaw clenched. "Don't make me say it, Aster." When I frowned, he sighed and gently tilted my chin until our gazes met. "I haven't been with anyone since you left me."

My stomach dropped, emptying me of a working heartbeat. "You're lying, and there's truly no need." Yet my eyes drifted back to the flowers, the pouch of sweets spilling onto the grass a few steps beside them. My words fell into a baffled whisper. "I told you not to lie to me."

"I know," he said, bringing my attention back to him. "And I'm many unseemly things, wildflower, but I wouldn't lie to you."

He couldn't possibly have been alone this entire time. "But it's been…"

"Eighteen months and ten days," he supplied quick and confidently.

I blinked hard enough to send the rapid gathering of fresh tears to my cheeks.

He wasn't real. No male of sane mind would keep themselves for someone they knew damned well they might never see again.

"I tried once," he said, as though reading my thoughts. He squeezed and stroked my cheeks. "I really fucking tried, but I couldn't even kiss her, let alone take her home, so I fled the tavern like a mutt with my tail between my legs."

I bit my lips, trying to keep from laughing when he muttered, "She and her friends likely had fun with that." He stared down at me with his thumb brushing the apple of my cheek. "I don't like it when you cry."

"Remember that next time you feel inspired to make me."

His eye danced, and he lowered his head to mine. "It won't happen again, I swear it. Not because of me—not because of anyone if I can help it. I just want to keep you, to get rid of this fear of losing you, and I don't know how."

I didn't know either. I couldn't reassure him or myself. But I wanted him anyway. I would have him anyway.

"You could start by kissing me," I suggested.

A ragged exhale heated my ear, then I was in his arms, and he was striding through the door. He set me on the counter, his mouth pressing to my cheek. He treated the other to the same, our eyes and noses meeting briefly, and then his mouth slammed over mine.

My skirts were lifted and torn and my legs opened.

His pants were pushed beneath his ass. Blood pooled over my tongue when his canine caught it, and I moaned when he licked and groaned. I was pulled to the very edge of the countertop, my thighs spread wide and the head of his cock rubbing through me, testing me.

Then entering me.

His mouth froze over mine with his hitched breath. Our foreheads met as he peered down to watch my body swallow all of him. "I don't deserve this," he whispered, almost as if to himself. "But that won't stop me from trying to."

My heart rattled. Needing to touch him, I snuck my hands beneath his tunic to explore his flexing back. I gasped when he slowly withdrew and then rammed back in, my nails scoring into his skin.

"I should apologize for taking you the way I did the other night."

"Don't bother," I warned, my lips skimming the coarse hair at his jawline and my legs clenching tight around his waist.

He held my thigh and the back of my head, fingers entangled in my hair. "Do you wish to be tied to my bed again?"

"I will be disappointed if that was the last time."

He hummed, turning his head for his mouth to steal mine. He kissed me with a lingering softness that radiated through me. "We can't have you disappointed, wildflower."

I pulled up his tunic, and he released his hold on me so I could tug it over his head. It fell to the floor. My hands immediately splayed

over his chest, fingers searching, rubbing, greeting every defined indent, scar, and smattering of hair.

He stilled inside me.

"I've thought about this for so long," I confessed and leaned for-
ward to place my mouth to his skin, right over his thundering heart.
The action made him press perfectly against the swollen depths of me.
I clenched around him, my legs beginning to tremble.

"Truly?" he rumbled, though he could read the truth in my desperate touch.

"Truly," I moaned, rocking into the pleasure.

He gripped my thighs. "Did you make these beautiful legs shake,"
he asked, rough and tentative, "when you touched yourself to thoughts
of me?"

"Yes," I said without hesitation. "So many times, I lost count."

A hand roamed up my back to cup my head and tangle in my hair
as he released a groaned breath. The shaken exhale made his heart
beat faster. I held him closer and trailed my lips over his chest to a
new scar at his shoulder.

I kissed it and felt his lips at my hairline. "I never stopped thinking of you."

"Never?" he asked, gruff.

"Not an hour could pass by, not even in my dreams."

I heard him swallow, and my mouth moved to his throat. I kissed
it too, my name whispered when I dragged my lips over his dark stubble to meet his. My thighs climbed his hips. My body rocked forward,
needing him to move.

He gave it to me. With a sharp thrust of his hips, he began to
fuck me in earnest. Clasping my cheek, he forced my head back. He
studied my every feature with parted lips and roughening breaths, his
hips moving faster.

I moaned, long and loud, and licked his thumb when he stroked
the corner of my lips.

He rumbled a hummed approval and aimed with that incredible
precision. I shattered so slowly, it was near painful, but he didn't slow

or stop. Not even when my nails sank into his chest. My breathy cries were hushed with a soft murmur at my ear, "You can take it, wildflower. We both know you can."

A croaked plea was my only response.

The wolf smirked as he leaned back just far enough to inspect my flushed and struggling state. "Did he ever do this to you?" When I didn't answer, for I couldn't, he added, "Did he make you beg for mercy, even though you wanted none?"

"No," I said, but I would say nothing more. I took his face within my tingling hands, and I kissed his nose, then nipped his mouth. "Never have I felt as crazed." I slid my tongue under his upper lip. "So out of control"—I met his eye—"as I do with you."

His mouth crushed mine, his hands gripping my cheeks and hair. Our joined bodies rocked, my hand reaching down to touch myself. His tongue left mine when he realized what I was doing, and he pushed my hand away. "Me."

I grinned when his eye widened upon the finger I placed in my mouth.

Scythe's nostrils flared when I sucked, his hips jerking when he shivered. "That was mine, too." I laughed, and he cursed, his shoulders shaking. "Beautiful, stars-sent creature." He stole my mouth again, my clit rubbed and pressed as he speared into my body with careful cruelty, over and over.

Pleasure took him in a trembling onslaught of hoarse expletives.

I trapped them all against my lips, kissing him, and so close, I knew I'd soon explode once more. Then he flicked me, and I was gifted a rasping chuckle when I came apart. His hands slid down to my ass and lifted—forced my hips to his body while he emptied inside me.

"I'm far from done," he said to the curve of my shoulder, his mouth caressing the skin. "So maybe you should quickly eat something…"

I smiled and lifted my gown over my head, revealing my bare breasts.

He blinked and took one in his hand. "You can eat later."

TWENTY-TWO

Scythe

T HE DAGGER WAS A DULL PIECE OF WEAPONRY, NO JEWELS OR fancy embellishments, but Aster still studied it with rapt attention while I sharpened it.

It wasn't fear that kept her staring. I could sense it was something else. She confirmed as much when she asked, "How many did you lose?"

"During the battle?"

Her fingers stilled over my head, which had made a home in her lap. I looked up to find her now watching me. "It must have been terrifying—all those humans crawling ashore and through your land."

I pondered that for a moment, noting the absent murkiness to her gaze. She was lost to thoughts of such a thing happening. "You could say it was unexpected yet wholly expected at the same time."

She frowned, tilting her head and blinking. "Why?"

I shrugged and ran the stone over my blade again. "We had it coming, Errin and Sinshell working together to stop our attacks, but I must admit"—I skimmed my thumb over the sharpened edge of the dagger—"we most certainly never expected an army of that magnitude."

Aster was quiet for some time. Her gaze drifted to my chest of drawers, absent yet again.

To say I was relieved she was still here, and that she still wanted anything to do with me after the way I'd behaved when I hadn't known what to do with her, was putting it mildly. I didn't deserve her. Not one piece of me deserved any of her.

But she seemed to want to stay regardless, so I would try to keep from losing my mind to worry.

Mere hours had passed since I'd last taken her upon the bed we laid naked on, and I couldn't help but fear that now I'd satisfied her enough to calm us both, that perhaps she was wondering what she would do next.

"Aster," I started, prepared to finally ask about the swine husband I wanted to erase from our memories.

But then she smiled, fingers stroking down my hairline to my jaw, and asked, "Could you make a tiny boat?"

I almost cut myself with the blade. "A what?"

"A boat," she repeated. "Kloon and Jats could do with a better functioning one for when they fish in the pond."

"Kloon and…" I muttered, and then my confusion cleared. "You mean the elves?" Surely, she couldn't actually care a thing about the rodents.

But her smile bloomed, breathtaking. My chest spasmed. As did my achingly hard cock, which I'd been trying to ignore since it last left her body, for I knew she needed rest.

"Do not encourage them, wildflower."

Her smile fell, and I wanted to immediately take back my words—to offer her anything she desired. "Why not?"

"They're pests. Royal pains in my fucking ass."

"They're not pests," she said, her cheeks reddening and her eyes narrowing. "They're little folk and rare."

"Not here, they're not."

Outraged, she demanded, "What have they ever done to you?"

"Besides trespass on my fucking land to help themselves to anything they want?" I huffed. "Their sheer audacity to continue existing, really."

Aster lifted my head and promptly dumped it upon the bed before scooting to the edge.

I grabbed her ankle before she could. She squealed, laughing when I tugged her back and loomed over her. "There it is."

"There's what?"

"That laugh," I murmured, lowering for my nose to brush her soft cheek. "That fucking smile." I kissed her cheek, inhaled her fragrance deep, and her thighs opened wider when my hips dropped and reared back.

Slippery and ready for me when the head of my cock nudged at the opening to her perfect cunt, she moaned when I sank inside.

"I could live inside you," I whispered, shivering when her hands explored my back and her body welcomed mine like a velvet glove made just for me.

"I wouldn't protest."

I kissed her jaw, and her head tilted for my mouth to fuse to her neck. "No?"

"No," she exhaled. Her nails dug grooves when I withdrew and took my time plunging back into her body. "All I want is this."

"My cock?"

A giggle squeezed my shaft, and I groaned. "You, wolf." She clasped my chin, bringing my eye to hers. "All of you."

Thrusting deeper, harder, I stared down at her with my heart in my throat and my soul on the line. "Stay with me." I swallowed, amending, "Stay here with me."

Her brows puckered. "Live here with you?"

I nodded, fearing I might not breathe until she gave me an answer.

A moment later, her searching eyes grew glossy with tears. Her thumb brushed over my cheek. "I would love nothing more."

Three pounded knocks on the door gave away Fang's mood before I even opened it, still pulling a pair of pants on.

He was too pissed off to crack a joke as I buckled them and stood shirtless before him. "You didn't show for family dinner."

"Shit." Due to the madness that had overtaken my brain, I'd lost track of nearly all else. Guilt punched at my chest. "I fucking forgot, okay? I'll head over there tomorrow and—"

"Mother's beyond upset." Fang's eyes flashed. His nostrils widened as he sniffed and peered behind me.

Aster was leaving the bedchamber. I turned to find her mercifully dressed in one of my tunics and waving at Fang.

Fuck.

"Well, well." Brows high and a smirk lighting his eyes, the asshole returned her wave with wiggling fingers. "And who might you be?"

I growled and stepped outside, forcing him back while pulling the door closed. "None of your concern."

"Nice try, but this is too fascinating. You never bring anyone here." He frowned, laughing a little with shock. "Shit, you barely let me inside this fucking hovel." He looked back at the door, and it dawned. "That's your captive?"

His features grew slack and then tightened. Before he could open his mouth again, I marched down the path and into the thin layer of trees that separated my home from the outskirts of the city beyond.

I'd known this moment would arrive before I wanted it to, yet I'd been too caught up in the female I'd never thought I'd see again to prepare for it.

"Stars stun me." He'd ceased walking, and I whirled when he said, "You don't have a captive, you lying asshole. You're fucking mated, and you're keeping it a secret?" He stepped closer and hissed, "Why?"

"It's…" I braced my feet apart and crossed my arms over my chest. "Still fresh."

"Bullshit." Fang studied me for a moment, his head shaking as he laughed low. "No, you've been even more torturous to be around than usual over these last few years, and she"—he stabbed a finger toward the cottage—"is the same female I scented in your apartment that time you didn't show at the Keep."

"You don't know what you're muttering about."

"But I do, don't I?" Fang pressed, his eyes alight with knowing. "I fucking do, and your unwillingness to share anything right now merely confirms it. She broke your miserable excuse for a heart, didn't she? And now she has returned to you." He snarled when I stayed silent, "So who is she? Why keep her a secret?"

"I don't need to tell you anything."

His brows lowered, and his features fell lax. "No," he said. "You don't, but if you want her kept a secret, it would be fucking nice to at least know why."

He was right.

He was also the closest thing I had to a trustworthy friend and a real brother. But I didn't know what to do or what to say. Stuck, I decided on some form of honesty. "She's not from here, okay?"

Impatient, Fang waved a hand before him. "Okay, and…?"

"And," I gritted, "after everything, it would not be wise for everyone to know that just yet."

He pursed his lips in thought, then cursed. "You mean to tell me she is indeed from *Wistensia?*"

I refrained from wincing, adding, "And she's married."

Fang tensed, his dark eyes comically wide.

He blinked, slow and then repeatedly. "I see." I nodded, thankful for that much at least. Though I hated having to even say it, the marriage was a huge problem. A problem I didn't know how to solve just yet.

What was I supposed to do? Kill the bastard? Simply try to pretend the marriage did not exist? It took two agreeing parties to terminate a marriage, and if he'd been willing, he'd have already let Aster go.

Fang rubbed at his cheek. "Leave it to you to break the law in every way you can possibly get away with." He chuckled. "Stealing some poor idiot's wife and claiming she's a war criminal in order to hide her."

"You think I want it like this?" I said, close to seething. "She's my mate, asshole."

Mirth left his eyes at that, and he sighed. "So what are you going to do?"

"Other than try to keep her from running away again, I honestly have no fucking idea," I admitted. "She only just came back."

"Why after all this time?"

"She'd heard of the human army, and she can warp."

"She feared for your life," he said with a snort. "How unnecessarily sweet." I gnashed my teeth, and he grinned. "You know..." His smile wavered. "Dade won't like this."

"It has nothing to do with him."

"Ah, but I think it does. Otherwise, you wouldn't have lied to him. You'd be marching around the Keep with the smug look of a male who'd found and thoroughly claimed his counterpart."

He let that sit there for some moments, and I surrendered a little more. "He'll want to speak with her. Ask her what she might know of the king who sent all those human soldiers here."

"And why would that be a problem?" he asked in a way that implied he knew it would be.

It shouldn't have been an issue. Yet I couldn't bear the thought of exposing her to our king—of letting anyone know where to strike to wound me beyond repair. "I plan to talk to her myself." For whatever Aster might know and however she'd heard of the war that had resulted in her return to Vordane, I had faith that she would eventually tell me.

Fang was quiet for a half minute. Then carefully, he murmured, "He does care, you know. He wouldn't harm her." He paused. "He wouldn't harm you, either. No matter what he discovered."

That remained to be seen, for we certainly couldn't hide this forever.

"When are you going to finally realize that not everyone is untrustworthy?" Fang asked, exasperated. "You've known and served Dade for nearly two decades now."

Indeed, I'd known the king almost as long as I'd known Fang. But although Fang knew my past was to blame for the way I was, he still didn't understand, and I wasn't sure how to make him.

Smoke puffed from the chimney of the cottage through the trees, luring my feet toward it. "Just keep it quiet until I figure everything out."

TWENTY-THREE

Aster

SCYTHE HAD RETURNED FROM WORKING WITH HIS LEGION mere minutes before there was another beating upon the door to his cottage the following evening.

We both glanced at the shaken wood, and Scythe cursed. He looked at me with his lip between his teeth, then at the door again. "I have to," is all he said before walking rigidly to it.

I frowned at his unusual display of fear as he hesitated before turning the handle.

"Dinner," a short and beautiful brunette said. "Thirty minutes." She crouched to catch a glimpse of me beneath Scythe's arm. "Hello there." A warm smile lasted only a moment. "I'll be expecting you, too."

Scythe said nothing in return. He closed the door when she left and stared at it, tense and expelling a violent, "Fuck."

I wasn't sure whether to laugh or demand to know who she was, so I did both. "Who was that?"

"Mariana," he said.

Oh.

I rubbed my lips, watching Scythe attempt to compose himself. "Seems to me like you might be in a touch of trouble."

"Your fault." He smirked when he crossed the room to where I remained in the armchair. Gripping it, he leaned down and whispered to my mouth, "Best get that gown back on and help me out of it."

He left me dazed and more nervous than I'd felt in months. The heady feelings made me smile as I slipped back into the gown I'd mercifully washed while Scythe had been carrying out his duties for the day.

It was still faintly marred with blood in places, mainly the sleeves, and torn at the shoulder and hem. I made a mental note to inquire about the gowns at Olivianna's as Scythe brought my clasped hand to his mouth, and we walked along the riverfront.

The moon was the same shape as his scarred eye. My stomach warmed when he rubbed my knuckles over his soft lips. "I'll murder Fang for his inability to keep his damned mouth shut."

"Why is she so displeased with you?" I dredged the courage to ask.

Scythe clutched my hand to his chest, pulling me into his side. "I missed family dinner last night."

I recalled Fang visiting him the evening prior and nodded. Relieved it was not because of me, at least, not entirely, I relaxed against him as the first row of houses bordering the city came into view.

"If you're worried, we don't have to go."

I squeezed his hand. "We do."

It was clear that this family of Fang's was also his own, even if that hadn't always been the case. Even if perhaps he was too afraid to admit such a thing to himself. They meant something to him, and anyone who meant something to this incredibly guarded creature was someone I knew I'd want to know.

The townhouse made from brown stone sat on the corner of the first block outside of the woods.

Its tall windows overlooked the river. Beneath them were white wooden boxes overflowing with crimson roses. The same dotted the hedges in the small front garden.

A white door with a brass knocker in the shape of a wolf waited above two wooden steps at the end of the garden path, and it opened before we'd even reached it.

Fang hurried out, his hands raised. "I know what you're thinking, but I swear, I didn't tell them a rotting thing." After a quick glance behind him into the house, he lowered his voice and spoke behind his hand. "You know how she is. She knew I wasn't telling her something, so she took matters into her own hands."

Scythe's jaw unclenched as he studied the male with long brunette hair. He was just as tall as the giant beside me but leaner with far less muscular bulk.

His dark eyes narrowed upon my hand in Scythe's, then widened when he truly looked at me. "This male?" he asked, blinking once and hard as he jabbed his thumb at Scythe. "Are you certain the fates chose right, and it is him you want?"

Rubbing his hands together, Fang grinned and stepped back when Scythe released a low, throaty growl. "I'm Fang."

"Aster," I said with a trained smile.

"Fang is short for Fanerin," Scythe supplied with obvious pleasure.

I smiled in earnest when Fang scowled at him. "You promised to cease calling me that years ago." His features hardened, and his eyes shined a brighter brown as he snarled, "I have it written in blood."

"And you should know better than to think I'd keep my word after you blatantly ogled my mate."

A swooping creature took flight in my chest at hearing him say that.

Fang's features twisted with annoyance. He groaned and entered the townhouse when a female I could only assume was Mariana called for him.

Scythe chuckled silently when she scolded her son, then led me inside.

I was immediately engulfed in a hug by the strawberry-scented female. She patted my arms as she pulled away with wet eyes and said, "Let me get a good eyeful of you." Her full lips parted, and her soft brown cheeks flushed as she gripped my upper arms and looked at Scythe. "Where in the stars did you find such a divine creature for yourself?"

Scythe's broad smile made my heart kick as he collected a fistful of peppered nuts from the small bowl on the kitchen island and tossed them into his mouth. "In a tavern."

Mariana frowned up at me. "What is a female such as you doing loitering in taverns?"

I laughed, taking her hands and saying, "I've heard wonderful things about you."

Mariana's eyes glistened again. She gave them to Scythe, who gave the female a devastating grin that had her releasing a thick song of laughter. "Oh, how can I stay upset with you?"

My own eyes grew a little wet when Scythe swallowed the tiny female in a hug. "Is there tart?"

Scoffing, she withdrew from him and gently smacked his chest with the towel she snatched from the island. "Out. Go sit."

"This is so warm," I murmured to Scythe as he took me by the hand and led me down the wood-floored hall. Portraits hung upon the wall of Fang and Scythe, and I halted by the last one I saw.

Scythe waited, his fingers tight around mine as I traced the younger version of him. His ruined eye was reddened, as though it had taken some time for the scarring to settle into the shape of the smooth scythe moon it now was. It was the fear in his remaining emerald eye that struck me cold. "How old were you here?"

"Fourteen years," he said, toneless. "I hadn't wanted my portrait painted, but Berk had ordered me not to break his wife's heart." He huffed lightly. "I barely lasted long enough for the painter to complete it. Berk had to compensate him for the stool I wrecked."

"Wrecked?" I asked, turning to him.

He dragged his eye from the portrait of his young self. "Deep claw marks."

I stepped into him and rose onto my toes to place a kiss upon his cheek, then I headed into the dining room.

He beat me to my chair and untucked it.

Fang stopped rocking on his own to watch us with mirth dancing in his eyes. "Never thought I'd see it."

Scythe's chair groaned when he seated himself next to me. "Shut your mouth."

Fang was not deterred in the slightest. "This male," he said, making sure he had my full attention before continuing, "he's never so much as purchased a beverage for a female before taking her home to bed."

My stomach squirmed. I bit the inside of my cheek to keep from showing how I felt about being made to think of this mate of mine with another.

"Last warning," Scythe growled and tossed an apple I barely saw him snatch from the fruit bowl at the table's center.

Fang caught it right before his long nose, then bit into the fruit with a grin that warned of more torment to come.

"I'm just stating a truth, though," Fang said, chewing the apple as Mariana entered the room to place steaming dishes upon the table. "And I've some more where that came from."

"Do not tease him," Mariana warned.

A repetitive clopping sounded over the floor outside of the room.

"You've never once told him to stop teasing me," Fang protested, mouth agape.

"Because you usually deserve it," said a male from the doorway. He lowered his head to kiss Mariana's cheek before she flitted back down the hall toward the kitchen.

Then the new male with shaggy mud-colored hair and a limp to his step entered the dining room with a walking cane. "Who have we here?" He gave a derisive snort. "Another one of Fanerin's attempts to..." He stopped, nostrils twitching, and looked from me to Scythe with wide brown eyes. "Yours?"

Scythe, rubbing at his chin, failed to hide his smile. "This is Aster."

I smiled once more and fought the urge to rise to my feet to greet him properly.

The male blinked down at me from across the table. He frowned as he searched my face and my form, perhaps even my posture, far too thoroughly for my liking.

"This is Berk," Scythe said, pointedly enough that Berk tore his studious gaze from me and continued to his seat at the head of the table.

Fang's brows wiggled at us as his father settled into his chair. "He's one of the most surliest creatures you'll ever meet, but you'll soon get used to it." Helping himself to the chicken upon the table, he tore off a leg and said with far too much pleasure, "You know, being that you're mates and all."

Berk grumbled something that sounded like, "I'll give you surly, you ungrateful shit."

"Manners," Mariana hissed and set the last dish on the table before taking her seat at the opposite end. "We have a guest."

"Can you even call Aster as much when she will be present at future dinners?" Fang asked, and Scythe seemed poised to leap across the table to wipe the smug smile from his face when he said again, "For they are mates."

Berk grunted and poured himself a large glass of whiskey from a crystal decanter. "And here I'd thought the stars would fall first…"

"Do not poke fun at a blessing," Mariana said. "Eat."

We did, and as my stomach grew impossibly full, as did my chest when Fang regaled me with tales of the pranks he and Scythe had pulled on Berk over the years.

All the while, Berk seldom removed his attention from me.

Suspicion leaked from his dark eyes. I did my best to ignore it— to enjoy the warmth from not only the fire in the small hearth in the corner of the room but also from the company of the family surrounding me.

Mariana cleared some of the dishes, but returned shortly after with a blueberry tart, of which I couldn't possibly dream of squeezing into my overloaded stomach.

Scythe seemed to sense this, and he curled his arm over the back of my chair to stroke the hair resting upon my shoulder.

"Oh, and once," Fang continued. "Scythe here took the liberty of fixing the old wolf's favored chair with an entire pot of glue after we broke it while fighting in the sitting room."

"To be fair, I was actually trying to help."

"Help?" Berk snorted. "I lost a good shirt and two layers of skin."

"But you did get the new chair you'd been whining about wanting for months," Fang said, licking beetroot sauce from his fingers.

"I don't fucking whine."

"Yes, you do," all three of them said in unison.

When the laughter settled, Mariana set her gaze upon me as she sipped her wine, and Scythe refilled my own glass.

"And what do you like to do with yourself, dear?" she asked. "I do hope it doesn't involve visiting taverns frequently. Those in this city are too often filled with males looking for a spot of trouble or a fleetingly fun time."

I bit my lips at that and shook my head. "I, well..." Having no idea what to say, I said the first and only thing that came to mind. "I love to paint."

"Oh?" Delight lightened her eyes. "How splendid. I work at the orphanage, which is now, unfortunately, undergoing some much-needed expanding. There are younglings who could do with more color in their lives, especially right now. Perhaps you could come by and show them a thing or two?"

Unable to stop myself, I looked at Scythe. He opened his mouth, then closed it with a frown as he stared at me.

Fang's mischievous grin waned as he watched us.

There was nothing else to do but smile as genuinely as I could and say, "I would really love that."

"Wait," Berk barked. "What was your name again?"

I tore my gaze from Scythe, who was scowling at Berk. I cleared my throat and said, "Aster."

"Aster," Berk repeated, as if scrutinizing every letter like he did my face. "Is that short for—"

Fang cursed when his elbow slipped from the table and knocked his glass. Water tipped into his father's lap.

Berk merely glared at him—knowing exactly what he'd been playing at.

I wasn't sure how much Fang knew, but I was grateful he seemed to sense an intervention was needed.

Mariana fetched a dish towel and tossed it to her son. "No need for that, Fanerin. My stars." She tutted, then rounded the table to pat my shoulder. "We're very good at keeping secrets, dear, don't you worry. Here, have some tart." She dragged the dish toward my plate before heading to her seat. "It fixes everything, even if only momentarily." Her chestnut, long-lashed eyes twinkled knowingly. "Sometimes a moment is just what we need."

Scythe took my hand beneath the table and stroked it with his thumb.

Later that night, as the stars shone through the window behind the bed, Scythe slept with his head upon my stomach. I'd been so full from dinner that he'd taken me slowly from behind before we'd both fallen limp upon the bed.

He woke with a grunted snore and turned to stare up at me. "Okay, wildflower?"

"Perfect," I said, and I meant it.

On the way back to the cottage, he'd told me not to worry about Berk. I wasn't worried about him, and I wondered if he could sense that.

"I know it was a lot," Scythe said after a moment, voice rough with sleep. "The dinner and—"

"No," I said, stopping him. "I loved it." I continued stroking his head as he nestled closer and kissed my stomach, whispering to the ceiling, "A little too much."

TWENTY-FOUR

Scythe

THE WAR ROOM WAS THE LAST PLACE I WANTED TO BE, AND SO I made quick work of eating the pastries Opal had brought with her before Fang pocketed them all to eat later. Which was what he'd done last time she'd brought treats to a meeting.

The nuisance mouthed the word, "Mates," to me from across the table and licked his sugar-dusted fingers.

I looked at the jam-filled pastry in my hand, tempted. He smirked when I chose to eat it instead of throw it at his head.

Fang's mocking aside, I couldn't help but dwell on the matter myself.

All morning, I'd wondered over Berk's reaction to Aster last night, and of all I knew she still hadn't divulged to me. It sat beneath the surface of her every look and touch—a trepidation she felt she couldn't yet give voice to.

I was far from patient. But I was so far out of my element that I would accept whatever she was most comfortable giving in hopes of not making her anxieties any worse than they clearly already were.

Dade slurped his tea, and I gnashed my teeth.

Fang chuckled.

Opal's gaze burned, and I finally looked over to find she'd been waiting. "What?"

Dade's teacup nearly cracked when he dumped it back into his saucer and said, "Manners, you miserable fuck."

"He's no longer so miserable, king," Fang supplied.

Dade's annoyance fell into a smirk. "And how is our captive?"

To better ignore and annoy him, I said to Opal, "You said something I missed, my queen?" Last I knew from when I'd been paying attention, they'd all been discussing Queen Nikaya—Opal's mother. Apparently, Sinshell's queen and her new lover, Silver, had gleaned little of use from a meeting with Errin's human queen.

Of course, Queen Sabrina could be lying through her teeth, especially after losing her son to the war he helped to create. But it was in her best interest not to if she wished to continue breathing after all she'd done.

Errin, the human kingdom of Nodoya, had sent out a call for aid to end Dade's attacks upon their half of the continent, and the gold-touched clothing had been used to gain that help. Sabrina had since admitted to Nikaya and Silver that no one had been interested in risking their lives.

No one except for King Marvis, from the Isle of Emerald.

Dead giveaway... that scar.

Unsure what to do with the knowledge I'd discovered during the battle with those who'd been sent to kill not just any faerie they happened upon—but to kill me—I had no choice but to keep quiet for now. Dishonest, most certainly, but after all these years, also extremely necessary. Even so, I'd made a mental note to talk to Berk about it as soon as I could catch him alone.

Yet I was also never more certain that I was not the sole reason all those soldiers had ventured across the sea.

Opal asked me, "She still hasn't talked?"

I gave my gaze back to my pastry and tore it in two, feigning a lewd drawl, "Define talking, Majesty."

Dade cursed viciously.

"No." My chair creaked as I sat back and smirked. "Not about anything that would be of use to any of you. Your gold," I said to Opal, to change the subject—and because a tiny part of me was reluctantly curious. "Can you still weave it or not?"

"Whether she is capable is irrelevant."

"I disagree, my king," Fang said, shockingly serious. "Now that everyone knows of her gift, we need to know if it remains in order to better guess at what might befall us in future."

Dade glanced at Opal, who nodded and sipped her tea. The king licked his teeth and sighed. "She has tried and has so far been unsuccessful, but it has been mere weeks since she released the glowing. What does it have to do with anything?"

Fang was now staring down at claw marks in the table. He was leaving this to me, then.

"If the ability remains, the gold stitched clothing Errin's royals sent offshore to lure those vermin to battle with us could make them try their luck again."

Dade captured my meaning, reclining back in his seat with less color to his cheeks. "You don't mean…"

But Opal understood. "I've wondered it myself," she admitted, trailing a long finger around the rim of her teacup. "If perhaps the goal was not merely to hunt and kill because they hate us and they'd been paid to do so, but to also find the source of the gold-woven clothing."

Dade's jaw went rigid, his eyes downcast upon the table. His stiff posture, the ire flaring his energy, made it clear he hadn't spared much thought for this.

I didn't rub the mishap in. For the better part of the past couple of weeks, he'd been healing alongside his princess—queen now— while also navigating the miserable task of cleaning up and rehoming the displaced who'd survived the bloody invasion.

But I did suggest carefully, "Something to ponder. I'll see what I can pry from the prisoners while we still can."

As it was, I'd made sure that only a few remained. They were quiet in the dungeon next door to the underground war room we sat in, no longer rabid and desperate for escape that would never arrive but slowly dying.

Fang eyed our king, the pastries forgotten.

I rose from my seat. "Until next time."

Unexpectedly, Opal offered a warm smile.

Stunned, I didn't return it, but I nodded quickly and took my leave before Dade's worry became a storm cloud heavier than those outside.

TWENTY-FIVE

Aster

THE SIGN UPON OLIVIANNA'S SHOP WINDOW SAID THAT IT WAS open, so I let myself in to escape the rain.

I didn't realize doing so would be a mistake until the wolf who had the seamstress pressed against the wall with his hand up her skirts stilled and flung familiar dark eyes over his shoulder. "Well, fuck."

Unsure what to do, I stood frozen.

Olivianna peered over Fang's shoulder with wide eyes, then laughed and smacked at his chest. "Put me down."

"No need," I said, then winced at the absurdity of saying such a thing and retreated toward the door. "I'll come back later."

"He was just leaving."

"I was?" Fang chuckled when she scowled at him. He kept his back to me as he adjusted Olivianna's skirts and his tight britches. "Fine, I was."

He then stalked past me with a fiendish grin and sang, "Be sure to talk all about me."

Olivianna rolled her eyes but smiled at his back.

I watched him go, looking at Olivianna when the door closed. "I'm sorry."

The talented seamstress waved her hand dismissively. "Don't be. The commander is but a lovely pest I can't seem to force myself to be rid of. You did me a favor."

I withheld a smile. "A pest?"

Oliviana made a face—an expression that said she was at a loss for what else to say—and gestured to the chaise. "Sit, we need tea." She then disappeared through a door behind her into a dark room.

I sat and listened to the clang of teaspoons and teacups, wondering what I'd just walked in on. Though, if her remark and reaction were anything to go by, it would seem Oliviana might often find herself wondering the same thing.

The word pest suggested Fang was a frequent visitor to Oliviana's home and place of business. I smiled down at my hands in my lap, glad for it if it brought her happiness after seemingly being let down by love before with little Ryon's father.

Oliviana soon reappeared and placed a floral spotted cup of tea upon the table. "Dare I ask if you and the angry beast have resolved things?"

She evidently no longer wished to talk of her own situation with one of Vordane's commanders, so I thanked her and wiggled aside so that she could join me on the chaise. "Enough for now, I suppose."

"You suppose?"

Indeed, there was much to still be discussed with Scythe, and although the terror of it all made my chest constrict, I knew I would need to tell him everything in order for us to figure out how this would work. For us to figure out if it *could* truly work, or if we were merely on borrowed time once again.

Rorn would never release me from our marriage. Scythe had vowed to never lose me.

It all seemed... irrevocably impossible.

So much so, I could hardly stand to think of what might lay ahead. But hiding the extent of the truth for too long would not help matters. It was time Scythe knew all of it.

And perhaps once he did, he would not be so desperate to make sure I stayed. I was tempted to snort as I imagined being thrown out of his cottage, my beautiful gowns of which I'd come to collect tossed to the grass after me before my beast slammed the door.

I sighed, both disappointed and immensely relieved to know that was unlikely, and picked up my lemon tea. "He's calmed down, but he was called to the Keep at first light. There's still much for us to discuss."

I'd left a note upon the dining table, explaining where I'd gone just in case he returned to the cottage before I did.

"Later, then," Olivianna said, blowing on her tea with a knowing glint in her eye.

I smiled and sipped. "Yes, later."

Little Ryon raced downstairs, jumping from the last two and landing with the grace of a wolf he was perhaps going to become. "You're back." I set my tea down as he hurried over, two pieces of parchment in his hand. "You forgot your pictures." He spread them over the table, nearly knocking my tea over.

I shifted it aside, smiling bright when I glimpsed the...

The handprint of blood upon a doorframe.

Olivianna hummed, the sound throaty as if she were withholding a laugh. "Quite good, aren't they? Very... realistic."

The other picture was of Scythe—or rather, of his scarred eye.

"Indeed," I said, smiling wide. "In fact, I don't think I've ever seen pictures quite like this."

Olivianna snorted, and Ryon frowned at her.

I tapped the picture of my handprint. "You are very talented. Just look at this detail."

He beamed, leaning on the table and kicking his legs out behind him. "Mama says you know the angry wolf."

I laughed. "I do indeed. Would you like me to show him this?"

Ryon nodded. "You keep them."

I feigned a gasp, pressing my hand to my heart. "Truly?"

His smile stretched, displaying a crooked canine and two dimples.

Olivianna stilled beside me, then set her teacup down in the saucer with a clatter. Ryon whirled to face the door.

A female with golden hair and eyes stood in the doorway. "I do hope I'm not interrupting. I can come back."

"Not at all." Olivianna rose and curtsied. "Come in, come in."

Ryon bowed, and rushed to hug her legs. "Opal!"

My stomach sank. Royalty.

If it weren't the show of respect and sudden tension in the air that gave that away, then it was her posture, the opulent gown of cream and crystal blue silk and gentle ruffles.

Belatedly, I realized I should rise too, and I lowered into a clumsy curtsy. Opal noticed, closing the door, and eyed me curiously. "I do not believe we've met."

"This is Aster. A friend..." Olivianna looked at me, finishing with, "A friend of mine."

Although I knew why she'd said it, I still felt that she'd meant it. My heart warmed. I gave her a smile.

"Aster, this is my friend and our new queen, Opal."

"The swan," I said before I could help myself.

Opal's smile waned, and color stained her cheeks. "It would seem that's a widely known fact now."

"Now that you've set the night ablaze with daylight to save our king, you mean?" Olivianna teased. "I don't know, possibly."

Opal laughed. Olivianna showed her to the armchair opposite the chaise, then we retook our seats. Ryon bounded over, stealing the queen's attention from me. He shoved the parchment right before her nose. "Look what I made for Aster."

"Oh my," Opal said, brows high. Gently, she took the artwork from him, her lithe fingers tracing the bloodied handprint.

"And this one," he said. Olivianna and I both tensed as he handed the picture of Scythe's gaze to her as well.

Opal studied them for a long moment—too long. Her golden eyes lifted from the artwork to me, then to Olivianna. She feigned a smile that looked nothing less than genuine and brushed her hand beneath Ryon's chin. "I fear I am feeling a little forgotten."

Ryon stilled in his bouncing. "Forgotten?"

"You've never drawn me a picture, that's why." A musical laugh settled the frozen youngling, as she then said, "They are so good, I simply must have one of my own."

Ryon gasped. "Okay." He then raced upstairs to get to work.

I watched him go, feeling the queen's eyes upon me like a kiss from the sun. Without meeting them, I picked up my tea and took a hearty sip.

Olivianna cleared her throat. "Vivid imagination, that one. Cup of tea?"

"Very," Opal concurred, and mercifully, she let whatever she was piecing together be. "No, thank you. I must be quick, I'm afraid."

"Still fretting, is he?"

Opal rolled her eyes, though her soft pink lips curved. "I've probably got a half hour before he finishes with his rounds, and then he'll be in a panic."

While it was somewhat comforting to know that most wolves seemed to be the same—overly protective and slightly neurotic—I couldn't help but wonder if King Dade was worried over the well-being of his swan after the war.

For what Rorn had alluded to had indeed come to fruition, and she'd unleashed the ancient glowing to save her mate.

A quick survey showed no sign of ill-health. In fact, I'd seldom seen a female as beautiful and radiant as she. Her long golden waves curled over her ample chest. Those high cheeks and rare eyes shined with contentment.

"You are well?" I thought it safe to ask, for it was what one of her citizens would do. That, and I was tempted to discover how she felt after such an overflow of power.

"Oh, I'm fine. It's been weeks, and I'm only getting stronger." Opal tilted her head. "And you?"

"Me?" I asked, close to balking.

"Was that not your handprint Ryon showed me just now?" As

though sensing she'd spoken out of turn, she winced. "Forgive me. I am overstepping."

"Not at all," I reassured her. "I cut my hand, and Olivianna's was the closest residence who would help me," I said, finding it easy for it was mostly the truth.

Staring at my tattered gown, at the bloodstain still present upon the sleeve, the queen chewed her lip. She nodded to Olivianna. "This is how the two of you met, then?"

"It is," the seamstress confirmed.

The lack of explanation for Scythe's unforgettable gaze hung between all of us like a smothering smog that was growing too thick to see through. I feared I might need to admit who he was to me, at the very least. Being that Opal didn't already know, I struggled to bring myself to.

Olivianna mercifully intervened. "The garments you requested are ready." She stood. "Though I did have some trouble sourcing the sky-blue cotton. My usual supply chains think it will be some months until stock isn't so thin after the war. I settled on a lovely teal instead."

Vordane's new queen rose from the chair and followed Olivianna to a rack at the very back of the shop.

Though I was tempted to take the gowns I could see hanging on the rack closest to the door and leave, I waited and finished my tea. Fleeing would only arouse more suspicion, and as I sipped, I felt foolish for even considering it.

There was nothing to be afraid of. The queen wouldn't know that I was one myself if she discovered that I was mated to the commander of one of her husband's legions. But I would talk to Scythe before I made a move as bold as letting our accepted bond be known in such a large way.

I finished the delightful tea while listening to the two female's faint laughter and chatter, wishing and perhaps hoping too heavily to one day find such companionship.

Scythe was in the kitchen, stirring a pot of what smelled like beef stew. "I met someone special today," I said by way of greeting and closed the door with my backside to keep from disturbing the gowns.

As it was, I'd warped to the front yard of the cottage to ensure their volume did not break anything on display in the city streets and so that nothing damaged them. I draped the gowns over the back of an armchair.

"There's a rack for them in the bedchamber," he said. "Behind the door."

I wandered to the room and plucked it out. I set it in the small space available along the wall by the bed, then fetched the gowns.

When I returned, Scythe tapped the wooden spoon upon the pot and placed it down. He leaned against the counter. "You might have left a note, but you failed to do something else."

I wrapped my arms around his waist and untucked his tunic from his pants, in search of the smooth skin of his back. "Oh?" I smiled up at him.

His lips twitched, breaking his stony expression. "You didn't kiss me as soon as you arrived."

"Is that a rule?" I taunted, rising onto my toes for my lips to near his.

"A requirement, really."

"And the note?"

He gripped my ass, squeezing, and whispered to my lips, "Unnecessary but appreciated."

My heart swelled, and I looped my arms around his neck as soon as our lips met. I opened his, felt the warmth of him invade, and welcomed it, my body both calming and heating.

He seemed to feel the same. His shoulders loosened, and a low groan rumbled within his throat. "Hello, wildflower."

I smiled against his lips. "Hello, wolf."

A peace so freeing settled within me. No matter his mood, no matter the numerous obstacles between us, I'd come to recognize its arrival whenever he was near. Uncanny, that it should exist. That such a thing could be gifted to me from a wolf who was not only capable of murder but who had also spent most of his life bathed in bloodshed.

"I will build you a wardrobe."

"You will not."

He frowned. "I will."

I kissed each corner of his mouth. "Such resources should be given to those who have nothing right now, wolf."

His eye narrowed slightly, as if he were dissecting my choice of words.

The stew bubbled.

He cursed and turned away to tend to it. Then he turned back, his mouth pressing hard to mine, and I laughed. "Sit," he gently ordered. "Tell me who you met."

I grabbed the bowls he'd set on the countertop and took them with me to the table. Cutlery, bread, and a carafe of water already waited at its center. "Your new queen."

He stilled, the question gruff. "Where?"

"She visited Oliviana's while I was there collecting the gowns. Oh, that reminds me." I hurried back to the bedchamber to the gowns where I'd left the pictures Ryon had created in one of the clever pockets Oliviana had sewn into all five of them.

Scythe was pouring dinner into the bowls when I returned.

I unrolled the pictures. "Ryon drew these. From the night I came back."

Scythe peered over at them, then grunted with a smile. "The cub's got a great eye for detail."

I laughed. "That's what I said." I placed the pictures upon the bookshelf. "He wanted to make sure you received yours."

"I'm sure you'll let him know."

"He called you the angry wolf."

"Suppose he's not wrong." Scythe set the pot on the stove. "Come and eat."

I sat down and dug straight in, smiling as he watched me eat every mouthful. "I didn't mean to, you know." At his raised brow, I explained, a little embarrassed, "The weight loss. I just…" I shook my head, unsure if now was the right time to delve into it all. There would never be a good time, I surmised, so I sipped some water and confessed, "I wasn't well."

"You were ill?"

I peered up at him beneath my lashes. "Not well in here." I tapped over my heart, then my head. "And here, I suppose."

Scythe lowered his giant mound of stew-soaked bread, nodding once. "I had wondered if it was something like that."

I ate another mouthful, then said, "I'm not proud of it, but I couldn't…" He waited while I searched for the words. "My life, everything I've ever known, was totally obliterated. I had to learn how to make sense of what it's become."

He seemed to know I wasn't merely referring to him—that he was only a small yet ginormous part of it. "I couldn't escape it," I said softly. "What he'd done and the repercussions. But I was expected to accept it. To move on and live with it."

"You don't have to accept anything you don't wish to now," he said, vehement and too still as he watched me. "You never have to again, Aster."

I nodded. "I wish that were true, and I desperately want it to be." Scythe scowled, and I attempted to ease his alarm. "I want to stay," I reassured him. "I do, but it won't be easy."

"So be it," he stated instantly. "For I'm not letting you go."

Cracks within my heart re-stitched, but my stomach tightened. I gave my attention to my meal.

After a minute, Scythe did, too.

We ate in silence. Lost to the fear and the need to tell him everything, it grew harder to even look at him. But I didn't need to look to know he never once removed his eye from me.

Knowing there was so much more trapped within me, Scythe

said, "If it troubles you, it can wait, Aster. I'm not going anywhere." He rose from the table. "Tell me when you're ready."

I watched him, unable to comprehend how I'd found a male so domineering yet so patient at the same time. But I understood. My wolf had demons of his own, just as Olivianna had warned in this very cottage. I wanted to learn them. I wanted to know every facet that made him who he was, and to let his darkness touch my own.

But I wouldn't force it—force him.

Maybe it was his own secrets that made him capable of such patience, such unexpected empathy. I didn't know. But I was grateful. Grateful yet still certain I could no longer wait. I wanted him to know all of me, and that was only possible if I was honest about what and who I'd run from.

Perhaps we'd stand a chance at making this impossible bond grow into something truly attainable if he knew why it was all so difficult.

Tomorrow, I vowed silently.

"One more night," I murmured while he filled the kitchen sink with soapy water.

Scythe froze.

A moment later, he tossed me a smirk over his shoulder. He shook his head and scrubbed the pot when I smiled at him. "As many as you need, wildflower."

While he cleaned up, I drew a bath.

Scythe built a fire before he rid himself of his clothing while I peeled my ruined gown from my body. He helped me into the tub to sit atop him. I splayed my hands over his chest, sliding them to his shoulders. "You can wield fire."

He did his best to keep from reacting to my statement, but I still saw it—the slight thinning of his luscious mouth.

"The fire," I said. "Every time, you've lit it yourself."

"Been watching me closely, wildflower?"

I grinned.

His mouth curled. "It's not something I flash around often," he said. "It's not an ability I believe I should have for though it's sometimes useful, I don't need it."

"Yet you do have it." I traced his collarbone. "Was one of your parents a wielder of flame?"

"My father," he admitted, and just those two rough and quick words were enough to feel like I'd earned a small victory. A part of me wondered if I could dish out morsels of myself in the same careful way. In a way that wouldn't alarm so much as it would invite curiosity to know more.

I refrained from snorting at the mere thought of casually mentioning anything I had yet to tell him. Ignoring the fear cooling my chest, I said what I'd already assumed to be true, "Your father was of alpha blood."

He nodded, and I sensed that was all I would get for now.

Though I longed to discover what had happened to his parents, to him, and to know why he'd ended up with Mariana and Berk, I let it be.

He would tell me in his own time, which he confirmed with a reassuring gloss of his fingers over my jawline.

My heart and lashes fluttered. "Did you mean what you said? About not going anywhere."

"I mean everything I say, even when I'm an angry wolf."

I rubbed his hair-dusted pectorals and smiled.

He tipped up my chin. "I like the way you give my heart warning."

"Warning?"

He tapped my nose. "This crinkles right before you unleash one of those murderous smiles." Lowering his mouth to my cheek, he said just above a whisper, "Though it warns me of what's to come, it still stops my heart…" He kissed the crest of my cheekbone and leaned back. "Every fucking time."

My cheeks flushed and stretched, and I laughed until his own mouth slackened into a beautiful smile in response. My smile fell as I gave into the urge to devour that mouth with mine.

Before we became too swept away, I gripped his shoulders and pressed my head to the side of his, my eyes still closed. "I want to know," I whispered. "I need to know that no matter what I tell you, you will still feel the same."

"Look at me." I opened my eyes to find that green orb burning bright. "I'm a wolf, wildflower, one with a million atrocities under my belt. I've seen and done too much for anything you reveal to scare me away."

I wanted to believe that. Desperately. "Swear it?"

Curling my hair behind my ear, he clasped my cheek and jaw to study me intently as he traced the arch. "Aster, maybe you should just tell me what happened. Let it out so it stops plaguing you."

"I swear I will, but right now, I just need to know that I won't ever have to go back. That you will still want me to stay." I swallowed. "With you."

"Nothing and no one will ever keep me from you." His eye searched mine. "I swear it on my life."

A weight unlocked in my chest, escaping me in a rushed exhale. I nodded, my eyes damp as I leaned forward to press my lips to his. "Thank you."

"Don't ever thank me." He brushed his fingers down my neck to my arm, gooseflesh rising in their wake. "You're mine. My mate. I'll give you whatever you need, always and gladly."

I reached between us to his length and gripped it. "And what do you need, wolf?"

He sucked in a breath through his teeth, then groaned when I rubbed myself over him. "Just you, wildflower." He brought my mouth to his as I brought him into my body. "Can I keep you?"

"Please do."

Scythe's snarl woke me before he shifted me from his chest to sit upright in bed.

Gently, he shook my shoulder, though I was well and truly awake. He whispered, "Get dressed." Snatching his dagger from the nightstand, he left the room while pulling on a pair of pants.

I didn't ask questions. I reached for the tunic I'd abandoned before heading to Olivianna's and put it on. There was no time for propriety. Scythe was more than on edge. He was prepared to spill blood.

The door to the cottage crashed open.

I hurried from the room right as Scythe went chest to chest with another male. "Hand her over," the stranger ordered.

Scythe growled and shoved the male back. "Over my rotting fucking corpse."

"Easily arranged, especially after a deception such as this."

"A threat?" Scythe stopped before the male. "You should know better."

"It's you who should know better…" The stranger trailed off when I stepped forward from the darkness of the hall and into the dim light of the lamp burning between the armchairs.

His hair was a blond so light it was nearly white. Though he was just as tall as Scythe, he carried less bulk. I didn't think that mattered. He might have been dressed in the black and crimson regalia of a warrior, but I knew that wasn't all he was.

Menace dripped from the intruder's blue eyes as he surveyed me, his features falling into shock.

He sniffed, then looked at Scythe with something akin to outrage and fear. "Of course," he said to him. "It would just have to be someone like her for you, wouldn't it?" Scoffing, he shook his head and turned for the door, his long coat sailing behind him. "Say your goodbyes. Her husband awaits."

I sensed him before I saw him standing mere feet beyond the entry to the cottage, his two favored guards beside him.

Rorn.

Scythe looked back at me, a promise he could no longer keep within his eye. He just hadn't realized it yet. "Wait here, okay?"

I shook my head, but he left before I could stop him. I followed, my heart in my throat and my pulse screaming in my ears when Scythe stalked outside, and I heard Rorn's shocked laugh. "The fates are indeed delightful."

Scythe stood just outside the doorway, unmoving. Perhaps not breathing.

"Scythe?" I whispered at his back.

He said nothing, but he flinched when I skimmed my fingers over his as I rounded him to leave the cottage.

Outside, the blond male stood a small distance from Rorn on the grass.

Rorn's attention remained fastened on Scythe when I stepped between the waiting guards. "If you truly want to wound me, Astrantia, then find yourself a toy with two eyes."

Roye, one of the guards, chuckled. Rollins remained stoic—poised and waiting and undoubtedly uncomfortable.

The blond male, of whom I'd now guessed was King Dade, sneered at Rorn. "Just take her and be gone."

"You've been most helpful, king," Rorn murmured, his gaze still upon my silent wolf, and Scythe's upon him. "I won't soon forget it."

Although the words were polite, Vordane's king understood the hidden meaning beneath them just fine, and he stiffened. "Careful now. It's my understanding that your war-ravaged kingdom cannot withstand much more than it already has."

Rorn tensed, his brows cinched with incredulity as he opened his mouth.

"We should go." I stepped forward before things could further escalate, all the while my heart bleated for Scythe to somehow stop this—to talk to his king. To try something.

Yet I knew his hands were completely tied. I knew it was best that he did nothing.

"Indeed," Rorn said. "We should." Without looking at me, my husband held out his hand, and I placed mine within his. His skin was cool, clammy, and his fingers bruising as they folded through mine. "But do you not wish to say goodbye?" he crooned, soft and daring.

I merely glared, though Rorn still wouldn't look at me.

Vordane's king watched, blue eyes flitting between Scythe and me, as the shadows congregated and split through the dark of night, and we left their land for Wistensia.

Moments later, the familiar yet no longer comforting scent of my paint parlor enveloped me.

The smog cleared to reveal Theenon, who appeared to have been waiting.

Iron manacles were instantly placed around my wrists, their burn burrowing through my skin to my bones. Afterward, Theenon stepped back with his nose in the air. As though he were so displeased with me, he did not care that what he'd done would wound more than my flesh.

I would not be warping anywhere.

Rorn stared at me for endless seconds. I stared back, unwilling to cower and refusing to say a word.

Finally, his ice-struck features cracked with the curling of his upper lip. He made a sound of disgust and turned for the door. "Welcome home, wife."

PART THREE
BLOODY LOVE

TWENTY-SIX

Scythe

DADE STARED AT ME FOR SO LONG, I WAS BEGINNING TO THINK it was a new torture tactic of his. "She was your mate."

"She *is* my mate," I corrected.

The shame of what I'd let happen threatened to split my chest in two until it bled out upon the table in the war room, where Dade had summoned me mere hours after Aster was taken.

Astrantia.

Her true name crawled through me like a parasite. An itch I could never hope to quell.

I should have been furious, and I was, but I couldn't find it within me to feel any more anger toward her. This wasn't her fault. In many ways, it was my own for not encouraging her to tell me the truth—for failing to make her comfortable enough to do so.

Instead, I'd wasted days being an ignorant, insufferable ass when I should've opened my fucking eye to what was truly happening to my mate. I should've realized she wasn't torn between two males—she was fucking stuck with no way out.

I'd known, had guessed, that she was bound in marriage to someone of importance. Someone not so easily deceived and deserted for another. But I'd have never guessed this.

That my past and my future would intertwine so intricately, I would need to claw what I needed free in order to somehow keep it.

Dade continued his slow pacing along the wall lined with maps of Nodoya. "The queen of Wistensia is your mate, and you didn't think to fucking say something?"

"I fail to see why I had to when it was nothing you needed to know."

But that wasn't entirely true.

"She is a queen," Dade repeated.

My teeth met and gritted.

"And you were not even aware, were you?" He slammed his hands down on the table and snarled across it. "You merely wanted to gorge yourself on something that wasn't yours to take."

"She is mine." I stabbed at my chest. "And like you can talk, *king*."

He straightened, his eyes alight with cold, cruel fury. "Now is not the time to act like a rogue prick."

A warning.

I ignored it. "Why did you bring them to my home?" He might have been left with little choice, but it was a betrayal all the same. "Why not make him wait here at the Keep until sunrise, and give me some fucking time to prepare?"

"So you could kill him and make matters worse?" Dade scoffed. "I think fucking not. When a king arrives on your doorstep in the middle of the stars-damned night, demanding for his wife to be found and returned to him, you do not dilly-fucking-dally." He paused, laughing bitterly. "You find out what the fuck is going on and do whatever it takes to avoid another conflict we cannot afford."

I leaned back against the wall, smirking. "So, to put it all simply, you betrayed me."

"I did nothing of the sort." Features twisting, Dade growled, "You betrayed *me*, and not just in this instance."

Silence arrived like an axe poised at our throats.

We both stared, our chests heaving, waiting to see if the other would finally acknowledge the wedge that had sat between us since the day we'd met.

I decided to touch it at the very least, for he was wrong, but he was also right. "You know to speak on it would do none of us any good," I said, low and careful. "None at all."

"And keeping quiet about it for all these years has served you so very well," he fired back smoothly. "Look at you now. Without a mate, without a name, and without a legion to commandeer."

Another blow to my already ravaged chest. Between my teeth, I said, "You cannot take them from me."

"But I can." I waited for the softly delivered threat. "For if you fuck this up any more than you already have, you leave me with no choice but to discharge you."

The dishonor of being discharged from service for anything other than disability was rare. As it was a humiliation most did not survive.

"Say exactly what you mean," I clipped. I didn't need him to spell it out, but I wanted him to make his position abundantly clear. There would be no dancing around words. If he was turning his back on me, he'd better turn it real fucking well.

Dade's upper lip curled. "If you go after this mate of yours, then you betray us all."

Unbelievable.

While I understood his concerns, they were not warranted. Hating that I had to, I tried to keep my temper in check as I grasped at whatever I could to keep this from happening. "You said it yourself. Wistensia is in no position to be warring with us, and they damned well know it."

Dade raised a brow. "You're certain of this, are you?" When I didn't answer, he laughed, his words growing growled. "For you must be when you know we are at our weakest, yet you still wish to skip across the Night Sea to anger another king by stealing his wife."

"And whose fault is that?" I growled back, entirely done with treading lightly and this conversation. "For years, I've done everything you wanted. I've killed. I've robbed. I've captured. I've burned livelihoods and homes to the ground. All for this kingdom. All for *you*," I seethed. "So forgive me for not giving one single fuck about keeping the peace when you are the one who encouraged me to disturb it so fucking thoroughly."

The room shook with his rage—with his need to put me in my place.

My blood roared and pressed at my skin. My flesh groaned. Every sense sharpened as the shift awaited the last trigger to unleash. I grinned, ready and hungry for it. "We both know I've followed your every command because I chose to, you pompous asshole, not because I had to. So you just go right ahead..."

Claws unsheathed from Dade's hands, his eyes glowing a lupine blue as his own wolf rose to the surface, ready to take over.

"Come on, now." I rounded the table slowly. "It's the only way if you wish to stop me." I let the gathered heat beneath my veins unfurl with my claws, rippling shadow encircling us both.

"Let him go."

We both froze mid-change. Muscle protested, and my skin swelled.

Opal entered the war room, her apricot skirts bundled in her hands as she looked between us and sighed. "She might be someone else's queen, but she is his mate, Daden. She returned to Vordane because she knows who and what she wants, despite the gargantuan risks." Opal walked closer to her mate. "You must let him try to find a way."

Dade, stiff and still glowering at me, said nothing.

Then she hit him hard with her soft question. "Would you want someone to stop you?"

At last, the king relented, his claws retracting as he rolled his neck with a tormented groan. Still, he said nothing.

I waited, prepared to do what I must even if it would cost me everything—the only place I called home.

But the king I'd fought too many battles for and alongside just stared at me in a way he never had before.

And I knew this game of hiding in plain sight was now done. Dade would allow it no longer.

I tried to tell myself that it didn't matter. That I'd never cared what he'd thought anyway. That he wouldn't know what true loyalty was if it bit him twice on his threatened ass. I tried, but I quickly gave up and stalked past Opal before warping back to the cottage to prepare.

I had a queen to find.

TWENTY-SEVEN

Aster

RORN PACED THE LENGTH OF MY PAINT PARLOR. NOW AND then, he would stop only to glower at me.

The glass in the windows had been repaired. A lone crack still lingered in the one closest to the door. I kept my eyes trained on it in an effort to keep my ire from making things worse.

After being left alone for the remainder of the night and the following day, I'd half-expected that not to change, and I couldn't say I was glad it had.

He'd arrived with dinner. Dinner I hadn't yet touched.

My wrists burned from the iron. The manacles clinked whenever I moved. Painting and reading were impossible. Eating was nearly as impossible. A fitting pattern for the way things continued to be.

Eternally impossible.

Nothing and no one will ever keep me from you.

I'd spent my solitude trapped with every heated word, every exchange—every promise I'd forced him to make yet had known he could never possibly keep. Knowing didn't stop the organ in my chest from bleeding, the burn of it a distraction from the ache at my wrists.

Scythe had expected the worst, all the while thinking there could be nothing worse than what I'd already divulged. I'd told him I was married.

I'd failed to tell him I was married to a king.

Perhaps, deep down, I'd known it would be too much. The enormity too high to scale. And perhaps that was why I'd already forgiven him for not even uttering a goodbye—for not saying anything at all as his king had handed me over like stolen goods being returned to its rightful owner.

I couldn't blame him.

I could only blame myself for falling prey to temptation yet again. For daring to believe that I deserved to be happy again. For thinking I wasn't selfish for wanting to somehow keep the happiness I'd found.

I might have been married, but it was not out of choice. It hadn't been my choice for a long time. I might have no choice but to stay in Wistensia and forget about Scythe and the burgeoning new life I'd tasted, but it was not because I wanted to.

I was so fucking tired of not being able to make my own choices.

Rorn rubbed at his chin, at the shocking amount of growth now decorating it. Not since his brother had died had I seen him with so much facial hair. It was almost a beard.

"Truth be told, I don't quite know what to do with you."

I didn't answer. He wasn't looking for one.

"I…" He laughed, the sound bitter and cold. "Well, I suppose I'm still stunned, really. I'd known what you were up to, yet to see it with my own eyes…" He shook his head, his steps faltering momentarily. "I'm torn between the need to bend you over and fuck you senseless and the need to have you executed for treason."

That raised my brows and opened my mouth. "Shouldn't you be executed too, then?"

Rorn laughed once more. He shook his finger as he paced from the door to the fireplace again. "It's not the same. What I do does not warrant the same ramifications."

I should've been scared. I should've spoken with care. But I'd lost the will to worry, so I rolled my eyes. "Rorn, this marriage was over nearly two years ago. Cease letting your ego get the better of you."

He stopped, glowering yet again. "You think it's merely my ego you've wounded?"

"You do not love me. Perhaps you did once," I said gently. "But now…" I didn't need to say anything more. Now, he had Carelda— and a queen who'd humiliated him by fleeing to another realm to be with the only thing he'd always lamented not being himself.

A wolf.

"Just because I've fucked another does not mean you know what I do and do not feel, Astrantia," he seethed, and heated enough to make me waver in my beliefs. Noting as much, he smiled, and the sight of the sad lilt to his lips alarmed. "It was not a choice I made lightly. And not something I would have ever even considered had things been different."

"Stop using my inability to have a babe as a weapon."

"That's not what I meant."

"Then what?" I dared to ask, but I knew he would say no more.

His throat bobbed and his eyes glossed as he watched me study him. Snarling slightly, he resumed his pacing. "Him," he spat. "Of all the fucking creatures to wound me with, you chose *him*…"

"Insulting Scythe is pointless, Rorn. I do not wish to—"

"Scythe?" he questioned absently.

"His name." I frowned, confused.

He expelled a burst of cool laughter as he turned away. "Of course, it is."

"Rorn," I said when he raked a hand through his hair and began to mutter to himself beneath his breath. I rose from the chaise. I had to go back and explain, at the very least. I had to try. "Rorn, I'm not staying—"

He froze, all of him stilling. "In case you failed to notice who I came to collect you with, you are no longer permitted in King Dade's territory, and that beast is most certainly not allowed in ours."

My throat closed, rasping my words. "He didn't say that."

"Did he need to, Astrantia?" I tripped, backed against the wall as Rorn advanced and loomed over me to whisper scathingly, "Do you really need a knife poised at your throat before you fucking realize you've made a grave mistake?"

I swallowed, officially afraid and unwilling to show it.

Rorn blinked, as if realizing it—scenting it, and he backed away.

His chest rose and fell heavily as he eyed me with such intensity, it was as if he were searching for me beneath my skin. He cursed. "Go upstairs and get some proper rest. I won't be sleeping in our rooms tonight, and I expect you awake with the birds to help Theenon with preparations."

Dumbfounded by the brutal change in subject, I asked, "Preparations?"

"For the first jewel ball our people have had in years, of course." My eyes closed.

He could lie to himself all he needed, but he could not hold such an event while his queen was busy creating a new life with her mate. I opened my eyes, tempted to laugh at the absurdity. At the reason he'd ventured to Nodoya to whisk me home when he had.

Duty awaited, and he would not be humiliated by my absence.

At my silence, Rorn ceased adjusting and brushing his tunic sleeves. "Before you left me to agonize over the differing ways another male was fucking you, you said you wished to be involved in our affairs again. So why don't you head upstairs and bathe?" His lip curled into a sneer as he turned and exited the parlor. "You reek of stray mutt."

A light knock sounded a moment before the handle turned.

Carelda entered, already dressed in a stunning emerald gown with an apple-green bodice. "Someone wanted to see you."

I smiled, tears smarting as Helvectus waddled into the paint parlor.

I'd returned last night after bathing as Rorn had requested, and my gown for this evening had been delivered by Dudley with lunch.

It was only minutes before Carelda's arrival that I'd finally removed my robe and donned the overflow of silk and chiffon.

The emerald mountain of skirts scrunched and hindered when I lowered to my knees to catch Helvectus before he fell and hit the table. "You're so sneaky to learn such a thing in my absence, little Hel."

"Asher," he said, poking my cheek.

Carelda closed the door. "He started saying it after you left."

I stole his finger and feigned eating it. He giggled so hard he folded to his knees, which only served to make him laugh more. I helped him up and righted his tiny charcoal vest over his green tunic. "I like it," I whispered, brushing his black hair back from his angelic, pinkened face.

"He's showing signs of a wolf within," Carelda said, and cautiously, as if afraid of what that might mean for her son. "Tremors and a glowing of his eyes when his emotions get too volatile."

Rorn would be pleased.

Admiring Helvectus' blue and emerald gaze, I stroked beneath his silken chin. He giggled again, saliva dribbling. "A fine wolf he will make." I rose and smoothed my skirts.

Carelda smiled her gratitude, though worry still tightened her mouth. Sighing, she said, "I wasn't sure you would ever return."

"I didn't want to," I confessed, quiet but resolute.

Carelda nodded, peering down at her cupped hands. Helvectus stole one of the dry paintbrushes from an easel and tossed it against the wall.

He laughed when it clattered and went to retrieve it while I struggled to find something to say.

I decided withholding the truth, in this instance especially, was cruel, and I was tired of hiding. I stepped forward to clasp her hand. "Not because of you, but because I was happy there."

"You've found another male," she said simply, for she certainly knew as much already.

"Quite some time ago, actually, yes."

Her eyes lifted, her fingers wrapping around mine. "Rorn was in a state, Astrantia. Wild like I've never witnessed before." I frowned, able to envision his anger and ready to apologize for leaving her to deal with it when she added, "He desires me, but he is still very much in love with you."

My heart sank so hard and fast that I felt the color drain from my face.

Unbalanced by guilt I hadn't expected, that I'd never thought I would feel regarding Rorn, I feared I would be ill.

Then Hel squealed with a large pot of paint in hand.

Carelda cursed and rushed to pry it from his fingers. He wasn't happy about it, but he was soon smiling again when I snatched a tulip from the vase on the tall table beside me and handed it to him.

"You owe me nothing, my queen, but I'm afraid I do need you to promise me something." Carelda plucked a rusted key from her pocket. "That you will not leave before the ball is over, or I will find myself in severe shit indeed."

Understanding what she'd come here to do, I laughed, the sound wet.

I wouldn't dare, and so I shook my head as she unlocked the manacles from my wrists. "After everything we've all endured, I wouldn't. I need to see this through." I rubbed my skin, then pulled the sheer chiffon sleeves over the red welts. "Thank you."

She dropped the iron chains to the floor, then took her son's hand.

Petals fell behind them as Helvectus kept the flower stuck against his nose, mumbling a song to it as they left.

TWENTY-EIGHT

Aster

THE BALLROOM WAS ALIVE IN A WAY I HADN'T SEEN IN TOO many years.

Free of dust and ghosts and shadows, the grand space had been restored to the bright, hopeful room that held so many of my most magical memories.

Emerald flowers of varying breeds stood vibrant within crystal vases in every corner. Vines looped and crawled across the ceiling, orbs of trapped fireflies strung with them through the rafters and along each doorway.

Gowns, dress shirts, and flowing coats and cloaks in differing shades of green soon flooded the giant space that had sat cold and abandoned for years. And although I would rather be anywhere but here, I failed to feel that way at all at that moment.

I couldn't think of anywhere else I should have been. After so much turmoil and uncertainty, this celebration for our kingdom was not one I could ever imagine missing.

Citizens of all ilk meandered and danced. Many talked in small groups at the edges of the room amongst tables holding an array of divinely scented treats. Hope and relief traveled within conversation and laughter. Within the buoyant tones of the flutes and fiddles from the rear corner of the ballroom and within every face we glimpsed.

It was over. For now.

Hopefully for good.

Rorn's hand laid across mine, and I'd almost forgotten the show of unity until his fingers gently curled over my own. "Incredible, isn't it?"

"I've no words, but yes," I said, a little breathless as my chest continued to swell. "I suppose incredible will do."

He leaned over the arm of his throne, a glint in his eye, and scratched his clean-shaven jaw. "You seem happy. Truly happy."

"I find myself in awe," I said sharply, but then I acquiesced, "And glad to bear witness to this. It's been too long."

"You do know I would have freed you myself, but she beat me to it." He eyed my wrists, the glimpse of red beneath the cuff of my sleeve. "Are you in pain?"

"No," I lied. The welts were already healing, so they itched more than they hurt.

Though I shouldn't have provoked him, I couldn't help myself. His audacity and his contradictory actions had altered the shape of my heart until he could no longer fit inside it—and he had no one to blame but himself. "And let us not pretend that you would care if I was."

"That you can even say that only further proves that you merely choose not to see it."

"See what?" I took the bait.

"That I still care far too much." He slowly righted himself, and I slid my hand from beneath his to place in my lap. He stole it before I could, and I glared at him. Ignoring me, his mouth curved as he nodded to Theenon when he requested to climb the dais to speak in his ear.

Wary, Theenon looked at me as Rorn considered what he'd informed him with flattened brows.

I smiled, harboring no ill will, even if the steward was displeased with my actions. He had to know I didn't mean to be cruel or cause concern—and that whatever he'd heard from Rorn was merely his side of the story. I never wanted to disappoint and hurt anyone. Rather, I merely wished for a little more understanding.

I wished for everyone to realize what I'd spent many months coming to terms with.

That this life and this role I'd once adored was no longer mine. It no longer fit, and trying to make it so did not benefit anyone. Not even Rorn.

But to my relief, Theenon nodded and offered a tiny smile before retreating into the shadows behind our thrones.

Rorn looked back to the joy before us, but his gaze was empty—unseeing.

A minute later, he murmured between his lips, "Next time you're tempted to lose yourself to thoughts of fucking a one-eyed beast, remember this. Remember them." Leaning closer, he whispered, "Remember *me*."

Disgusted and shocked, I stood and smiled at a few onlookers. Then I made my leave.

Guards followed, but they slowed and waited in the adjoining hall containing the stairs that led to the staff chambers and kitchens. Assuming I was headed for the privy we were to use during events such as these, I was mercifully left alone.

Though the quiet I encountered made it clear that it wasn't only disgust that had me running for the solitude I'd once lamented.

It was shame.

I didn't regret it. Not one second spent with Scythe could ever be considered a mistake. I'd made a choice. One that I would own and be grateful for no matter what this eternally long life delivered next. My time in Vordane with my wolf had given me so much more than a much-needed escape—it had helped bring me back to life.

But that didn't mean I was proud of what I was coming to realize.

That I'd indeed hurt Rorn. That maybe in his own narcissistic way, he truly did still care for me.

I closed the door and walked down the first flight of stairs. The chatter and shouting from the kitchen staff beneath the next tower echoed down the tunnels of halls below. A comfort as I leaned back against the stone on the landing and tried to slow my heart.

The door opened and closed.

I nearly whimpered as I tried to muster the courage to tell Rorn to give me a few more minutes, and as I tried to ignore the desire to apologize for something I could never be sorry for doing.

His scent was a cool compress in the middle of an unbearable summer night. "Nice crown, wildflower." The green of his eye shined in the dark of the stairwell. He slowed as he took the last stair to where I was flattened to the wall of the landing.

"What…" I swallowed, without words, and blinked continuously. "*How?*"

A black top hat shadowed his scarred eye, but it was him. My wolf was here, and dressed in a fitted black ensemble that hugged his impressive physique far too well.

Scythe looked me over from head to toe, taking his time—as though we had all of it to waste. Then he seized my waist and my face, and my lips with his.

Ice melted within my chest.

My body fell limp against the wall. His mouth was soft, but his kiss was hard and still, his inhale of breath searing.

I sighed, clasping his shoulders, then I remembered myself and broke away. "You cannot be here. How are you even…?" My heart began to race. "Scythe, it's not safe."

He dragged his nose over my cheek, undeterred. "I made you a promise, and then I failed you."

"You didn't. I know it was…" I peered over his shoulder to the low-lit stairs beside us, fear locking my spine. "A shock."

"It was, but it doesn't matter. I intend to keep it." He kissed me again, softer and groaning. "I intend to keep you."

"How?" I asked, both relieved and tempted to shake some sense into him. "I cannot simply leave. You cannot—"

He hushed me and squeezed my waist, pressing his lips to the corner of my mouth.

Then he tensed and seized my wrist. "He cuffed you?" The question was a low snarl I didn't need to answer as he inspected the other. "No. I think we'll stay a short while." He kissed my reddened skin and stepped back. "Just to make a few things clear."

"Clear?" My eyes widened. "What do you intend to do?" He couldn't mean to do anything, surely, but then why else would he be here… "Scythe, no. You mustn't do anything."

The shadows around us darkened, and I was left chilled by his warm chuckle as he disappeared.

Fighting the desire to vomit, I remained on the landing long enough for one of the guards to open the door atop the stairs. Doral ceased descending the steps when he saw me and sniffed, then he hurried down them to peer into the next row of stairs.

Finding nothing there, Doral stared at me and frowned.

With my heart pattering in sharp bursts, I climbed the stairs before he could ask questions I wouldn't answer, and the guard trailed me closely back to the ballroom.

Rorn was standing before his throne, his gaze upon the crowd as he saw me exchange pleasantries with a few nobles. More guards soon hurried me along, and I apologized to the curious guests who'd been waiting to speak with me before returning to Rorn.

He captured my hand to help me to my smaller throne, then retook his seat in his own. "You worried me."

I whispered, resituating my giant skirts, "Am I not allowed a moment to relieve myself?"

"Of course, but you were gone…" He stilled, nostrils flaring. Ice veiled his eyes as he swung them to mine. "I smell him."

My mouth opened, and I feigned confusion with a frown. Rorn looked at Rollins, and the guard began to walk over to the dais. But it was too late.

The sea of green revelry parted.

Voices lowered to murmurs.

My ears rang with the ensuing quiet. My blood churned cold

through my veins as Scythe stalked through the center of the ballroom with a leg of chicken in hand.

Helvectus, wearing a wet grin and waddling toward the dais, cried out in greeting to his father.

Rorn cursed but scooped him up. Carelda hurried through the crowds at the side of the room but realized she could go no farther. Retrieving Helvectus would cause a scene. Rorn still hadn't permitted a space at his side for her in any form.

Scythe faltered at the sight of Helvectus.

His calm features rearranged into feral fury until his gaze met mine, and I shook my head—just once. Enough for him to tilt his own and narrow his eye. After glaring at the king beside me, Scythe then understood. He laughed silently as he neared the dais.

Whatever he had planned, he needed to stop before he was stopped.

But the guards were too slow, or perhaps too stunned to act, when the intruder removed his hat and tossed it at Rorn's feet.

Gasps sounded from some of those watching what was unfolding.

Helvectus, clinging to Rorn's neck, had stopped bouncing on his lap. He dropped to the dais while Rorn sat like a statue about to crack beneath the sun's heat.

Hel scooted down the stairs on his rear to collect Scythe's hat.

Scythe studied him, flashing his teeth as he chewed the chicken.

Rorn finally woke up. "Touch him," he warned with lethal softness, "and you won't live to greet another sunrise."

Scythe raised his hands. Helvectus wobbled closer, the wolf's hat in hand as he babbled and offered it to him.

Rorn snarled and stood.

I didn't breathe.

Carelda broke through the crowd, uncaring of the threat everyone seemed to sense within this strange male who'd infiltrated our celebration.

Scythe stood back from the infant he'd been watching, and Carelda paused as he stated more than asked, "The cub is yours."

She nodded, snatching her son.

"It would seem I have myself a cousin." Taking another fleshy bite from the chicken leg, Scythe returned his attention to me as Carelda rushed from the ballroom with a protesting Helvectus. Looking at Rorn, Scythe grinned. "The fates are indeed delightful."

Confusion lowered my brows and pushed a shaken exhale from me.

"Fear not, dear uncle." His smile fell. "You can keep your precious throne." He tore into the chicken with relish, then threw the bones at our feet. Gaze tight on mine, Scythe licked his fingers slowly, lewdly, and bowed deeply toward me. "I've come for your wife."

TWENTY-NINE

Aster

PINNED STILL WITH SHOCK, I FOUND IT HURT TO BREATHE AS Scythe's gaze refused to relinquish mine.

His lone eye glinted with mischief, but his jaw was clenched. His lips parted when I merely continued to gape at him—to stare at him with new vision and feel every inch the fool I was.

For I hadn't so much as considered it. That this wolf of mine was not crimson like most of those in Vordane.

He was emerald.

Rorn cursed and ordered, "Would someone seize this drunkard already."

But we knew he was not drunk. I knew with certainty that Scythe had probably never been this sober.

Uncle.

Keep your throne.

His missing eye. An eye that I now knew had once been blue.

An eye that would have told all who he was—the alpha. The true king of Wistensia.

My stomach roiled and shrank. I covered my mouth as a choked sound escaped. Tears sprang forth, burning as I forced them not to fall.

Scythe frowned and made to climb the dais.

I shook my head and drew in a deep breath, willing the wet to dissipate.

The ballroom fell utterly silent.

Then Rorn rose. His guards finally snapped into action.

Scythe took one large step back from the dais. His attention stayed fixed on me as he offered his wrists and merely waited.

"No," I mouthed. "*Leave.*"

Scythe gave a maddening smirk.

The guards nearing him paused, confused by his willingness to surrender.

"Stop," I said, rising and glaring at Rorn. "He's not a criminal."

"The queen is right." Scythe flashed his teeth when the guards shackled him. "I'm just another bastard-born heir who's come for what is rightfully his." He looked at me as he was dragged toward the doors, guests parting and gasping. "My queen."

Rorn leaped down the steps of the dais and whispered something to Theenon, who nodded and got to work on calming everyone.

And then Rorn left.

One by one, our guests began to follow suit and headed to the exits to their awaiting transportation, or to the guest rooms within the towers. Many lingered, and when I felt the curious press of their eyes upon me, I pulled free of the shock that had held me immobile.

I hurried from the ballroom and down the hall I'd seen Rorn take, calling after him when I caught a glimpse of his gold embossed emerald coat before it winked out of sight at the hall's end.

"Rorn, wait."

He ignored me.

"Rorn, please."

He stopped and murmured to the guards who were trailing the entourage escorting Scythe to the dungeon.

"Don't do this," I pleaded when we were alone. "Just let him go, and I'll make sure he leaves."

Rorn's smile was not one of pleasure but of pain. "Bloom." He wiped a trembling hand over his mouth. "I fear I cannot even stomach the sight of you right now, so it would behoove you to return to your parlor while we fix this unfortunate mess."

"Fix?" I asked, incredulous. "If Scythe is as he says, then he does not wish to have anything to do with Wistensia."

Rorn laughed, shocked and shocking. "You didn't know, did you? And you still have no idea."

"I suppose it never mattered to him enough to tell me." I knew that was a lie, and it was just the opposite.

It meant too much for him to dare whisper it to anyone.

"Astrantia." Rorn's gaze flared, his eyes dancing wildly. "You didn't know who he was, and he had no idea who you were. Am I understanding this correctly?"

I swallowed and reluctantly nodded, then I stepped back against the wall when he clasped my chin. He followed, tone edged like a blade. "You just let the beast fuck you seven ways from the skies to better forget me and what I did to you, is that it?"

I nearly refuted that, but I found I couldn't entirely. "At first, yes. That was exactly what it was. I met him in a tavern."

Rorn huffed, then searched my face with something akin to disgust and nostalgia. "It was only me. I was the only male you'd ever allowed inside you. Just me. Why did you have to ruin that?" he asked, the words whispered as though he hadn't meant to say them. "And with him, of all creatures."

"Because you ruined it first, and so thoroughly that I couldn't see a way back to you."

I was pushed against the wall, his forehead almost touching mine. "Couldn't?" he taunted. "Or was it that you merely did not wish to?" His fingers brushed my cheek, and the heat of his rage blended with the acidic scent of fear he could not hide. "Do you have any idea what you've now brought upon us?" he asked, and so gently, I found it hard to hold his gaze. "What you've brought upon me?"

"Scythe is the son of Helvectus, isn't he?" I asked with a twinge in my chest. "He's a wolf, and his missing eye was—"

"No." Rorn's fingers dropped. He glowered, gritting, "My brother had no son."

"None that he would've shared with the rest of us, Rorn." I grasped his wrist, urging, "Think about it."

"Think about it?" He flung my touch away. "I've done nothing but think about you with him for never-ending days. He will lose more than his remaining eye for that, Astrantia, and for daring to come here to arouse suspicion in my people."

"Oh, they're *your* people now?" I foolishly sneered. "It's just as I thought then. You brought me back merely to put me on display and to make sure I'm not there with him."

His glower eased. "That's not true and..." Growling, he smacked the stone wall beside my head, and lurched backward. "If you wish to prove your loyalty to this kingdom and for me to stand a chance at forgiving you, just do as I say and return to your fucking parlor."

As much as I still cared, I didn't care enough to want or need his forgiveness.

"I don't want your forgiveness, Rorn. He's my mate," I blurted, for I had nothing else. Nothing that might help. "That's why I found it so easy to do what I did. That's why I cannot give you what you want," I admitted softly. "Even if I could forgive you."

"Enough," Rorn rasped, paling more by the second.

"No, he's my mate, and if you harm him, if you kill him..." I swallowed thickly. "You know damned well you might as well kill me, too."

Rorn staggered back. His eyes swept over me before he stalked down the hall.

THIRTY

Scythe

THE DUNGEON WAS JUST AS SMALL AND MISERABLE AS I remembered.

I stared at the cell across from the one I'd been locked within, unable to forget the way she'd stood there, staring at me with tear-stained eyes. Staring at me with so much regret, it had stalked my dreams ever since.

We hadn't asked for much. I hadn't asked for anything. But she had feared we wouldn't make it on our own. So she'd asked for help—for just enough to get us by while she grieved a mate she was never allowed to publicly claim.

They'd said her request was a bribe. Our mere presence a threat. And that there could be no risks taken.

"Giselle was her name," I told the poor asshole who'd been tasked with keeping watch on me. He didn't acknowledge me, but he seemed to stir awake from the nap he'd been taking while standing against the door. "My mother. You might remember her. Short black hair and a stricken yet beautiful face. The last time I saw her"—I lifted my fingers from my forehead to point straight ahead—"she was in that very cell."

The wolf had stiffened, and he peeled open an eye to narrow it at me. "I care nothing for your stories. So kindly shut the fuck up."

I grinned and continued, "Some coward took her from that cell, and do you know what she told me as she was dragged from it and taken to her doom?" I told him before he could say a word, "Everything will be all right."

The wolf said nothing.

"It wasn't all right, though, was it?" I feigned a tormented sigh, yet my chest burned when I recalled the moment I knew I would never see my mother again. "She was taken to the woods and butchered. Never to be seen again." I shrugged. "Or so I hear."

The wolf spoke then. "You will likely meet the same fate, should you find yourself lucky."

"Maybe," I mused, for I'd no plan outside of convincing this king I longed to kill to surrender his wife.

He should be dead. I'd had ample opportunity to fulfill that desire twice now. But although it would make me sleep better at night, I didn't want his crown. I wanted no part of this miserable kingdom.

I just wanted their queen. Finding a way to keep her would be vengeance enough.

"Or maybe, I'll get rid of your spineless king for you," I supplied, more of a suggestion than a threat. "What say you?"

"I say you're insane and irritating as fuck."

"I have been known to be a little... unhinged."

A snort. "Your father was, too."

And there it was.

A crack. I widened it by asking, "You knew him, then." Telling silence followed. I grinned. "Ever wonder what he'd make of all this?"

"The dead do not have opinions."

The male I remembered was as kind and quiet as he was fierce and quick to anger. There had been many a night I'd lain awake, waiting for his inevitable return to the small farm he'd purchased for my mother upon discovering she was expecting me.

We might have been kept hidden, but we'd been loved, so their arguments had never lasted long. The way he'd spoken of this place...

I could see it now. Feel it. The rot that stalked the halls in a cool caress. The soulless stone that harbored copious ghosts of those who'd met untimely and unjust deaths.

A curse, my father had always claimed, one he'd never wanted us exposed to. While my mother had always harbored a fear that the king had been ashamed of us. Over time, as more people met their ends and the news of burning towns and villages arrived in warnings delivered by the breeze, she came to learn his intentions were honorable.

I'd never known what to believe.

Not until a knife was taken to my face upon the sand of Nodoya's coastline.

I'd lost an eye that night, but I'd never seen clearer since.

"Let us say they do have opinions, Doral," I said casually. "Then I would think my father's would have only grown in conviction. This place is nothing but a cursed wasteland of spreading poison."

The warrior stilled. "You remember me."

"I remember everything," I said, rising and kicking open the door to my cell.

Doral advanced in a heartbeat, only to be met by my fists at his coat collar.

"So…" I tightened my grip as I said through my teeth, "You can either try to stop me and join the ghosts trapped within this putrid shithole, or you can go and take a piss and simply fail to comprehend how the fuck I managed to slip past your excellent observation skills."

His bright blue eyes narrowed to slits, his body vibrating with the need to change. "I didn't know what Rorn would do to you and your mother. Helvectus was my friend."

"A friend you failed. You let that pompous excuse for a king drag his mate from this very dungeon right before your pretty eyes, and you did *nothing*."

His teeth gnashed, said eyes shining with both anger and regret. "I didn't think he would have her killed."

We both knew he wouldn't have been able to stop it even if he had known—therefore, he wouldn't have even tried. "Go take a piss," I reiterated softly. "I'll be back before anyone knows I was gone."

"With the exception of the queen," he said, a brow rising. "Right?"

I released him and brushed the leather lapels of his coat. "I'd mind your fucking business if I were you, Doral."

I could have stood there and watched her sleep until the sky lightened with the incoming dawn, if it weren't for the way she tossed and turned upon the chaise.

A damp sheen coated Aster's forehead. Her lips parted and closed and twisted as though wherever she'd gone in her dreams, it was just as stressful as the world she'd briefly left behind.

With the exception of my parents in the years after they were taken from me, never had I ached for another in the way I did for this queen I'd found myself fated to. Never had I felt another's pain so acutely as I had hers upon seeing that waddling infant in the ballroom.

I'd known at first glance that he wasn't Aster's son, yet I'd still panicked. The guilt of it had flayed me wide when I'd gotten a better scent of the youngling who'd been audaciously named after my father.

All my mate had been through…

All she'd been forced to endure for the sake of this rotten land, and while I'd done nothing but unleash my fury upon others, believing she'd simply chosen her lousy husband over me…

It had never been that simple.

I could see that now, and I could see why she'd been too afraid to explain it all. If I were any other male, then taking a king's wife would be a death sentence and therefore out of the question.

Luckily for us both, the stars had decided she was stuck with me.

Paintings stood upon easels, all of them propped near the long row of windows and in various states of neglect. They still stunned me. The moon swam across the parchment, capturing each brushstroke and coaxing the eye to trail each deepening hue.

Along the far wall before a tall set of half-filled shelves were hundreds of paintings. They lay in stacks and stood tall upon canvas against the stone wall. A few, in particular, caught my eye and my nose, and I lifted parchment until I found them.

Paintings of me.

My fingers shook as I carefully lowered them, and after a series of light snores, Aster stirred with a snorted gasp.

I crossed the room quietly and knelt beside the chaise to place my hand over her mouth. "Bumblebee."

Her eyes opened wide. A rushed exhale warmed my palm when she saw me through the dark. The sun would soon rise, but I had to see her. I had to know that despite whatever happened, she did not loathe me for my deception.

"I'm sorry," I whispered, leaning down to tuck my nose into her neck. "I was cruel. A selfish, arrogant prick. I thought you'd simply chosen him. I didn't know..." I cursed and brushed my lips over her jaw. "Say you'll forgive me."

Taking my hand from her mouth, she kissed and hugged it to her cheek. "You weren't to know because I was too cowardly to tell you." I was gifted a soft, stomach-easing smile. "It would seem we've both been keeping secrets, wolf."

My cock ached, as did my chest, from the sight of her relief at my touch.

Her lashes fluttered. "I tried to see you, but I wasn't..." She stopped and pushed upright, her nose an inch from mine. "You shouldn't be here." Looking over my shoulder to the door, she then gripped my shirt. "You need to go back to the dungeon right now. Oh, stars, you should just warp home." Her eyes widened. "You didn't kill anyone, did you?"

I bit back a chuckle but smirked. "I needed to look at you." I licked my lips and gently pushed her down. "I'll return to the dungeon." I moved to the end of the chaise. "Right after I've helped you get back to sleep."

I opened her robe and tugged her legs over my shoulders.

"Scythe, this isn't the time to be—" she moaned when my mouth met her clit, and I kissed it.

"Can't have you worried," I said, licking her slowly from bottom to top. "And I most certainly can't have you upset with me."

"I'm not upset, but you can't fix everything with sex."

I dragged my tongue through her, and she flooded my mouth. "Your magical cunt says that is a lie."

Her essence soaked my tongue—fueled me in a way nothing else could. I tortured and enjoyed her, wanting to never leave, but she released all too soon with a silent cry. Her thighs clenched my head, and her back arched off the chaise.

"Always so delicious, wildflower." I lapped up every drop of pleasure I'd forced her body to produce and rubbed my nose through the swollen silk of her to savor for later. "Has he tried to have you?" I trusted Aster, but I sure as fuck did not trust the male who murdered my mother and looked at my mate as if she were his own.

"No, wolf." I reluctantly acquiesced when she pushed to her elbows. "And this parlor has been my sleeping quarters for a long time."

I licked her flavor from my lips. "How long?" I couldn't help it—had to know.

Her beautiful eyes rolled, but her lips curved. "Since I met you." My relief must have shown, for her expression softened, her fingertips glossing over my cheek. "You need to go back. Go home. If you're the rightful heir..." She didn't need to say it, and she swallowed as I carefully lowered her legs and righted her robe. "I'm afraid of what he might do, Scythe."

"You know I'm not leaving without you."

"But we can't just leave. The trouble we'll cause..."

"Not leaving yet." I tightened the ribbon ties to better ensure no one walked in here and saw any part of her. "Not until we're certain you never have to return."

Her hand took mine. "Tell me what happened to your eye."

I looked at her then and just smiled. "Sleep. We'll talk tomorrow."

"It is tomorrow."

I kissed her forehead. "Then in a few hours."

"Scythe," she said, confused. "You don't know what will happen, what Rorn might do…"

"We'll find out soon enough." I kissed her nose. "So get some rest." Stars knew she deserved a lifetime of it after all she'd endured from the male who had made vows to cherish her—from the foolish fuck who had impregnated another instead.

"Helvectus was your father." She whispered, urgent, "Tell me your real name."

I crawled over her and said to her lips, "When you tell me yours."

"You already know it." I did know, but I kissed her until she surrendered the information I wanted. "My father called me Aster."

The secret I'd never shared with anyone left me with unexpected ease. "My name is Helvectus Jade," I murmured to her lips, "and this stars-forsaken isle will burn before I let your husband keep you."

I claimed her mouth again, hard and groaning when her arms wrapped around my shoulders and her fingers clasped my head. And then I forced myself to leave her as she reached for me, her lips swollen and her gray eyes murky with fear and desire.

Doral was sharpening a blade by the door when I returned. He didn't so much as glance at me as I shut myself back inside the cell. "What game are you playing, Helvectus?"

I laughed low and settled against the wall for a few minutes of sleep. "I've no fucking idea, Doral, but I do intend to win."

THIRTY-ONE

Aster

"**R**ORN WISHES TO SEE YOU," THEENON SAID WITHOUT knocking.

I ceased gnawing at my fingernails and crossed to where he stood at the parlor door. "Where is he?"

I'd struggled to sleep after Scythe had left. Instead, I'd tried and failed to find Rorn to attempt reasoning with him again. No one would tell me where he was.

"The king?" Theenon lifted a brow. "Or the prisoner?" I glared, crossing my arms, and he sighed. "They're both in the dining hall. Rorn is finishing breakfast."

I asked nothing else and hurried down the stairs, my robe threatening to open and a chill sweeping into my bones.

Doral stood guard by the doors with a younger wolf, and they both eyed me with unveiled interest. I ignored them and pushed open the doors myself. They thudded to a close behind me as I froze and beheld what awaited within.

Scythe was seated at one end of the long table. His hands were bound in iron to the wooden armrests of the chair. He watched me, a gleam in his eye that tried to convince me he was fine.

Rorn sat at the other end, dabbing a napkin at his chin. "You could have at least dressed, wife." He set the cloth down and pushed his chair back to recline slightly. "We have ourselves a guest, after all."

Words left me in a pitched pant. "What are you doing, Rorn?"

He gestured to the place setting beside his. "Waiting for my wife to join me so that we can make a united agreement on the threat that has stolen into our home."

"He is no threat."

The pursing of Rorn's lips was followed by a sad smile. "Come here, Bloom."

But I didn't move.

Rorn looked to the corner of the room, where a wolf I hadn't sensed upon my arrival came forward, a hammer in the guard's hand. A nod from the king and the wolf unbound one of Scythe's hands from the chair. He splayed it over the table, the chains around his wrists clanking.

My heart thundered. "Rorn..."

The wolf positioned a nail over Scythe's forefinger and waited.

"Did he place that finger inside you?" Rorn asked, and too casually for me to believe he wasn't a moment from snapping.

A screeching flooded my ears as my heart stopped.

The wolf with the nail poised waited. The others outside could no doubt hear, too.

My cheeks instantly caught fire. "Rorn, please."

He nodded again. Scythe hissed through his teeth as the metal was smacked into his finger.

I screamed and ran to free him.

Rorn caught me at the waist and gritted into my hair, "You'll find answering me is the best course of action, Astrantia."

"Stop it." I whirled and slapped at his chest, tears entering my eyes. "Please, this is fucking insanity."

Rorn just watched my eyes fill, his expression void.

"I do hope you've got more nails," Scythe said and drummed the fingers of his other hand over the table. "Every single one of these undeserving digits has had the pleasure of exploring my mate's perfect cunt."

Rorn's veneer cracked, his jaw creaking.

The hammer rose, and I threw myself over Scythe. It met the wood behind my head, the guard cursing and looking at Rorn.

"Don't do that again," Scythe warned, his lips brushing my cheek when I righted myself in his lap.

"She won't," Rorn assured him.

He grabbed and set me upon the table mere inches from Scythe, who cursed and groaned when another nail was imbedded in his next finger. Blood soaked his hand, crawled in a small river beneath it to drip from the ruined table to the floor.

Rorn clasped my chin, forcing my eyes to his. "Kiss me."

"What?" I almost shouted, for he couldn't mean to torture Scythe by using me. "What is it you hope to achieve here, Rorn?" A tear fell down my cheek. He ducked, licking it before it reached my chin.

Scythe snarled.

His energy curled around us as he began to shift, but the iron chains and nails stopped him. He fell back into the chair, panting, smoky tendrils wafting from him as he tried to pull the nails free of his hand.

"He stole something that wasn't his to take, and now, the last thing he'll see before he dies is my wife returning herself to the male of whom she truly belongs to. So kiss me, Bloom, lovely and soft just like you enjoy."

Horrified and without breath in my lungs, I choked. "I can't..."

The hammer rose. Another nail stood poised. This time above Scythe's hand.

"There was a time when you'd barely let my lips leave yours." Rorn turned my head back to him and whispered to my cheek, "You break my heart more as each day passes. Fix it, Astrantia. Help me fix us and fucking kiss me."

The chains rattled. "Don't you dare," Scythe seethed. "I'd rather he take my other eye than—" His words fell into a low groan.

Sickened, I turned away from Rorn's advancing mouth.

Scythe was smiling. My wolf was smiling as the guard frowned and backed away. "Piece of cake in comparison, wildflower."

But he couldn't continue like this. Eventually, his hands would be destroyed. Perhaps past the point of being healed.

And then he would die.

I closed my eyes, trying to think of a way out of this madness when I could scarcely think at all.

Opening them, I looked up at Rorn. "Promise me you won't kill him." My chest heaved, and Rorn's eyes dropped to my breasts, which were almost exposed courtesy of my robe opening. "Promise me, and I'll do whatever you want."

Rorn opened my knees and stepped between them, scenting what had happened mere hours ago in the paint parlor before dawn. His nostrils and eyes flared, his grip on my thighs turned bruising. But I clasped his face and brought it close to mine.

Scythe growled, "*Aster.*"

Rorn's ire slipped but still remained. I trapped his gaze with mine. My thumbs brushed over his sharp cheeks, my smile real when I recalled caressing them with my lips after the first time we'd made love.

I'd thought him a dream.

One I never would have believed would become nothing more than a nightmare.

His breath hitched. His eyes closed as I pressed my lips to each corner of his. It was all I could do not to flinch when the table rocked violently with Scythe's fury.

Rorn groaned and clutched me tight at my thigh and the back of my head as I encountered the soft ruin of his mouth with mine, and I kissed him in earnest.

Then he cried out when my knee encountered his hard groin.

Guilt ensnared me, softening my angered words. "Stop acting like an infant who's had his toy stolen." Rorn stumbled back and fell, his legs cinched and agony reddening his face, and I hurried to free Scythe.

He'd already freed himself.

The guard tore his eyes from his king, realizing too late.

Scythe snatched the hammer. It connected with his head, and the guard fell to the floor with a gut-dropping thud.

Blood covered and poured from Scythe's hand. I looked at the table. Only skin and nails and more blood remained...

My hand flew to my mouth. "Scythe, my fucking stars."

He'd ripped his hand free of the nails.

"Now," Scythe said with an eerie calm, as though he hadn't just been severely wounded. He unwrapped the chains from his wrists and used one of them to seal the doors, then he stalked to Rorn. "This is how it's going to go..."

I could only stand there, shaken, torn, and in disbelief, while Scythe seized Rorn by the hair bound at his nape. He dragged and fastened the king to the grate over the fireplace with the other chain.

Then, with a fevered wildness to his features, my wolf came for me.

There were no orders. He picked me up and set me upon the table, his injured hand cupping my cheek as he stared at my mouth and rasped, "I don't care if someone's about to pierce my fucking heart, Aster. The sight of you kissing another kills more thoroughly than any death."

"I had to for it—" I was quietened by his mouth and by the rising of my robe as his unwounded hand crawled up my thigh to my stomach and opened the silken material.

His blood coated my cheek. His tongue plunged inside my mouth, taking and claiming and robbing me of memory of where we were.

"Scythe," I panted, pulling away when it came back. "Show me your hand."

His nostrils widened with his displeasure, his dark brows low. Then he grinned, blinding and beautiful, and slid his thumb to my mouth.

I opened, the copper taste of him invading and heating me to dangerous heights. I sucked and searched for more when he stroked my teeth with the digit and the hardness straining his pants against my core. "Always so well behaved for me."

My eyes closed as yet again, I realized what I was doing.

Scythe cursed, his low voice both rough and soft. "We'll stop." I collapsed against him, wanting him but grateful, for I didn't want him like this. He held me tight to his chest with his fingers woven through my hair and murmured to the top of my head. "Close your robe, wildflower."

I reached between us and retied it, then lifted my chin upon his chest.

Torment sharpened his features as he gazed down at me, but he still vowed to my forehead, "It's going to be okay."

We both knew it was a vow he had no idea how to keep.

My eyes closed over tears when the doors crashed open, and he pressed his mouth to my temple.

Scythe made no protest as he was seized and returned to the dungeon.

Swallowing thickly, I looked over at Rorn. He was still on the ground, his wrists shackled to the grate, and watching me with enough contempt to burn down the sun. "Please," I said, crossing the room to free him. Crouching down, I untangled the bloodied chains and pleaded, "If you ever loved me at all, you will stop this."

Between his teeth, he gritted, "It is because I love you that I can't."

I stared at him for some moments. He stared right back, his ire never lessening.

Sighing, I rose on unsteady legs and took a seat at the table, where I watched my husband sit up and rake a hand through his hair. It fell from its tie around his shoulders, much like Scythe's had before he'd cut it.

I snatched a bowl of chopped melon from the array of barely touched food and stabbed at a piece with a fork, waiting to see what this king I was tied to might say or do next.

But he merely remained slumped beneath the window, eyes unseeing as he stared at the doors.

I chewed the melon slowly before finally asking what I'd been too afraid to know until now, "Who took Scythe's eye, Rorn?"

He tensed as if he'd forgotten that I was still here. Then he scoffed. "Irrelevant, wouldn't you think, Astrantia?"

"But it's not." I smiled down at the fruit. "It's not irrelevant at all because it was blue, wasn't it?" I asked, but I already knew. "He had one blue eye before you took it."

I waited, but there was no reaction. Rorn stood and made his way to the table.

Unsure what he would do, I gripped the fork and stood.

He looked at it, then at me, and smirked. "Do you wish to maim me for something that happened before you even knew of the bastard's existence?"

Anger rose within me, a storm I'd barely kept at bay. "I would maim you for far more than that."

"Your threats are good for nothing more than exciting me," he whispered and closed the space between us. He stopped when I dug the prongs into his throat. "You cannot do it, Bloom."

The fork punctured the first few layers of skin, blood bubbling and coating the silver crimson.

Rorn's eyes widened, and he laughed. "At least let me get my cock out before we skip past foreplay."

I scowled. "You're aroused."

"Anything you do arouses me, but if I'd had known how feral you liked to be, I'd have chained you with iron in our rooms and fucked you free of want for anything but me a long time ago."

His attempt to deter me wouldn't work. "Why?" I demanded between my teeth. "Why take his eye?"

He sighed, accepting that I wasn't going to let this go. "Why do you think, Astrantia?" He reached for a grape, causing the prongs to dig deeper into his skin. "It was that or kill him."

An amused voice sounded from the doors. "For he'd just been crowned king, and to surrender such a thing so soon to his bastard of a nephew would not do."

THIRTY-TWO

Aster

S CYTHE LEANED AGAINST THE DOORFRAME, HIS IRON manacles hanging from one wrist and an apple in his other hand.

Rorn rounded the table. "Who set you loose, mutt?"

"The power you lack that I just so happen to possess, of course." Scythe eyed the blood-tipped fork in my lowering hand and smirked. "Come to me, wildflower."

"Move, and he dies, Astrantia."

But Rorn wouldn't take his anger and jealousy that far. For he now understood there was no surer way to lose me.

Done breathing the same air as the male I'd given too many chances to, I crossed the room to Scythe. He tossed the apple over his shoulder and took my hand. "Think quick, *king*," he warned Rorn. "For if I need to take a crown I do not want just to get what I need, I will, and I'll wear it with a shit-eating smile for the rest of my days."

Scythe then warped us away from the towers.

We rematerialized in a field of demolished homes, the swaying wildflowers tickling my bare ankles. "Would you have told me?" I asked, tearing at the end of my robe with the fork. "That it was Rorn who maimed and banished you?"

Scythe watched me, unsheathing a claw. "Eventually."

I dropped the fork and lifted the robe for him to slice the corner of it with ease, then I took his uninjured hand and led him to the creek at the field's edge. He didn't so much as wince while I washed the blood from his hand and carefully cleansed the punctures.

He stared with rapt focus. "You've done this before."

"When I returned from that first week with you, I fell prey to it all. Too much time was spent merely perishing slowly." I lifted his hand to my lap and gently wrapped it with the strip of silk from my robe. "After some months, I knew I had to do something to keep from losing the little sanity I had left. So I began doing what I could to help in the infirmary."

"Eighteen months and ten days," he said.

I smiled. Tucking the silk beneath his palm, I brought his hand to my mouth. "Eighteen months and ten days."

His thumb brushed my lips. I kissed it, then squealed and smacked at his shoulder when he picked me up to place me in his lap. "Your hand."

"Farthest thing from my mind." His length dug into my core through his pants. My legs twined around him, but he merely held me. My racing heart slowed, and the tight tension faded from my limbs with every trail of his fingers over my back.

"Where do we go from here?" I couldn't help but ask after some much-needed minutes of recapturing my breath. The uncertainty felt like another war we couldn't escape.

"We find a way, or we force it."

"A way that does not involve Rorn dying?" Scythe tensed, and I lifted my head from his neck. "I know it's not what you might want to hear, but I did love him, and though a part of me longs to kill him with my bare hands for all he's done to you..." I shook my head, unable to fathom it all. "His death would not fix or erase any of it."

Scythe tilted my chin, and his brow furrowed as he searched my eyes. "I do not intend to kill him."

My lips twitched. "But you would like to, and I don't blame you."

His eye dropped to my mouth, his own curling. "I've imagined doing so more times than you'd care to know." His smile fell, his attention still upon my lips. "If I'd have freed myself from that chair faster, I daresay I would have." His features scrunched, and his eye closed. "Never appease him or anyone like that again."

"I needed the chance to end his antics," I said, loathing that either male had been in such a position. "It worked."

"I do not care," Scythe rumbled. Shifting my hair over my shoulders, he rubbed my arms and sighed. "As much as I want to free my cock from my pants and slide it between your legs to remind you to never make my heart stop like that again, we should soon head back before we make matters worse."

I shivered, liking that idea too much, considering all that'd just happened. "They cannot get any worse," I said, smiling sadly.

"Believe me, they always can." He scented my unfurling desire and cursed. "I should probably tend to you." His teeth nipped at my ear. "Just in case."

"In case things go further astray?"

"Exactly."

I laughed when he licked my pulse, and I cupped his cheeks. My thumbs stroked as I forced him to look at me, nearing the corner of his scarred eye. "He did this to you."

"He was right when he said he could've killed me instead. I was all of thirteen years, and the only training I'd had was from my father when he could escape his duties and come home every other day."

I leaned forward to place my lips upon the forever-closed eyelid. Scythe stilled, but only for a second. A soft exhale loosened his limbs, even as his hold on me tightened.

While he'd been discarded and left to die on another continent, I had been marrying the new king responsible for the ruination of his life.

As if sensing exactly what I was thinking, the shame and sickness crawling through my chest cavity, Scythe kissed my jaw. "The fates are unforgiving, wildflower, but also strangely merciful. I wouldn't want any of this cursed land, even if it hadn't robbed me of all I loved. It's no longer my home. It never will be."

I blinked away tears. "Home." I pondered that, Helvectus having another home, and found it did not surprise me. He'd spent such little time at the towers from what I could remember. "And your mother?" Scythe's lack of response both hardened and sliced at my heart. "No," I whispered. "Tell me he didn't."

The list of Rorn's atrocities, such unforgivable actions, just continued to grow. Soon, I wondered if I'd be able to see past it all to the male I'd once known.

Scythe looked beyond me to the trees and licked his teeth. "I'm not certain it was him, but I do know he would've ordered it. He would've been there. And I'll never forget that he took my eye on that beach, for his henchmen couldn't bring themselves to."

My stomach roiled, but he went on, "He had us both locked in the dungeon when my mother came to ask for help some months after my father had died." He released a huffed breath. "We were there for all of one night before he decided there was no more time to waste."

My mind skipped backward to that brighter time—to the darkness Rorn had carried with him after Helvectus' death. "It slowly changed him. Festered," I murmured, mostly to myself, for I knew he wouldn't care to hear it. "I'd thought it was his brother's death, but now I see it was his own misdeeds."

I rose with help from his shoulders and did my best to walk off the tears that didn't seem to want to abate for longer than a few hours.

A monster.

All this time, I'd been married to a monster, and I'd had no idea.

"So much horror and heartbreak…" I laughed low. "Just so he could keep the throne."

"He'd just taken it," Scythe said. "The shame of stepping down and handing it to some youngling he'd known nothing about would have undone him worse than what he did to keep it."

"No." I stopped pacing when Scythe grabbed me from behind, his large arms enfolding me. "No, he can't get away with this."

"You just said you do not wish him dead."

"That doesn't mean he should get away with it," I seethed, turning in his embrace to glare up at him. "He cut out your fucking eye and killed your mother. He stole your entire life and forced you to make a new one, and you would've been so scared and in so much pain…" I drew in a gasping breath, unable to see through the wet filming my eyes. "You could've died. You—"

"Breathe, wildflower. In case you haven't noticed, I've already won." He framed my face and dropped his head, his thumbs wiping the tears from my cheeks. "Breathe."

I tried, inhaling deep. My exhale caught, hitched into a violent hiccup, and the beast chuckled. The sight of it instantly calmed me, and noticing that, he whispered, "Cease pushing me deeper in love with you." He rubbed my cheeks, his expression near pained. "I've fallen too fucking far as it is."

He didn't seem to care that my eyes bulged wide and that he'd stolen my breath all over again, nor that I didn't say anything back.

My wolf lifted and crushed me to his chest, and my nose smooshed into his neck.

"Berk found me," he said, as though I weren't still reeling in his arms. "He was in really bad shape. His injury was about to get the better of him when he saw me below the cliff, almost swallowed as the tide rolled in."

Shocked yet again, my head rose. "He was going to jump?"

Scythe nodded, curling my hair behind my ear. "The rocks below are sharp enough that it probably would've worked too."

"You saved his life."

"And he saved mine." Scythe's gaze grew wet, and he cleared his throat. "He likes to say that he was just taking a late evening walk due to the pain, but I knew, and he knows I'm well aware."

"What about Mariana?"

"Deep down, she knows. It breaks her heart. He breaks her heart. But they make it work."

A heavy moment passed of staring at one another, and I had to acknowledge it. "I do believe you just said that you love me."

"You're surprised." His brow rose. "Did you think a brute like me incapable, wildflower?"

I kissed him gently and only once, even though I longed to smatter his face in adoration.

"But Aster…" He pulled away and murmured, "I can't give you this type of life." I frowned, though I knew what he was referring to. "I have plenty of coin, but I still can't give you anything remotely like what you're accustomed to. I could damned well try to take it, and that is my right, but I don't want it. In fact, I hope to never set foot here again. I can't give you castles and staff and fancy parlors—"

"Stop." I pushed my finger against his lips, and his brows jumped as he smirked. "I don't want it either. I don't want any of it, and I have to wonder if I ever truly did." His features creased with confusion. I smiled. "I wanted the magic I'd believed would come with it. I wanted what I was promised."

"Promised?"

I nodded, climbing down from his arms. "Can I take you somewhere?"

He frowned, nodding once.

I took his hand. His fingers instantly snuck through mine, and I gestured for him to lean down. I was gifted a rare smile when I rose to my toes to kiss his cheek, then I clasped his other hand and tried my best to prepare for what I might discover as we left the fields.

"Your eyes are still closed," Scythe said at my hairline, humor in his voice.

He kissed each one, causing me to smile and each eyelid to rise. He turned atop the small knoll we'd arrived on, its bulk still weathered from many a warping journey by my father and myself. "This was your home?"

My feet bare, I carefully traipsed closer to the wreckage.

Tears welled at the sight of the rubble, the exposed remaining bedchamber. "I haven't been back. Not since I heard it had been destroyed." The cottage that sat in the foothills of the mountains containing the towers, as well as a portion of the forest surrounding it, had been burned.

New life had unfurled. It crawled over the darkened bodies of trees and among the remaining stone of the home I'd grown up in.

"My father was a wolf," I said. "One of great power that would see him become a general in the king's military. My mother died not long after giving birth to me, so it was always just us. He would often return home with tales of his ventures with the king. Living here, we were close enough to the towers that he was able to come home each night and still be sent for if needed, yet far enough from them and the town village beyond these woods that it was peaceful."

"It is," Scythe said, peering up to the canopy of trees above the cottage, and to the remains of the small animal shelter some yards behind it. "Peaceful."

"I miss it." I released a humorless huff. "I'd spend so many days wandering the forest and the creeks, dragging our runt of a horse with me while pretending to be a princess."

I circled a pile of blackened stone and glowing shrubbery while my wolf lowered onto a large rock, watching me. "Will we need a horse to keep the chickens company, then?"

I halted, staring over my shoulder at him.

"Did you think I'd forget?"

I smiled down at my feet, saying quietly, "Chickens will do."

He continued to watch me as I roamed the grounds I'd once called home, unsure how it was possible to feel so much joy and so much despair all at once.

"I was sixteen years when I attended my first jewel ball—when I first saw Rorn. It was there that a ruby-haired sorceress with snakes upon her shoulders and blood in her eyes found me standing alone in the corner of the crowded ballroom."

"Silver," Scythe said, and without a trace of uncertainty.

I paused. "You know of her?"

He nodded, fingers steepled beneath his chin. "She lives and works in Sinshell. Berk took me to her after finding me, seeking help to heal my eye."

"She couldn't save it, then."

"She wasn't sure if it would be possible, but somehow, Berk came to realize it was best I live without it. So they made sure it stayed closed."

"Berk knows all of who you are?"

"He acts as if he doesn't, and he's never asked, but I think he figured it out long ago." He cocked his head. "Tell me what happened with Silver."

Still stunned that he knew the same sorceress and that she hailed from Nodoya, it took me a moment to remember what I'd been saying. I couldn't help but laugh a little as I did. "She told me I looked terribly bored but not to get too comfortable, for I would one day find true love in a king."

I could still recall the flickering flames within the crystal chandelier and the leafy emerald wreaths and garlands touched by white roses. "Not a moment after she'd disappeared, there he was, a prince scowling at me from across the ballroom."

I gestured to Scythe. "Much the same as you are now." His scowl deepened before he eased his features, and I reconsidered what I was about to divulge, my voice lower than I'd intended. "You probably don't want to hear the rest."

He pondered that, staring down at his hands between his knees. "I really don't fucking want to, but I..." He exhaled roughly. "I also do." Sensing my confusion, he looked up at me beneath his lashes. The sun crested the trees, igniting the jeweled orb of his remaining eye. "I want you. I want all of you. Everything that has made you who you are and who you're becoming."

Burning breath sat trapped in my throat.

He shrugged. "So although I loathe it, that asshole is a huge part of that." He flicked his chin, lips tilting a fraction. "So tell me, wild-flower. Tell me the rest."

I nodded, looking back to the cottage as I forced my emotions to settle. "I didn't have the courage to approach Rorn that evening. And at the next ball, I was seventeen years and still without enough bravery to do anything more than watch him. But before the night ended, he asked me to dance. Before the sun rose, I asked if he was going to kiss me. I can still feel the way my heart had sunk through my legs when he said no. I feared I would cry right there in front of him." I laughed and sniffed. "Until he smirked and said that I would kiss him."

Scythe scoffed.

I continued. "A game ensued for months as I made sure to accompany my father to the towers as much as he would allow. Rorn's teasing with other females would leave me incensed and wondering if the sorceress had been toying with me. But then I decided to tease him back by taking one of his warrior friends with me to the forest fair. The last before the humans became a larger threat than we'd anticipated."

"Rorn stepped in as soon as we'd reached the starlit dance floor and claimed that he'd been waiting for me. I told him if that were the case, then he would be waiting forever, but before I could finish talking, he kissed me." I stopped as I remembered those endless minutes—as he'd kissed and kissed and kissed me. "After that, every single thing I'd ever known changed. The moment I reached eighteen years, we were wed."

Scythe had gone unbearably quiet and still.

"All of the magic, our beliefs that the world laid waiting at our feet, began to unravel when my father died as the war intensified, and Rorn was crowned king when your own father died mere months later. Now I know why." Anger and grief warred and swam in circles inside my chest. "And now I remember."

Walking over to Scythe, I lowered to my knees between his and placed my hands upon his thighs. "This sorceress, Silver, she told me that my true love would be a king." A small laugh escaped me as I saw her meaning so vividly now.

Scythe glared down at me, speaking gently but through his teeth. "You've told me that part, wildflower." He stared over me to my family's ruined home.

"But when she'd said that, I had immediately looked at Rorn, and as she'd vanished…" I clasped his chin and tilted it down, making sure I had his eye. "She did so with a taunting laugh."

Scythe's brows fell heavily, his jaw rigid beneath my touch.

"Don't you see?" I asked, and his jaw slackened when I stroked it. "I didn't then, of course, but now I do." I rose and pressed my nose to his, whispering, "It was you. All along, always you."

An exhale trembled from him and heated my lips.

He studied me as my smile bloomed and I let the tears gather in my eyes. "I was supposed to love you, and I do," I said, for there was no denying that he'd crawled inside my heart long ago. "I do love you."

He'd crawled inside it to plant a seed he'd watered and nurtured with every moment spent with him. With every knowing touch, every soul-healing action, and every honest word, I was gifted safety unlike any other, and a desire to believe when I'd lost the ability to.

I had been gifted a love that wanted only to love me in return.

I laughed when Scythe grabbed and hauled me into his lap.

He silenced me with his mouth, clutching my cheek as he kissed me with a ruthlessness that spoke of undeniable relief. He pulled away long enough to stare at me, as though checking I was real and that he finally had me in every way he'd wished for.

I stroked his cheek, smiling, and he kissed a tear from mine before fusing our lips once again.

Searing moments later, he murmured, "My turn to show you something." The large hand palming my ass beneath my robe squeezed.

I wanted him inside me, all over me, but we both knew it was unwise to do so here. For although we were alone, we wouldn't be for long. Rorn knew of most places to search for me.

Together, we rose and warped farther inland.

We materialized by a large dam, spotted with reeds and lily pads. Beyond it stood a generous wood and stone structure, smoke rising from its chimney. Hedges, well-tended and riddled with roses, surrounded the home. Wooden fencing stretched for miles either side of it, encaging livestock.

A small farm.

I looked up at Scythe. "Yours?"

He was staring at it, his expression clean of emotion. I still saw it, had come to notice his tells after obsessing over his features, both in person and on parchment with paint. His jaw rocked ever so slightly. His eye was squinted—just enough to know there was effort given to keep from showing what he felt.

"You don't have to do that," I said, squeezing his hand. "Not with me."

"Hard to shake," he said, bringing my hand to his mouth. His gaze stayed fixed on his old home. "The last time I didn't need to watch every move I made was when I lived right here."

My heart splintered at the thought of him spending all these years within the walls he'd built to protect himself. Berk and Mariana, his found family, had likely spent many of those years trying to see past them, and although he'd let them in more than the rest of the world, he still held even them at a distance.

"I'm surprised it's still standing," I couldn't help but admit. "Most homes this far inland were deserted long ago due to passing human squadrons stealing crops and weaponry." I looked at the hillsides of the valley. "They would kill so many of us, even if we surrendered."

Scythe's skin had grown clammy, his fingers squeezing mine. "I cannot bear an opinion when I've done the same."

"I suppose you have," I said carefully, for there was no use acting like all he and his king had done was right. "But perhaps you've been a touch less murderous."

That roused a huffed chuckle from him. "Murderous?"

I smiled up at him. "Am I wrong?"

He cupped me beneath the chin and lowered his head to mine. "I've never felt more murderous than I have these past few days." He kissed me before I could respond, swift and thoroughly distracting me from our surroundings.

"Perhaps it's not fae who dwell here anymore." He straightened and looked back to what had once been his home so long ago. "And therefore, we should be going."

But we took the dirt road leading to the nearby town lit up from the midday sun, prolonging our inevitable return to the towers.

"What was he like?" I asked. "Helvectus."

"I assumed you'd met him?"

"Yes, but I did not know him well. Not in the way you did." I swung our hands and grinned when his lips twitched. "There's a portrait of him in the towers that I think you might like to see."

"I've no need." He was quiet for a minute, then he said, "He always read for two hours before bed, no matter what. When I asked him why, he would always say why not?" He slowed as the town became less of a blur, his voice low as we passed an abandoned field. "It would make me fucking incensed."

"Until you began to read yourself," I surmised.

In answer, he smiled at the ground. "In the months before he died, he began to drink a lot. I didn't understand it then, but now I see it was the worry over what was happening and being unable to control it."

I remembered how much less we had seen of him at the towers and how quiet he'd grown when we had. "Did you ever meet your grandfather?"

"No, but he was aware of my existence. He didn't agree with my father's secret life—which was what he'd called it—but although he didn't understand, he never betrayed his son by telling anyone. Not even Rorn."

"All that changed when the skirmishes became what no one wanted to call them—war. Then my father began to instruct me on how to fight in earnest. He told me religiously what to do should something happen to him." He shook his head, and my stomach sank. "He knew, in some way. He knew it right down to his bones. And in the end, I didn't try hard enough to stop her. I didn't keep my word."

"You tried to stop your mother from going to Rorn for assistance?"

"Yes, and when that failed, I tried to reach her before it was too late. She was already at the towers seeking entry when I found her. So

I did the only thing I could," he said. "I accompanied her and hoped that my father's affection for the brother who'd resented him for his alpha status and abilities would not let us down. I knew it would not go well, but not once did I think he'd…"

"You never thought he would see you as a threat after he'd gotten what he'd thought he'd never have," I finished for him when he couldn't.

Rorn had never longed to be king. At least, I hadn't noticed if he had. But he'd risen to such unexpected power so quickly, and he was not the type to surrender anything.

Scythe nodded. "My father began to bring more coin home with him. He could never take too much for fear of Theenon growing more suspicious than he already was. He feigned a gambling problem, but it didn't matter. It wasn't enough. It was too late, and what we did have didn't last nearly as long as we'd hoped it would."

"Your mother would have gone to Rorn regardless of how many times you stopped her."

Scythe's jaw rotated, and he sighed. "But he warned us. He told us that no matter what, we were to live free of them. To never seek a thing from anyone at the towers." He cleared his throat. "I know I was just a cub, but I've lived with it ever since."

"The alcohol," I questioned, smiling when Scythe steered me around a small but sharp rock in the road.

"I saw my father rely on it, and when I started drinking, I was too young to understand that it wouldn't actually help. I was in so much pain. Every type of pain. Even when it dulled, the discomfort of my eye, of the life I was then expected to adapt to…"

I nodded, taking his arm and clutching it tight.

Scythe stopped suddenly.

I looked up at him, uncertain of what he was doing. Then I sensed it, too. The unnatural silence that had flooded the woodland and fields on either side of the road we'd taken.

The smoke now rising from just beyond the town up ahead.

"Well," Scythe said quietly. "If they weren't already here, they certainly are now."

Screams sounded, faint and few but heart stalling all the same. "We need to help them."

"Too many," Scythe said, scenting the air and watching the smoke. "And you're without shoes and clothing."

"That doesn't…"

Hooves pounded from within the woods to his left, and Scythe immediately pulled me close before we could greet the enemy racing toward us.

We warped back to the towers. To the very dining hall we'd left mere hours ago. There was no longer blood on the floor and table. The breakfast dishes had been cleared and replaced with a lunchtime feast.

Scythe tensed as the king of Vordane turned from the window and eyed us both with a growing smirk. "How lovely of you to finally join us."

THIRTY-THREE

Scythe

"**W**HAT ARE YOU DOING HERE?"

"Rude," Dade said, scowling with a twitch of his arrogant nose.

Opal, at his side and dressed in a flowing gown of gold and crimson, made to speak when footsteps neared the doors behind us.

I pulled Aster aside before they were flung wide open.

Rorn entered with an embarrassing number of wolves trailing him. They picked posts along the walls while Theenon stared at me as though he were seeing a ghost. With a slight shake of his head, the steward bowed toward his king and closed the doors upon taking his leave.

"It would seem your prisoner has returned," Dade said, humor thickening his tone.

"Indeed," Rorn said. "Let us now get to the reason for this visit, king, so that you can take this rogue mutt of yours back to his hovel and away from my wife before I'm left with no choice but to kill him."

Dade said nothing, but Opal bit her lips as though tempted to laugh.

Looking at Aster, his gaze filled with icy promise, Rorn clipped, "For my patience has come to an unshakable end."

My hackles rose, and I stepped forward.

Aster gripped my hand, halting me. "There's been another attack," she said, then released me to tighten her robe.

I'd have protested if it weren't for the fact I wanted her to make sure the asshole never saw her body again.

He kept her waiting, and Dade raised a brow as his amused gaze flitted between all of us. Done with selecting a handful of nuts from the platter on the table, Rorn asked impassively, "Where?"

"The town of Curmin," I supplied roughly.

Rorn stilled.

He turned slowly, a knowing gleam in his eyes as he dragged them over me with his jaw working too hard as he chewed. He looked at one of his wolves. "Inform Jyll that there's been another."

"Another?" Aster queried as though this were news to her.

"You would know of such matters had you not been otherwise preoccupied with the wrong"—Rorn tossed more nuts into his filthy mouth, then grinned—"*thing.*"

Dade cleared his throat far louder than necessary. "Good, we're on topic then," he said, and Rorn reluctantly tore his undeserving gaze from my mate. "I'm afraid I need my commander back, and you'll need to surrender your wife to him to make that achievable for me."

"Careful, king." Rorn leveled Dade with a reproachful glower. "For I'm thinking I'm already done with this conversation."

Unperturbed in the slightest, Dade lifted a shoulder. "I would not be standing here watching you eat if I did not have something of interest to offer you in return."

Disbelief straightened my spine and momentarily stole my careful focus from the king and his wolves. "What?"

Aster took my hand again. She tugged it, and I knew she was telling me to shut the fuck up.

Dade noticed and nodded to Opal.

Rorn's brows lifted as the queen of Vordane stepped closer to the table. "While it's terrible," she said softly but strongly, "what is happening to your beautiful realm, it's also clear that it cannot be stopped."

Rorn smiled at the queen in a way that made Dade stiffen. "This conversation is now over." He looked at the wolves, and they advanced toward Aster and me. "Enjoy the refreshments, then see yourselves out."

Dade growled, and the wolves halted.

Opal took the chance to quickly say, "I know a sorceress capable of providing wards. Wards we've recently put in place along our coastline to better guard against another attack."

The emerald king's attention was officially retaken.

Though he tried not to show too much interest as he waved his warriors back to their posts and looked at Dade for confirmation.

Expressionless yet tense with growing loathing, Dade nodded, indicating that what his wife had said was true. That he even had to confirm as much pricked at both of our skins, our beasts riled and waiting beneath the surface.

"Interesting," Rorn said, eyeing Aster. "And how might one go about having this sorceress put such a thing in place?"

"You must pay for them," Dade clipped. "And dearly, for they will be forever bound to her."

Rorn's jaw clenched.

Aster, although still in her robe, stood like the queen she was, her shoulders back and her chin high, as she stated confidently, "I'm afraid our coffers are too drained to afford it."

"We will compensate her for you," Dade said, his gaze fixed upon Wistensia's king.

Rorn rubbed at his chin, laughing low beneath his hand. "Of course, and dare I even ask what you seek in return?"

"Your wife and nephew's freedom," Dade said, his lips quirking. "Of course."

Rorn returned his smirk. "Of course." He then looked at said wife, and my mate stared back. "No," he said.

His wolves shifted in their boots. I had no doubt they wished for the assistance the wards would give them.

Aster's knees quaked, and my grip on her hand tightened.

"No?" Dade questioned, and far too softly. "Forgive me for assuming, but I do not think I am mistaken in doing so..." Hardening his cold gaze on Rorn, he stated, "You are going to lose this war. Any advantage you could have had was lost when you chose not to act while the vermin skipped across the sea to terrorize my own people."

"We needed to be certain of what they were doing," Rorn said, tone scathing. He then looked at me with a dismissive flick of his hand. "If I'd known Marvis sought the beast, I would have found him myself and handed him over."

"Yet I hear it was you who tipped his men off as to his whereabouts."

Aster gasped, her fingers falling from mine.

Opal winced before glaring at her mate.

Dade shrugged. "Did you think we would not find out? While the promise of gold and a hatred for our kind was likely enough, we knew there had to be something more that would encourage an otherwise occupied battalion to cross the Night Sea."

I couldn't keep from looking at Dade. He merely glanced my way before giving his attention back to Rorn.

I should have told him.

He'd always known, but I'd thought if he'd never known exactly who I was then there would never be any real issue.

Guilt nicked at my chest.

All those lives lost and altered. It was not my fault, I knew that. For I never would have expected anyone besides Rorn himself to come for me. If I had expected an army, then I'd have spoken.

I might not have been the sole reason for their attack on Vordane, but I had been the determining factor when the kingdom of Errin had put the call out to neighboring continents for aid in defeating Dade and our legions.

"But it's not only the true heir that these humans seek." Opal broke the stilted silence carefully. "It's every member of your family. It's your family's kingdom. It's this entire isle. It's the extinction of faeries from a land they deem as theirs. You cannot hope to keep fighting them at all without more assistance, and this will help you. These wards will provide you with the opportunity to better ready yourselves and therefore protect your people."

Aster was still looking at Rorn—staring at him with her fingers curled into her palms and her chin trembling.

Rorn tore his gaze from her and gave it to Opal with a rough exhale. "What we need is that Marvis's head on a pike."

"And have you tried as much?" Dade said, knowing full well this king had not.

"Once or twice, but only during rare sightings of the coward when he journeys," Rorn said. "Any attempt to warp inside the fortress he's built for a quick assassination would only further rile his bloodthirsty people, should we even succeed."

"And any heirs he has surely sired, too, and then the next to rise into power will come for you and your own heirs," Dade said smoothly. "It never ends. Not until you gain enough strength to make them believe they will not succeed."

"We had that," Rorn snapped and turned for the window. His back bowed as he splayed his hands upon the sill. "At least, I thought we did. Then they started to flee, and we thought…"

The silence screamed of all he wouldn't admit to himself—they'd never had this under control.

They never would.

"Rebuild and reinstate that strength in the ranks you have left," Dade said, gruff as though tempted to shake some sense into Rorn.

I'd have liked to throw him from the window he'd cowered against. Instead, I kept watch on Aster and the emerald wolves. She was now staring at the ground, her regal posture stolen by the knowledge of yet another betrayal from Rorn.

I was tempted to tell her it didn't matter. But it wasn't about me. My reassurances wouldn't help when it was about *him* and his never-ending deception.

My teeth gritted. Perhaps I'd throw him from the window after all.

Lost to thoughts of his broken limbs in a tangle around his

insufferable head on the drive below, his blood dotting the gardens and his eyes staring unseeingly at the sky as he waited for a healer, for a chance he did not deserve, I nearly swayed backward when Dade spoke.

"Rebuild and refocus on what is important. Too much is at stake. Take the wards and let go of what is no longer within your grasp."

Rorn remained quiet. So quiet that I sensed another refusal was heading our way.

Dade sensed as much too and sighed. "Do they know, Rorn?"

Rorn cursed as though tired of our presence and merely awaiting our exit. "I will hear no more, king."

"Do your people know?" Dade enunciated each word with lethal quiet. "Do they know that your pride is larger than your desire to protect them?" Taking Opal's hand, he hummed. "Perhaps they ought to know that you would keep your wife from happiness out of spite and jealousy, and you would therefore ensure their doom."

"If you love that swan of yours, then you know what you ask of me is fucking impossible."

That made Dade pause, but he was a king raised on brutality and blood, and it was not within him to shy away from troublesome truths. "You might love her, but it's evident to all that this marriage ended long ago." He then led Opal to the doors and said with crystal-sharp finality, "So give Astrantia to her mate and give that love to your own."

"Mate?" Aster asked, paling more.

Fuck.

So the mother of Rorn's son was his mate.

Pure venom scoured down my spine, locking it as it sped through every limb. If I was furious, then I couldn't even begin to imagine what Aster must have felt.

Stars, how I fucking hated this.

Each breath drawn burned hotter than the last. I refused to lose myself to jealousy over Aster's reaction, but I didn't know what to do. I didn't know if there was anything I could do.

But I knew I had to touch her. I needed to remind her I was here, so I stole her hand.

Aster said nothing, but her trembling fingers latched over mine as though she needed the tether to something real while the husband who'd hidden this from her—the husband who'd tried to keep both a wife and a mate—refused to even look at her.

Dade had stopped at the doors as though now aware of the consequences of what he'd divulged. Opal hushed him when he opened his mouth to say something more.

Though he remained where he was, Rorn hung his head between his shoulders and finally spoke. "They will need to die." Everyone stilled at that, even his three wolves. "Both of them can no longer exist, or Marvis might eventually come for her."

My teeth gnashed.

Before I could say it didn't matter, that I would run from continent to continent to ensure they would never find us if need be, Dade's boots creaked as he shifted his weight from one foot to the other.

A sign to stand down.

"That can be arranged," Dade said, watching the king with both curiosity and apprehension, for he sensed what I could feel brewing—Rorn was close to snapping.

We needed to end this before we lost the ground we'd gained.

"Have this sorceress arrive before the week's end and let it be done," Rorn demanded, voice thickened with barely leashed fury. He then pushed away from the window and strode for Aster.

I braced, my blood and bones humming, ready to shift and lunge—

Rorn marched past her without a glance and straight through the doors.

Opal pulled Aster into a hug.

I longed to pry her free and comfort her myself, but when the swan queen rubbed her back and whispered something that sounded like, "Stars, you deserve a lifetime of peace after this," I backed off and waited outside against the wall.

Aster appeared a few minutes later. Though her eyes were still damp, the adoration beneath the gleam ripened my hunger when she neared me. "Dade has taken Opal home, but he said he will return."

I nodded and waited.

Finally, she sensed what I wanted and erased the tiny distance between us to fold her arms around my waist. The ache in my muscles melted as I held her close and laid my mouth and nose atop her head, breathing her into me.

"I'm sorry," she whispered to my chest.

I fucking loathed that she felt the need to say such a thing. "You have nothing to apologize for."

Pulling away just far enough to gaze up at me, my heart gave me a sad smile. "I have to see him," she said, and I tensed, ready to say that no, she absolutely did fucking not need to, when she rasped, "I won't be long, but Scythe…" Rubbing my hips, she whispered, "It's something I must do."

Torn between the desire to leave right away, to never let him lay eyes on her again, and the desire to ensure she had as much closure as she needed to move forward without ever looking back, I found myself unable to speak.

Stepping back, Aster placed her palm over my cheek, her mouth pinching as her fingers brushed the corner of my scarred eye. My throat tightened, bobbing painfully when I swallowed, and she flattened her hand over my racing heart.

"I won't be long," Aster repeated and captured my hand. She lifted it to lay a kiss upon my palm. My warmed skin grew cold as she released me to walk away.

Aster turned right before I caught her by the waist when she neared the stairs.

She smiled as I pulled her back into my arms. My lips seized hers, and she instantly softened beneath their claiming caress. Her hands splayed over my chest, fingers curling into my shirt, as she yielded to every taste I had to have.

Breathless, she blinked up at me in a beautiful daze when I broke away to roughly warn her, "I'll be counting every fucking second." Then I traced her damp, luscious mouth with my thumb. "But I'll wait as long as you need me to."

Her gray eyes flooded, and her lips trembled.

Before I changed my mind, I released her and forced myself to walk back toward the dining hall. Forced myself to keep from so much as looking over my shoulder as the beast pressing at my skin writhed with the desperation to do what we needed. As my wolf whined for us to take her and get the fuck out of here.

Minutes that felt like hours later, the air warmed with his impending arrival.

I ceased pacing by the window at the end of the hall.

Dade exited the dining hall and stopped when he saw me. "Well?" he said, making an unnecessary show of peering around. "I see no guards." Then he frowned. "Where is your mate?"

"Saying her goodbyes."

Dade pondered that with a low whistle. Tucking his hands within his coat pockets, he came to lean against the wall beside me.

"Thank you," I murmured after too many seconds of tense silence had passed.

Dade stiffened. "I didn't quite catch that. Could you repeat it?"

I glared at him, and his eyes glinted before he chuckled.

But I truly was thankful, and I hoped he knew that. He certainly did not have to involve himself in matters such as these. If anything, he should have avoided it. He should have done his utmost to punish and be rid of me.

Instead, he'd decided to help my mate and me.

"I suppose I owe you one," I said, at a loss for what else to say, and crossed my arms and ankles.

"A continued lifetime of servitude should suffice," he drawled, though we both knew I was destined for as much anyway. He lifted a shoulder, staring at the stairwell ahead, and scratched at the growth on his jaw. "A little birdy might have told me this is merely what friends are supposed to do."

Slightly alarmed by the warming of my chest, my teeth met. I released them to mutter, "I'm not hugging you."

He laughed once more.

"And what are we to do about this?" I asked when the silence settled, this time without the earlier tension.

He raised a brow, and I gestured back and forth between us with a flick of my fingers, indicating the issue of Vordane containing two alphas. Dade stared at me with those cold blue eyes, his wolf staring at mine.

But there was no challenge. It was merely an assessment of what he'd always felt simmering beneath the surface of who I allowed people to see.

I let him look, and I didn't cower. I never had. It seemed Dade now understood that while I would prefer to hide it, and that I would continue to, all that I was wasn't something I could simply change for him.

Smirking, my so-called friend winked. "I'm afraid I have no idea what you're talking about." He looked straight ahead again. "Just make sure this king holds true to his word. Your legion is positively feral in your absence."

My lips twitched, but I couldn't help it. I laughed, too.

THIRTY-FOUR

Aster

RELIEF WAS SOON MET WITH AN ONSLAUGHT OF GRIEF I hadn't expected to still be capable of feeling.

Not for the king seated in our rooms, staring at the crown he held between his spread knees. My crown.

No longer mine.

"I know you loathe me," Rorn said. "But I cannot find it within me to apologize, for once I discovered those portraits you'd painted of him, I simply had to."

"Did you know?" I felt compelled to ask. "Did you know that Scythe was my mate before you told those that wish he and every single soul in this family dead where he was?"

Rorn's shoulders rose with his long intake of breath. "I had my suspicions, but Astrantia…" He exhaled slowly. "It wouldn't have stopped me."

My eyes closed as my heart shook within my chest. I opened them and did my best to keep from looking too closely at the contents of the bedchamber I'd shared with him. It seemed a different life, and now, new ones had torn us apart.

Fate had intervened.

"Why didn't you tell me?" I asked. "That Carelda is your mate."

"Because I didn't want her to be," he said to the crown. "I've not wanted anyone but you since the night I first laid eyes on you." He huffed. "But the moment I saw her in that destroyed village town, ready to fight one of our warriors with nothing but a fucking stick for daring to take fruit from her mother, I knew it didn't matter what I wanted. I felt it. A connection happened. I intended to do nothing about it. To merely ignore her and reject it."

I recalled the way he'd tossed Carelda from these towers like unwanted goods.

He hadn't only been trying to remove her for my sake—for the sake of our dying marriage. He'd been attempting to rid himself of temptation to better keep the life he'd known, the life he'd chosen. Even at the detriment of his son.

Rorn's lithe fingers smoothed over one of the emerald leaves of the crown. The jewels, and the silver and gold they clung to, glinted in the glow of afternoon.

I could hardly believe that he'd finally agreed to let me go, and the sudden weight of knowing I'd never see him again formed icicles that threatened to erase the warmth that had engulfed my heart just minutes ago.

For despite all he'd done, a part of me would always care for him. He might not deserve it, and he might have lost my love long ago, but he had been the largest part of my life for too many years. He was woven into the fabric of who I was. I could move on, but I knew forgetting such a thing, forgetting him, would only prove impossible.

"But you stayed, Rorn." I wrung my hands. "You didn't ignore her. You evidently ended up staying with her." It shouldn't have mattered. Not anymore. But I couldn't help but wonder if he had told me the truth, then would I have tried harder to forgive him? Could I have held on to that love for just a little while longer before it faded to the intrusion of a growing longing for another?

Many a creature had lost love when a fated mate came along. Many also decided to fight it, to ignore the painful pull toward another and commit to living their lives without it—without them. Regardless of what anyone chose, there were often casualties for all.

"I didn't," Rorn said. "Not at first. We left, but the town was so ravaged, the people so distraught, that we needed to escort them to new shelter before we returned to the towers."

I nodded, though he didn't see, not needing to know the rest. "You still haven't accepted the bond." Which was probably why I hadn't been able to scent too much of a difference with him—to know he was spoken for in that way, as he was already spoken for in marriage.

His silence was answer enough.

"Please know that I loved you," I said, barely a whisper. "Perhaps more than was ever good for me."

"You'll find having a mate to be just as consuming, Astrantia," he argued, and his voice lowered with the muttered admission I assumed he'd rather withhold. "If not more."

I refrained from saying it would indeed be different.

He didn't need to know that I wouldn't shape my entire existence around one person again. That I planned to live my life for me, and to be grateful that my mate was there to share it with.

"I know you loved me," Rorn said when the silence grew too loud. "I know because I watched it bleed from you for months until nothing was left, and I couldn't stop it. I couldn't…" He squeezed the crown. "I couldn't make that love stay."

My cheeks grew wet with an immediate flood of tears.

I had to go.

I had to leave, yet I didn't know how to say goodbye. I didn't know how to say goodbye to someone I'd never thought would exit my life.

As each second cooled, the sun sinking lower, I thought perhaps it was best I didn't, and that I simply whisper instead, "Make sure you fight, Rorn. For all that you want. For Carelda and for Helvectus. For your people and for your life."

Finally, I turned to leave.

He seized me and turned me into his chest.

He held me so tight, I wasn't sure he'd ever let go. I surrendered and held him back when I felt it—the silent anguish that shook through him. "Bloom, I can't do it. How am I supposed..." His choked words ended in a groan, his hands shaking as he grabbed my cheeks and pressed his wet lips to my forehead.

For seconds that ruined, he breathed me in, then forced the crown into my hands and himself to move away. "Go," he ordered and turned his back to me. "Go before I tell them to fuck off because I choose you."

I rocked on my feet, unable to see through the tears.

At the doors, I gripped the wood as he rasped, "Because you are my choice, Astrantia."

I wouldn't have known what to say even if I could've managed to speak, so I made myself leave. I made myself walk as what he'd said sank deep while I descended the stairs of our tower.

Steadying myself with a trembling hand upon the stone outside of my paint parlor, I struggled to breathe, knowing he'd meant it when he said he'd chosen this for me. In his own twisted and cruel way, almost everything he'd done had indeed been for me.

The crown felt too heavy in my hand. My heart far too heavy to carry in my chest.

He'd intended for me to keep it. I couldn't. I couldn't take any part of this life with me if I was truly doing this. I wiped quickly at my cheeks but soon gave in when the tears refused to stop. Leaning back against the stone, I slid down it and bit my fingers to keep from making noise as what I was doing rattled through me.

It was right, but that didn't mean it was easy.

Some minutes later, I took the stairs down to Carelda's rooms.

After one knock, she called for me to enter. Her eyes widened when she saw me, and she rose from the bed. "Forgive me, my queen. I was distracted. I didn't realize it was you."

I smiled at Helvectus, who was squashing grapes beneath a bowl on the floor.

Then I sniffed and motioned for her to sit. "That is no longer who I am." I pulled the door closed behind me so Helvectus didn't escape to the stairs beyond. "And that is why I'm here," I said, revealing the crown from behind my back. "This belongs to you."

"You're crying," she breathed, her eyes lifting from the crown to me. Disbelief scrunched her features. "You're truly leaving?"

I crossed the room to where she sat on the edge of her bed. "We all know it's well past time I did, but eventually"—I placed the crown atop her head—"he will earn your forgiveness."

She reached up. "Astrantia, I cannot—"

I took her hands and cupped them within mine. "Do not forget who you are and all you are capable of when you surrender."

The wind had never felt more alive than it did upon the precipice of the cliff ledge we stood waiting on. It forced my hair to fly over my shoulders and lashed at my cheeks in both greeting and warning.

"Ready?" Scythe asked, and I knew he was referring to more than just the deadly stunt we were about to hopefully pull off.

He had been waiting where I'd left him below the stairs in the tower, and after he'd held me until he was satisfied I was okay, we'd not waited another moment.

Now, we waited for the carriage ambling down the mountain pass to come into better view. To ensure the driver, and perhaps even the occupants within, would see us.

I didn't look back at the towers in the distance.

I refused to fall prey to the crack within my chest. I'd been given too many at the hands of this land and its ruler. No matter how much it hurt to walk away for good, it was indeed past time to move on.

It was time to start again.

Tense with anticipation and apprehension, I swallowed at the sight of the raging river crashing against the sharp rocks below. We would be fine. I'd done this enough that it would work. And should I fail, I knew the powerful male standing beside me would not.

I nodded. "Ready."

The carriage drew closer, trundling toward the towers. We would give them news to take with them.

The news of our demise.

Scythe backed up, then roared to make sure we had their full attention. My heart fell into my stomach as the sound shook the skies, and he made a show of charging and causing me to fall back over the ledge.

I should have screamed.

Instead, I could only smile as death loomed close and reached for me with cold, welcoming hands. It didn't scare me. It couldn't when I'd felt its embrace before.

And I'd survived.

Scythe's hand captured mine right before we crashed into the river. Shadow enfolded, stealing us from this cursed isle, and I took my wolf home.

EPILOGUE

Scythe

Three years later...

THE SORCERESS ARRIVED IN THE DEAD OF NIGHT.

Uncurling from Aster, I rose from the bed with my claws already unsheathed. They retracted slowly at the sight of Silver standing in the doorway to our room.

Aster startled awake with a gasp. "Silver?" Moving her tangled hair from her face, she sat up and snatched her robe from the end of the bed, pulling it on as she rounded it. "Stars, what happened to you?"

But the sorceress was staring at me.

Her shoulders and arms were bare of her snakes. Blood ran from a deep gash upon her forehead. The scent of smoke and death wafted from her form like a breeze.

Silver gently clasped and lowered Aster's hand when she reached for her face to inspect her injury. "I'm fine." And I knew before she said it, her crimson gaze unmoving from me. "The towers have fallen."

Aster stumbled back, her hand clapping over the pained sound that left her mouth. Her gray eyes met mine, filled with the horror of heartbreak.

Every instinct screamed to gather her within my arms and soothe.

But Silver had come to me for a reason.

I stepped into a pair of leather pants that were folded and waiting upon the drawers for the morning, uncaring that Silver had seen us both naked. It mattered not when she was here with such news. News I'd foolishly thought I'd never be delivered.

For three years, we'd not heard a word from Wistensia, and we hadn't wanted any.

"He is asking for you."

Aster remained stone-still in the corner of the room. Her fear and anguish smothered, even if she chose not to voice it.

Mercifully, Silver was not referring to my heart. She was referring to me.

I pulled on a tunic and grabbed my dagger, then slipped past the sorceress to fetch my swords.

She appeared before me and placed a hand on my arm. Her red eyes shined with urgency. "You won't be needing them, but you must hurry."

"No," Aster called, following. "Silver, he can't go back…"

I sucked in a breath through my nose and nodded to Silver.

Then I slid my dagger into the holster within my sleeve and turned back to meet my mate. I framed her face and kissed her. "I'm not leaving you, and when I am forced to, it will not be for them," I vowed to her lips.

Aster swallowed, her eyes closing.

Tears still escaped as I pressed my lips to her forehead and inhaled her.

Silver took Aster's arm when I released her, and she directed her to the armchair. A discreet nod from the sorceress said she would not allow my mate to warp from the cottage. She had the power to make sure she couldn't follow.

I'd promised to never return to the isle—had thought I would never have to.

But there was no quelling the pull I couldn't name, and so I let it drag me back one last time.

Fire choked the mountain hillside I arrived on.

It rose toward the dark sky from the highest windows of the only remaining tower. The other towers were nothing more than debris that covered the mountains and drowned them in plumes of smoke.

Soldiers, in the same silver armor I'd seen crawl throughout the lowlands of Vordane a few years ago, ran to and from the burning eruption of stone and mortar. Many laid dead from both sides, their armored remains akin to gleaming flowers that spotted the land for miles in either direction beneath the moon.

Though victory had evidently been met, the sounds of battle still raged on.

It was not victory they sought. It was vengeance. There was little to celebrate until the last living royals of Wistensia were no longer, and the entire isle was free of fae.

Which was why Silver had said to hurry. Somehow, they still lived.

The dungeon was empty and overflowing with rock and dust. Warping, I continued my search, hoping I wasn't seen by anyone else after needing to burry my dagger in the throats of two unlucky assholes who'd been injured and trying to escape a hall they'd been trapped in.

The king was in the throne room, crouched over a fallen body.

The body of a female stuck beneath a pillar.

Her eyes were closed. Blood pooled beneath her like a bed of crimson to cushion her over the stone.

Carelda.

Before I could reach her to remove the pillar, Rorn stood and stopped me. "She's already gone."

I cursed, twisting to better see every destroyed angle of the room as a bone-trembling boom sounded from outside the tower. "You need to get out of here." Truth be told, I didn't care if Rorn lived or died. I'd ceased harboring such hatred toward him the moment I knew that despite all of his monstrous efforts, I'd won a battle I'd never known I was fighting.

But he had a son. He had a duty to a land he'd gone to great lengths to ensure remained his to control.

Rorn didn't move. He held his son close and hushed him when

he squealed in fright. Inhaling his dark hair, he asked me with far too much calm considering the circumstances, "She is well?"

Now was not the time to rub anything in, so I merely nodded.

The king's smile was tremulous yet genuine, as he swallowed and nodded in return.

He kissed his son's head, his eyes closing momentarily, then said, "I should not ask anything of you, I know, but my son…" He smoothed a hand over his head. "He is your blood, and Astrantia has love for him." He pushed him into my chest, and the tiny cub reared back to get a better look at me.

Stunned, I caught him before he could fall and held him tight.

"I do not expect the same of you, Helvectus, but I know your mate will love him as he deserves to be loved."

"Rorn," I started, shifting to the side and covering the young male's head as rock crumbled above us.

"He deserves to live." Rorn gritted his teeth, evidently pained as he stepped back from his son and me. "Just make sure he lives and that he never tries to come back." Withdrawing his sword, he shook his head when I made to remove my dagger from my sleeve as shouting sounded behind us. "Your father…" Rorn swallowed, ducking as stone plummeted from the ceiling. "My brother was right. This isle is cursed. There is nothing to come back to."

Battle cries sounded from the hall, screams of agony soon following.

Rorn pleaded, "Protect him. If not for his innocence, then for your father." He gave one last watery glance at his son. "He is just like him."

Then with a roar forged from anguish and blood-red fury, the king of Wistensia charged into the hall with his weapon to the advancing human soldiers who'd sieged the towers.

There was nothing to be done. Nothing.

I still stood there and watched as blood sprayed the hall beyond the throne room, and metal met metal as Rorn gave the soldiers what sounded like the fight of their lives.

But it didn't last long.

Helvectus whined and hid his face in my neck, his small hands fisting my tunic. I held him tighter as I forced my body to quit trembling and focus—as I forced myself to remember what was and was not within my control—and we left right before the surviving soldiers could check the throne room.

Aster was pacing the length of the cottage.

As soon as she sensed us, she froze. Her hand fell from her hair, and when the tiny male unlocked his arms from my neck, she fell to her knees.

And wept.

Silver, staring at the youngling, nodded once and vanished.

"Asher?" Helvectus wriggled.

I set him down, suddenly unsure what to do without his weight in my arms to give me purpose.

Aster's head rose from her lap.

She swiped quickly at her cheeks as Helvectus, dazed and terrified, stumbled toward her. She held out her arms, and he fell into them with an ease that said his parents had not let him forget who she was. An ease that told me they'd feared this day would come.

And they had chosen to cease fighting fate.

Scythe

Eight years later…

Aster was still tidying up when the sun met the horizon.

Helvectus leapt through the door of what had once been my apartment and dropped his training gear by the wall. Wet paint brushes in hand, Aster whirled toward us with a smile that would forever stun me still.

Hel picked her up and spun her around. "I'm finally free."

"Just for two weeks," I reminded him for the tenth time since we'd left the training yard.

He'd completed his junior training—and a year earlier than what was expected. Most assumed it was because he wanted to keep up with Ryon, who was a couple of years older than Hel's twelve years, and he never bothered correcting them.

They might suspect, but no one would know that the young wolf with one blue and green eye was an alpha hiding in plain sight. Though Hel had figured it out years ago when he began training to one day join Vordane's royal legions, he was content with the way things were.

He was also well aware that there was no kingdom left for him to claim. Any survivors from Wistensia—if they hadn't in the years prior to the tower's downfall—had since scattered across both Sinshell and Vordane. There were likely not enough to claim as his own.

And given all they'd been through, I'd made it abundantly clear that a good ruler would simply leave his people be to enjoy a hard-gained peace.

Aster laughed and fussed over Hel's long hair when he set her down. He stood still and let her smooth the black locks over his broadening shoulders. Already half a head taller than her, I was expecting he would grow taller than me.

"You need to bathe," Aster said, her nose crinkling.

"I know." He kissed her cheek and grabbed his gear, then bounded from the apartment. "I'll meet you there."

"Make sure you're on time," I warned.

"Always am," he sang back.

I scoffed.

Aster looked at the door Helvectus had slammed closed behind him, her lip between her teeth. "Do you think he truly wishes to join?"

Nowadays, Vordane's wolves were given the choice to join Dade's legions of warriors. Most still did, being that it was ingrained within us to serve and protect, and therefore hard to ignore the desire. Aster worried, as the next phase of training Hel would enter in a few weeks meant he was signing on for a future as a warrior of Vordane. A commitment she feared he was too young to make.

She wasn't a wolf, and therefore I couldn't make her understand. I could only reassure her.

I plucked the paintbrushes from her hand and dumped them onto the closest table, then I took her by the waist. "He does."

"You're sure?" Grasping my arms, she blinked up at me, wholly unaware, or perhaps uncaring, that she had a giant blue smudge of paint upon her cheek.

Smirking, I nodded as I licked my thumb and gently rubbed her skin.

She scowled. "I told them to tell me when that happens."

"And you expect a bunch of younglings to actually do such a thing?" A roll of her eyes had me tilting her chin so I could fuse her lips to mine.

During the months after leaving Wistensia, Aster hadn't known what to do with herself. For a time, that had been necessary. It had been best for her to do nothing more than acclimate and grieve. Although she'd never seemed unhappy, her heart and soul had needed the rest.

I'd offered her the apartment. I'd even had some more clothing made and delivered to it, as well as soaps and food. But Aster had laughed and said that she'd spent more than a year just trying to survive, most of that time spent on her own, so the last thing she wanted was too much solitude.

I'd been so relieved, I'd immediately warped the things I'd purchased for her to the cottage.

It would be a handful of months later that she'd ask for the apartment after all, but not purely for herself. To offer paint and reading classes to the disadvantaged and displaced youth a few days a week. She spent the other days visiting the orphanage with Mariana to do the same there.

Aster tugged my tunic free of my pants, her teeth dragging my lip into her mouth.

"Dinner," I foolishly reminded her, but I would be the one Mariana chose to scold if we were late. Never Aster, and certainly not Helvectus.

"You wish to wait?" she said to my mouth, a smile within her voice. She knew damned well I didn't.

In answer, I picked her up and laid her over her desk, her skirts

324 | ELLA FIELDS

gathered and pushed out of the way. Parchment and inkpots were knocked aside, Aster's laughter ending when there was a crash. I grinned, promising, "I'll clean it up," and then I erased her displeasure by pulling her undergarments aside.

My fingers encountered soft, wet flesh. A musical exhale threatened to undo me when I parted her with my thumb. Pushing up with her elbows on the desk, Aster brushed her mouth over the corner of mine. "I've missed you."

It was always the same.

Even if we were only separated for a couple of hours, I was gifted the same heart-bruising words. "I know," I teased, dipping the tip of my finger into her welcoming body. Long lashes fluttered, her hands roaming up my arms to cup my face.

I shoved my pants down over my ass, and her thighs opened wider in invitation. We both groaned and watched, her head upon my shoulder, as I eased my cock inside her sweet cunt.

I gripped her thighs as searing heat swept through me in a rippling shiver. Never would I get enough of this female of mine. Never had there been a day—stars, a fucking moment—when I didn't crave her.

Groaning low, I pushed all the way in. She received me with a greedy, clenching tightness and a beautiful gasp of breath.

"Look at me," I said, and she gave me those stormy eyes. "Tell me."

At my jaw, she feathered her lips with the declaration I never went a day without hearing, even when I'd pissed her off. "I love you."

My chest swelled with my cock.

I caught her mouth with mine as I began to thrust. My fingers dug into her thighs, and she moaned her approval against my lips. Deeper, I delved and aimed, her body both softening and tensing.

With a grunted cry, Aster made to break away. I refused to let her. My eye remained open, watching as hers flared and then drooped with the onslaught of building pleasure that began to rupture through her.

The sound of her heart dancing faster with each panted breath satisfied me like nothing else could.

I could've stayed inside her for hours, as I'd done as often as I could, but I let myself follow. She swallowed my curse, her hand snaking up my back beneath my tunic to clutch my body tight to hers.

"I'm afraid we'll need to be late. I haven't seen your tits since last night," I complained.

Aster laughed, a little breathless. After a quick kiss, she left me to clean herself up in the bathing room. "A good thing, seeing as Hel didn't lock the door."

Little prick, I thought with a smirk. I wrapped my arms around Aster from behind at the wash basin and stuffed my nose into her neck, groaning. She reached back to trail her fingers down my cheek. "Later," she murmured. "We'll be late."

She was right, so I tidied the mess we'd made, and we finished making ourselves as decent as possible before warping to Berk and Mariana's townhouse.

At the door, Aster stopped me with a tinkling laugh and tucked my tunic back into my pants.

I might have left it that way—might often leave many parts of myself disheveled—just to have her fuss over me. If she'd figured that out, then she didn't seem to mind. Rising onto her toes, she kissed my jaw while knocking on the door.

Fang and Olivianna were already there, of course, but Fang's mother-pleasing nature never stopped his father from throwing scathing barbs.

"If you'd have told him properly instead of making those mumbling sounds that fall out of your mouth like a fish who's decided to learn how to talk, then maybe he'd actually listen to you."

I tucked Aster into her chair. Olivianna moved closer with the decanter of wine to fill her glass.

Fang sighed, kicking my chair out as I went to take a seat beside my mate.

I caught it and kicked him in the shin. He cursed, wincing as he said, "It's been a decade, oh lovely father of mine, let it fucking go."

Berk jabbed his glass of whiskey toward his son. "A decade of which they've probably spent plotting our demise."

"Nothing new to report," I said, and I'd said as much too often, for Berk scowled. "Dade has even finally agreed to form a new treaty with Errin." The kingdom that once mostly contained only humans had opened its borders mere months after the war in an effort to welcome fae of all ilk.

We weren't fools. It escaped no one's notice that the human royals were number one on Dade's shit list. Still, at Opal's urging, he'd decided to leave them be and to hear their excuses for their actions.

But not without careful use of their fear.

We now had a permanent fixture of warriors within Errin, as well as along every coastline. Should Marvis, the human king who'd seized control of Wistensia, decide to try his hand with us again, he would not succeed.

It would seem he was well aware of that, as there had been no sign that he'd set his sights on us.

As far as he knew, I was dead. And if he didn't believe it, then perhaps he was satisfied by my willingness to play dead. That, or he knew he didn't stand any chance of ridding me from existence. Not without consequences.

And now that Sinshell and Vordane were once again united as we had been in the past, the consequences would be more than he could afford.

Regardless, I could understand Berk's worry. I still harbored a healthy amount of it myself now that I had a family—a life I never would have imagined would be gifted to me.

But should trouble come our way again, we would be ready. We had too much to fight for. Too much to lose. So we were always prepared.

Berk stewed on what I'd said for another minute while Mariana placed the herb-flavored mountain of chicken upon the table, his eyes on me and his jaw tight.

Mariana clasped my cheek. "Where's my pup?"

I kissed her when she leaned down to do the same to mine. "I warned him."

She narrowed her eyes. "Not well enough, and your hair needs brushing."

Indeed, I'd taken to wearing it long again.

Fang hadn't left me alone about it for the months it had taken to grow it back because he knew why I'd done it. This time, I didn't keep it trimmed to my shoulders. I'd somehow ended up in a competition with Hel to see whose hair could reach their ass first.

Unfair if you asked me, being that the cub was still growing his brawn and I had too much of it, which put me at a slight disadvantage.

Said cub arrived late, as per usual, and with Ryon in tow. Both of them ceased their shit-talking when they saw Mariana standing in the doorway, a dish towel tucked within her hand at her hip. "What am I to do with the both of you and your tardiness?"

"Love us," Hel said, hugging the female around her neck. "For we certainly love you and your magical cooking."

Ryon kissed Mariana's cheek. "What he said."

She swatted them away with the towel. "Oh, sit and eat."

"Rotten suck-up," I muttered to Hel when he took his seat on the other side of Aster.

"Learned from the best," he said, and he wasn't referring to me.

Aster and I laughed when Fang glared. "Enough with the teasing."

"Stop giving them reasons to," Olivianna said and scooted back to her seat beside him as her son joined her.

Fang turned his scowl upon her. It melted when she whispered something in his ear that made his eyes and teeth flash with a sickeningly pleased smile.

Despite neither of them wanting to commit beyond friendship with certain benefits, the seamstress and the commander had made it last, and slowly, it had turned into something permanent.

Olivianna's mate was, unfortunately, still floating around. He served in Dade's legion. There seemed to be an unspoken agreement between them that the king's seamstress and friend was not to be discussed.

The male who'd never given Ryon the time of day was well aware not to mistake that for approval of his actions, but Olivianna had lost any hope for a relationship with her son's father long ago. He was married, and he wanted to remain that way. As the years had raced on, it was clear she did, too.

I could respect that. It was the wolf's absence in his son's life that I would never respect.

But if Ryon cared, and if he cared that he might one day serve the king alongside the father who abandoned him, then he showed no signs of it. He had Fang, who was more friend than father, but admittedly a far better role model than the rest of us.

"Treaty," Berk spat, tucking a napkin into the collar of his shirt. "Waste of fucking time, just you wait."

"Stars, Berk." Mariana dumped a dish of roast vegetables onto the table. "Must you insist on spending the rest of your days worrying over things that will likely never happen?"

"Someone damned well needs to. The human swine will have us all swimming in mud if they aren't better kept within their cage."

We all laughed, and Berk glowered at each of us.

"Eat your dinner, Berk," Mariana scolded gently.

He glared but picked up his fork, and we all laughed harder as he grumbled, "Who's being teased now?"

As we walked home along the river, the question I'd been waiting some years for finally came, but not as I'd expected.

Hel waved a stick before him as though it were a blade. "Ryon calls Fang his father."

"He does," I said, and though I didn't know what had prompted it, Ryon had thought of Fang in such a way for a long time. Perhaps he always had.

Helvectus slowed, eyes upon the stick he picked at with his fingers. He was nervous. "Sometimes," he began. "At the training yard, I mean, the other wolves will call you my father, and others…" He scratched at his cheek. "Well, they ask me if you are."

Aster squeezed my hand, then walked on ahead when I slowed.

"I see." My chest grew tight. "What do you tell them?"

There was no hesitation, just a slight shrug as Hel admitted, "That you are."

Neither of us spoke for a minute.

My gaze glued to Aster, the wool of her pale yellow gown floating behind her with her caramel hair. Despite giving us some semblance of privacy, I knew she still heard every word exchanged.

And despite all the years that had passed and that she loved me and this life we'd created, I knew it still haunted her. Not regret, but a sadness for the souls she'd known who were now lost. For all Helvectus had barely known and had lost.

As the path forking toward the woods that contained our home came into view up ahead, Helvectus stopped. I did, too, as he asked carefully, "Is that okay?"

I couldn't seem to speak, and he mistook my silence, rushing on in a ramble, "I know you're not," he said. "I know that, but it still feels like you are." He swallowed. "Does that make sense?"

Fucking stars.

I blinked hard but then decided it didn't matter if he saw my state. I pulled him to my side and kissed his sweat-scented hair. "Makes perfect sense, pup." His shoulders relaxed under the heavy weight of my arm.

Then he asked the question I'd expected before the father talk. "Did he do that to your eye? Rorn?"

His rare gaze was upon Aster, of whom he still called Asher even though she was a far better parent to the cub than me. He knew who she really was—that she would always be his mother.

"No, some other asshole," I finally said and watched Aster falter as she entered the cottage. "Go make your mother a tea and get cleaned up properly. Your hair still stinks."

Shocked, Hel looked at me with wide eyes. "Do you think I could call you both—"

"Yes," I growled. "Now piss off before you make me weep like a babe."

Laughing, the cub I'd never expected to love as though he'd never been anything but mine ran ahead while I rounded the cottage with a shaking heart.

Setting the axe upon the grass, I lowered to the stump and listened to Helvectus as he panicked and ordered Aster not to cry. "Stop it, please. Right now."

I smothered my laughter with my hand. Then I groaned and hung my head, wiping at the wet that had leaked from my eye.

After many a discussion, Aster and I had decided that we were content without a babe. We were not entirely opposed to having one, but even if it were possible for Aster, given her family history of death due to delivery, I was more comfortable living this life with just the three of us.

Stars knew Hel was enough for us both. Should we again want to stress ourselves with the joy of raising another youngling, then we would likely look to those who hadn't any parents or caregivers.

A rustle sounded in the bushes. I knew who it was and quickly swiped at my face before he appeared. "What's got you acting so out of character, beast?"

"What are you doing out here at this hour?" I barked back, withholding a snort at the sight of his long nightcap. A pompom at its end, the bright silver hat that matched his nightgown fell to the grass beside matching slippers.

"Ruth escaped," Kloon said pointedly. "Again."

That damned chicken was not a chicken. It was a winged, clucking waste of good food that failed to produce any for us in kind. When she did, she'd make sure to lay somewhere the elves could reach first.

"Not to worry, for I braved the night to put her away," Kloon said and jumped up to sit on a tiny rock across from me. "You're welcome."

"Not paying you."

He scrunched his crumb of a nose. "Aster does."

"Not in coin."

"You're right," the elf said, his smirk and the fluttering of his lashes warning me of what was to come. "With her love and her time. Shall I expect the same of you?"

Rising, I dusted my hands together and headed for the cottage. "Go to bed, Kloon."

"But the boat you so cleverly made has done us such wonders, truly. The glorious craftsmanship, beast. Such skill should not be wasted. At the very least, you must take the idea of a matching wharf into consideration, then we could—"

I closed the door behind me and made sure the rest of the cottage was locked. There was no need to fuss in such a way, but old habits were hard to shake. The instinct to protect was impossible to squash.

Hel had bathed and sealed himself inside his dungeon of a room.

Aster, already in her robe, waited upon our bed with the giant book we'd spent the past week reading.

She placed the novel over her stomach and greeted me with a tremulous smile. Knowing I was not adept at filtering and storing an onslaught of such unexpected emotions, she thankfully didn't touch on the mess the young wolf had made of them.

"I know it's not just Berk who worries." She rubbed her finger over the book's spine. "I know you do, too."

I kicked off my boots and nudged them beside the door. "You do not?"

She smiled once more.

I sighed and set my dagger in its nightly resting place on the windowsill behind the bed, then stripped free of my clothes. "It's hard not to after so many years of being trained to believe the enemy lies everywhere and that everything can be taken from you in a heartbeat."

"That is also why Berk worries so much? As he was also trained to."

"Not as thoroughly and as brutally as those of us who came after the death of Dade's parents, but yes. That"—I leaped over top of her, snatching the book and setting it facedown beside us—"and he has little else to do but dwell."

After the arrival of Helvectus and the falling of the towers, Aster and I sat Berk, Mariana, and Fang down to tell them everything. None of them had been shocked. They'd already known about me, and Berk and Mariana had assumed correctly about Aster.

And we'd all agreed that unless Helvectus required it, then it was safest to never speak on it again.

Concern etched Aster's brows low. "Is there not something more he can do?" It was not the first, nor the third time Aster had found herself worried over Berk's well-being. Though she knew there wasn't a task in the world that would shake the surly from him, she still thought it would do him good to have more to focus on. We both did.

"Dade and I have been talking about giving veterans military roles many of them can still handle. He seems to be heavily considering it."

"Which means after Opal and I talk of it, he will inevitably agree," she whispered to my throat and then licked it. Indeed, with Aster and Opal being such close friends, it would likely not be long before Dade implemented such changes.

"Inevitably," I concurred, untying her robe to feast upon her chest.

Aster discarded the moss-green silk and clutched my head. A mewl escaped her, her back curling off the bed when I ran my fingers over her soft stomach and danced them teasingly atop her mound.

Hel made a loud show of leaving for the woods, items placed upon the kitchen countertop with a clang and the door slamming.

Aster had refused to move when I'd claimed we needed more room as Hel had grown. For some years after the towers had fallen, Helvectus had been prone to nightmares, so we'd let him sleep with us. Which had made it difficult—but certainly not impossible—to carve out some time from each day to spend inside my mate's body.

Eventually, he'd requested a room of his own.

I hadn't wanted to move either, so I'd made more space by adding an extension to the front half of the cottage. One of the new rooms was for Helvectus. The other was for Aster to paint. But it was times like now, when he was still awake, and I didn't want to wait, that I wished I'd built a larger extension.

Stars, a room for him within the fucking woods.

Aster laughed, and I snatched her nipple with my teeth, causing that laughter to break into a hissed intake of breath. Fingers sank into my hair and over my scalp, smooth legs climbing my back. I gave her other tit the same treatment and slipped my fingers over her mound, two sliding with dizzying ease into her cunt.

She whimpered when I withdrew to stick them in my mouth. I sucked them clean before laying down and ordering, "Climb on."

Aster spent agonizing moments trailing her fingers over my chest. Reaching my cock, she gave her eyes to me while her fingers dragged down it. "Your mouth or your cock?"

Fuck. "I could listen to you say cock for the rest of my days." At her raised brow, I grinned. "You decide."

Not a second later, she was straddling me. My hands roamed her thighs to hug the addictive flare of her hips as slowly, she rose to her knees.

Then with a breathy moan and fluttering eyelids, she worked all of me into her body.

For so many years, I'd let the days blur together without a plan or hope for anything. I'd simply existed. I had done whatever I had to in order to survive without truly living at all. I hadn't even known what I was trying so damned hard to survive for, yet ignoring my lack of purpose had become part of the mindless routine.

All that changed the night I'd walked into a tavern in search of someone who was looking for an evening of escape, and I'd found myself a miserable faerie queen.

I'd never expected her, and I'd certainly never expected to feel the way she made me feel for anyone. Love had never been something I'd thought I would need. Now, it was everything I couldn't survive without.

And I would guard hers with my life.

Aster rocked her hips until she'd taken as much of me as possible, and only then did I rise and wrap her legs behind me.

Her back arched beneath my hand as I caught her, and I kissed her throat. "Wildflower," I whispered, kissing under her chin. "Breathe." Her chest deflated with a shuddering exhale, and I stroked the indent of her spine as she inhaled and relaxed against me. "Okay?"

"Perfect," she responded thickly.

334 | ELLA FIELDS

I chuckled silently and licked her racing pulse. "Indeed. I love you."

Nails gently scraped over the ridges in my shoulders. I pushed her so close that her tits were squashed against my chest. Then I pulled her hair aside to better access her scent, her skin, my lips glossing over the light sheen of sweat at her collarbone.

I'd asked her almost every other month for the past decade, but her answer was always the same. Her refusal didn't hurt me. I knew it was not due to a lack of faith in me but rather a lack of faith in a union that had broken and robbed her of everything she'd once known so unexpectedly.

It also didn't deter me.

One day, she would surrender. Not to please me, or she would have already agreed to it, but because she was ready. So I would keep asking—and I would keep waiting.

"Marry me, wildflower." Tilting her chin down, I whispered to her lips, "I want to make you my wife." I didn't brace for her response. I did what I always did and kissed her before she could give me that teasing smile of hers and laugh as she told me no.

But Aster didn't laugh. She didn't smile.

My counterpart returned my kiss, and so softly that my lips fell still over hers.

My heart lost its beat, and my eye burned when she gripped my face to kiss the tip of my nose. "Then please do."

ALSO BY ELLA FIELDS

NEVER MISS A THING!

Follow on Instagram
www.instagram.com/ellafieldsauthor

Website
www.ellafields.net

Made in the USA
Monee, IL
16 November 2024